Christopher Brookmyre was born in Glasgow in 1968, and has worked as a journalist in London, Los Angeles and Edinburgh, contributing to *Screen International*, *The Scotsman*, the *Evening News* and *The Absolute Game*. In 1976 he became a St Mirren supporter. He was at the Hammarby game. This may explain a great deal. His first novel, *Quite Ugly One Morning*, was published in 1996 to popular and critical acclaim, winning the inaugural First Blood Award for the best first crime novel of the year. This success was followed up with the bestsellers, *Country of the Blind*, *Not the End of the World*, *One Fine Day in the Middle of the Night* and *Boiling a Frog*. His next novel, *A Big Boy Did It and Ran Away*, will be published in Little, Brown hardback in October 2001.

'*Country of the Blind* is a veritable Alton Towers of a novel' *The List*

'A writer to watch' *Mail on Sunday*

'Considerable elegance and verve . . . [Brookmyre] is not afraid to be passionate and partisan' *Guardian*

'Snazzy writing . . . droll characterisation . . . good fun' *Herald*

'Deeply satisfying stuff' *Literary Review*

'A comic and nourish critique of the nature of power' *Arena*

'In Parlabane he has created a nicely amoral hero for our times' *Irish Times*

'Brookmyre knows how to plot excitingly and with daring touches of strangeness' *Guardian*

'A high-octane political thriller doused in stinging satire' *Sunday Times*

'Its undeniable strength is Brookmyre's ability to create characters you care about' *Scotsman*

Also by Christopher Brookmyre

QUITE UGLY ONE MORNING
NOT THE END OF THE WORLD
ONE FINE DAY IN THE MIDDLE OF THE NIGHT
BOILING A FROG

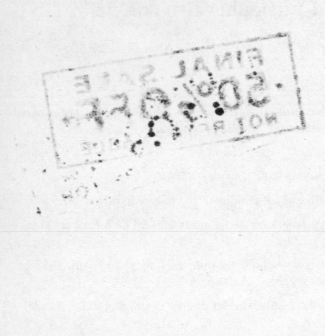

COUNTRY
OF THE
BLIND

Christopher Brookmyre

An *Abacus* Book

First published in Great Britain in 1997
by Little, Brown and Company
This edition published by Abacus in 1998
Reprinted 1998, 1999 (twice), 2000, 2001

A CIP catalogue record for this book is available
from the British Library.
ISBN 0 349 10930 3

Typeset in Times by M Rules
Printed and bound in Great Britain by Clays Ltd, St Ives plc

Abacus
A Division of
Little, Brown and Company (UK)
Brettenham House
Lancaster Place
London WC2E 7EN

www.littlebrown.co.uk

For Mum and Dad

THANKS:
Karen & Hugh Curry (true believers),
Roger Dubar
and, especially, Marisa Haetzman

I

"We are a party whose sole purpose through the centuries has been to win and retain political power."

– Malcolm Rifkind
Conservative Foreign Secretary, 1996

ONE

If Nicole Carrow was being absolutely honest with herself, her most substantial reason for believing Thomas McInnes was innocent was that he had made her a nice cup of tea. She hadn't been a lawyer long, but she still suspected she might need more than that in court. Her two weeks experiencing the practical application of Scots Law had demonstrated a few divergences from its more familiar English cousin, but she'd yet to find precedent for a special defence of Refreshing Herbal Infusion.

Nicole had anticipated an uncomfortable breaking-in period in Glasgow – acclimatising herself to the city, the people and the notorious weather – and was prepared for feeling like a fish out of water in the job for a while. However, her vision of in-at-the-deep-end had nonetheless proven short-sighted: she'd naively assumed it would be a bit more than a fortnight before she was representing the accused in a crime that had shaken the world.

Obviously the contents of the oh-so-mysterious envelope had raised her hopes and stiffened her resolve, but the sober reality was that – as Mr Campbell had pointed out – they merely thickened the plot her client was embroiled in, and apart from briefly

3

delighting a few conspiracy theorists, would ultimately be of more use to the prosecution.

The cold facts remained that McInnes, his son Paul, one Robert Hannah and one Cameron Scott had been apprehended fleeing the grounds of Craigurquhart House in Perthshire, that the Dutch media mogul Roland Voss, his wife Helene and their two body-guards had been found murdered within, that when Paul McInnes was detained he was soaked in blood, and that an attempt had been made to open Voss's bedroom safe.

McInnes and Hannah had been members of the "Robbin' Hoods", as the tabloids had tagged them, a gang responsible for a series of country-house break-ins over a short but prolific period during the mid-1980s, the name referring to their profession of pil-fering from the rich, and conveniently ignoring their omission of the giving-to-the-poor part. A speculative early spin on the story was that their loathing of the wealthy must have become intensified during their embittered prison terms, and that – whether entirely for their own motives or willingly assisting someone else's – they had meted out terrible revenge upon their perceived oppressors by mur-dering Voss, an international icon of arrogant, even decadent – and some would say thuggish – tycoonery. This seemed to be borne out by the police's revelation that while the bodyguards had been shot (once each, middle of the forehead – very quick, very clean, very efficient), Voss and his wife had been tied up and their throats cut. It hadn't taken a pathologist to work out that Helene had been murdered in front of Voss before they dispatched him too.

It had been a particularly cruel and vicious crime, undoubtedly evidencing a heartless brutality borne of violent, furious hatred. And there had been something sickeningly demonstrative about it, thrusting its depravity before the public and forcing them to look at it. It seemed to crave their disgust, to solicit their repulsion, while at the same time its very publicness sought to rob Voss of his aura by the posthumous humiliation of such a sordid and con-spicuous death. Death often built legends, lent greater stature to mere men and granted them the immortality of public mythology.

4

But murder could be insult *through* injury, a faultless disgrace in an irredeemable theft of dignity, which burnt the oil portrait of a proud man and replaced it in the public eye with a grainy police b/w of a withered corpse, helpless and bested by no worthy foe, but some – and by extension any – rogue whelp.

Nicole couldn't help but feel a sense of *déjà vu* as she remembered Robert Maxwell's watery demise, the unreality, the *impropriety* of death paying a visit to one of the untouchable Three Rs: Rupert, Robert and Roland. Maxwell had seemed a figure so proverbially larger-than-life, a looming presence in and behind the media, and a figure she had, young in years, grown used to assuming would always be there. Someone the everyday realities of life wouldn't touch, whose very irritatingness seemed to guarantee he would be around forever so you'd better get used to it, like the common cold or washing powder ads.

She remembered how the radio bulletin had sounded like a joke. Rich tycoons don't fall off boats; if they do, they turn up later, safe and sound, then write a book about it and bore us all on chat shows, telling the world how the publicity – sorry – their *lives* flashed before them. Even while he was missing, those uncertain hours of anxious speculation and dismal journalism, she had assumed Maxwell would be found boomingly alive, having spent the whole time enjoying the amorous advances of a short-sighted minke whale. But no, the only whale they found was the dead one floating off the Tenerife coastline, and the colossus had indeed been felled.

And actually, after all, no, the world didn't miss him.

Even before the pension-fund stories broke, he had started to become a smaller and smaller figure, just a dead businessman whose appetite for self-publicity had meant there was no-one left to blow his trumpet now he was gone. He wasn't a giant after all, and history would make less and less of him with every passing day.

The famously ebullient financial health of Voss's empire and his status in the UK as one of the Conservative Party's favourite businessmen meant that the inevitable eulogising and necro-sycophancy by sufficiently important figures would safeguard his stature in certain circles for at least a while. However, the reality was that ultimately he would be remembered more for being murdered than for any of his achievements while alive. God, who could tell you *two* things about Lord Mountbatten, for instance?

Ee-aye-ee-aye-oh.

It was like that joke about the shepherd who, in addition to his traditional duties, had built half the houses in his village, repaired two dozen boats and knocked out all-comers in unarmed combat, bemoaning the fact that he was never referred to as Hamish the builder, chandler or boxer. "I shag *one* sheep . . ."

Nicole remembered someone once saying that killing a man takes away all he is and all he might ever be, but some murders can also take a sizable swipe out of everything a man ever *was*, and this was one of them.

To say the country was shocked wasn't even clearing your throat, never mind an understatement. In the six months since Dunblane, the people of Britain had become reaccustomed to a world where unimaginable atrocity took place only beyond the removes of oceans or fictions. A spring and summer dominated by images of confused bovines – inside *and* outside Downing Street – had provided a comfort blanket of mundanity as they reassimilated themselves into the very British realm of the unremarkable. Then this.

It had been a slow burn, starting from the first sketchy and seemingly incredible reports, breaking at the tail end of the BBC news, that police had found a number of bodies in a country mansion in Perthshire. Nicole remembered the panic in the reporter's voice – perhaps contemplating the consequences if they got this one wrong – as he stated that "although it is as yet unconfirmed, we have reason to believe that the media magnate Roland Voss has been staying at Craigurquhart House with his wife Helene; so far the police have stated only that the bodies of three men and one woman have been discovered, and that they are treating all four deaths as murder".

By the first ridiculous BONG! of ITN's late-evening bulletin, the bodies were "believed to be those of Roland Voss, his wife Helene and two bodyguards". Five minutes in, it was confirmed

6

that Voss and his wife had been staying in the house. By twelve minutes, the police had told the programme's "Scotland Correspondent" that the killings were "sickeningly brutal and sadistic", but further details were not yet available (stay tuned!).

The nation was allowed to relax briefly while they learnt that their anuses need never again suffer the ravages of plain old bog roll now that the scientific breakthrough of the decade had delivered a quilted version; that two Eighties refugees with a coffee fixation still hadn't shagged; and that nineteenth-century French peasants derived materialistic comfort from paying over the odds for a bland, gassy chemical passing itself off to the gullible as beer.

After the break, the day's "other main stories" were shunted out as it emerged that the police were holding four men in connection with the deaths, and by the end of an extended programme, it was stated with bass-toned gravity that a terrorist motive "had not been ruled out". Nicole had noticed that the situation was deemed to be so serious and the mood so sombre that Trevor didn't even try to revive the viewers' spirits with an amusing *And Finally* . . . clip. This meant the scheduled report from Wigan about a hamster who could play "Waltzing Matilda" by farting into a series of colour-coded test-tubes would presumably be held over until the next night, when the last story might be about a plane crash in Zambia which, despite claiming 230 lives, had pathetically failed to turn up one corpse holding a British passport and was therefore not important.

By the time the specially convened and unprecedented *Sunday Newsnight* went out, the cops were getting less reticent.

"Police initially thought that tonight's tragic and bloody events might have been the result of a burglary gone wrong, or even that the killings were part of a contingency, but they are now saying that, given the profile of Mr Voss and his well-known links with the Conservative Party – together with the sheer ruthlessness of the killings – they have to consider all possibilities at this stage."

Yes, Nicole had thought. Especially when the Prevention of Terrorism Act allows you to hold your suspects for six days without letting them talk to a lawyer.

"Although Roland Voss was best known in the UK for his newspaper and pay-TV interests," the strainingly stern-faced reporter continued, "it should be remembered that his empire spans many countries, many businesses and many industries, including arms manufacture. As a result, Mr Voss had no shortage of enemies, and seemed sometimes to publicly revel in the fact, playing up to what he liked to call his 'prizefighter image'. Indeed, you may recall that after the 1992 General Election, when his newspapers were accused of some very low blows in their campaign coverage, it was hinted by Labour sources that were they ever to win power, his would be one score they would not forget to settle. His words at that time were, famously, 'If the British Labour Party was the most dangerous enemy I had to worry about, I'd sleep easier tonight. In fact, if it was in the top ten, I'd sleep easier tonight.'

"That is perhaps why the police are anxious not to jump to any conclusions regarding the motives behind tonight's atrocities. As one police source told me, the fact that the bedroom safe appears to have been tampered with does not necessarily mean robbery was the principal objective, especially as at this stage it has not been established whether anything was in fact stolen."

Eventually, out of facts and out of quotes, they moved on to reaction, which in most cases was blank disbelief. You could see it on the faces of the few establishment grandees who could bring themselves to be interviewed: System error. Does not compute.

Ordinary people got murdered. Poor people got murdered. Black people got murdered. Women got murdered. *We* don't get murdered.

Occasionally one of us manages to off himself by mistake with the wife's knickers over his head or gets found upside-down in a septic tank after a share crash, but we don't get done in by the unwashed when we're trying to enjoy a spot of hunting and fishing in the countryside. We're *safe* from that sort of thing.

Aren't we?

One by one they struggled to make sense of it, in a repetitive litany of incredulity, confusion and white-faced horror solicited by the noticeably unsettled anchorman, who was plainly wishing it wasn't Peter Snow's night off.

And as no-one could make sense of it, thoughts turned instead to retribution; the only way forward after such a senseless loss of precious human life was to . . . er . . . kill someone else.

Rentaquote time.

"This is an outrage of *unprecedented* proportion," blustered one ruddy-faced Tory backbencher – perhaps forgetting about an awful lot of dead Irish people, perhaps not – "and if there was ever a stronger argument for the return of the death penalty, then I can't think of it."

No, I'll bet you can't, Nicole had thought.

". . . lack of the death penalty as a punitive sanction in a case like this makes a mockery of British justice," said another apoplect, as one by one they hitched their agendas to the back of the bandwagon of indignation rolling out from Perthshire.

". . . well documented that Roland Voss was a strong advocate of the death penalty and it would certainly be his wish that these men were made to pay that price for what they have done tonight . . ."

". . . how long will we continue to listen to so-called liberal excuses over the death penalty as outrage follows outrage, atrocity follows atrocity, murder follows murder . . ."

And soundbite follows soundbite.

". . . of course with the autumn party conference coming up soon in Blackpool, the annual calls for the return of hanging are bound to be all the louder, and all the more difficult to shout down."

Ah yes. There was the rub. Need *something* to resuscitate the party faithful at the last get-together before the election in the spring, if they can hang on that long.

By the time the first-edition front pages were flipped briefly before the camera at the end of the show, the mood of the lynch-mob had reached hysteria.

"HANG THESE BASTARDS NOW!" led Voss's own flagship tabloid, one frothing voice amidst a baying clamour.

"SCUM FOUR MUST DIE!" screamed the next.

9

"FOUR LIVES FOR FOUR LIVES," demanded yet another, with a strap elaborating: "VOSS MURDERS: Nation calls for return of hanging".

It struck Nicole that The Nation must have called the paper directly, given the short time between the story breaking and its going to press, but who could say. The Nation had clearly made up its mind, and it would be a brave or foolish person who stood before it and argued the contrary.

"God help whatever poor bastard ends up defending that lot," she had muttered to herself as she switched the TV off, before taking her empty cornflakes bowl into the kitchen then going to bed.

Her radio alarm clock woke her up the next morning with the news that she was a poor bastard in need of divine intervention.

". . . holding the men overnight under the Prevention of Terrorism Act, with the approval and, indeed, we are told, concerned assistance of the Scottish Secretary, Alastair Dalgleish. Two of the men, Thomas McInnes and Robert Hannah, served seven-year sentences for their parts in what became known as the "Robbing Hood" break-ins, and police say they are investigating possible political motivations and exploring any links these men might have established with terror groups, particularly European left-wing factions, given Mr Voss's media interests on the continent."

Nicole sat bolt upright in bed, turning the volume louder and listening in frustration to more pompous conjecture as she waited for the names and their connections to be repeated, just to confirm she hadn't been confusing the remnants of her last dream with the words from the radio that had stirred her.

She remained glazed-eyed and entranced for a few more fuzzy-headed seconds as her just-woken brain struggled to cope with the pace of her thoughts. She reached over and switched off the radio with a tut, its tinny burbling an irritating distraction as she attempted to process the information she had just received.

Last night, like everyone else in the world, she just couldn't believe it, but had been gradually forced to accept the truth of this incredible development as the stark fact was coloured in with

10

details, quotes and human emotional response. Nonetheless, there had remained an unreality about it, in common with all truly momentous events, perhaps because the "news industry" had for so long made its living from over-dramatising the banal.

Disbelief was a reaction borne of so much wolf-crying, with the public so desensitised by the hyperbole with which the most tedious events were related (and the deceitful exaggeration with which the most harmless quote could be twisted or recontextualised to create "a sensation" where there was barely a story), that when something truly remarkable happened, you just couldn't deal with it. The media, having robbed every superlative of its meaning through misuse and over-use, did not have a vocabulary with which to convey such import. Once you've used up all your language of astonishment on Hugh Grant getting his cock sucked, how do you express the shock of thirty schoolchildren being gunned down in a gymhall, or of one of the world's most powerful businessmen being forced to watch his wife bleed to death before having his own carotid opened as his bodyguards lie slain in the hall outside?

Usually, it all got more real in the light of day, as you woke up and found that you hadn't dreamt it, and (most importantly) as you realised that the world had failed to stop – and that apart from having to listen to tail-chasing discussions on the subject, it wasn't actually going to affect *your* life.

But this morning, the confirmation that it was all still there ("Voss still dead shocker") had been accompanied by the realisation that it *was* going to affect Nicole's life. Thomas McInnes. This was a man she *knew*, that they were talking about, no longer some face in the paper or a name on the radio. A man who had sat down in front of her only a matter of days ago, a man whose voice, clothes, face she could remember. And by extrapolation he was one of the men all those MPs and journalists last night had said they wanted to see hang. One of the perpetrators of the most audacious crime of the decade. One of the men who had slaughtered four human beings in cold blood.

11

Which was where it broke down.

And with his son involved, too – how could that possibly have come about? What was this, *The Generation Game* does armed robbery? Brucie: "Let's see, they got the toaster, the teasmaid, the fondue set, the cuddly toy . . . okay, they lose marks for the four dead bodies, but other than that, didn't they do well?"

She could not believe it.

Blank, staringly, simply could not believe it.

A mocking voice told her she sounded like a serial killer's nextdoor neighbour. "Eeeh, you'd never have thought. He was so quiet, you hardly knew he was there. Very polite to speak to . . ."

So she searched for something solid, some rationale that could support her instinct in the face of all the evidence that was already in the public domain and all the evidence that was bound to emerge in the coming days and weeks.

Exhibit A, your honour: one cup of tea. Milk and two sugars.

The defence rests.

God help us.

In mitigation, it *had* been a very good cup of tea.

After the self-doubt maelstrom of the first two days, she had thought that if she could get through the first week of the job she might find her stride, start to galvanise herself, get into the role and gradually remember the plans she had and the ambitions that had driven her this far.

And she did, battling through with her eyes fixed on Friday evening like a shipwrecked sailor's on the shore ahead. She had been most grateful not to know anybody in the city, because if she had begun to unburden herself, she feared she would crumble completely. She had gone out for a drink after work with her bosses on the Monday and with Ian, her fellow subordinate, on the Wednesday, but in a way she had still been in character. None of them knew her from any other context, so she could hide behind her mask until she felt confident enough to take it off.

Unfortunately, it's the second week that gets you.

That's when you realise that last week wasn't hell because you were new and inexperienced, but simply because that's what it's like to work here. When you see an eternity of all the things you hated most on that first Monday morning, prioled out towards the horizon: the dingy Portakabinesque offices, like a candidate for demolition in a street otherwise embarrassed by its wealth of architectural splendour; the musty smell of suspiciously damp books; the rows of hideously Seventies grey-metal filing cabinets, like a set left over from a Monty Python sketch; the flickering strip-lighting and the glowering low cloud outside the draughty windows. That's when you realise that this is not a game, but what you do when you grow up.

Thomas McInnes had appeared in the afternoon of that awful second Monday, right after her meeting with Mrs McGrotty.

Her first appointment of the day had been with a shrivelled-looking man called Mr Taylor, who explained at great length and with much historical detail – a great deal of which seemed some-what tangential, which is saying something when you're working in a legal context – that he wished to sue the council because it had taken them three years to mend a broken gutter-pipe around the roof of his house.

"Why didn't you try and get it mended yourself?" she had asked, with unintended insensitivity.

"What the fuck you talkin' aboot, how didnae I get it fixed?" he exploded animatedly, deeply wounded by her apparent lack of compassion. "S'no up to me to get it fixed, is it? Up to the fuckin' cooncil to get it fixed. S'how we pay wur rent and wur poll tax, innit?"

"Look, just to help me get this straight," she said, trying to couch her words in as conciliatory a tone as possible. "Couldn't you have arranged for it to be repaired and then submitted the bill to the council?"

"Assno the fuckin' point but, is it?" he yelped, a flurry of upper-limb gesticulation. "Issi principle of the thing. S'no up to me to go runnin' aboot after plumbers and then try chasin' the

13

fuckin' cooncil for the cally. Be easier chasin' fuckin' Red Rum and hopin' it shites gold."

"So you wish to complain to the council for their laxity in responding to your complaint, and their delay in carrying out the repair to your guttering?" Nicole asked.

"Naw, ya stupit bitch," he said, eyes ablaze with incredulity at her persistent obtuseness. "I want to sue them for the *psychological damage*. I've been up to high doe ower this cairry-on, so I huv. Fuckin' post-dramatic stress hingmy. Three years of listenin' to the drips on the windae ledge – like Chinese water torture. And aw the cairry-on of phonin' them up and askin' when somethin's gaunny get done. My nerves are shot to fuck, so they are. I'm on tablets, you know."

By lunchtime she had dealt with half-a-dozen more such victims of a troubled world in need of Manson & Boyd's assistance in their heart-rending battles for justice, including one man wishing to contest his ex-wife's custody of his two children on the grounds that her new boyfriend was "a prodisant" and that their spiritual welfare was under serious threat; and a woman seeking compensation from the Strathclyde Passenger Transport Executive after twisting her ankle alighting from one of its orange double-deckers, who was able to furnish Nicole with figures for her settlements down the years from the city's other main operators as a guide to how much they should ask for.

Inexperienced as she was, Nicole nonetheless feared none of them were terribly likely to qualify for legal aid in pursuing their cases.

Ian had joked last week about the mythical "Manson & Boyd Justice Fund", which he suspected clients would readily believe existed, and which might assist in legal crusades when legal aid applications had been rejected. Just fill in the form: give your name, address and a brief summary of the case you are fighting. Then tick the appropriate box which best explains the moral rectitude of your cause:

(1) It just isnae right. ☐
(2) It's against God's law. ☐

(3) They cannae do that, can they?

Over the course of the morning, she had been directly insulted eight times (five instances prefixed with the distastefully emotive epithet "English"), been referred to as "hen" (which she suspected was seldom applied in affection) more times than she could remember, and been asked twice by male clients if she would make them a cup of tea "while they waited for the lawyer".

This last had happened several times the week before, too.

"No, I'm rather busy right now. In fact, I'm so tied up, would you mind nipping out to the chemist and fetching me a packet of tampons," she had promised herself she would say next time, but of course didn't.

And then Mrs McGrotty had come in.

She was an elephantine creature in a shapeless brown coat that looked like it had been fashioned from dog-pelts and then dragged behind a heavy goods vehicle for a couple of days, its sleeves over-reaching her arms so that it appeared that she had shopping bags instead of hands. The door had burst open before her as two accompanying children – one about seven, the other nearer four – formed a noisy vanguard-cum-herald, and the two young girls had continued to burble, argue and occasionally trade punches throughout the early exchanges of Nicole's conversation with their grandmother.

"They're no mine, like, they're oor Angela's, but she's fucked aff withoot tellin' us anythin' this mornin'. Fuckin' cheek of her, me comin' up here to try and sort this shite oot as well. Treat you like a fuckin' skivvy, so they dae. Think you're just here to look efter them and they don't need to tell you anyhin' if they don't waant to. It's nae wunner I'm up to sixty a day, between this and her Barry bein' back in the Bar-L. Mind you, polis stitched him up for that wan. He never hut that boay – well, no much, but wance your face is known they'll just pull you in for anyhin'. Six months just like that, bloody liberty – boay was oot of hoaspital in a fuckin' fortnight. Right enough I've said to her enough times she'd be better aff withoot him, but they never listen at that age, do they, specially not when they're aw misty-eyed like that. Ach,

15

you should've seen him when the weans were born but, picture of young love, so it was. Puts it aw in a different light when you've got wee yins, just forget aboot everyhin' when you look at them playin' you come ower aw sentimental, so you DEMI! I'LL TAKE MA FUCKIN' HAUN AFF YOUR FACE IF YOU TOUCH NAOMI AGAIN, RIGHT?"

Followed by injured wailing on the part of the chastised and a competitive tearful bid for further sympathy by the oppressed sibling.

"So Mrs McKechnie, what exactly were you . . .?"

"HERE!" she suddenly barked, Nicole placing a relieved hand on her chest when she realised it was not she who was being thus addressed. "Yous sit nice while I talk to the lassie. 'Mon. Play wi' this."

Nicole watched in horror as Mrs McGrotty's yellow hand removed a ring binder from the desk and offered it to the older sprog, who took this as a cue to help herself to a further clutch of folders and a box of highlighter pens that had been sitting nearby.

Nicole found herself rooted to her chair and helpless as Demi and Naomi began to tear documents from the folders and Mrs McGrotty looked challengingly at her, demanding full attention as she resumed her stream of consciousness.

". . . way that scheme's been goin' it's nae wunner there's nae bulbs in the lights in hauf the closes and it's not like I don't know my ain business cause I've tell't thon yin a dozen times faimlies like that can get singl't oot, specially when there's cairry-on like that nonsense last year with the new railings they were puttin' in . . ."

Nicole felt herself slump inside, knowing her eyes were gradually glazing but aware Mrs McGrotty was less concerned about her victim's on-going attention levels once initial capture had been accomplished.

". . . oor Chic gettin' laid aff by that cheeky bastart ower in Milton just cause he was late a coupla moarnins, as if it was his fault the bookies wasnae open on time that day, and after him comin' in on a Sunday the week before as well . . ."

16

Demi and Naomi coloured in a few affidavits in streaks of luminous yellows and greens, then disappeared around the side of the desk, out of Nicole's view, giggling and chattering, occasionally silenced by an interruption to the Joycean catharsis.

Nicole made a couple of attempts to interject, to perhaps maybe kind of sort of ask what legal matter Mrs McGrotty wished to pursue, or even to inquire whether she might have mistaken these offices for those of her GP, but got no further than the words "So Mrs McKechnie . . ."

". . . no easy when you've weans runnin' aboot I've tell't them but do they care? N.O. N-FUCKIN'-O. Too busy givin' oot grants to darkies and sendin' wee thugs on hoalidays tae Kenya to be worryin' aboot the state of . . ."

Demi appeared on the outer reaches of Nicole's vision; or rather, her hand did, swinging something white on a string.

"DEMI!" came the throaty rasp, this time accompanied by a reaching, haymaker of a slap. "Leave the lassie's bag alane. That's the lassie's fanny pads you're in at there. You've no to touch them."

Mrs McGrotty smiled understandingly as Nicole felt the colour drain completely from her face, leaning over the side of the desk to see the contents of her bag abandoned randomly within a short circumference surrounding the two little girls.

"Fuckin' law unto themsels this pair. Just never know what to dae aboot them, dae ye?"

Nicole knelt down, frightened for a moment that she might succumb to tears as she gathered up the remaining Lil-lets, her car keys, purse and other items. She found herself at eye level with Demi, and tentatively held a hand out to receive the pendulous tampon for disposal. The girl stared at her in apparent deep puzzlement.

"Can I have that please?" Nicole said in a croaky, plaintive half-whisper.

Demi's brow creased into a determined furrow.

"NUT! GETTYFUCK!" she suddenly decided, and lashed out at Nicole with an open-handed swipe that caught her painfully around the bridge of her nose.

"HERE! THAT'S BAD," stated Mrs McGrotty, further clarifying the moral position with another clout to the offending granddaughter.

"I'm awfy sorry aboot that, hen," she offered, then deciding another show of penitence and retribution was appropriate, slapped Demi yet again. "You're in for it noo," she warned darkly. "Showin' us up in front of the lassie, ya ignorant wee hoor. Noo just sit doon and shut up fae noo on.

"But that's what I'm talkin' aboot here, see? What chance have you when there's that kinna hing . . ."

Nicole's eyes were now watering, as was her nose, both in reaction to Demi's blow. She pinched the bridge and held her head back for a few moments, blinking hard until her vision cleared.

"MRS McKECHNIE," she barked firmly as she brought her head back down, beginning to appreciate that volume was the most valid currency of debate. "I'm sorry, could you please tell me concisely what it is you think I can help you with."

"What?" Mrs McGrotty asked in disbelief, eyes filling with offended anger. "What the fuck do you think I've been talkin' aboot here the past hauf-an-oor, ya stupit English cow. The poofs! That's what I'm talkin' aboot. The poofs next door! There' two of them, right in the next hoose."

"And have they been bothering you in some way? Loud music or something? Late comings and goings perhaps?"

Mrs McGrotty looked at Nicole like she was the thickest human being ever to have walked the earth, which by coincidence roughly matched Nicole's own self-assessment at that moment.

"What do you mean? They're poofs! Zat no enough? I've tell't the cooncil a dozen times, but they'll no listen, and I waant them oot. I mean, we've got weans livin' in that hoose. I'm no wantin' Demi an' Naomi exposed to any filth. Weans have to be protected. What kinna upbringin' dae the cooncil want them to have? Tell me that. An' you're askin' me what's wrang? Mind you, I'll bet the likes of you hinks it's fine, long as you've no to live there. In fact, here I'm are, pourin' ma heart oot an' you could be wan o' thay lez-beans. Probly hink I'm the wan that's no normal, zatit? Probly hink there's nuhin' wrang wi' poofs. Well mark ma words, hen. If they're sayin' poofin's awright the day, it'll be child-molestin' that's awright the morra. Christ, don't know what I'm daein' here. Waste o' ma fuckin' time. Demi! Naomi! 'Mon!"

And with that, they were gone, as if sucked back out of the room by a tornado of indignation.

As the door slammed, Nicole put her head down on the desk and cried, hearty, snuffly, snotty sobs, the anguish of someone who not only felt very lost, but who feared she was reaping what she had arrogantly and headstrongly sown.

She used to think Rob had been her self-inflicted punishment for her teenage rebellion, but she knew now that he was merely a separate, self-contained disaster, an integration of sin and retribution, mistake and consequence. The real invoice had just arrived for her, here in Glasgow, September '96, humiliated, lost, alone and found out.

This is what you want – this is what you get, as John Lydon put it.

Jesus. Being fourteen once had a lot to answer for. The dark years. Black clothes and heavy eye make-up, and the obligatory Cure albums providing their soundtrack of facile angst-platitudes, essential listening for huffy teenagers. But you don't just rebel. You need something to rebel *against*, and in true Blue Peter fashion, you can use an ordinary household item, like your father.

It should have told her something that she opted for politics; she had choice of weapons and picked an inflatable squeaky hammer. Annoyance and attention, but no damage. Dad was an Old Tory, sure, and his father was an Old Tory, and politics was in the blood, but it was an enthusiasm, not a vocation. If she had wanted to hurt him, she could have chosen any number of tried and tested methods. Maybe she had just been trying to show off. Little girls like to do that in front of Daddy.

And so it came to pass that Nicole did declare herself a Lefty. Her pal Monica, who was into Howard Jones at ten and The

Smiths a bit later, had declared herself a vegetarian (her father owned a bacon-curing business).

She met Rob at university in London, after a meeting at the student union to discuss plans for protest about some reactionary outrage that she couldn't now remember. It had been one of the first such events she attended, a hall full of young people desperately looking for a common cause and a set of shared beliefs; what they needed wasn't politics, it was religion. There was an overwhelming sincerity and worthiness, *earnestness* about it all, a reverence that seemed, well, again, religious. Until, of course, the SWP mob fell out with the RCP over some minute point of interpreted socialist principle, and the Labour Group got shirty with the Marxist Group about what slogans to put on their placards, and the Intergalactic Socialists for a Marxist Universe started a spat with the Vegan Organic Hamster Protection League . . . And so on.

Her older flatmate, Pippa, who was in her final year and had been round the houses with this stuff before, had sung her a song when she announced her intention to attend:

> One Trot faction, sitting in a hall,
> One Trot faction, sitting in a hall,
> And if one Trot faction, should have a nasty squall,
> There'll be two Trot factions, sitting in a hall.
> Two Trot factions . . .

Her faith had been restored slightly in the bar afterwards, where she recognised a guy from the meeting, someone who had seemed refreshingly aloof, watching events from the back, arms folded and wearing a sardonic expression. He was very accurately caricaturing some of the speakers, and cutting ruthlessly through all the bullshit and posturing to get to the issues that the meeting should have been about. Nicole took one look at him in action, drink in hand, surrounded by a laughing audience, and would later blush at some of the thoughts that popped into her head. Unfortunately, thoughts were all she'd ever have. His name was Eberhardt – his father was German and his mother a West Indian from East Ham – and his wit, intelligence, laughing brown eyes and flowing dreads all belonged to Martina, the drop-dead blonde sitting on his right.

Rob was the consolation prize. Nicole made the mistake of thinking, because she had seen him laugh at Eb's jokes, that he had (a) understood them and (b) a sense of humour.

She had seen Martina on TV in recent months, presenting some Channel Four kids-and-chaos affair, and had heard her romantically linked to several B-list celebrities. Funnily enough, the last time she saw Eb was on TV too, but it was on the news. He was working in Rwanda for an aid agency, surrounded by a rag-bag of children who were shrieking and laughing at everything he did as they followed him around the refugee camp. His hero status remained very much intact.

By contrast, Rob's stock had fallen, it would be fair to say. The humourlessness that she had mistaken for integrity, the ideological snobbery she had thought was political commitment. She still felt embarrassed for the green first year who had fallen for it, but she couldn't blame her for not seeing through him right away. He was very good at emotional manipulation, at eroding your bases from within, making you feel worthless without him. Making you need his approval, making you feel that he was a pillar without which you couldn't stand up. This, of course, he achieved by subtly chipping away at your self-respect, and cutting you adrift from the values and beliefs you had moored yourself to.

Her most frequent mistake was thinking he was listening to her. She thought he understood what she was saying about her family, her relationship with her father, when really all Rob latched on to was that her father was an establishment gargoyle from whose clutches he could rescue her. It was his fantasised ideal of their relationship. He was always trying to take her by the hand and lead her through the streets of London, like she was the bloody pit-owner's daughter who needed her eyes opened. The bizarre, sliding-scale inverted snobbery that made him think he had been afforded priceless insight by being brought up by parents who earned less than hers, even though it was still in a middle-class

21

house in a middle-class neighbourhood with a middle-class school, middle-class friends and middle-class values. Amazing, apparently, the difference in your ability to understand the world, depending on your mum and dad's combined take-home and the size of their bloody drawing room. Wasn't this what they were trying to get away from?

But then Rob wasn't very big on irony.

He couldn't see the joke in his class-warrior act any more than he could see that his use of – for want of a better expression – "political correctness" was in itself a vehicle for his own prejudices. Actually, there wasn't a better expression, that was the problem. Nicole didn't think political correctness existed as an entity or a code or a system or anything else. It was a phrase that certain conservative elements had thought up because they needed a stick to beat back at the liberals with. It was a phrase coined by people who resented the fact that you couldn't treat niggers, yids, shirt-lifters, bints and cripples the way you used to, who wanted to believe that it was all part of some organised agenda (and therefore reversible), rather than a natural, gradual, evolved process of increased understanding and therefore tolerance, which was leaving them all behind.

Rob, however, used it to look down on people and social groups in what he thought was an ideologically sanctioned way. A new snobbery for the Nineties. His sneering disdain when he heard someone address a woman as "luv" or "pet" or "darlin'", for instance, thinking there was a crime in the language, unmitigated by innocuous intent. People who didn't recycle their newspapers. People who bought the wrong newspapers in the first place. People who talked about "girls", not "women". He never realised that what he was really sneering at was that they were somehow less than him, beneath him. And the fact that they were almost invariably working-class was probably significant. (Just maybe.)

God knows how, but they lasted more than eighteen months. In the end it was taking him to actually *meet* her parents that finished it, but then maybe, in a devilish way, taking him to meet her parents had been her *way* of finishing it. She must have known what would happen.

Rob just wasn't programmed for it. It did not compute. Her father was warm, welcoming, genuine, generous and, above all, magnanimous. Rob must have been shattered not to find himself perceptibly disapproved of, nor any great strain between Dariusz Carrow and his younger daughter. Her dad didn't agree with her politics, but had (almost infuriatingly) refused to be upset by her apostasy; indeed he seemed amused (in a not quite the full hundred per cent patronising manner, though close) that she had turned out this way. But that was him through and through. He was someone who was entertained by life's twists and surprises, rather than constantly disappointed by its failure to meet his expectations (which, she too late understood, rendered her efforts at rebellion rather futile).

To Rob, politics was about good guys and bad guys, knights and dragons. He never had the grace to acknowledge positive aspects of political opponents, couldn't admit to qualities of humour, wit, generosity or conscience in a Tory. He saw them as non-persons, sub-human, or (of course, thank you Mr Bevan) vermin. Nicole had heard such terms before, but more importantly, so had her grandmother, in Poland.

She could read his mind at the dinner table, see him find all sorts of ideological significance in the constituents of the delicious menu her mum had prepared for them (he must have been shattered at the absence of servants), but the overall atmosphere of warmth and civility was what finally flipped him out. He was one of the knights, and he clearly felt duty-bound to slay the dragon, despite the dragon's hospitality and conspicuous failure to breathe any fire.

Her dad didn't rise to it at first, trying to be both diplomatic and polite in changing the subject. But Rob had to fight, needed to fight. Even though this was being served up unprovoked at his own table, Dariusz was clearly prepared to let it go rather than cause a scene that would upset his daughter. However, a combination of annoyance that *Rob* was upsetting his daughter and the fact that his wife had already weighed in and been subject to

23

some moral accusations that were as insulting as they were bizarre, meant that the gloves had to come off.

And Nicole enjoyed it. She really, utterly, massively enjoyed it. It was like watching the All Blacks against her old school team. Her father was a trial lawyer, for God's sake – what chance did the goateed pipsqueak think he had? She could see the look on his face, the defeat, the self-disgust, the realisation that he was finally playing for his team, fighting for his side, wearing the jersey – and getting an absolute trouncing (or gubbing, as they'd say round here). The desolation of seeing his supposedly infallible moral sword blunted and useless, the first time he'd ever really got to unsheathe it.

And it wasn't fair. Not fair at all. She knew that. She could not possibly have condoned some of the stances her father took or the tactics he employed, but his technique was nonetheless breathtaking to watch.

Rob couldn't face her, and she knew that too. There was no big scene, not even a heavy phone-call. In fact he never rang again, and tended not to be around the same bars, clubs, meetings or buildings as her after that either.

She saw a bit more of her parents, though. There had been a few shared glances between her and her father during his demolition of Rob, a few mutually noted glints of enjoyment, a joke just the two of them were in on. So she made a greater effort to go home the odd weekend, and her father made a greater effort to be there when she did.

They were able to talk politics together from time to time, and although he never attempted to change her views, and she definitely couldn't accept his positions, he did nonetheless teach her a few things.

"We're not monsters, Pepper, that's the first thing you've got to appreciate," he once said. "This demonisation, it's not healthy, not constructive. You *know* I'm not some rampaging oppressor; neither are my family or your mother's family. And we're not 'the exception that proves the rule', either. Don't fall into the trap of thinking everyone who doesn't agree with you is some kind of alien whom you can't possibly relate to or communicate with.

"I know that shouting a few slogans and lobbing some metaphorical rotten apples at a few aunt sallies can help get a head of steam up, but it's no substitute for political debate. It's also not a million miles away from what your man Orwell was on about. You go back and read about the Two-Minute Hate next time you see a bunch of protesters chanting hysterically on some demo. What this country needs, as a democracy – maybe now more than ever – is an exchange of ideas, some discourse. And you can't have that if you don't respect the other side a little."

"Well I don't think anyone ever told Thatcher that, when she was talking about 'wiping socialism from the face of the Earth'," Nicole replied. "That didn't exactly do a great deal to engender an atmosphere conducive to reasoned debate, did it?"

"No, it didn't," he conceded. "It certainly reduced the currency of debate – I think deliberately. After years of consensus politics, she knew it was going to be a time for really taking sides, and it stiffened a few spines to mix it like that. Some would see it as a deft political manoeuvre, but certainly it left a bad taste in a few mouths. None more than your grandfather's. I know you'll find it hard to believe, but we used to argue about politics a great deal, while you and Gillian were tucked up in bed upstairs. Your grandfather was what was called a 'Wet'. An Old School Conservative who saw politics as a more gentlemanly affair than it has become today. He always said he found Thatcher and her accomplices . . . rather 'thuggish', was the word he used."

"And you?"

"I was younger, and it was a climate for a younger generation. I've got my reservations in retrospect, but at the time, Pepper . . . Well, it was *exciting*, let me tell you. It was intoxicating. Things were really changing, rapidly. And I know you'll tell me that while the champagne was flowing and the Porsches were lining up around the Square Mile, the bill for the party was being met elsewhere – in the North and in Scotland – but by God it shook the country up. It changed it, moved it forward. And there will be winners and losers every time there's change, so don't tell me to feel guilty because I was one of the winners this time. For despite the aspects that seem rather distasteful in hindsight, if I went back there I'd sign up to be a part of it all again."

"You'd vote for her if she made a comeback?"

"No, no. I just mean that I don't regret the choices I made back then. Different measures suit different times. I don't believe I was wrong, *we* were wrong or even she was wrong, even though I do regret some of her legacies."

"Like what?"

"Well, like this mutually suspicious politics of hatred that we've been talking about. I know it's hard, but you've got to put it behind you, rise above it. It's no good me saying 'don't reduce politics to a slanging match' and you replying 'well, your lot started it'. At some point you've got to write off the old scores and look ahead to a new game. And although I know you don't respect the people in the Cabinet just now, you have to look beyond them, too. It's about ideas and values, not slogans and personalities.

"I don't know, maybe I've turned into an old Wet like your grandfather, or maybe it's just the lawyer in me, but I think politics is more fun when there's two strong sides squaring up, no quarter asked or given, and respect on both sides. Because if you don't respect your opponent, you're not respecting the game, and that means you're not respecting our parliament."

"What, so you're telling me after all this time that you respect the Labour Party? That you respected Neil Kinnock?"

"I respect the fact that the Labour Party has always been an advocate for, well, sections of society that have perhaps not been so high on the Conservative agenda. And *you* have to respect the fact that the Left's agenda doesn't cover the whole spectrum either. I know it sounds trite to say that 'it's all very well looking after the poor but someone needs to look after the rich', but there's a grain of truth in it nonetheless. And that truth is that in Britain we need two sides, two advocates, each reminding the other about the issues that aren't on their agendas, the parts of the board that their plans don't cover."

"It might help if a few of the current cabinet thought that way too," Nicole said.

Her father had arched his brows, seemingly troubled by unspoken thoughts.

"Yes, well," he said. "I'd have to give you that one. I do often wonder what your grandfather would have made of the likes of Portillo and Swan. He was a great admirer of Lord Home in his day, of men who saw their role in government as one of service. The problem with those two is that they are very much creatures of current politics. One gets the impression when one of them drafts a paper or makes a speech, they're less concerned with how the idea would affect the country than how its reception will affect their standing within the party. I never thought I'd hear myself say it, Pepper, but I do fear that it's a symptom of a party too long in government."

"Well, it seems there's at least one thing we're agreed on."

However, there had been another consequence of her father's humiliation of Rob back then, something that strengthened Nicole's resolve to make her own way in law, something that confirmed the difference between them. She had enjoyed his mastery, certainly, and thrilled at his oratory, but was disturbed not only by his use of arguments that she found abhorrent, but more by his use of arguments that she knew *he* found abhorrent.

There were lawyers, she knew, who although they would (obviously) never admit it, nonetheless took pride in achieving a verdict they knew to be unjust, considering it a testament to their own prowess that they could play the game so expertly. Lawyers who well knew that their client had done it, for instance, but whose egos it boosted to win the case, to let their own abilities wield more power than the facts. And she knew that it wasn't all down to egotistical misanthropy; whatever his or her beliefs or intentions, a lawyer has to do whatever is in his or her power to win the case, and can soon forget the morality of it as the race gets faster, the contest heats up.

27

But there was still something very distasteful about it, something that underlined how it was just a game to the lawyers when it meant a hell of a lot more to the other people inside and outside of the courtroom. Gods playing with the mortals for their sport.

There was a look on Rob's face, fed up with him as she had been, which she recognised and which bothered her. She knew it from courtrooms, from the many spare mornings and afternoons she had spent watching trials. The bewildered, frustrated and – most significantly – impotent look on the face of the poor sod on the stand, as he sees truth, fact, logic and reason implode and disintegrate under an onslaught of semantic gymnastics, molecule-width hair-splitting, near Dadaist reinterpretation, and mean, downright sophistry. And she didn't just mean the accused or the plaintiff; how often had she seen the honest eye-witness, or the casualty officer who treated the victim, or whoever, stagger back into the body of the courtroom feeling like they had been unmasked up there as a malignant liar, an incompetent moron, or both?

The devil, it seemed, was never short of an advocate. The ordinary punter, however, was often less spoilt for choice in his representation. And so what if it sounded naive? She wanted to assist people as they cowered before the imposing and forbidding complexity of this machine which otherwise sucked them in, twisted them, stretched them, turned them inside out and upside down, and then spat them out, telling them as they lay there, dazed, whether it had (by the way) found for or against them.

A guide through the maze, a Sherpa on their climb.

Nicole's real sin hadn't been a rebellion, but a vanity. While her father expertly worked the machine, she thought she could take it on. This is what you want: to defend the ordinary Joe who is being buffeted, abused and toyed with at the unknown whims of a shapeless entity he can no more understand than he can control.

This is what you get: "Post-dramatic stress hingmy."

"Don't touch the lassie's fanny pads."

Careful what you wish for.

*

When the sobs subsided, she remained in place with her head on the desk for a while, wondering whether she should attempt a Major Major-style exit out of the window, only never to return again. Trouble was, she was two floors up over West Regent Street.

She heard the door open, then looked up slowly to see a man standing before her, holding what was locally known as a tammy in both hands. He looked mid-to-late-fifties, tall and broad, carrying excess weight in places that paradoxically suggested he was once a lot more trim. Formidably so, even.

"Oh God, I'm sorry," she said with a sniff, suddenly sparking herself into action, tidying a few items on her desk and harassedly moving around to gather some of the debris from the office floor.

"Let me get those," he had said, almost to himself, placing his tammy on a chair and kneeling down to pick up a few sheets of paper.

"No no," she said, failing hopelessly not to sound flustered. "I'll manage, I'll manage." She sniffed again, her tubes still a little choked, her face feeling conspicuously puffy. "I just need a moment here . . ."

"Look, tell you what," he said in deep, soothing tones, "why don't I make you a wee cuppa tea while you take a wee minute to sort yoursel' oot. Maybe even nick oot for a bit of fresh air."

"You know, I'm perfectly capable of making myself a cup of tea if I decide I want one," she snapped, not taking her eyes off the multicoloured documents scattered around her. "I'm not . . ."

"Miss Carrow," he interrupted, the voice again soft but lent persuasion by its diaphragmic bassiness, "I'm sure you're extremely capable of makin' yoursel' a cuppa tea, and plenty more besides. But you look like you've had a helluva rough day, an' I'm just sayin' let me make you wan while you . . . recompose yourself, if you like."

She suddenly stopped fumbling around on the floor and looked up at the man, closing her eyes for a second and then giving him an apologetic smile.

"I'm sorry," she half-whispered, shaking her head. "I don't mean to be rude. You're right. I have had a hell of a day."

29

He held a hand out to her to help her climb back to her feet. Nicole grasped it and laughed a little.

"A cup of tea would be just lovely," she said. "Mr . . .?"

"McInnes. Tam McInnes."

Mr McInnes had looked to the kettle and mugs while she finished gathering up the stray stationery and opened a window. He placed the steaming mug on the desk in front of her and took a seat opposite.

Nicole took a few warm, restorative gulps and sighed, a long, slow exhalation.

"That bad, eh?" Mr McInnes inquired.

"You've no idea," she said, and then began, inexplicably, to rant to this total stranger, letting go everything from the past couple of weeks and far beyond between mouthfuls of tea, while he sat there and nodded sagely, or responded with understanding, unjudgmental comments.

"My own fault, really," she had said during one of the more lucid passages. "Being a such a bloody-minded and impetuous creature. Such a bloody stereotyped middle-class daughter, trying to rebel against Daddy for reasons I can't even begin to understand, and that I don't think Freud understood so well either. Do you have children, Mr McInnes?"

He nodded with a smile, his eyes straying just long enough for her to detect the conflicts of love, hope, disappointment and regret.

"Aye."

"Well, forgive them," she said, "for they know not what they do. My father's a lawyer. His father was a lawyer. Two of his brothers are lawyers. I suppose if I really wanted to rebel I should have gone into the arts or something."

"Or become a crook," Mr McInnes offered.

"No. Two sides of the same coin. If you're going to play fast and loose with the law anyway, you might as well get a bit of security."

"So what was your big rebellion?"

Nicole laughed. "Coming here, I suppose, among other things."

"To Glesca?"

"Yeah, sort of. Well, partly. Maybe. I don't know. I don't know."

She had another gulp of tea.

"Daddy specialises in libel law, and I grew to see that as a way for rich, successful people to make themselves even more rich and successful because they'd never heard the phrase 'sticks and stones may break my bones but names will never hurt me'."

"I wouldnae be so sure they hadn't heard it," Mr McInnes offered. "Seems to me being called a few names hasn't hurt a few of them, financially speakin'."

"Yes, but that's precisely my point. It just seemed to be about money, nothing but money. Among people to whom only money meant anything, my father included, and that was something I could never understand."

"Well, it certainly comes in handy when you're peyin' for the messages."

She shook her head, laughing sadly at herself.

"I know, I know. It's pathetic. I'm a collage of clichés. I don't know. I don't know what I'm doing here. Some bunch of reasons that seemed so important once upon a time but suddenly didn't seem quite so inspirational this morning.

"I came here because I wanted to prove I could make it on my own, away from all that . . . benevolent familial support. I also had some insane notion about helping people. Maybe some adolescent Gareth Pearce fantasy, I don't know."

"Why here?"

"Well, I didn't want to leave England, and I couldn't think of anywhere more different from London, more removed from what I was used to. It's also a different legal system, which meant an awful lot of extra studying and even a few correspondence courses, but it meant that I'd be working within something my family – and I suppose I really mean my father – were excluded from."

31

"So did your father dae somethin' to upset you? Ach, sorry, that's none of my business."

Nicole shook her head and waved her right hand placatorily.

"No, no. You're quite right. It's a logical enough question. But the fact is quite the opposite. He provided everything for me. Put me through school, university, and was ready to set me up in the legal profession for life. I always loved him, dearly, but I don't know . . . I wasn't trying to bite his hand; I wasn't trying to throw it all back in his face. I don't know what the bloody hell I was trying to do."

"Maybe you were tryin' to make him proud of you," Mr McInnes said flatly, a notion that made her suddenly sit up. "You could have been a good wee lassie and gone and worked for his firm, but then you'd only have been a good wee lassie. Maybe this way you're tryin' to show him what you can achieve on your own, even to repay him for everythin' he'd given you."

Nicole just sat and stared, fixated by the sad-smiled man opposite, and thinking that his words were quite the most disarmingly perceptive ones she had heard in several years.

Another part of her wondered at what mistakes he had made and what harsh lessons he had learnt as the price for such understanding.

"So, Mr McInnes," she eventually said, after some polite smalltalk had cleared the ashes of their previous discussion. "I hope after all that that there is actually something I can do for you."

"Aye," he said, rather darkly, and produced an A4 brown envelope from inside his jacket.

"I need you to look after this," he explained, placing it on the desk. "I need you to record that I've gie'd you it, sealed, then haud on to it until next Monday afternoon. If I don't pick it up before then, open it."

"What's in it?"

"If we're baith lucky, you'll never find oot."

TWO

"**Bastards! Bastards! How** dare they! Who the hell do they think they are? Killing him just like that, arbitrarily putting an end to the man's life without the merest thought."

Carefully carrying a couple of mugs of morning coffee into the bedroom, Sarah Slaughter was slightly perturbed by her fiancé's uncharacteristic hawkishness as he sat, red-eyed and ranting at the radio. He usually turned over and slept on after the alarm went off and she got up to have her bath, but he had obviously heard something of profound interest – and irritation – while she lay in the tub.

She handed him his coffee now that his arms had temporarily ceased their agitated gesticulation.

"So who's dead, Jack?"

"Didn't you hear? Roland Voss. Roland fucking *Voss*. Cops have four guys in custody."

"Really? My God," she gasped. Then "Ah," suddenly understanding his upset. She put her coffee down on the bedside table and took his left hand in both of her own, then leaned over and kissed his neck in a proven method of calming his spirits. "That's a shame," she whispered sympathetically.

33

He put his own mug down, switched off the radio and sat back against the headboard, his tousled hair making him look like Oor Wullie meets a Van de Graaf generator.

"Sorry to get so worked up, Sarah, but I just think it's such a tragic, tragic waste."

"It is, it is," she agreed softly.

"I mean, there must have been thousands of people in this world biding their time until they could get their own back on that slimy nyaff, and now these four clowns have gone and spoiled it for everybody. Inconsiderate arseholes."

"Come on, you can't blame them completely, darling," Sarah reasoned, her soothing English tones a balm against his early-morning Glaswegian croak. "Maybe they didn't know who he was."

Jack Parlabane's eyes widened with frustration.

"Well, that's a matter for some conjecture. But the thought that they might not have is what's so bloody tragic. If they had taken the time to get to know him even a little, or to learn just a wee bit about him, I'm pretty sure they would have decided that death was too good for the devious, Machiavellian son of a bitch."

"Well, I'm certainly relieved to hear you say that. For a moment I thought you were upset because you had been planning to kill him yourself."

Jack raised his eyebrows and grinned, a mix of aw-shucks bashfulness and RKO-villain malice that she found in equal measures unsettling and endearing. Sarah remembered an uncomfortable few seconds about eighteen months back, during which she had feared Jack *was* going to kill someone, right in front of her. Retrospectively it had seemed a rather ungrateful gesture, considering that it was the man who had effectively brought the two of them together, but in Jack's defence, he *had* also tried to murder the pair of them. It would make great small-talk when they met long-lost rellies. So how did you two meet? Oh, familiar stuff. Boy meets girl, boy meets slaughtered corpse of girl's ex-husband, boy and girl uncover massive conspiracy, that sort of thing. Same old same-o.

"So what happened?" Sarah asked. "When was all this?"

34

"Last night. Amazing what you can miss when you're pished out of your face, isn't it."

Sarah reached again for her coffee and rubbed the side of her head.

"Tell me about it," she said mournfully.

She had been on-call over the weekend, but had the rest of Monday off once she got home around ten. After a couple of hours' kip and a long soak, they had hit the Cask for lunch and remained there for an inadvisably long time afterwards. Somewhere amidst the blur she could hazily remember an inevitable curry and some very clumsily executed but nonetheless enjoyable sex. The next flashback was of staggering woozily into the kitchen at about three a.m. for some Irn-Bru and a couple of paracetamol. Significant world events had, curiously, not featured.

"I can hardly believe it," Jack mumbled. "Voss dead. Actually dead. I mean, guys like Voss don't die. Good guys die. Arseholes live forever. John Smith dies, John Major lives. Bill Hicks dies, Jim Davidson lives. After all these years, it's so hard to believe the slimebag is just suddenly gone."

"So whodunnit? Who are these guys the cops've got?"

"Christ knows. Couple of them have form for turning over some country mansions back in the Eighties. Cops are invoking the Prevention of Terrorism Act so they can turn the screw without any interference from lawyers, but from the sound of it, they're still entertaining the possibility that it was a burglary, and that killing Voss and his missus was just part of the deal."

"They killed his wife too?" said Sarah, appalled.

"Yeah. And two bodyguards. Which makes it sound to me that killing was definitely on the itinerary; it was certainly an eventuality they were prepared for. These guys were shot through the head, standing outside the VIP suite, presumably so that they didn't interrupt."

"And Mr and Mrs Voss?" asked Sarah.

Jack winced visibly. He drew a finger quickly and unhistrionically across his neck, looking away from her. Sarah's ex-husband had become an ex-person in roughly the same fashion, and although his loss hadn't exactly devastated her, it was still the method of violence least likely to be mentioned in a romantic dinner conversation between them.

"So why did they . . . do that when they had shot the body-guards? I mean, if they had guns . . ."

"I was beginning to ask myself the same question," he said, with a look of concentration she had long ago learnt to be wary of.

"Oh dear," said Sarah accusingly. "I can see your antennae beginning to swivel. Conspiracy glands starting to secrete?"

"Just a little," he confessed, smiling. "A smidgen."

"Well at least wait until you've heard some more details before you start cooking up any theories."

"Oh sure," he offered. "But I was just thinking that the – shall we say – *inconsistency* in the manner of execution does lend itself to the possibility of a terrorist, or at least vengeful, motive."

"So would it make you feel better to think that someone had specifically set out to kill *him*, rather than to kill whoever happened to get in the way?"

"Well I'd hate to think whoever did it didn't appreciate what a privilege it was."

"You're a sick bastard, Jack Parlabane, do you know that?"

"Well, just remember you've opted to be Mrs Sick Bastard, Dr Slaughter."

She stood up and reached for a dress, letting the bathrobe slip to the floor.

"It's a decision that's seldom far from my thoughts," she said, with a stern tone but a devilish glance.

Parlabane wasn't just being facetious or gratuitously offensive, even though he had an effortless talent for both. Unlike the many thousands of people who would be having a little chuckle over their cornflakes this morning, or maybe an extra drink before bed last night after catching the late news, his score with Voss was personal. Mutually.

And Sarah knew that, which was why, despite her efforts to hide it, he could tell she had been a little on edge before going out to work. She obviously hadn't wanted to overstate her case, but he could read the point she needed him to consider:

People do just get killed. Murdered even. It can happen to anybody. Even evil, scheming, right-wing billionaires. Just because his demise would cause wider ripples than normal didn't mean there was more to Voss's death than met the eye.

Hey, hey. My, my.

Parlabane was a connoisseur of conspiracy theories. It had been remarked that he was so paranoid, he should have been a Catholic; better yet, a Celtic supporter. He considered his own thoughts on Voss that morning. He couldn't just die, not someone like that. Even if there was a revenge motive, even a terrorist motive, how could four guys – two of whom had to be well into their fifties – circumvent the kind of security there must have been, and take out two trained bodyguards?

But then he could hear Sarah's voice talking again about the mythology that seems to grow like a fungus upon the corpse of a dead celebrity. Some people can't deal with the loss, with the thought of a world darkened by the snuffing out of *that* bright star. Voss hadn't exactly brought light to Parlabane's world, but he still had a very special place in his thoughts, in that most volatile of compartments, the one marked "Unfinished Business".

And that, Sarah would surely tell him, was the problem: he needed Voss to still be there; and with no more life, he had to find greater meaning in his death. Like Elvis Presley. Like John Lennon. Like Marilyn Monroe.

Like JFK?

Nah.

Sarah was probably nervous because of the timing. Less than a month to the wedding, promises made and (so far) promises kept. Then this.

The Last Temptation of Parlabane.

"Look upon it as a challenge," she had said, as much in consolation as encouragement. "You can still be the world's most paranoid and irritating investigative reporter; you just have to do it without playing fast and loose with the police, the security forces or the laws of physics."

It was what he had to agree to before *she* would agree to becoming his wife. No more recourse to his, ahem, less conventional journalistic techniques; viz, picking locks, scaling buildings, burgling offices and hacking computer systems.

"There's no point in me marrying someone who's soon going to end up in prison or even dead."

"Why not? Your last husband was dead when you married him."

"No, Jack, Jeremy was *un*dead. There's a subtle difference."

"Well, he looked pretty fucking dead the last time I saw him," he *hadn't* said – evidencing one of those amazing changes he had gone through since meeting Sarah, prior to which certain former girlfriends had described him variously as "Captain Sensitive", "subtle as a belt in the baws wi' a bag o' bools" and "as romantic as a bucket of shit". Love Is: being able to keep your fucking mouth shut.

So he had been a good boy so far, and Sarah must have been afraid this reappearance of a ghost from his past might send him off on some last crusade, a disappointingly male demonstration of his suppressed virility. So near to the wedding, she was probably worried he might consider it his own equivalent of a stag night.

He shook his head, laughing a little at the thought of her anxiety and at what now struck him as the ridiculousness of certain past antics. Jack Parlabane: sniffer of a million scams, fearless, intrepid, resourceful, incisive, and quite clearly, in vivid retrospect, in need of serious spiritual and emotional guidance. He saw images of a furtive-looking bloke in a black polo-neck and black jeans, climbing out of windows, dozens of floors up, computer disks and photocopied documents strapped to his chest, shinning up ropes, hanging off gutters and drainpipes.

Oh yeah, and getting shot at.

What the fuck were you *doing*? he often asked himself.

Ah, Sarah, he thought. Didn't she remember what he had said back then, in response to her request?

"I'm too old for all that carry-on."

In a simple equation: if he was mature enough to finally want to get married – and he meant really, really, *achingly* want – then he was too mature for "all that James Bond stuff", as she called it.

Still, didn't mean he couldn't take an interest.

If Roland Voss had got his way, Parlabane would still be in jail right now for Class A possession with intent to supply, in little danger of seeing any more of the twentieth century first hand, especially since that tit Howard – the one who seemed to have such difficulty achieving the relatively simple feat of pronouncing the letter "L" – had attempted with embarrassing desperation to win some votes by mooting the abolition of early remission. Parlabane's crime was to let Voss know, with trademark subtlety, that he knew the Dutchman had been using him. Neither was infringing any laws: what Voss was up to – getting Parlabane to do hatchet jobs on his business rivals in his flagship Sunday broadsheet, Parlabane unaware of the fringe benefits of his exposés – was as legal as it was difficult to prove. Parlabane, for his part, had simply resigned and made no threat to embarrass Voss publicly with his knowledge. But within a matter of hours his Clapham flat had been turned over, and he discovered and disposed of a large slab of party powder with moments to spare before the cops turned up looking for it. Jack was a man who could take "fuck off" for a hint. He shipped. Put most of his gear in storage and took off for California, on a promise from an old friend who was now Metro editor of the *LA Tribune*.

Perhaps Voss had him set up with the coke just in case, but Parlabane suspected it was simply a punitive sanction to demonstrate the folly of having the audacity to oppose the Dutchman's will in any capacity whatsoever.

He was an evil, evil man.

The Monopolies and Mergers Commission seemed afflicted by chronic cataracts as it failed to notice anything amiss throughout his acquisition of newspaper after newspaper after radio station after pay-TV channel, making Parlabane wonder whether the government body's senior staff actually knew what the word "monopoly" meant. Either that or they had misunderstood their remit and thought their role was to help *create* the things.

But by a staggeringly unlikely coincidence, all of Voss's media voices just happened to be singing the government's tune, whatever their previous allegiances. Which obviously had no bearing whatsoever on the blind spot that Voss seemed to occupy in the MMC's field of vision.

Parlabane saw the tabloids as Voss's own private Cerberus, a multi-headed bulldog baying its ugly howl of racism, misogyny, homophobia and moral repression in a seething ferox of hatred. Cerberus would defend to the death the ordinary Brit's right to remain ignorant, underlining for its readers that just because the person telling you something is the world authority in that particular field doesn't mean he knows any better than you. Safe sex? Pah! AIDS is a poof's disease, innit. If you're not an arse-bandit, you've nothing to fear. Guildford Four? If they didn't do that one, they're bound to have done something else. If we'd been able to string 'em up back then, British Justice would never have been called into question. Greenhouse effect? Bollocks! If it's getting warmer we should celebrate. Save us splashing out on foreign holidays and handing over our hard-earned to a bunch of dagoes.

With obscenity barked so loud and so long, people got used to it, desensitised. Stopped seeing the harm. Thus is the political climate altered.

Voss also had a couple of prestige broadsheets (two-hundred-year reputations soiled almost instantly by the touch of his leprous hand) for window-dressing, but the Dutchman's main British media trade was in ignorance. He packaged ignorance, marketed ignorance and sold ignorance – to the ignorant. Millions of acres of pine forest, millions of gallons of ink, legions of hacks, subs, photographers, all combining daily to tell people . . . nothing.

"Famous, important, reputable married man and young, attractive single woman in role-playing/kinky/S&M/back-of-the-car/hotel-room/privacy-of-their-own-home sex romp shock."

Sub editor please.

"Famous married man and single woman have sex."

No, still some redundancies. Neater please.

"Married man and single woman have sex."

Just the bones of the story, space is tight.

"Man and woman have sex."

What a scoop. Hold the front page.

Drive that common denominator lower. Distract the proles with drying-green tittle-tattle so they don't notice anything of what's actually going on in the world.

Jesus, when he thought about it, Parlabane had probably hated Roland Voss more than he hated any other human being on the planet, even Jimmy Hill.

How many revenges had he fantasised? How many poetic come-uppances? How many gruesome, lonely and humiliating deaths? However, they were only fantasies; Parlabane was not a violent man. But it wasn't the pain or the violence that was the turn-on. Entirely. It was of penetrating Voss's invulnerability, rendering him human. Of him suffering the things he was so protected from, the everyday reality of normal people that he never experienced but still cast judgment upon, and which he could greatly affect. "Mile in my shoes" stuff. Fantasies of Voss suffering poverty, joblessness, discrimination, as much as of him being beaten up by homosexual martial arts experts after his papers declared gays were "not man enough to be in the armed forces". It was the thought of him being forced to pay dues for his words and actions. Being forced to acknowledge that there *was* a price, even for him, the mighty Roland Voss. And the fun of the fantasy, the *source* of the fantasy, was its sheer impossibility.

But last night someone had cut Voss's wife's throat right in front of him – probably forced him to watch – and then made sure it was the last thing he ever saw.

Voss didn't deserve *that*. Neither did his wife. No-one did. No-one. A solid, full-blooded boot in the balls, maybe, but not that. Detached postures of schadenfreude were one thing, but the visceral reality of Voss's death made Parlabane sick. And if it could make him sick, it would make anyone sick. Which was why the media was loudly asking itself who these men were that could bring themselves to do such a terrible thing. "A dire, extreme consequence of the Left's politics of envy," suggested one generously superannuated pundit, making the most of the Robbin' Hoods angle throughout the frustrating delay in the cops tossing them a terrorist motive they could really get their teeth into.

Parlabane didn't care who had done it. And although naturally curious, he wasn't particularly consumed by wondering *why* they'd done it – Christ, pick one motive from a thousand.

What he really wanted to know was *how* the fuck they had done it.

DS Jenny Dalziel opened the cold can of diet Irn-Bru with a practised action of her index finger, holding it up with her right hand and clanking it against Callaghan's Sprite as he leaned against her desk, not taking her eyes off the report in front of her. She made to reach for a pile of change amidst the clutter that ringed her peripheral vision like crime-scene ghouls, but Call waved a hand dismissively and pulled away from the desk.

Jesus, you needed Call on a day like today. In fact, it was in these moments after the fan had liberally redistributed the Douglas Hurd that he was usually at his best, adversity and chaos provoking a laconic, unflappable air; as if just a plain ol' normal day somehow didn't provide the right sort of stimulation. You got the impression he was there for you, or at the very least that he understood, even if it was just the shared secret of a subtly abusive gesture, like half an hour ago when he had cupped one hand around the right side of his chest after that MI5 bear started shouting at everybody.

When his missus sprogged last year, Jenny had feared Callaghan might, like many before him, turn into a jumpy, obsessive goo-ball or a tired-eyed Grumposaurus Rex, but there had so far been no evidence of either. Thank fuck.

Her phone started ringing as Callaghan walked away, prompting him to turn around and grin archly. He held up nine fingers, in reference to their last conversation.

"A fiver," he said.

Jenny just fixed him with an "I don't need this" look.

"Answer it. A fiver."

She rolled her eyes. "Go away, Call," she said, eyeing the phone resentfully. He held up the nine fingers again then turned away.

The phone kept ringing.

She really *didn't* need this.

When she walked into the building this morning, it was like someone had been through and sprayed the place with oestrogen repellent. The British Olympic team for the Male Self-Importance event had invaded Lothian & Borders HQ, a rampant infestation of facial hair and Y chromosomes. They had been parading around the place with a brusque arrogance that was just dying for an excuse to tell you how much more serious their business was than anything you might be trying to get on with, such as the body of Fiona Dickson, prostitute, found bludgeoned behind Commercial Street in Leith. Fiona didn't own any newspapers or TV stations, so manpower was likely to be a little thinner on the ground when it came to the investigation of her death, what with everyone having to impress the Scottish Office with a result on the Voss killings.

Wankers.

The station hadn't been besieged, it had been taken over. Anyone not directly involved with the Voss investigation was being treated not only as irrelevant, but with a hostility that bordered on suspicion of complicity. The atmosphere was horrible.

There were more desperate men outside the cells than in. To paraphrase the great WB, the worst were full of passionate intensity, and right now they lacked a conviction.

And of course this whole thing had to follow a weekend largely dominated by one of Angela's periodic episodes of psychoanalysing her own sexuality, another bout of "am I really a lesbian, I mean, am I just reacting to my upbringing, is this a phase, I'm so confused, I find you attractive but then I sometimes find some men attractive although I'm not sure I'd want to do anything with them, you know, sexually, it's just that, oh, I don't know . . ." Etcetera. It was funny how these soul-searching crises of sexual confusion always coincided with the approach of one of Angela's law exams. And funny also how Angela was less uncertain of her desires and orientations when she was licking ice-cream off Jenny's stomach on summer Sunday afternoons after a stroll round the Botanics.

She was used to it. It would pass. But now wasn't a good time; Jenny felt at the moment that *she* should be the one being indulged a bit of erratic or self-pitying behaviour.

Still the phone rang. Wearily, she reached over and picked it up.

"Hi Jenny, guess who?"

"I don't need to," she said gravely. "I already knew. Why do you think I let it ring so long? It's a fucking circus over here, and Callaghan was just saying he gave this entire situation a Parlabane factor of nine, making it only a matter of time . . . and now here you are."

"It's nice to be wanted."

"You're not fucking wanted," she said, trying to sound mordantly humorous but failing to hide the harassed tones in her voice.

Jack Parlabane. Or, to give him his full name, Jack Bloody Parlabane. Also known as Trouble. Jesus Christ's arrival had been precursorily heralded by the appearance of John the Baptist. Parlabane's had been preceded by a ridiculously mutilated corpse overlooked by a gigantic jobbie on a mantelpiece. It could not have been more appropriate. Carnage, chaos and dead people

44

seemed to surround him like an aura, and after his passing, there was always plenty of shite to clear up, with Jenny usually the one left wielding the shovel.

His involvement infallibly ensured that a situation would imminently go out of control on a scale she seldom had the stomach to anticipate; and if it was already disintegrating, Parlabane was a guarantee that you hadn't seen nothin' yet. However, it remained a fluctuating matter of internal debate for Jenny whether he was more trouble than he was worth. She knew that her career had been enhanced by having been the one who put the collar on certain high-profile scumbags whose deeds would have remained undetected without his unorthodox and frequently unnerving interventions, notably that NHS big-noise last year. But there was, at the same time, the gnawing question of what opportunities may have been lost to the time she spent either clearing up after him or trying to warn him off for his own good.

Because that was the real fear. Parlabane wasn't a catalyst; he didn't stroll through the wreckage and the rubble, oblivious to the havoc he was precipitating. He was a danger to himself and others. While he could often be the one who saw through the facades, who had the intuition and the sheer balls to break a case right open, there was always and equally the possibility that he'd bring the whole thing down on top of himself and anyone else who happened to be in the vicinity.

All of which made him the last person she wanted anywhere near her on a day like today.

"Are you okay, Jen?" he asked, concerned. He had once described her as "as phlegmatic as a spittoon at a bronchitics' convention". It wouldn't take much for him to clock that all was not peachy.

"Look, nothing personal, Jack, but fuck off," she said quietly, eyeing the testosterone casualties stomping loudly about the office. "That's not an instruction, it's a piece of advice, you hearing me?"

"I'm listening, but I'm not picking up much sense. Qu'est-ce que c'est le Hampden?"

45

"You want to know the score?" she replied in an agitated near-whisper. "Well as I'm sure you know, somebody just popped the Conservative Party's chief meal-ticket, with the result that they're wheeling out the fucking dancing girls in putting on a show of official reaction. The building's suddenly full of guys with stern faces and smart suits but no name-badges, if you know what I mean. It's like a bad 'tache society reunion. Nobody knows who the fuck these guys are, but the vibe is that they get to ask the questions and you get to do whatever the hell they say."

"G-men types?"

"If it's G for goon squad, aye. Call it a hunch, but I've got an irrational suspicion they know absolutely bugger-all more than anyone else, as the word is that the men in custody aren't saying much that anyone wants to hear, and what they are saying is posing more questions than it answers."

"What do you mean? What are they saying?"

I'm not getting into this, she thought. Not today.

"I don't know," she said. "I don't want to know and that's just as well, because it's pretty clear us plain old cops aren't supposed to ask. But whatever it is, it has obviously not been enlightening and constructive. That's the problem: these morons are always ten times as dangerous when they don't know what they're looking for.

"Listen to me, Jack, I knew a guy who was on duty in Brighton the night of the bomb in '84. He said they got orders to round up every Irish person they could find. I mean *every* Irish person. Like fucking *shamrocknacht*, you know? He says they lifted pretty much anyone with an Irish accent, Irish name, anyone who'd ever visited Dublin for a stag night, anyone who'd ever drunk a pint of Guinness and anyone who'd ever been to Parkhead. Panic, Scoop. Panic and the political *need* to be seen to be taking massive and decisive action.

"That's what's brewing here. They've got four guys in custody with – literally – blood on their hands, but they still don't know what the fuck's going on, why the thing went down, anything.

46

Consequently it's time for Hunt The Motive. They're already out knocking on doors across the country. Lefties, union officials, anyone they can think of. And if memory serves, you crossed swords with the corpse yourself once, didn't you?"

"Something like that."

"Well that would be enough for these eejits. Like I said, Scoop, fuck off. Keep your head down and your mouth shut. I know you've got a personal interest, but you'd be wise to stay well away from this mess."

"You know I can't do that," he said, with what would normally have proved infectious humour.

Jenny sighed. Stay out of this, Jack. Take a holiday.

"Christ, I wish *I* could," she said. "I've got better things to be getting on with. Another dead prostitute in Leith, and the male public being as forthcoming and cooperative as ever, the hypocritical bastards. Mother of three, but who cares, she's just a pro. Could be some nutter on the loose and I can't get any bodies on to the case because of this Voss fiasco. In fact I could hardly get out the fucking station for TV cameras. It's a media menagerie out there – I got swamped nicking out for a roll and bacon a wee while ago. I'd have had to starve if they hadn't started queuing up for their shot at this lawyer who's been making a nuisance of herself."

"Who she?"

"No idea. She showed up about half-eleven, apparently, claiming to represent one of the suspects. She knows fine she can't speak to him, so she started making noises about wanting some evidence to support the use of Prevention of Terrorism powers. Callaghan said she was getting short shrift until she produced some document, upon which she was immediately wheeched into an office by a couple of the 'tache team. They took their own stat of whatever it was, but Call says she insisted on accompanying them to the photocopier, wouldn't let the thing out of her sight. Half-an-hour later she's out front and the telly's lapping her up. She'll be all over the lunchtime news."

"Brave woman," Parlabane said.

"What do you mean?"

"Well anyone demanding rights for those guys – other than their right to be taken forth from this place and hanged by the neck until dead – is gaunny get some kicking in the press, just doing her job or not. I take it she was pretty young?"

"Yeah," Jenny said, remembering. "I only saw her from a few yards away but she looked a wee bit like her mammy probably didn't know she was out. How did you know?"

"She'll be from some major firm. They'll be happy enough to be involved in this case, for the publicity, but none of the big names will want to be seen sticking up for these guys, not at this stage anyway. I mean, given the climate of bloodlust and retribution over this thing, most firms would see their "defence" role as little more than the formality of delivering their clients into the hands of the sentencing judge."

Oh no. He was off.

"Maybe they've got something, who knows," he continued. "But it sounds to me like they're not sure themselves, otherwise it would be one of their famous names talking to the cameras. Instead they'll send in someone junior – ideally photogenic – who can be 'young and idealistic' in pursuing her cause. They're angling. If it works out, the big man takes over and they wheel her out every so often because the cameras like her. And if it goes nowhere, she can be 'inexperienced and naive' in chasing up a blind alley, and the big man can join in the condemnation of the baddies with everyone else."

Jenny glanced up at the clock. She was in real danger of being sucked into his vortex. Time to eject.

"Well, tell you what, Scoop," she said. "I've got to go. Why don't you tune in and find out. I can't. I've just spotted a formidably solid-looking wall down the corridor and I could really do with banging my head against it."

Parlabane sat back on the settee, having wandered around the room for fully five minutes in a second vain attempt to locate the

VCR's remote control before admitting defeat and making the gruelling six-foot journey to the telly to start the tape recording. Pulling his legs up on to the settee, an indulgent luxury of Sarah's absence, he felt a lump under one thigh and proceeded to fish the errant electronic device out from between two of the cushions.

"Good afternoon," said the newsreader, in a stern tone of voice that suggested it should be anything but; He is dead! He is dead! Anyone caught not mourning to be reported to Conservative Central Office immediately! Parlabane recognised the anchorwoman as one of those media phenomena that just showed up everywhere, like some kind of human corporate logo. Fashion shows, chat shows, consumer relations and even the news, an abject lack of discernible talent, intelligence or personality having proven no impediment to a rocketing career. He distantly wondered for a moment whose cock she had had to suck to enjoy such success, then realised that on this sort of scale, as Hicks would have suggested, it was probably Satan's.

"Inside information may have played a part in the murders last night of Roland and Helene Voss," she led off, subtly relegating the two dead bodyguards to the appropriate proletarian status of Total Fucking Nobodies. "It has emerged today that the four men apprehended at the scene of the crimes may have been assisted by someone connected with the security operations at Craigurquhart House."

Parlabane snorted in mild amusement at her pronunciation, "Craigurkew-hart". Right up there with "Tannadeechee".

The programme cut to the location reporter, one of their bigstory first-team, no doubt dispatched to replace last night's "Scottish affairs correspondent" as this was of national importance and therefore had to be presented in a Home Counties accent and a trenchcoat. He was standing somewhere in Princes Street Gardens. It was nowhere near L&B HQ, but having the Castle in the background was presumably obligatory for broadcasts from Edinburgh – in the same way that, in London, a backdrop of Buckingham Palace wasn't.

"This latest dramatic development followed the arrival of a lawyer representing one of the suspects, Thomas McInnes. Nicole Carrow, of Glasgow law firm Manson & Boyd, gave police a letter she claims was written by her client more than a week before the murders, in which he says he had received vital information about the security arrangements at Craigurquhart House, and that this information would be used to plan a burglary."

The image cut to a petite figure in a light blue skirt and jacket, walking down the steps of the police building, being swarmed upon by an insect-like infestation of multi-limbed creatures – arms, hands, booms, mics and cameras. The purpose of the chaotic footage was, of course, to underline just how bloody important *this* news programme was when she appeared talking exclusively to them in the next shot.

The autumn breeze blew her straight black hair erratically around her pale, girlish face as she spoke, nervous but determined. Parlabane realised then how flustered Jenny must have been; even if Carrow wasn't one hundred per cent exactly the policewoman's type, she was certainly cute enough to have normally elicited comment. Such declarations of desire were a running joke between them; Jenny indulged in the occasional ostentatious pastiche of dykiness when in Parlabane's company, and he steadfastly made no reaction to it. Neither was ever quite sure who was taking the piss out of who.

"I received an envelope from my client at the beginning of last week," she began, English accent, surprisingly husky voice for her age and size, "and was told he would collect it again today. If he did not, I had instructions to open it. Inside wuh . . ." She cleared her throat, brushed some straggly hair from one eye. "Excuse me. Inside was a letter from my client stating that he had been in receipt of information from someone he believed to be connected to the security staff at Craigurquhart House. But most importantly, he states that this information was being used to plan a *burglary*, as he had been informed that, and I quote, 'someone very rich would be staying there from September the twenty-first to the twenty-fifth'.

50

"I have presented this letter to the police because I believe it proves not only that my client's motive for breaking into the house was robbery, but also that neither he nor his accomplices knew the identity of this 'very rich' guest. Nonetheless, the police have persisted in refusing me access to my client under Prevention of Terrorism powers, even though what I am in possession of casts a great deal of doubt upon the notion of a plot to assassinate Mr Voss."

"So you believe Thomas McInnes and his gang simply intended to murder and rob *whoever* they found in the house?" the reporter interjected, suddenly having some sort of Jeremy Paxman delusion.

"No," she said, fixing the off-camera interviewer with a scolding, don't-be-so-fucking-stupid look, "and as a matter of fact I don't believe my client murdered anyone. Right now we're seeing an awful lot in the way of hand-wringing and hysteria and very little in the way of evidence, and until those proportions change I will be persisting in that belief."

"Ha-ha!" Parlabane clapped his hands in appreciation. "Get that up ye, ya poe-faced bastard," he muttered, momentarily distracted from the nagging thought that something she said earlier was bothering him.

"However," continued the poe-faced bastard, now straight-to-camera once more in his editorialising, This Is The News voice, "the police take a different view of what Miss Carrow's letter implies. Detective Superintendent David Garloch, who has been coordinating an investigation involving police from two different Scottish regional forces, believes it could be a deliberate red herring."

Cut to a tired, middle-aged man in a crumpled suit, looking like he could use a sleep, a coffee and a shower. He was sitting at a desk in an open office area, uniformed officers buzzing around looking serious and busy. The next shot was closer up, without such ambitary distraction. He spoke in tones intended to suggest he was a reasonable man trying to remain mannered and calm in the face of unnecessary frustration, like it wasn't enough he had all this to sort out without some daft tart insisting on rocking the boat.

"I appreciate that in light of how dramatic and distressing last night's events may have been for many people," he said, "any new development may be bound to cause great excitement, but it is vital that we keep our feet on the ground. In this climate of uncertainty, it would be easy to imagine Miss Carrow's apparent revelation as a twist in the tale, but in fact it merely confirms what our investigations have been increasingly leading us to believe – that some kind of security leak facilitated last night's tragic events. And indeed, we are already involved in efforts to establish the source of the leak right now. However, it strikes me as disingenuous to suggest that a few handwritten words can in any way clear the suspicion of a terrorist motive."

"And why do you believe that?"

"Well, Miss Carrow's paragraphs do not actually *prove* the suspects didn't know the identity of whoever would be staying at Craigurquhart House. Indeed it strikes me that by going on about 'some rich person' it sounds very much like McInnes was deliberately attempting to cover up the fact that they *did* know, and you have to ask yourself why that might be. You have to ask yourself why Mr McInnes would deposit such a letter with his lawyer prior to taking part in this atrocity. It seems to me the only reason could be as a damage limitation exercise in the event that he was caught. If he has written a letter claiming he intended merely to rob some anonymous rich guest, and that he did not know that rich guest's identity, it would suggest that Mr Voss was not a premeditated target, as well as protecting whoever might be behind the operation – by suggesting that *no-one* was behind it."

The policeman held up his hands in an explanatory gesture. "At this stage," he continued, "we cannot for certain say that this *wasn't* just a very bloody and ruthless attempted robbery, but nothing we have seen gives us any reason to rule out a terrorist motive either, and for that reason we can't afford to relax our position. These men have already managed to murder one of the most powerful businessmen in the world. If there *is* a terrorist group behind them, then it is a very merciless and very resourceful one, and if this is a demonstration of their capabilities, I think it is vital to the security of not just our own country that we do everything in our power to hunt them down."

Fair enough, thought Parlabane, but something was still discomforting him, some half-formed realisation that had got lost along the way, an irritation like trying to remember in which movie he had previously seen some minor-role actress – and whether she might have taken her clothes off in it.

He jogged the remote control to picture-search Rewind, watching the figures and talking heads suddenly turn black and white, and jiggle, newsreel-style, at jerky high-speed. The cop disappeared, replaced by the reporter, replaced in turn by Nicole Carrow, Parlabane all the time trying to remember what had sparked his truncated revelation.

There, he suddenly thought, watching her hand place hair into her eye in a sharp, precise movement. He hit Play and the image slowed, lurchingly, restoring itself to colour a moment before sound returned.

". . . ot, I had instructions to open it. Inside wuh . . ."

Sudden look of uncertainty in the unobscured eye, glancing quickly off and back before she cleared her throat and then swept the offending strands clear. Offending strands that hadn't been bothering her for the four or five seconds they had already been sitting there.

"Excuse me. Inside was a let . . ."

Something was wrong. Something had slightly knocked her off balance.

He jogged into reverse once again, that hand plonking the hair faithfully back into her eye a second time.

". . . open it. Inside wuh . . . Excuse me. Inside was a letter . . ."

She had given something away, or rather was afraid she had.

". . . uctions to open it. Inside wuh . . . Excuse me. Inside waw . . ."

He listened to the accent, the inflections and emphases.

". . . it. Inside wuh . . ."

He had it. She was about to say "inside *were*", not "inside was". That's what was bothering him. She had talked about an envelope first, not a letter.

She had something else. McInnes had given her something else.

The tape played on, Parlabane's blind wondering about what more had been in Carrow's envelope giving way to wondering why no extracts from the letter were being thrown up in any tediously overblown computer-animated graphic sequence to accompany the report, or at least read out by the poe-faced bastard in the trenchcoat. The only explanation for this was that they hadn't been given a copy, and as he couldn't imagine the cops sticking any kind of injunction on the letter and then blabbing on about its contents to the cameras, it must have been Carrow who denied them.

Why?

At this stage, with no evidence on the table, the name of the game is publicity. Why not give the media a copy, get it right into the public domain? Unless she was holding something else back, too.

". . . as disingenuous to suggest that a few handwritten words can in any way clear the suspicion of a terrorist motive," said Garloch again.

"And why do you believe that?"

"Well, Miss Carrow's paragraphs do not actually *prove* that the suspects didn't . . ."

He sat up straight, hit Pause, leaving the policeman open-mouthed and palms-up on the screen in front of him, trisected by two vibrating lines of interference.

A few handwritten words, thought Parlabane. Miss Carrow's

54

paragraphs. Never mind what else she was holding back – she hadn't even let the cops see the full text of the letter.

Sarah rested her head on Parlabane's chest as she lay along the settee, eyes on the TV screen, attempting to digest the latest assault in his chili-laden campaign to defoliate their colonic flora. He lowered his head slightly as he sat, enough for his nose to touch a few stray strands of that cascading red hair, and breathed in her smell as she wriggled cosily against him. She was losing herself in the video; he was losing himself in her. Again.

"Surprised to see you here," she had said when she arrived back from work and found him in the kitchen, thoughtfully stirring a voluminous pot. "I thought you'd be up in Perthshire causing trouble, and asking awkward questions."

"Who, me?" he asked, feigning indignant disbelief, arms wide like an Italian full-back who's just decapitated a winger. They were both making light of it, tiptoeing their way around a dangerous obstacle. She had to joke because she didn't want to sound too accusatory, or to lay her worries on too thick. He had to joke back to assure her that he wasn't offended and that she had nothing to worry about anyway.

And she didn't, he had gradually come to realise.

"There's no angle," he said as they ate. She had brought the Voss thing up, probably hoping that he might benefit from a certain amount of catharsis, and hoping equally that what she heard would reassure her. "I'm interested, of course, but really just from a spectator's point of view. I spoke to Jenny today, and it sounds like they're under martial law."

"So they're really going for this terrorist thing? What do you reckon about it?"

"Couldn't say. That lawyer on the news knows something more than she's letting on, but what she's said doesn't change the fact that these guys went in *very* well prepared and took out four people in an incisively clinical exercise. They knew what they were doing, and whether it was for purposes of robbery, revenge,

55

terrorism or their idea of a laugh on a dull Sunday night seems of secondary importance to me."

"So if they knew what they were doing so much, how come they all got caught?"

"Don't know. Cops haven't said yet. In fact, there's a lot of things the cops haven't said, but I can't say their reticence either surprises me or makes me suspicious. Whatever went on up there, there's some bad bastards involved, and I'm more than happy for it to be the cops who find out who they are and what they're about. Whether it's cops and robbers or cops and terrorists, I don't care. Either way it's cops and very dangerous people, and that's my principal consideration."

His eyes were on the screen, but he wasn't watching the movie. He'd seen it a dozen times and he'd see it a dozen more when he *would* be paying attention. But what was weird was that it wasn't the Voss murder that was distracting him; it was the fact that the Voss murder wasn't distracting him.

Sure, there were a few tantalising contradictions and enticing inconsistencies in the information being issued, but somehow none of it seemed enough any more to have him sliding down the Batpole and into action. Not off this settee with the scent of Sarah's hair in his nostrils, the warmth of her shoulders in his lap and his left palm rested on her left breast, pressed into place against her T-shirt by her own right hand.

He realised that all of this meant he was changing; indeed had changed, and he wasn't even sure whether he should feel sad about that. He felt a confusing mixture of excitement, envy and comfort when he thought about Nicole Carrow, recklessly playing cat-and-mouse with the cops, driven by a belief in some unknowable cause, running on adrenalin and hiding her fear behind a glistening sheen of arrogance. Excitement at recognising someone he once knew, someone that age, who had shown the same raw, enervating energy and promise, with a glint in the eye that said "I'll find out all your secrets, but you'll never know mine." Envy that that person still had so many exciting paths to explore back

56

then; at the thought of what was to follow. And comfort at the thought that someone from the Resignation Generation actually looked like picking up the torch.

"We're going to fuck you up the arse," said the government, all the time. In his adolescence the collective response was: "Come ahead and try it, ya bass. See what you get." These days they would just drop their trousers then drop some eckies so that their acquiescent complicity was a fun and trippy experience.

But maybe it was the sight of Nicole Carrow that had underlined the detachment of his position: it wasn't his fight any more.

He liked to think that it was Sarah that had changed him. All the hackneyed old bollocks actually *applied*. He *had* never met a woman who made him feel this way. He was feeling emotions not only that he had never experienced before, but that he had previously concluded were not applicable in his case. (So many things had seemed not applicable in his case, which was itself part of the greater problem.)

However, the fear was that it was because he had *already* changed that he felt this way about Sarah. That at another time she would have passed him right by, no possibility of him recognising what could lie before them. Or, more simply, that he would have blown it. The thought of having missed her, of her not being there, was a shivering cold one. And along with it came the attendant doubt that he might well have already met women who would have made him feel like this, but . . .

No. That way madness lay.

But did it matter? Either way, this was how he felt, this was how it was. They were together now – fate, serendipity or whatever.

Unfortunately it did matter. Because he still wasn't entirely sure why he was content to be sitting on his settee at a time like this. He'd like it to be all the right reasons, all the cute, cosy and even mature, adult ones, but he wanted to know how big a factor fear was in the equation. What had he said? It was cops and very dangerous people, and that was his principal consideration.

It never used to be.

Once upon a time it had been all and anything for a bloody story. The risks, the gambles, the dangers. The death threats. All for the scoop, for the exclusive. Oh yeah, and THE TRUTH, of course, in hundred-foot letters of fire, burning high on a mountainside. That idol he had made so many sacrifices to.

Parlabane had never been afraid of dying, he had always known. He had taken actions, decisions out of fear for his life; but fear for your life and being afraid to die were two very different issues. Fear for your life was a basic, unignorable instinct of self-preservation, dictating action and reaction in certain situations. Being afraid to die was what kept most sensible people out of those situations in the first place.

Once, he had suspected it was because he was daft enough not to believe it was ever going to happen. That it wasn't applicable to him. That he didn't fear death because he had never been forced to really contemplate it.

Then he had been forced to contemplate it pretty close-up.

Twice he had stared death in the face and on both occasions found that even the Grim Reaper wasn't immune to a sudden attack of self-doubt when it caught that gleefully malevolent glint in his eye. Bollocks, Death must have thought. Do we really want this guy loose on the other side?

So what had changed?

Well, for a start, he thought, he had someone to miss. Someone he craved and jealously guarded his time with. Someone whose company he looked forward to enjoying for as long as possible. But that wasn't it.

Responsibility. A new thing.

He couldn't leave her behind and didn't like the thought of her on her own. She wasn't some pathetic soul who couldn't cope without him – Sarah was a resourceful and some might say formidable woman – but he didn't want her to have to.

And he had made promises. Obligations. If he wanted to marry her, then that meant he had to want to always be there for her.

Doing something that could get himself killed or imprisoned would suggest otherwise.

But that wasn't it either.

It was this: he could feel *her* fear of his death.

A coldness, an emptiness, chasmic and desolately lonely. A fear like none he had ever known.

He could feel how *she* would miss *him*.

In the past, when he was contemplating his next recklessness he hadn't considered even how his parents would miss him if he died; he knew they'd be sad, but . . . In a relationship based so much upon his needs of them, he hadn't appreciated that there were ways in which they needed him. In fact he had never appreciated that there were ways in which anyone needed him – not like that.

He felt how there was something he gave Sarah that she could never replace if he was gone. A preciousness she could not bear to lose, and that he must do all he could to protect.

In short, he sensed the receipt of his own love, and it was a revelation far more devastating and unexpected than anything he had ever splashed across a front page.

He held her a little tighter on the settee.

It didn't mean he was opting for some culture-of-contentment, lifestyle-pages yupped-up existence with his beautiful new bride, though. He wasn't about to simply accept that black was black and white was white, start writing a weekly column with a picture byline and do profile pieces for the Sundays. But it did mean his guerrilla days were over: if something was wrong and conventional investigation failed, then maybe it was time for someone younger to prove it.

Ken Frazer swigged back a can of juice and pored over the b/w laserproof of tomorrow's front page, feeling a hollow tingle in his guts where there should only have been the dull grind of his sausage supper in slow digestion. He was familiar with the feeling, half-instinct, half emotional memory; the distant suspicion that something was missing, something hadn't been accounted for. An uncertainty that had its roots in arriving at the school gates and suddenly remembering that it was PE day: your gear was in the washing machine and your arse was out the window. The dread of that moment when you realise (a) what was bothering you; and (b) that it's now too late to do anything about it.

He shook his head. Probably nothing. It was an ailment of being the news editor, of having always to be on the alert for potential screw-ups; a phantom symptom, like feeling itchy when someone starts talking about headlice. The kind of nagging worry that was bound to happen on a night like this when he was endeavouring particularly hard to anticipate the pitfalls. This evening's latest and most bewildering twist in the Voss saga required delicate and dextrous hands. Between the presses rolling and the punters picking up their copy of *The Saltire* in the a.m. there were hours enough for further hairpin bends in the script. He had instructed the subs to excise anything too speculative regarding the motives or connotations of what had taken place; stick to the facts and the quotes. The tabloid shitrags were happy to wipe their past clean every night and ignore the previous day's statements and positions when events proved them diametrically wrong; they knew their readers had memories even shorter than their attention spans. But Ken had a professional pride those pricks would never understand. Maybe that made him a dinosaur, but he'd still be a dinosaur who was never embarrassed by the sight of yesterday's front page.

He had another gulp of juice and looked away, then quickly back at the proof, an old trick of checking what was the first thing that caught his eye. Nothing was amiss. No unintended insensitive puns in the headlines, no unfortunate juxtapositions. It was fine.

"Send it," he told the chief sub, and in that moment of surrendering his option to change anything, realised with a wry smile that what was missing was nothing to do with the page. What was missing was John Lapsley Parlabane, known to his accomplices as Jack.

He hadn't heard from him in a few days, which was not in itself unusual, as *The Saltire* was just one of several newspapers here and in London labouring under the misapprehension that Parlabane worked for them. They all frequently sent him large sums of money as retainers in vain attempts to entangle him in this deluded fantasy, but at best they were just buying a ticket for a raffle, and Parlabane was the one who decided who was going to win the prize of first look at whatever he had unearthed. Mostly it depended on who he felt would handle the story best, which paper he thought it suited, and sometimes he had deals worked out with the Sundays to run a big overview piece as a follow-up to something he broke elsewhere earlier in the week. But as he only lived ten minutes' walk from Saltire House, *The Saltire* and *Saltire on Sunday* tended to see more of him out of sheer geographical convenience.

Nonetheless, his arrangements were never sufficiently formal for him to see fit to show up on anything other than a random basis, but with a story as big as the Voss one going down, it was odd that he hadn't phoned or popped in to shoot the shit and cast an eye over what they had on it. Especially as Jack and Voss went a long way back, although not exactly in a drinking-buddies manner.

It wasn't a question of putting your best man on the case or anything like that. These big feeding frenzies were the last place you'd find him; the rest of the hack-pack might wait patiently for the bounteous bovine of the police press office to squirt another pasteurised bulletin into their greedily gaping gubs, but Jack preferred his untreated. You didn't send Jack Parlabane to a press conference. In fact, you didn't *send* Jack Parlabane at all, as Jack very much did what he fancied then fucked off again.

Jack's name carried respect – if seldom affection – in any newsroom in the country; and to a lot of the paper's younger reporters, he was a legend, a figure they might have considered mythical if they hadn't seen him in the flesh, having heard tales from older hacks that they had previously assumed were made up or at least greatly exaggerated. Ken wasn't sure what any of his charges really believed about the devious wee Paisley bastard, but he was sure none of the apocrypha was as far-fetched as the truth. Jack for his part stayed tight-lipped about his reputation and his, ahem, "methods".

He was a good man to bounce ideas off, and he was usually around somewhere when there was a big story going down because – like Ken – he loved the buzz of a newsroom in full panic. That he and Jack hadn't exchanged any words at all since Voss's murder was – and should have struck him earlier as – bizarre.

Ken knew Jack had promised to go straight as a pre-nuptial condition, but had put the notion to the back of his mind, filed somewhere between sceptical "I'll believe it when I see it" and worried "How am I going to cope if it happens?". He had reckoned that if the recidivist reprobate was actually serious, then the acid test would be something like this, and Ken doubted he would pass. Yet here they were, one of the stories of the decade unfolding round about, with a personal angle for Jack to boot, and there was no sign of him. It appeared he really was hanging up the black polo-neck and the grappling hook.

Say it ain't so, Jack. Say it ain't so.

The movie ended and Parlabane hit the Stop button on the remote as the image of Dennis carrying new bride Ellen around their apartment faded to black beneath the credits. The poe-faced bastard in the trenchcoat appeared, steam from his breath picked out by the lighting as he looked with brow-furrowed concentration into the camera.

". . . believe that he must have taken some kind of poison, possibly cyanide, as he was only alone for a matter of minutes. Police are trying to maintain as much calm as possible at this time, but the possible ramifications of this apparent suicide are obviously very sinister, and potentially very far-reaching, with the circumstances surrounding the death of Roland Voss becoming increasingly bizarre."

"Do you fancy a cup of coffee, honey?" Sarah asked, pulling herself upright and standing by the arm of the settee, a hand running through Parlabane's hair.

"Yeah, please," he said, and she turned and walked out of the room.

". . . appears to answer the riddle of who may have leaked information to the four men still being held under the Prevention of Terrorism Act, given his involvement in coordinating security at Craigurquhart House, but poses many more disturbing questions as the mystery begins to assume trappings more usually associated with James Bond films."

The image of PFB Trenchcoat suddenly shrank to fit a screen in the studio, where the anchorman sat addressing him from his desk.

"But curiously, isn't it true that Mr Lafferty came forward *voluntarily* this afternoon?" the anchorman asked.

"Yes he did. Mr Lafferty had in fact been involved *in* the investigation at the Perthshire end, and was asked to come down to Edinburgh to help look into the allegations of a security leak. There has been speculation that he decided to take his own life after discovering the police knew something he thought they didn't, but it's far too early to draw any kind of conclusions. All I can tell you is that I spoke to Mr Lafferty a few hours beforehand, as he entered the station, and that he seemed very nervous and agitated. He . . ."

"Ex – Excuse me, Terry," interrupted the anchorman, "but I believe we have those pictures just now."

And Parlabane's heart stopped.

Donald Lafferty was standing in the light drizzle, a few hours ago and less than a couple of miles from where Parlabane sat. He looked about fifteen years older than he should, pale as a virgin at a vampire stag night, trembling visibly, eyes darting suspiciously to and fro.

"Obviously veh-very shocked at what has taken place, ah-and am eager to cooperate in eh-any way that can assist the ih-investigation. I am devastated at what has happened and intend to ss-stop at nothing to find out how our security arrangements weh-were circumvented."

"And do you have any suspicions about the source of a possible leak?"

"I'm afraid I can't really comment on that, f-further than to say I don't know much more than you about it at this stage. I-I've been busy at Craigurquhart since the eh . . . since it happened, and I haven't really had time to c-catch up on developments down here at this end of . . ." He looked suddenly straight into the camera. ". . . of the arena."

He cleared his throat.

"It's not as if I've been sitting around listening to my favourite music, although I think a lot more people should. Excuse me," he muttered, and moved off-camera.

"As you can see, he did seem very concerned about some-thing," stated the reporter as the clip ended.

"Yes," rejoined the anchorman, "and his last remarks seemed *very* curious."

"They did indeed. At the time they struck me as the words of a very distracted – and I suppose extremely tired – man, but as you can imagine, in light of the strange and tragic events that have fol-lowed, there has inevitably been speculation as to whether this was some kind of coded message. However, if that was the case, your guess is as good as mine as to what those words might have meant."

But Parlabane, tears welling in his eyes as he knelt trembling on the carpet, knew exactly what they meant.

They meant black was white, white was black, something was very, *very* wrong – and only he could prove it.

THREE

The death of Donald Lafferty hit Nicole like a fall from castle walls in darkness.

As Monday had progressed, she had become distantly aware of the thought that her world was changing, unexpected doors and pathways opening before her and leading to unexplored chambers, unknown heights. An insecure concern that she was being urged or even led through, along, up – that someone somewhere had a role, a place for her. Fate, if you like, telling her great things were afoot; you took difficult decisions but made the right choices, and here is your reward, your future.

There had been the usual detachment she tended to feel during momentous events, the rest of her functions and processes carrying on efficiently while her emotions lagged behind like an old woman carrying too many bags. She had seen herself on TV when she got home, and couldn't remember saying a word of what she was hearing. It might as well have been someone else playing her; or was it just that she had been playing someone else?

Then there had been the phone calls, of course. Mum, then a couple of friends (not Dad; not home yet; not unusual). Saying how thrilled they were to see her on TV. How they could see her becoming a big legal personality, this was just the sort of thing that got you off to a great start, oh isn't it exciting . . . Nobody mentioned multiple murders or terrorism, but then that was, literally, last night's news. Mum talked about the well-known TV reporter, what was he like in the flesh; about how she had looked, was she nervous, it didn't show; and had she videotaped it, as Mum still couldn't operate the dashed thing. It was as if she had been appearing on a game show.

How do you feel about sticking up for those accused of the crime of the century?

Who is this man you're defending?

Do you really believe he's innocent?

Do you think you've any chance of saving him?

If not, how many millennia will he go down for?

Nobody asked those things, and during those conversations, she didn't think about them either. But then that was law. Footballers, she reflected, tend not to agonise over how the ball might be feeling. Law was other people's nightmares. Nightmares of the victims, nightmares of the accused, nightmares of the guilty, nightmares of the convicted. All on the other side of the big screen, except that they were the ones helplessly, passively watching *you* in action.

She had got to be a player for a day.

Open the mystery envelope and see what you've won, Miss Carrow. Congratulations, a sensational day-trip to Edinburgh! And what a prize it is! You'll get to talk tough to some policemen, produce a sheet of paper like a rabbit from a hat, then enjoy the spectacle of several pompous middle-aged men suddenly ceasing to treat you like an eight-year-old girl. After that you will be interviewed and taken very, very seriously by some very, very serious men in suits, and finally, to round off your trip, you'll get to address the nation on BBC Television! Just set that video-recorder for an instant memento of *your* day as a legal hot-shot!

She still felt a nervous exhilaration as she sat at home later, feeling satisfied, important, part of something. Then she saw the latest news and discovered herself to be in a world whose nature she had entirely misunderstood.

Normally the lawyers don't get involved until the action's over, when everyone who's going to die is dead. When all the pieces are on the board, and they can play out the moves between themselves. Donald Lafferty's death knocked the board to the wall and scattered the figurines; tore down the screen and revealed her to be among the corpses and the villains, part of the same story. She hadn't known him, hadn't set eyes on him, hadn't spoken to him. She hadn't even seen his baffling interview when it first went out, only catching it when it was repeated post-mortem. But his death still felt very close. Very, very close.

She had produced evidence that suggested someone connected to Craigurquhart was behind what had happened, and that Thomas McInnes and his colleagues were there to carry out a robbery, not an execution. Big news, dramatic development, in as much as it affected what was already known, moved the pieces already on the board.

Lafferty comes to Edinburgh to assist in the *investigation* of a leak, not as the suspected source, but then kills himself with a poison pill as soon as he's left alone for five minutes. If he had hanged himself with the belt of his trousers, or chucked himself off the roof, then it would have been the last confessional act of a guilty man who couldn't face a future of harsh consequences, not least those of his own self-loathing for what his greed and scheming had led to. But cyanide pills? Not something you just happen to have on you, in the jacket-pocket or shoulder-bag pharmaceutical cache: paracetamol for those strip-lighting headaches, antihistamine for the occasional bout of hay fever, and cyanide in case you suddenly feel the need to top yourself and aren't going to get home for *hours*.

All the assurance and confidence she had drawn from the idea that someone was behind McInnes soured and dissolved as she wondered, blindly, graspingly, at who was behind Lafferty. What body, what organisation, what person could inspire such loyalty or such fear, that taking one's life was preferable to betrayal? That

67

taking one's life – in cold blood – was an option one was prepared for so readily as to carry the means at all times? And if Lafferty was behind McInnes, and someone else was behind Lafferty, how many layers deep did it descend?

Suddenly the world turned in upon itself; convex became concave, the image shifted and changed.

She thought she had come along when the moves were complete and the action was over, but it looked now like the game was still in progress; in fact it might be just beginning.

Whatever pride and satisfaction she had felt at being the centre of attention was transformed into a sickening fear that she was exposed in the midst of matters beyond her ken and far out of her hands. The excitement of being seen by millions on television changed to a naked vulnerability, as the whole world now knew who she was.

She thought of Thomas McInnes, what his letter said, and what had followed. It said someone on the inside – as it turned out, Lafferty – had been behind what was only supposed to be a robbery, even given the letter's other strange claims. This contradicted the idea of anything larger, anything more sinister, being at work (as if four murders weren't sinister enough). But now she wondered, as that cop had suggested, was McInnes acting to protect someone, something? Had somebody set up and used Lafferty, the same as they had set up and used McInnes?

She needed more than ever to talk to her client; previously it had been so that she could help him, but now the relationship was likely to be more reciprocal.

She felt disorientated and exposed. Whatever was afoot, whatever forces were abroad, she was now part of this. She was *involved* – and no longer as a player in the game, but as a piece on the board.

Morning had been a long time in coming, after comfortless waking episodes like irritating stops at minor stations on a lengthy train journey, the normally caressing pillow transformed into a sack of Meccano pieces with a built-in face-heating filament.

When it did arrive, morning had apparently had a rotten journey too and was in a remorselessly uncooperative mood. There was no hot water for a shower, as she had inevitably managed to bugger up the central heating programme, having still failed to master a computerised LCD panel that seemed to have been built for surfing the net rather than regulating the labours of the boiler. The time machine that was an unadvertised built-in feature of her fridge had once again altered the "best before" dates on both the milk and her sausages, so she had to make do with black tea and toast, the latter thoughtfully burnt by the toaster, which had neglected to eject its contents as part of its on-going "vigilance training" regime.

By the time she had driven to work, she had become sufficiently aware of being grumpily paranoid as to be getting fed up with it and with herself, which was why she paid less heed than would have been normal to the feeling that she was being watched as she walked from her car to the office. What also proved efficacious in expelling it from her mind was the mental projection of acting on the impulse to tell someone about it, picturing her forthcoming meeting with Finlay Campbell.

"I've got this feeling that I'm being watched."

"Yes, dear, you were. By about ten million people. It's a thing called television. Us Scots invented it, don't you know."

Sod that.

Another tiny voice queried whether it was possible that awareness of being paranoid might cause over-compensation in ignoring the feelings of paranoia that would be vital in warning a person if "they" really were out to get you. And still another queried whether she might be going out of her fucking mind.

There were cheers and some applause when she walked into the office, the inevitable cracks about being a TV personality, and Ian West holding out a notepad and a pen as if seeking her autograph. She said nothing in reply, keeping her head down and holding up her right hand in the widely recognised "wanker" gesture. It was almost reassuring to see that it was still all a game to some people. She could see Finlay Campbell on the phone, his office door wide to the wall, and upon catching her eye he gestured her to come in.

Nicole sat opposite his desk as he finished his phone-call, booming-voiced and overbearingly jovial, certainly for that time of the morning. He leaned over towards the cradle of the telephone as he wound up the conversation, as if moving the earpiece gradually nearer its place of rest would in itself make the person at the end of the line do likewise. She caught the glare of his shiny-bald crown, surrounded by black shoulder-length strands of hair in a bad mid-Eighties West-Coast post-glam style, the overall effect described disparagingly by Ian as "a Hateley cut". She hadn't known who Ian was talking about, but when he showed her a couple of pictures of the former Rangers striker and hairdressing casualty, she had laughed out loud. "Just be grateful Campbell doesn't go to the same tailor," Ian added, "embarrassing as his suits may be."

Yesterday morning was the first time she had experienced a conversation with Mr Campbell that had lasted more than thirty seconds. He hadn't been among those who interviewed her for the job, so she hadn't really known where she stood with him. He struck her as a little slimy but generally good-hearted, and when you're talking about lawyers, *a little* slime is probably not worth making much fuss over. He was in his late thirties/early forties, dressing smartly but perhaps a little too flamboyantly for his age. She saw in him an affable fellow, generous of spirit but perhaps over-keen to be liked. A one-time looker, probably a ladies' man, who had screwed up at least one good relationship somewhere along the line and was trying to recapture youthful glory days because he couldn't recapture whatever he had regretfully thrown away. It was a lot to read into a bad haircut and silly jacket, but she did have a good track record on this sort of thing.

The place had been in a ferment over the fact that one of the Voss accused was a client. And when they opened the envelope – working on the reasonable assumption that Thomas McInnes was unlikely to show up in person to retrieve it – Campbell had ushered her into his office and closed the door.

"I'll make this brief because I've got to be in court in half an

70

hour," he had said. "But the first thing you should know is that I defended Thomas McInnes, Robert Hannah and associates during the Robbin' Hoods trial. That's why McInnes came to Manson & Boyd with this," he added, in response to the involuntary widening of Nicole's eyes. "When I say defended, I suppose I should really say represented, as there wasn't much defending to do. They pleaded guilty. That wasn't on my advice – they had decided on it well before it reached that stage. When the game was up, the game was up, was how they saw it. Kind of the opposite of 'it ain't over till it's over'.

"My job was really to present them as remorseful and penitent men, who posed no danger to society and who had committed their spate of crimes – first offences, incidentally – in circumstances unlikely to be repeated, etcetera etcetera." A sad look of pity and regret passed over his normally indefatigably smiley face.

"I have no idea whether I was any good or not," he continued, shrugging, "because I could have stood up and said, 'Your honour, my client would like to state before the court that you suck horses' cocks and your wife shags donkeys,' and it wouldn't have been much worse. These guys had been screwing the homes of the great and the good and they were going to get it up the arse with a chainsaw for their troubles, no matter what mitigation I presented. Normally, poor people just steal from other poor people. And back then, Scottish country mansions simply didn't *get* burgled. The establishment were affronted at the sheer temerity of it, that some bunch of oiks could even *dare* to attempt what they had done. But what really sealed the Hoods' fate was that insurance premiums on such properties soared as a result; before this, they were – ironically or not – regarded as comparatively low-risk. Like I said, nobody stole from these places. After the Hoods hit the headlines, the insurance firms saw things a wee bit differently. So these four men's actions hadn't just deprived a few toffs of some trinkets – their repercussions were going to hit the pockets of every member of the landed gentry across the UK. Including the judge, Lord McLean."

71

"And I suppose an exemplarily harsh sentence would be seen as a deterrent to further such offences, and thus smiled upon by the insurers?"

"You got it. Seven years."

"Jesus," Nicole gasped.

"Unprecedented and unbefuckinglievable. Not only that, but their parole was messed about with and various strings pulled to make sure they served just about all of it. The establishment made sure they got every ounce of their pound of flesh. So I took it as a measure of the man's character that McInnes actually came *back* here for legal assistance. Blamed no-one but himself for what happened. A man of dignity and humility.

"He got pulled in for questioning a few times about rural break-ins, first year after he got out, and always got in touch with us for a brief. He even handled all *that* stoically as part of the price he was paying, and fortunately the cops gradually got the picture that he was an unlikely repeat offender, and gave it up. I never dealt with him personally again – I had moved onwards and upwards by the time he was out and about once more – but we exchanged a few words the odd time. He even gave me a wave through the door last week when he was in seeing you.

"But what I'm getting at is that I believe what's in this letter, as much as I *can't* believe he was part of what happened last night. It just doesn't add up, and we won't be able to make much sense of it without talking to him in person. I want you to go to Edinburgh . . ."

He finally put the phone down, then sat back in his chair and turned his attention to Nicole.

"It's getting interesting, isn't it," Campbell opened.

"Indeed," she replied, with a furrow of the brow.

"Interesting, as in 'may you live in interesting times'," he confirmed, expressing his awareness of her discomfiture. "Another day, another dead body. Question is, where does it put us?"

"I've been asking myself that all night."

"Well, the simple answer, for the time being, is that it puts us

72

right here, until our client is actually charged and we're allowed to speak to him. Whatever progress you might have made yesterday – and you handled the whole thing extremely effectively, I have to say – has been undone by Mr Lafferty's DIY demise."

He picked up a pen, toying absently with it, its turning in his fingers like a wind-turbine powering his thoughts.

"Although the police were right in saying that our letter was of no intrinsic value in terms of proof," Campbell continued, "I think it nonetheless depicted a very plausible scenario that people might be ready to believe, especially in the continuing absence of any substantial alternative. Public opinion would have been with us, even if public sympathy obviously wouldn't. Everyone was bound to be getting bored of conjecture over possible terrorist motives for killing Voss; we offered something a lot more realistic: robbery. What better reason for breaking into the residence – albeit temporary – of one of the richest men in the world? People understand greed a lot better than they understand the politics of intra-European sub-factional splinter-groups. If Voss was an Arab or an Irishman, different story. And of course, if Lafferty had done himself in more conventionally, something a bit more obviously spur-of-the-darkest-moment . . ."

"I know, I know," she commiserated. "Mind you, the postmortem report could still show up something different. Sub-arachnoid haemorrhage or . . ."

Campbell shook his head and frowned, as if impatient with this futile and misguided optimism.

"I've got some police contacts. PM results won't be through for a while, but they know he took a pill; whether it was cyanide is incidental. The word is that the bloke who found Lafferty walked into the room and saw him pop something into his mouth and swallow it, upon which – get this – he said 'bye-bye' and sat down. The bloke tried to get him to cough up – Heimlich manoeuvre or whatever – but was fought off. Whatever he took, the result was that he was dead in minutes. And the result for us is that suddenly it's all very cloak and dagger again, and this terrorist crap has come crashing back down like a bloody anvil."

Campbell leaned back in his chair, running a hand through his thinning locks and widening his eyes in frustration

"I don't know what to think any more," Nicole confessed, breaking a growing silence. "If Lafferty was working for someone, or even just being used by someone . . . what does that do to what McInnes gave us? It looks now like Lafferty was the middle man, but maybe the whole operation *was* just to kill Voss. Thomas McInnes told us he was being coerced into carrying out a robbery, but could the letter actually be a cover-up after all? Could he even have been coerced into writing the letter as part of the deal? I mean, if the letter is genuine, why didn't it tell us he was being coerced into carrying out a murder?"

"Nicole, Nicole," Campbell said quietly, attempting to calm her storm-tossed thoughts. "There are millions of baffling questions flying around, and it's infuriating that we can't answer them, but what we mustn't do is let them distract us from what we know *for sure*."

"What do you mean?"

"Well, you've met him. Do you believe Thomas McInnes could have carried out – or been party to – those murders?"

"To tell you the truth, this whole thing's getting so weird I don't know what I believe any more."

He rolled his eyes gently and smiled. "Look at yourself, Nicole. You're forgetting which way is up. Do you know who Tam McInnes is? What he did?"

"Only very roughly. Really just what you told me yesterday."

"He was a burglar. Not by profession, just by, well, a combination of circumstance, naivety and probably a bit of booze, in the first instance. He and his pals robbed country mansions; you know that much. The first one was the home – *a* home – of the man who took the decision to close down the car plant where they had all worked, because labour was cheaper in the Third World. They had intended the robbery as a protest, a stunt, if you like; said they were originally planning to give the gear back. However . . . to cut a long story short, when it became apparent that nobody had a bloody clue who had done it, they decided to keep their mouths shut and ended up doing it again somewhere else. The spree lasted a few months; they hit I think seven, maybe eight places. But the thing is, they mostly hit places when they were empty; and if someone was going to be home, they made sure they were in and out without a soul knowing. Do you see what I'm saying?"

She nodded and smiled, feeling a welcome moment of comfort as some aspect of solidity, of reassurance returned.

"They never hurt anyone," she said.

"Exactly. Not the proverbial fly. Not then, not before, not since. No knives and no guns. Not even a big stick with a nail through it. But that's only half the point. The reason I sanctioned your wee publicity tour yesterday was that, knowing what I did about McInnes, it seemed at least *plausible* that somebody might enlist his services – forcibly or otherwise – if they wanted to burgle a country mansion, especially if they had inside knowledge that someone as moneyed as Voss would be filling the wardrobes for a few days. And the kind of coercion he's described made sense because as far as I know, Tam McInnes has never committed another burglary since back then, and would be unlikely to be tempted, whatever the potential rewards. What doesn't make sense is murder. Even discounting our generous opinions of Tam's character and morality, the fact is, you don't hire a joiner to fix a burst pipe.

"Now, this suicide business might suggest there's someone else lurking in the background, but to us that's irrelevant. Whether no-one else was behind it or Ernst Stavro fucking Blofeld was behind it, no matter what might have gone wrong, no matter what happened in that bedroom on Sunday night, Tam McInnes went into Craigurquhart House to rob the place. Why there were four corpses behind him when he left is something we aren't going to find out without actually talking to him, so until we're allowed to do that I'd suggest we both distract our tired minds with other matters."

"Like what?" Nicole said apprehensively.

"In your case, this morning, a Mr McCandlish, an octogenarian who, if he's being consistent, probably wishes to sue whoever is top of the charts for plagiarising a radio jingle he wrote thirty-odd years ago. According to the senior partners, he used to do a lot of this in the Sixties, and everyone had assumed he'd died or given up. Unfortunately bands like The Stone Roses and Oasis came along in recent years, and by ripping off the songs he got upset about back then, they've inadvertently set him off again. Good luck."

The fear and the uncertainty, the high stakes and the precipitous sense of danger drifted away as the morning went on, and it wasn't down to the soothing qualities of the music she was forced to listen to. Mr McCandlish had brought along the most dilapidated-looking item of audio equipment she had ever seen, a bulky, bakelite reel-to-reel tape player that gave off a worryingly smoky smell as its spindles turned with arthritic labour and a syncopated squeaking. It looked heavy enough to have induced a heart attack in the wiry and animatedly cantankerous old soul in his efforts to transport it upstairs to the office, but unfortunately he was made of sterner stuff than he looked.

To illustrate his point, he played each jingle three or four times on the reel-to-reel before resorting to his other museum piece, the oldest functioning micro-cassette player in existence, for a tinny rendition of the offending lines or bridge from the suspect song. As he insisted on singing the corresponding couplet from his allegedly plagiarised jingle over the top of the later composition, Nicole felt he was somewhat prejudicing the demonstration, although the chorus from Oasis's "Don't Look Back In Anger" did have spooky echoes of the McCandlish-penned "Buy Mulligan's tripe – the stuff that you'll like".

Nicole was as polite and constructive as she could manage, but the meeting ended in what she was beginning to consider familiar (and inevitable) acrimony when she felt bound to point out that Mr McCandlish's jingles had last been aired some years before Noel Gallagher's birth – and even then only in central Scotland.

"It's a conspiracy!" he declaimed, before the door closed with its now equally familiar slam.

76

The only re-intrusion of her greater concerns came in the form of Finlay Campbell, sticking his head around the door and asking for The Envelope.

"I'm sorry, I don't have it," she told him. "In fact, I don't think I've had it since yesterday morning, before I went through to Edinburgh."

"Bugger," he winced. "Ach, never bother. I was really just asking on the off-chance. I can't find it and if you had it, it would have saved rooting through that office of mine. Look, I've got to nip out for a few hours. Could you ask Linda to hunt for it when she comes back from the stationers? It's buried in there somewhere, along with Lord Lucan, Shergar and the Stone of Destiny, probably."

"Will do."

He had driven around the block a couple of times, looking for the car. He had the make, colour and reg number, but between the one-way system and the parking restrictions, there was no guarantee it would be anywhere near the office. Someone was pulling out of a space close to the corner of the junction opposite the building, so he flipped the indicator to left instead of right and manoeuvred into the spot. He had a good view of the main entrance from there, and unless there was a back door he would see her coming out; with any luck she would be having to feed a meter somewhere, so he could follow her. He wouldn't intercept her then; he'd find out where the car was and weigh up the options for when she returned.

He had the home address, courtesy of his invaluable police contacts, but that was a last resort, as you never knew who might be watching. And for all his experience, getting in might not be a picnic. He was sure he could manage it, but if it came to that he'd have to make sure he left no trace. If she came in and spotted something that told her all was not as it should be, she might panic, freak out screaming before he could get to her, and then he would have all sorts of inconveniences to deal with.

There was a noise from across the road, the reluctant grind of a stiff and heavy iron window frame being laboriously swung open to let in some air. Looking up at the first floor he noticed with a shock that it was her. He glanced down at the picture on the front of this morning's paper, inset into the bigger one of Lafferty, for a final confirmation. She stood with one hand on the frame for a moment, letting the smoggy but cool breeze fan her face and hair, then retreated further inside.

He experienced a curious feeling of disbelief that she could appear so ignorant of her predicament, of being watched. There seemed such an intimacy about it, the way it placed her in his grasp, that it seemed impossible she couldn't feel anything through her part of it. Such ignorance, such vulnerability made her seem puny and frail.

Maybe it was this perceived weakness that made the predator despise the prey.

A man emerged from the main entrance, striding purposefully on to the road as the lights changed to let him cross, looking like he might have been visiting Manson & Boyd to enlist them in preparing a claim against whichever incompetents had advised him on his haircut and jacket. He cut diagonally across the junction, past the car, and disappeared into a narrow gap between two buildings on the smaller road that crossed West Regent Street going north. A few minutes later he was in front of the car again, but this time behind the wheel of a large, blue BMW which had apparently emerged from nowhere. The traffic lights changed and the BMW took off at speed.

He got out of his car and headed towards the gap that the sartorial casualty had disappeared into, and discovered that it concealed the entrance to an underground permit-holders-only car park.

He ducked under the card-operated barrier and trod quietly down the tightly spiralling ramp, on the balls of his feet. Sticking his head around the last bend he saw four lines of cars, two rows back-to-back in the middle, each facing another row against opposite walls. At the nearest corner was a yawning gap, presumably left by the BMW upon its exit.

He continued inside, his already light footfalls muted further by the lagging material on the low ceiling, and spotted the car he was looking for, one space from the far end of the row against the right-hand wall. He was about to approach when he saw something that made him grateful for his stealth. There was a pair of trainer-shod feet between the front wheels of the red Golf, the right one twitching arhythmically, like a nervous tic. He then heard a dull but unmistakably metallic sound, some weighty and solid steel implement being placed on the concrete floor, and the scrape-cum-rattle of another being dragged a few inches before being picked up.

He retreated from the subterranean chamber with continued caution, returning to his car and scanning the pavements now for a different vehicle.

There it was.

"Cowan's Garage," advertised an anaemically off-white Escort van, the paintwork of the sign in far better condition than that of the bodywork. "Breakdown recovery and on-road repair service."

Hmmm, he thought.

He took note of the address and telephone number, picked up his portable and began to dial.

Nicole sat in the traffic queue and regretted for the nth time that her geographical grasp of the city was so poor, and that she had neither taken steps to rectify this, nor even explored an alternative route home from work. She had decided that whoever planned and designed the Kingston Bridge must have had an abiding love of the Clyde and the Glasgow skyline, enough to devise a feature that would not only afford people a magnificent perspective upon it, but hours and hours to enjoy the view without such distractions as having to push the accelerator and move forward.

"Does it improve when there are no roadworks?" she had asked Linda, Finlay Campbell's secretary.

"I wouldn't know," she replied. "I've only been driving for twenty years."

She switched on the car stereo but was instantly irritated by the mid-Atlantic accent that seemed to be a standard requirement of DJs on Scottish music stations, wishing that the mid-Atlantic was where this particular drive-time jock was right now, preferably without the assistance of anything buoyant. She turned the dial a few degrees and heard the more authentically Scottish accent of a female newsreader.

". . . ritage Secretary said he would be fighting the proposal tooth and nail, saying it wasn't for Brussels to impose its own low standards on Great Britain.

"Detectives in Glasgow are appealing for more witnesses after a man was found stabbed to death in Partick this afternoon. The man, who has not been named until relatives are informed, is believed to have been the victim of a mugging. Police say a wallet was discovered close to where the body was found, and one witness saw two youths running from the scene . . ."

Nicole reached in front of the gearstick and grabbed a tape from a compartment cluttered with torn pieces of roadmaps, flyers removed from beneath her wiperblades, and gradually biodegrading travel sweets, which were working slowly to bind all the surrounding constituents into one amorphous paper and plastic nest. The various sensations of slimy stickiness and fluffy dust on different digits triggered a vague, finger-wagging guilt about how long it had been since she last cleaned the interior or exterior of the vehicle.

She slammed the cassette into the player and the radio was silenced, replaced by the wobbly sounds of an ancient compilation tape. She always felt bad about switching off disturbing news; it sometimes seemed the least you could do was listen to what was going on, as you weren't the one having to cope with the tragedy first-hand. But there had been a little too much death on her plate over the last few days, and stories of murder and violence, especially in Glasgow, made her that bit more nervous now that she was living alone, and in a city where she really had no-one to turn to. She glanced to her side and took one hand off the wheel to push down the doorlock button.

The sound quality began to improve at roughly the same time as the traffic, and she was allowed to move out of first gear occasionally as the conditions gradually cleared. She found herself giggling as an old Stone Roses track rasped through the speakers. It hadn't been one of those under scrutiny today, but she couldn't help wondering whether it had an unknown subliminal precursor in a Sixties pile-ointment commercial.

Reaching the stretch that climbed gently alongside the twin glass towers of Scotland Street School, she cranked up the volume as she was finally able to move up the gears and put her foot down, the swell of the power chords and the surge of acceleration bringing a liberating sense of escape.

A couple of hundred yards back on the M8, another driver was rather surprised and more than a little disappointed not to see Nicole die in a horrific fireball, as her car quite inexplicably failed to go out of control and plough into the back of the slowing traffic ahead.

The action of her key in the lock was not as smooth as usual – there seeming to be a grinding sensation as it turned and she pushed the door open. First signs of it buggering up, she feared, remembering a frustrated few hours waiting for a locksmith on the doorstep of her former home in Blackheath, after she and her flatmates had concertedly ignored the ancient Chubb's progressive deterioration. She would have vowed to get this one seen to right away but for the fact that she was renting this place and would probably be out of it in a few weeks, and that there was a white sheet of A4 staring up at her from the screaming red swirly-patterned carpet.

It was lying several feet from the door, a lot further away than her mail usually came to rest, even allowing for a certain distance of gliding. What was more suspicious was that it was dead straight, uncreased and equidistant from the hallway's two bubonically Anaglyptaed walls. And if its improbable positioning wasn't enough to draw maximum attention to itself, it also bore the words "READ THIS NOW NICOLE" in large, handwritten capitals across the top.

She put her bag on the floor as she knelt to pick it up, her heart beginning involuntarily to pound as her mind raced to anticipate the possibilities. She began reading as she stood upright again, her hand reaching automatically for the small brass knob on the door, although which side of it she planned to put herself before locking it was unfamiliarly in the balance.

"I have written this so as not to alarm you," it began, with unconscious irony, "as this warning should lessen the shock when you discover that there is an intruder in your flat."

She looked up from the paper, beginning to tremble, hand turning the lock, eyes frantically scanning the doors that now seemed to loom menacingly before her, having previously merely loitered aimlessly in the hall, like bored teenagers with their hands in their pockets.

"Bear in mind that if I meant you any harm I would not be tipping you off before you got to me. Please do not scream, run from the house, telephone the police or do anything else to attract attention. I know you have no reason to trust me at this stage, so I apologise wholeheartedly for having to distress you like this, and ask that when you proceed to your living room, you do not resort to physical violence at least until you have heard what I have to say."

Nicole opened the front door slightly, leaving it ajar to facilitate a quick exit, then began her slow approach to the living room, a distance that had never seemed a quarter of this length before. Her heart had suddenly become sixteen-valve, fuel-injected, thumping viciously in her chest like an alien preparing to make its traditional entrance. In that time-suspended walk, that limbo in the hallway, she changed her mind back and forth a dozen times about whether to turn and run or see what fate awaited in the living room, that snug but twee little pocket with its cheesy old gas fire and fraying hessian on the walls.

Passing a cupboard she remembered the big golf umbrella given her by a friend who had lived in Glasgow for a while, and who had informed her: "Believe me, what you get in London isn't rain."

She took hold of it, comforted by its heft but unsure which end to grasp: the handle, so that she could stab at him with the grey metal tip, or the tip itself, so that she could bear down with the formidably sturdy wood of the handle. She opted for gripping the handle, as a stabbing motion might prove more effective at close quarters, where she would be unlikely to get in much of a swing.

Nicole backed up against the wall opposite the open living room door, seeking the maximum angle of perspective upon who or what lay within, and thus affording herself a few feet more of a start if events dictated that flight was the best option for self-defence. Edging forward ever slower and by decreasing distances, she caught her first glimpses of the room's interior. Coming teasingly into her field of vision first were the closed, snot-green curtains and the dusty magazine rack full of *People's Friend*s in the far corner, next to the turd-brown, corduroy-finish armchair that farted up a cloud of dust every time she sat in it. She leaned over, her feet refusing to move any further forward, and saw the far end of the hateful fireplace with its glass cabinets, before a hand came into view. Trying to calm her loud and tremulous breathing, she stretched her head and shoulders still further, a length of black sleeve becoming visible past the doorframe. It led to a shoulder and then a dirty-blond, mop-topped head, at which point she leaned too far and fell over, landing with a crump as the umbrella rolled away from her.

She rolled on to her bottom and scrambled backwards against the wall, looking up to see the intruder before her, ten feet away, standing still in the centre of the room. He loomed tall in her terrified vision, black boots leading to black jeans and a black polo-neck, missing only the ski-mask to complete the effect. Instead there was a face that she would ever after associate with more danger, trouble and chaos than a black balaclava had ever connoted. His posture indicated he was both uncomfortable and impatient, his quizzical face suggesting he was concerned but bemused.

"Let me help you," he said softly, local accent, and began to move towards her.

"Get back. Stay where you are," she warned, grasping the umbrella once more and climbing to her feet by the ungainly method of sliding backwards up the wall.

He put his hands in the air and backed himself against the fireplace.

"I told you," he said, "I mean you no harm. We need to talk. Urgently."

"Well talk," she barked, still trembling but now having added the feeling of clumsy stupidity to her catalogue of discomfiture.

"Can't you come any nearer?" he asked, in a tone that she was furious to realise suggested he thought she was being unreasonable.

"I'll move nearer when I hear something that interests me enough."

The man shrugged.

"Fair enough," he muttered with a sigh. "Would it interest you to know that someone tried to kill you today?"

She swallowed, trying to prevent tears from forming. His words seemed to have no meaning, no significance that she could relate to consciously, but somewhere deeper they were making an announcement her whole body was listening to.

"That . . ." she croaked, then cleared her throat and took a couple of quick breaths, "that would interest me. But you'd better not be selling insurance."

"Would that I was," he said flatly. Genuinely.

"H-how do you know someone tried to kill me?"

"I'm the one that saved you."

She stared numbly at him, baffled as to which emotion she should be feeling, and shook her head minutely, open-mouthed as a fight broke out in the impatient queue of questions jostling for the use of her tongue.

"How did . . .? When . . .? Why wou . . .?" She breathed once. "Who's trying to kill me?" won.

The man looked at the floor for a few seconds, weighing up his words, seemingly reluctant but forced to answer.

"Someone who's put a lot of time and effort into convincing the world that Tam McInnes and his pals killed Roland Voss, and who is not very happy about anyone suggesting the contrary."

If there had been any colour left in the pale cistern of her face, then the last words she heard hit the flush lever. She felt the walls lurch around her and slid back to the floor as her legs decided to withdraw cooperation. He started moving towards her again. She shouted and tried to crawl away from him but he was too fast, crouching before her and grabbing her flailing wrists as she struggled, then pinning her left arm against the wall with his elbow as he covered her mouth with his right hand. She tried to look around herself, even to close her eyes, but felt her own gaze drawn into his, intriguing, sympathetic, challenging and penetrating all at once.

"I'm very sorry," he said softly. "I know how hard this must be for you, but unfortunately neither of us has much time for you to get used to it. I know how scared you are, Nicole, but the bottom line is that you're going to have to trust me. If you run out screaming into the street, they'll kill you. If you phone the police, they'll kill you. If you get into your car and drive out of town, they'll kill you. The world as you remember it doesn't exist anymore. You're somewhere over the rainbow and the bad news is the munchkins are not fucking friendly."

He took his hand away from her mouth, let her arms go as the fight went from them.

"Who are you?" she asked in a whisper.

"My name is Jack Parlabane. I'm a journalist. And I'm not here because I believe Tam McInnes is innocent. I'm here because I *know* Tam McInnes is innocent."

FOUR

"This is fucked. This is well fucked," Paul muttered nervously, shaking his head and biting his nails. This was a difficult enough combined manoeuvre, but the handcuffs and the random rock and sway of the bus added an unwanted element of challenge. The effect was more cheese-grater than emery board, and his fingers looked like something the dog had found round the back of the butcher's. His eyes were bloodshot from fatigue, fear and a rationed allowance of self-pity, his throat sore and swollen from the sustained effort of not crying.

Tam McInnes looked over at his son from the seat opposite, feeling gagged by the sense of futility that shouted down every word of reassurance he could think to say. Even the desire to reach out and place a paternal hand on the distressed young man's shoulder was made less difficult by the handcuffs than by the notion that he had long forfeited the right and ability to play the wise and protective father. Nonetheless, he hadn't forfeited the right to have a go, so he shuffled across the narrow aisle and sat on the orange squeaky vinyl seat.

"Haw. What's goin' on back there?" shouted their guard, looking up from his *Daily Record* and interrupting his gloat over the prospect of Rangers' latest European misadventure. The young policeman had given up on playing the Imperial Stormtrooper and had sat down, loosening the strap on his semi-automatic so that it lay across his lap under the dismal tabloid.

"Ach, leave them alone for fuck's sake," barked Bob Hannah. "Can you no see the boy's upset?"

"He'll be mair upset if I've to come up there," came the retort, with the unconvincing and clumsily wielded authority that marked low-ranking British officialdom in all its manifestations, from menopausal primary teachers to nervous screws and bum-fluff polismen.

"Aye, he'll be fuckin' shattered," said Bob witheringly. The guard got up from his seat and began to move forward. Bob held his cuffed hands out together before him, palms up.

"Look, son," he said quietly. "After everythin' we've been through recently, and everythin' we're up against, the only way you could scare that boy is if you threaten to make him visit *your* dentist. Do yoursel' a favour. Sit back doon and read your paper."

Bumfluff stopped, frowning, and began backing away again, with a but-this-is-your-last-warning wag of his finger. He leaned back against the darkened glass panel that partitioned off the driver's cab and picked his *Daily Record* back up, a look of intense puzzlement and concentration on his face. Tam half-expected to see his lips move as he read.

"So is the boy afraid of dentists, like?" Bumfluff eventually asked.

Bob rolled his eyes and swallowed back a dozen obvious comments.

"Eh, aye," he stated, and looked away, shaking his head.

"What's the matter, son?" Tam asked, nudging Paul with his shoulder. "Is it the fact that we're all gaunny spend the rest of our lives in the jile, or is it just that your seat's no very comfy?"

Paul laughed involuntarily, the tension finding its own way out whenever it saw a gap.

"Naw," he said, glancing at the blacked-out windows. "It's the view."

Tam smiled and caught his son's eye. Paul's partaking in the time-honoured Scottish denial-therapy of bullets-bounce-off-me humour had been a brave gesture, drawing on God knew how depleted reserves, and had been as much for his father's benefit as for his own. But in Paul's look Tam saw that the time for blame and accusation was gone, or at least postponed. And for the first time in Christ knew how long, neither was ashamed to admit he needed the other.

Paul was, understandably, the most visibly disturbed of the four. He had been the force of sustaining energy in the preceding days and weeks, giving himself up to possession by a desperate nihilism and a sometimes cacklingly black enthusiasm for the pervading absurdity of it all. A man so violently hurled towards the end of his tether can sometimes gain propulsion from the whiplash. And when Paul wasn't acting like it was the ride of his life, he was acting like he didn't believe it was real, so maybe that made the crash all the more violent when he went into the ante-room and found out just how real it was.

Tam feared he would never look at his son's face again without remembering that look of horror and incomprehension as Paul sat on the carpet, the choking, gurgling man lying back in his arms, bleeding to death all over him, four feet from the body of the man's similarly slaughtered wife.

Tam wasn't entirely sure what day it was now, how long had passed since that moment. Panic, confusion, flight, pursuit, polis, interrogation, guards, guns, and now this van/bus affair with its frustratingly blacked-out windows and waftingly intermittent smell of stale pish and diesel fumes. The creaking hulk had been the site of their joyless and pale-faced reunion after separation in the cells and interview rooms, a few minutes' stilted conversation enough to establish that none of them knew any more than the rest, and that their cumulative knowledge was far from extensive.

The bus had been backed up to the covered walkway at the rear of the police station, the reverberating bleeps and white noise of radios punctuating the hubbub from beyond the open door at the vehicle's tail as they sat and waited for unseen forces to once more decide where to place their four playthings.

". . . kidding? More than a wee bit unusual," Tam had heard a polisman – carrying the somehow very British combination of a sub-machine gun and a clipboard – say to a man in plain clothes as the pair passed the door and walked around to the side of the bus.

"It's not the fuckin' corporation number nine. I mean, do you realise who I've got in this bus?"

"And do *you* realise who's signed this order?"

Which had apparently been the decisive statement in the argument.

Shortly after that, the greasy-haired wee scrote with the rifle and the *Record* had boarded from the rear, before the door was closed and locked from outside by the polisman with the clipboard, who then climbed into the cab up front beside the driver, placing his own weapon on the wide, shelf-like dashboard with a heavy thump.

"Where are we goin'?" Bob asked the scrote as the engine struggled bronchitically into life.

"It's a mystery tour," the scrote sneered. "You'll find out when you get there."

The bus had pulled away with a couple of unsure jolts and had jiggled its miserable contents over a couple of speed bumps before picking up pace with a clunky change of gear and a determined growl from the engine.

Tam had sat staring ahead, trying to make out the road through the heavily tinted panel behind the driver's head, but the monochrome kaleidoscope of metamorphosing shapes in the glass only strained his vision. Bob turned round briefly, rolling his eyes and sighing.

To Bob's right, Spammy sat – or more accurately had deposited himself; sitting entailed more coordination than Spammy was generally prepared to apply – and bobbed his head to an imaginary soundtrack, seemingly as oblivious as it was possible to be without ascending beyond the realm of the physical. Tam shook his head as he looked at him. In fact, Tam shook his head almost every time he looked at him.

89

"Don't call him Spammy. That's cruel. The boy's name is Cameron," Tam had told Paul sternly when his son was about nine, not wanting him party to the pack-instinct weirdo-baiting that kids enjoy and anthropologists enjoy even more.

"Call me Spammy," Spammy insisted, when Paul brought him along as the fourth member of the team.

He was a gangling, hairy galoot whose face always seemed to be saying "I'll be back in a minute" and who could probably contrive to look sartorially dishevelled in just a pair of swimming trunks. Tam and Paul *had* to do this job. Not an issue. Bob had agreed out of friendship, loyalty and a desperate old man's need to ride out and taste the action one more time. But if anyone knew why Spammy had signed up then it sure as shite wasn't Spammy. For a while Tam had assumed Paul must know – some bond, some friendship thing, a debt, a favour – but when asked, Paul euphemistically explained that Spammy "kept his own counsel", quietly confiding that the Yeti's recent and most radical drug experimentation – abstinence – had made him even more inscrutable than anyone was used to. "If he gets hold of some acid and gets a handle on this situation from a perspective he's used to, he'll probably freak out and we'll never see him again," Paul warned, the morning before the job.

"Riding along in an army truck / In a humpity bumpity army truck," Spammy sang to himself, then giggled. The scrotey polisman/guard glared at him with a mixture of contempt, bafflement and wariness, which reminded Tam of Spammy's mysteriously protected status on the scheme in Meiklewood. "It's like a force-field," Paul had explained. Not even the hard-cases, psychos or the Meikle teeny "Kick to Kill Krew" hassled him. "He's just too weird."

Without conversation or a view it was impossible to track time or distance as the bus continued its journey, only the frequent halts, gear changes and turns suggesting that the surroundings must still be urban. Even speed was difficult to gauge, as the metal cabin seemed consistently shoogly regardless of velocity.

The vehicle took a very slow, strainingly sharp left turn, and failed to pick up momentum afterwards, which made Tam suspect they were climbing a hill until he felt two bumps underneath and heard more bleeps and radio interference outside. The bus slowed still further, each of them glancing fervently at the others, uniformly unprepared for whatever the next chapter might bring, reluctant to lose the comparatively easeful limbo of transit. It would be time for deep breaths and once more withdrawing into the self, pulling down the mask, hiding scared behind a stone face.

There was an excruciating, extrapolated moment of purgatory as they realised the bus had stopped and awaited the silencing of the engine, with all it would herald.

It never came.

They heard a door open ahead, and saw PC Clipboard hop out.

More voices. Authoritative tones. Posh accents. Crap jokes. Sycophantic laughter.

Then the rear door was opened and the Wee Shite climbed in, cuffed and smirking, a cocksure erection of sinewy limbs. Tam clocked him right away, one half of a fight, impatient and unfussy about finding a partner. *Keelus Glasguensas Vulgaris*, the lesser-brained Glesca Keelie. A specimen so archetypal he should be in a zoo, where he could be exhibited for educational and instructional purposes. No, thought Tam. Make that a museum. They're infinitely less bother deid.

"Woah-ho," the Wee Shite announced, taking his place on the backmost seat, relaxing as if it was his own personal stretch-limo. "I'm in the presence of greatness. Yous kill't that Dutch cunt, didn't yous."

"Fuck off," Paul snapped as the door was slammed to once again.

The Wee Shite put his hands up.

"Awright. Nae bother, chief," he said, all mock gravity. "I'm not messin' wi' yous cunts. Yous are fuckin' mental. Fuckin' hard bastarts, eh? Better watch my fuckin' mooth, eh?"

"Just ignore him, Paul," Tam stated flatly.

"Aye, that's right, faither," the Wee Shite yelped. "Don't be consorting with the likes of that scruff," he added with theatrical articulacy. "You might end up in the jile."

At this he cackled throatily for a while; then, content that he had reaffirmed his status as the world's wittiest man, he sat back in his seat, cuffed hands behind his head, and began to whistle *The Sash*.

PC Clipboard clambered back into the cab, minus the eponymous article, and looking rather distraught for the loss of it.

"Bloody circus, so it is," he told the driver. "Waving orders from on high, and you've to jump when they clap their hands. As if it's no stupid enough comin' over here to pick that wee shite up, they've took my records off me. Comin' out with all this Top Secret, Need To Know shite."

"So what happens to the order, the file?" the driver enquired.

"Fuck knows, Davie. *He*'s away with it. I says I need a copy as well, but he gie'd me more shite about orders from above. I tell't him, I says if anythin' happens, I've no record of who's on this bus. Prick just says 'Well you'd better not let anything happen then.'"

"But he's got record of it, hasn't he?"

"Aye, but . . ."

"Well it doesnae matter if you haven't."

"Aye, but it's the principle."

"Aw, haud your wheesht, Alec," said the driver with a small laugh, putting the bus into reverse and pulling away.

After that, time seemed to dissolve. Tam could see less through the tinted panel and guessed the light was starting slowly to fail outside. The jolts of junctions and the pull and drag of turns had ceased, he realised, gradually appreciating their absence. Open road, maybe even motorway. There had been a syncopated beat beneath the wheels – ka-clomp, ka-clomp, ka-clomp – which he took to mean they were crossing a bridge, and he guessed at the Forth. After that, the disorientation was complete, with nothing to suggest change in direction, speed or distance. They could have been circling Knockhill race-track for all they knew.

The numbness of it was frightening. It fuelled paranoia, like you had a bag over your head and your hands tied behind your back, and you had been forced through a door into a room that might be full of boxers or might be full of nothing at all.

All thoughts turned inwards and backwards. That was when Paul had started to panic, and Tam had tried to comfort him.

"Aw, that's dead touchin', so it is," offered the Wee Shite, who had temporarily given up baiting his travelling companions in protest at their concerted policy of ignoring him.

"That's like, hingmy, the softer side of the beasts or somethin'. Cold-blooded killers wi' hearts of gold an' that, no?"

"We never fuckin' killed anybody, right?" hissed Paul, shooting him a furious glare.

"Aw, it's an injustice case, is it? We'll have to get a campaign goin' well. 'Free the Dutch Cunt Four'. That's got a ring to it, eh? Free the Dutch Cunt Four. Free-the-Dutch-Cunt-Four," he started chanting. "Free-the-Dutch-Cunt-Four."

The Wee Shite began stamping his feet and clapping his hands in rhythm with his chant.

"Now see what you've done?" Tam muttered. Paul rolled his eyes apologetically.

"THAT'S ENOUGH OF THAT," the guard yelled, throwing down his newspaper and standing up, hands on his weapon, upon which the Wee Shite desisted. "Christ's sake," the guard mumbled, sitting back down. "Like a bloody school trip."

The sound of the engine and the passing cars outside filled the bus, seemingly louder as a wordless vacuum grew.

"I'm bored," Spammy suddenly and loudly decided, probably an hour after everyone else had arrived at that position. "Anybody for a gemme of I-Spy?"

Tam, of course, shook his head.

"Aye," shouted the Wee Shite, thus declaring that he was the only one not to get the joke. "I spy with my little eye, somethin' beginnin' with . . . hingmy, M C."

Bob sighed loudly and turned to the black window, pretending to stare out of it, then began banging his head against the glass.

"A muwllyin green bottles, hangin' on the wall," sang Spammy.

Bob banged his head harder.

"Do yous give in?" asked the Wee Shite, ignoring the fact that none of them had given any indication of actually taking part.

"Awright," he announced triumphantly. "I'll tell yous. It's . . ."

"Miserable Cunts," said everyone else, including the guard, in monotonal unison.

This had the satisfying effect of shutting the Wee Shite up, but obviously made it unclear whose go it was next, had anyone wished to continue the game.

The driver and PC Clipboard, being in the cab at the front, were not included, but just out of interest, what they saw with their little eyes – for all of a quarter of a second before they hit it at sixty miles an hour – began with C.

What Tam would mainly remember was the noise, a single, percussive, metallic BANG that seemed to boom at them from all four walls of their steel chamber, imploding upon them with a fury and ferocity he'd never known sound could possess.

The room *had* been full of boxers.

With the eruption of terrifying sound came a rapidly accelerating lurch to the left, which threw all of them to the right. Tam was cushioned by Paul's body between him and the window, and he gripped the handrail on top of the seat in front, pulling against the G-force to prevent his bulk crushing his son against the wall. Bob was thrown towards Spammy, but slammed into the side of the seat opposite rather than directly across the aisle, as the angle of swerve altered erratically.

The guard was thrown like a teddy in a tantrum from his rear-facing fold-down seat, flailing along the front panel and meeting the outside wall mercifully below the glass.

The Wee Shite, with both cuffed hands gripping the rail and his right foot wedged hard against the base of the seat in front, was the only person sitting on the left not to leave his position.

The driver's consciousness returned from a terrified moment's suspended animation, and he turned the wheel furiously against the swerve. This had the inevitable effect of throwing everyone in the bus back towards the left, although with less force and, vitally, less suddenness.

Feeling the gut-shifting lurch as his innards suffered whiplash, Tam clenched his fingers tighter around the rail and jammed his left leg into the aisle, keeping himself in position and forming a barrier to prevent Paul being thrown past him. In fact, all of them managed to get a grip on something as the bus swung back against its previous momentum. Unfortunately these measures weren't quite so effective when it tipped over on to its side.

There was a scream like a thousand steel-gauntletted fingers down an old blackboard in an echo chamber, the soul-piercing shriek of a hyena with its balls cut off – in fact possibly at that very moment of deep personal and physical loss – as the bus skidded grindingly along the tarmac.

When it came to a halt, there was a fleeting moment of intense silence, just long enough for Tam to appreciate the pitch and volume of the ringing in his ears, a moment of stillness and paranoid anticipation, as if they each suspected a further unseen onslaught.

Then came the sighs and exhalations of the relieved, and the strained moans of the injured.

They had all finished up corralled on the side of the bus, partitioned off from one another by the rows of seats, squatting or crumpled amidst the fragments of black glass. Facial cuts seemed to have come as standard. Paul was nursing his upper arm, which was bloody and raw-looking through a rip in the sweatshirt the cops had given him. With the window shattered, his shoulder had been scraping along the hard road surface for a few seconds before he could drag himself clear of the gap.

Tam had rattled both thighs off something metal, probably a seatback, when the tipping motion sent them all into the air. The dull ache was like having the whole weight of the bus rested on his legs, but he knew he'd be all right to walk – albeit painfully – after a few moments. He had taken whacks to the same place in his footballing days from centre-halves carrying more bulk than the bus. He just wished someone had a magic sponge.

Spammy was the first to stand. He shook his shaggy black locks and a small shower of glass fragments precipitated from them, like fairy dust, giving him an even more ethereal appearance. Apart from the basic minimum of a small cut on his right cheek, he seemed completely unharmed. He didn't even look any more dazed than usual as he opened his eyes wide and took in his upturned surroundings.

Tam remembered a theory that a man would sustain fewer injuries from a crash or a fall if he was asleep at the time, as his relaxed state would make him more supple. Spammy's general unscathedness seemed to bear this out rather convincingly.

The Wee Shite was clutching at one knee with his cuffed hands, swearing and muttering, but apparently out of annoyance more than distress. It was as if he was furious that you couldn't get through a high-speed crash these days without hurting yourself.

"Aw, fuck's sake," mumbled Spammy ominously, stepping over to squat beside Bob, who was grimacing and spluttering, his hands tentatively feeling their way down his leg. His foot was trapped amidst a tangle of bent metal, a long splinter of wood from the wrecked seat-back jutting into his calf, from where blood was steadily trickling.

"Want to give us a hand here?" Spammy said, not taking his eyes off Bob's foot, but waving a hand above his head in case anyone was in doubt as to who was talking.

Tam and Paul trod delicately across the hazardous surface, watching where they placed each step amongst the newly formed stalagmites of glass and twisted metal.

"Aw Jesus," Paul said, but he wasn't looking at Bob.

Beyond the last double seat, the guard lay slumped, contorted and broken. His blank eyes stared forward above a smashed and gushing nose, his head twisted at an impossible angle to his shoulders, his neck snapped like an expired cheque card by the strap of his gun, which had snagged on a loose bolt as the bus tipped on to its side.

Paul crouched before him, automatically feeling at the polisman's wrist for a pulse despite not really knowing how to find one.

He released his grip on the limp arm and let his head fall into his hands, taking deep breaths and swallowing hard.

From behind there was a throaty rumble of effort and an angered scream.

The rumble was from Tam as he pulled at the crushed metal frame gripping Bob's foot, the scream from Bob as the splinter was wrenched from his leg. Spammy held Bob from behind, his hands under one shoulder, and gently helped him pull himself a yard back, his feet clearing the mangled seat.

The old man looked down reluctantly, gritting his teeth, levering himself up gently on one elbow, and a guttural growl built up slowly from his diaphragm.

"Awwwwrrrrrrrrrr PISH!" he lamented, staring accusingly at the end of his leg. The wound from the splinter was more messy than painful or serious, but below it his ankle had been violently twisted when the weight of his body strained against his trapped foot. In about ten minutes it would probably be the size of a melon.

Tam rapped on the tinted panel at the front, remembering the two souls in the driver's cab.

"Yous all right through there?" he shouted.

There was no reply.

He hammered on it harder.

"Are yous all right through there?"

He heard a noise from above, and looked up to see a figure staring down at him from one of the smashed windows on what was now, technically, the ceiling.

"You'll need to get us oot o' here," he yelled. "There' a man deid and another in bad shape."

"The polisman's away with the keys," shouted the driver. "You'll need to hang on."

"Well where the fuck's he away to wi' the keys?" Tam spluttered in incredulous exasperation.

"He cannae reach the lock with the bus on its side. He's lookin' for somethin' to stand on."

"Jesus Christ," Tam spat, shaking his head. "So what in the name of God happened?"

"We hit a motor. Came oot o' nowhere. No lights or nothin'. Just appeared, headin' straight for us, then bang. Christ, it looks in some state."

The driver's face was suddenly bathed in bright light from outside and he shielded his eyes, looking away from the bus towards the source.

"Aw, thank fuck," he said, then looked back into the wreckage below. "Another motor. And here's Alec back as well. We'll no be a minute." Tam saw the driver clamber out of sight and heard some thumps as he made his way down off the hulk and on to the road.

More silent, unknowing time passed; could have been two minutes, could have been twenty seconds. Tam heard muffled words from outside but the content could not be deciphered, only a final "NOW" as one voice got louder and more heated towards the end of a sentence. Then they could hear activity at the front of the bus, a metallic clinking and scraping, before further footsteps alongside the crippled shell as it lay across the roadway like an upturned beetle.

Only the Wee Shite seemed to remain unperturbed, and indeed was sniggering to himself as they looked frantically about themselves in nervous confusion.

"The hell's goin' on?" Paul asked no-one in particular as the door stayed frustratingly closed and the anticipated contact from outside remained suspended.

They heard a laugh and turned to see the Wee Shite at the back, leaning against what had been the floor with an exaggerated nonchalance.

"Wee surprise boys," he said nasally.

With a rusty creak and a slam the lock was released then the door swung open and down, like the gangplank on a ferry. PC Clipboard's colourless young face appeared in the gap, looking quickly at the scene of devastation within, before focusing more intently on the Wee Shite.

"C'mon well," the prisoner demanded, and astonishingly, the polisman threw his ring of keys to him, whereupon he proceeded to unlock and remove his handcuffs.

The Wee Shite made his way down to the front of the bus, and now that he wasn't obscuring the doorway, Tam could see the tall figure at PC Clipboard's side, pointing a pistol at his head. The policeman's semi-automatic was slung around the man's neck, his side-arm tucked into the front of his belt.

This was no accident. This was an ambush.

The Wee Shite extricated the heavy weapon from around the dead man's head and pulled it over his own, then knelt down and searched the body, producing a pistol from an under-arm holster. He got up and clambered back to the door, moving obliviously between the other four frozen, gaping prisoners like they were part of the inert wreckage. The young officer then offered a shaking hand as the Wee Shite climbed on to the makeshift gangplank.

Before jumping down, he turned to face his erstwhile travelling companions.

"Don't say I'm no good to you," he said, tossing the keys to Paul, whose handcuffed swipe in the half-light failed to catch them. They clattered across the floor and out of sight.

It took a couple of frantic minutes to find them again, nestled amidst a shadowy sprouting of twisted metal and broken glass; and still more time to find the right key for each set of cuffs.

Tam climbed on to the gangplank first, noting with confusion that there was no-one outside. No matter, he thought. One thing at a time. He crouched on one knee and took hold of Bob as he was passed up by Paul and Spammy below, hauling him through the gap amidst loud cries of strain and pain. Then he descended to the road and waited for Paul to climb past Bob and hop down beside him. Spammy remained on the gangplank and took Bob by the under-arms, passing him down now to the pair on the ground.

"Where the hell is everybody?" Bob asked breathlessly as he stood on the tarmac on one leg, an arm around Paul's good shoulder.

Another sudden, shuddering BANG shattered the air, shaking

all of them into momentary panicked thoughts of whether the bus had been hit again as it lay wounded and helpless. Such thoughts were dispersed by a further BANG, less than a second later, its reverberation diminishing into the skies and hills.

There was a sound of footsteps from behind, and Tam looked past the exposed underside of the bus to see the Wee Shite and the tall figure jog briskly towards a car sitting across the road, its headlights trained on the wreck.

"I'll treat it as gratitude if yous keep your fuckin' mouths shut," the Wee Shite shouted to them, hauling off his prison overalls.

The tall figure opened the boot of the car and they each threw in their semi-automatics, then he produced some clothes and handed them to his companion. He quickly slipped the trousers on and climbed into the passenger seat, pulling a top over his head as the car moved off, swinging around at 180 degrees and passing the stunned gathering. The four of them watched in glazed incomprehension as the Wee Shite's hand waved – royalty-style – from out of the rolled-down window and the vehicle accelerated into the deepening twilight, unimpeded, unpursued.

"So where's the polisman?" Paul asked, the first to find a voice.

Tam caught Bob's worried eyes, then Paul's, then closed his own.

"Aw Jesus," he heard himself saying, walking at an increasing pace around the wreck "Aw Jesus, Jesus, Jesus."

Tam made it to where the driver's cab edged a surface of grass and gravel by the side of the hard tarmac, and saw what he saw. He turned to stop Paul, who had been following him, but was too late.

Paul halted and recoiled like he had run into a glass wall. He shook his head minutely, like a slow tremble, then closed his eyes, clenched his fists and breathed out heavily, twice, before being convulsed by body-shaking sobs.

Tam wanted to hold him, to lead him away, but he felt too dazed, exhausted and disgusted. He leaned back against the bus and looked to the darkening heavens, then turned away from the corpses handcuffed to the radiator grill, and vomited.

FIVE

Nicole splashed water on her face, the bracing cold an attempt to prime her wits after the soothing warmth of the stuff she had used to wash the flecks from around her mouth and off her hands. She had thought she was beginning to reconstitute herself, recover some semblance of composure, even if it was just a front. But then he had shown her the device, and the fear, upset, tension and confusion had finally served their eviction order on her lunch.

That was when it had moved from the realms of the theoretical to the physically tangible with a sickening jolt. The best evidence does that.

It looked like a metal tile, or a transportation bracket for a cooker or washing machine. Then he turned it over to reveal the parallel steel strips that had fitted into a slot cut into the chassis of her car.

He pointed to a black box between the strips at one end, with a small, red, transparent plastic bubble on top, about half a centimetre in diameter, inside which a tiny light was blinking at half-second intervals.

"This is a radio-controlled switch," he explained. "But most of this wee box is just housing a battery, which is what these two wires are coming from."

The wires led along the inside edge of one strip, to a complex but nasty-looking arrangement at the other end, reminiscent of a mantrap.

"Is . . . is it a bomb?" she asked, eyes bulging at the stuff of Joel Silver movies suddenly appearing in this most tawdry and mundane of living rooms.

"No," he said with a dry laugh. "Almost shat myself for a second when I was unscrewing the thing and I saw the wires, but no, it's not. Watch."

He placed a pencil between the strips and slid it along to the end, between the two jagged steel jaws of the "mantrap", which were each connected to three tiny pistons. With a small screwdriver he flipped off the top of the black box to reveal a tiny circuit board resting on top of the flat, rectangular battery. Then he pressed upon an indentation near the radio pick-up and the six pistons gave out a minute hydraulic hiss as the jaws slammed together with a dull, tooth-grinding clash and the two halves of the bisected pencil leapt into the air and tumbled to the carpet.

"There were two of these wee gizmos under your car; I'm not sure whether one was a back-up or if your car has a parallel system. But the pencil is your brake cables."

That was when she ran to the bathroom.

She returned to find him sitting on the brown armchair, opposite the TV. Now able to focus properly, if not actually relax, she had a closer look at him. He was a lot smaller than she had initially thought when he was towering before her, and in her slightly less hysterical frame of mind she realised he appeared almost as worried as she did. He looked mid-to-late thirties, although there was a bright youthfulness about him that seemed to contradict his dark dress and solemn demeanour.

She held a towel in one hand and a glass of water in the other, and took a seat on the matching sofa, whose curled ends meant its shape complemented its colour.

"I'm sorry," she said. "I'm not really used to this. I'm trying very hard to make some sense of it, but you'll need to bear with me. I've a thousand questions. But what I don't understand first is, why go to all this trouble? Why not just cut my brake cables down in the car park?"

"Because you'd notice your brakes were gone right away and you wouldn't drive anywhere. This way, they wait until you're heading for a red light, or bombing along the M8, then blow your fluid lines and . . ." He waved with his right hand, a blank expression upon a face that didn't want her to think he was closely contemplating what would have happened next.

"Jesus Christ," she mouthed. "So why didn't you warn me? Why didn't you just give me a phone call or come into the office? And why did you have to break into my flat and scare the living daylights out of me?"

"Because, Nicole, they're *out there*. They're *watching*. There'll be a guy in a car somewhere on this street right now, wondering why his wee radio transmitter didn't work when he pushed the magic button, and deciding what to do about it. He would have been watching you all afternoon, ever since his pal finished work on your chassis, waiting to drive off behind you after work so that he could pick the right time to zap your brakes. Ironically, with the devices removed, you were safe *as long as he thought he could kill you*. This might be a nightmare to you, but the nightmare scenario for these guys is you finding out they're trying to murder you – they simply cannot afford for that to happen. If they suspected you had been warned, or that you were on to them in any way, then I'm sure there would have been a contingency that you definitely don't want to speculate about.

"If I had called you up – gambling on the million-to-one possibility that your office phone's *not* tapped – or I had come into the office and shown you what I have here, you'd still have had to get into your car and drive home. Any deviation would tip them off. And you'd have been doing it scared shitless, so how could you stop yourself looking pale and nervous? How could you stop yourself

103

stealing a look over your shoulder? Or maybe taking a different route home, maybe avoiding the motorway or fast dual carriageways, doing a steady thirty in case I hadn't found all the surprises?

"These guys were going to blow your brakes so that your death wasn't suspicious, so that it didn't attract much attention. 'Young lawyer dies in M-way smash. What a tragedy. She lost control of her car at 70mph. Colleagues said she had been working very hard and had been under a lot of pressure recently.' Does that sound plausible enough to you? The cops wouldn't even bother to examine the wreckage, what was left of it. But that was just their ideal score. If they couldn't get you like that, they'll have instructions to get you some other way. And if they think you've rumbled them, they'll have instructions to take you out ASAP, any way, any how."

Nicole reached for her glass of water and took a long gulp, having feared for a moment that she would need to make another quick exit to the bathroom. The nausea passed, but her eyes were filling with tears again. She knew that it was shooting the messenger, and that it was even rather ungrateful, but she could feel nothing but hatred for this man before her who was saying these things, tearing down the painted backdrops of the world she thought she lived in to reveal the black, damp, hewn stone of dungeon walls.

Amidst the swirl of thoughts, facts and fears, one consideration came suddenly into focus at the heart of the maelstrom.

"They'll be coming for me, then? Coming to kill me, here, tonight?"

He ran both hands agitatedly through his hair, looking down at the ugly carpet for a moment.

"Not necessarily," he said, wrestling with possibilities. "That's why I had to pick your lock and sneak in. I had to let you come all the way home without knowing about this. Like I said, you're safe as long as they think you're under control. Right now they don't know you've found out about them. They just think they're going to have to change their radio supplier. They'll reckon they've still got plenty of time to fix up something else that will look like an accident. They might have somebody outside watching the place all night, or they might decide you're safely ignorant and tucked up for the evening, so they can come back before you get going again in the morning. You can't make a run for it right now, though. You can't afford to make them nervous, because they can't afford to take any chances. That's why they set out to kill you in the first place."

"So what do I do? Enjoy one last kip and then offer myself to them in the morning?"

He smiled, which she grudged to admit made her feel a microscopic bit better.

"Well, you can't stay here any more," he said, "which is a helluva shame with you having decorated it so nicely."

"Ha bloody ha."

"You'll have to come with me. We'll wait until they think you're asleep for the night, then make a break for it. My car's parked round the block, so we can get there across the back greens and out a different close."

"Where are you planning to take me?"

"Somewhere you can lie low. Somewhere safe, comparatively."

"What about work?"

"That'll be staked out too, especially once you've given them the slip. I'm sorry, Nicole, but your life is on hold. This isn't hide and seek. They won't give up after a few days and say, 'Okay, you win.' This is a race: we have to find out who's behind them – and prove it – before they find you."

"How did you know?" she asked, both hands clasped around the coffee mug she was clutching to her chest, the comfort of its warmth the smallest of consolations. She sat at the kitchen table, slumped low on her wooden chair, feeling bedraggled and deflated as her pulse cautiously decelerated and the terror gave way to exhaustion. Her voice was croakier than usual, her throat suffering from the swelling of suppressed sobs.

The man in black, Jack Parlabane, sat opposite, his chair backed tight against the wall so that not even his shadow was visible to anyone who might be looking from outside at the closed curtains.

"I saw someone working under your car," he said. "There was a van parked across the road purporting to be from a recovery service. I called the number painted on the side but got that 'number non-existent' tone after about four digits. Then I phoned directory inquiries and gave them the name and address. Never heard of them. So I waited until he was gone and had a wee deck at his handiwork."

"No, I meant, how did you know these people, whoever the hell they are, would try to kill me?"

"Because they've got a lot to lose and they're not playing a percentage game. They'll kill anyone who poses a threat, whether that person knows it or not. They killed Roland Voss and then set up four guys to take the rap; four guys who look so guilty that nobody's worrying too much about the on-going lack of a plausible motive. You don't really need one when you catch them fleeing the scene, covered in large samples of the appropriate blood group. Then *you* come along and start asking awkward questions, showing the cops parts of a letter claiming Tam McInnes was being fed information."

She put her mug down and leaned over the table, placing her head momentarily on her folded arms, then looking up at the man in black.

"But if the police have already seen the letter, what good would it do these people to kill me now?"

"Because it's not the letter they're worried about. Not what you've shown the cops anyway. It's the fact that you've *not* shown them the whole thing. And you haven't shown them whatever else was in McInnes's envelope."

She sat upright, taken aback.

"Come on," he said disparagingly. "*I* worked out you weren't quite coming clean from your TV interview, so it seemed a fair bet they would too. McInnes gave you more than just a letter, I guessed, and so did they. So why didn't you produce everything at L&B HQ?"

She sighed, buying time to take in the revelation that so many people seemed to know things she thought were securely secret.

106

"Law can be a game of bluff sometimes," she offered defensively, her feelings of vulnerability fuelling a desire to restore her credibility as an intelligent human being. "You don't show your hand until someone pays to see it. I only showed the police what I needed to at that stage. To extend the card metaphor, I was waiting to see what they played in response."

Nicole took a quick swig from her mug.

"It's as much a public relations game as a legal one. Think of the Scott Report, for God's sake; it doesn't matter what the evidence says, or how blatantly it says it – it's how you present it, and how your opponent responds. It's spin. If I give three good reasons, three pieces of evidence to back up my argument, all at once, and the police come up with a good way to refute just *one* of them, the public perception, the *media* perception is that I've been discredited. If I shout about the fact that they haven't answered the other two issues, I just look like a sore loser. But by playing them one at a time, I would be forcing the police to counter the arguments each issue raised individually."

The man in black grinned, raising an eyebrow.

"Very smart," he said. "Theoretically, very smart. But with the unknown drawback that you made certain anonymous individuals as nervous as Ian Paisley at Parkhead. They wouldn't have anticipated Tam McInnes's wee surprise package in the first place, so they needed to know what was in it and how exposed it left them."

He paused and took a breath, evaluating.

"To be absolutely honest, I didn't know for a fact they would come after you," he admitted. "Not so soon, anyway. I knew they'd be *watching* you, but I didn't think they would make a move until they were sure of how much a threat you constituted. The reason I came looking for you was to find out what else you knew about this. I was looking for your car so that I could intercept you on your way to it from the office, so that it looked to unwanted observers that I had just bumped into you. When I found the vehicle in question I realised that events were already at a rather advanced stage."

"What do you mean?"

"Well, the intended manner of your demise suggests that discretion is a consideration for these guys, putting them in the 'evil but not psychotic' category. This isn't a killing spree, it's a cover-up. The more corpses accumulate, the more people start asking questions, and worse still, making connections. If they have to, they'll kill someone without a thought – but if they don't have to, they'd probably rather not add to the body-count. What you said on TV yesterday will have given them a serious hard-on for that envelope, but just suspecting you know more than you're saying might not have been enough for them to decide you were for the off. So between then and this morning they've encountered something that tipped the scales. Did you see the envelope today?"

"No. My boss was looking for it, but his office is such a . . ."

"Aw *fuck*. Then it's gone," he stated flatly. "They must have broken in last night."

"*What?*" This was insane. She was growing exasperated and angry as he revised and extended the catalogue of impossibilities he had brought for her to look at.

"No," she said firmly, slapping the kitchen table and looking accusingly at him. "My boss had it. He just couldn't find it among all the stuff in . . ."

"It's *gone*, Nicole," he rebuked, eyes flashing with a compelling mixture of fire and regret. "You've got to understand: these people are from the No Fucking About school of operations. They needed to see what you had, so they broke in. That's their logic, that's their *gig*. If they had given the contents of the envelope a quick swatch and decided it was no threat, they would have put it back where they found it and left you alone, but they didn't."

She lowered her head back on to her arms on the table, momentarily closing her eyes against the pain that was beginning to throb behind them.

"You make it sound as if they're everywhere, that they can do anything," she protested.

He looked at the ceiling, steadying his thoughts.

"They're not, and they can't," he said softly, staring into her eyes with a look that she found both sympathetic and cautionary. "But you're going to have to start acting upon the assumption that they are and they can."

His appellant expression suddenly changed, his facial muscles seemingly deactivated as if someone had switched off the power to his head. Whatever was pumping colour to his cheeks was also apparently running off the same supply.

"Jesus," he said. "You said your boss had the envelope? It was in *his* office?"

He reached down to the duffel bag (black, bloody natch) he was carrying and produced a portable telephone.

"Manson & Boyd has a 24-hour emergency line, doesn't it? I've seen the ads. Who's in the office?"

"Woman called Margaret operates the nightline."

"Call her. We've both got to be sure about this. Ask her to have a look for the envelope."

"Oh for goodness sake, I . . ."

"Do it," he insisted impatiently.

"I thought you said it would be tapped."

"Yeah, but nobody'll be monitoring while the office is shut, and this could be an emergency. Do it."

She lifted the phone from his palm across the table and dialled the number, glancing up from the ugly moulded plastic device to launch a few more daggers at her tormentor.

"Hello, Manson & Boyd," said a female voice. Nicole considered the tones unusually shaky, but dismissed the thought as a combination of her own fragile state and the portable's typically crap reception.

"Hello, Margaret, it's Nicole here. I was just calling to . . ."

"I know, it's terrible," the voice interrupted, now undoubtedly wavering with distress. "It's so terrible." The snuffle of tears was audible despite the audio interference.

"I'm sorry, Margaret, what's happened?" Her pulse was off the blocks and gaining speed yet again.

"Oh hen, don't you know? Oh Nicole, pet, I thought . . . It's Mr Campbell. Oh God, the poor sowel, and him wi' weans as well."

"What's happened, Margaret?" she asked again, this time in a dread whisper.

"He's dead," she replied, breaking into sobs. "Aw hen, aw pet. They found him this afternoon, over in Partick. He'd been stabbed. They were after his wallet. Killed him for a few quid. A few *quid*. Some pair o' wee thugs."

"Ha-have the police arrested them, Margaret?" she breathed, swallowing.

"Naw, pet. The wee . . . *bastards* are still runnin' aboot. Probably spent his money on the drugs by now."

He sat with his elbows resting on the table and both hands holding his head, tangled sprays of hair jutting out from the angled gaps between his spread fingers. In the lengthening silence, neither could estimate how much time had elapsed. Nicole had cried gushingly, bending over the kitchen sink as the waves of grief rocked her body, taken there by some daft notion that cold water on her face would stem the flow from her eyes. She knew she couldn't pretend she was crying just for Mr Campbell. He was a nice man, a good man; at least these were her impressions from the few conversations they had shared. But in truth the news of his death had served to jettison all of the turbulent emotional flotsam that had been swilling around uncomfortably inside her.

She felt a hand on her shoulder but she knocked it away and glared furiously at him. *He* had done this, she told herself, briefly, unfairly and knowingly indulging her aching need to blame. He returned to his seat, and she followed some moments later.

"Sorry," she sniffed.

He made a slight gesture with his hand as if to dismiss her concerns, and allowed her to retreat into her silence.

"I heard the story on the radio," Nicole eventually said, her voice hollow. She stared into nothing, her eyes gazing wide, her head turned away from the wall. "The victim hadn't been . . . Mr

Campbell hadn't been named. They said a witness saw two youths fleeing the scene. His wallet was . . ."

Parlabane exhaled slowly through his nose and looked up from the table.

"Witness probably saw two men with neddish haircuts and shell-suit jackets," he said quietly with another small sigh. "Maybe a Celtic top or a Public Enemy T-shirt. Youths from all but the closest distance."

"Oh for Christ's sake," she snapped. "You can't possibly be sure of that."

"Well it's a bit of a fuckin' coincidence, wouldn't you say?"

Nicole had no response to that. She knew she believed him, but part of her was still fighting to deny it, to hang on to the rules, the logic of a reality that was becoming terrifyingly obsolete.

"Why?" she eventually asked him. They were mirroring each other now, one elbow on the table, hand supporting jaw, temple resting against the wall, eyes flitting back and forth from the wooden surface to the face opposite.

"Why did the mafia kill Einstein?" he replied.

She screwed her face up in bemused confusion. What the fuck are you talking about now, read the expression.

"He knew too much," Parlabane explained with a sad smile. "They found the envelope in Finlay Campbell's office. They must have known he was your boss and therefore sanctioning your actions, ergo they figured if they got rid of you, he'd just step into the breach."

"My boss," she said stumblingly. "He represented Thomas McInnes during the Robbin' Hoods trial. Would they have known that?"

"What do you think."

"So they'd have known he knew McInnes well enough to find the murder accusation hard to swallow."

"It certainly looks that way. So he was a threat, you were a threat and this envelope was a threat. And at this point, according to their plan, there'd be no you, no him, and no envelope."

111

"But you said they wouldn't want to attract attention. Wouldn't two deaths at one law firm seem a conspicuous coincidence?"

"Not that conspicuous. Manson & Boyd's not a family solicitor's, remember. It's got, what, twenty offices across the West of Scotland, maybe a dozen in the East? And we're not talking about execution-style killings. One death by street mugging, one by car crash, same office, same day . . . tragic coincidence maybe, but not necessarily a suspicious one."

"But as far as *they* know, other people at the office could have seen the envelope too. They can't kill everybody."

"No need. Knowledge of the envelope's contents is useless if you can't produce them. And it's no good claiming it's been stolen, because anything you didn't give to the police effectively now never existed. You might entertain a few conspiracy enthusiasts with the story, but it's not going to cut much ice in court, is it?"

Nicole felt like she was climbing a staircase in an Escher painting, fearing her expression of baffled consternation might become a permanent feature as their circumlocutive argument continued to spin dizzyingly back and forth upon itself.

"But if that's the case, why would they still have to kill me and . . ."

"Because it's not this letter, this envelope that they fear. The letter was just a weapon, a catalyst, even. The danger to them is someone being motivated enough to start poking holes in what the rest of the world is perfectly satisfied is an open-and-shut murder case. The danger is someone believing not only that Tam McInnes and friends weren't there specifically to kill Roland Voss, but that they *didn't* kill him, full stop. You said that on TV, remember, in front of several million viewers, most of whom until that point were expecting this whole thing to unfold without hearing a single word of dissent against the idea that those four men did it. Jesus Christ, I mean, did you ever hear *anyone* say they thought Fred West didn't do it?"

"No," she conceded.

"But there *you* are, saying the unsayable, and suddenly some

112

viewers out there in TV-land are wondering whether there might be more to this one after all. Suddenly there's a few people asking themselves: 'What does she know?'. And unfortunately that included the bad guys, who had a more urgent need than most to find out. Like I said, if it turned out you had nothing much, the bad guys would let it go. You'd be just a silly wee lassie with her knickers in a twist and the media would soon get fed up watching you bang your head off a brick wall. But you didn't have nothing, did you? And my guess is you had proof not just that McInnes was receiving inside information, but that he was being set up. Tell me I'm wrong."

Nicole glared at him.

"You know, you're doing so well on your own, I can't work out what you need me for."

"Don't get huffy. We can't afford it. What was in the envelope, Nicole? What did the letter really say?"

She sighed, leaning away from the table and back in her chair. Body language of resignation and cooperation.

"McInnes was being *blackmailed* into carrying out a robbery," she stated. "He didn't know who, just where. There were photocopies of floorplans of Craigurquhart House, diagrams showing the positions of closed-circuit cameras, electric fences, alarm triplasers, the works. There were also photocopies of security-camera stills showing McInnes in the act of burgling three different business premises, which were being used to ensure his participation. McInnes swears in the letter that the pictures are fakes, says he's never committed a burglary since leaving prison.

"The letter says whoever was behind it contacted him several times by telephone using a voice disguiser. McInnes was instructed to rob the safe of the house's VIP suite, as someone very rich would be in residence. It would be a safe with an electronic lock, the combination programmable by the distinguished guest, but there was an over-ride access code which would be supplied to McInnes at the latest possible moment in case it was changed. He wasn't told what was expected to be in the safe, just to take whatever he found and that he would be contacted again afterwards about handing over the spoils, upon which he would be paid a generous percentage."

Nicole held up her palms as if to say "that's it".

"Now," she said stiffly, "maybe this is me being naive, or perhaps my judgment might be clouded by a conflict of interest, but I can't see why they would want to kill me just because I know this. Surely, if anything, this information only serves to explain why McInnes was there. Obviously there is a factor of mitigation regarding his being coerced into doing the job – though that won't be worth a monkey's toss against a murder charge. But there's nothing of use in actually proving he and his colleagues didn't carry out the killings."

"That's not the aspect of it that worried them," Parlabane said. "It's not about whether or not people believe McInnes is guilty. It's about *them*. It's about who *they* are."

"I'm sorry, Mr Par . . ."

"Call me Jack. I know you don't like me very much, so it's not supposed to be a term of endearment, but it's easier."

"Jack. I'm not following this."

"Right," he said, pulling at the sleeves of his polo-neck as though he might be about to produce a bunch of flowers from one of them. "Let me put it this way. Here's their ideal situation. They kill Voss, McInnes and co are caught for it, and go to jail. McInnes whines to the cops about being given inside information, and the terrorist scare caused by the high profile of the victims forces the cops to look into this possibility. However, with no evidence, the trail goes cold. Bad guys live happily ever after. End of story.

"Situation number two: they kill Voss, McInnes and co are caught for it, and a lawyer shows up with a letter saying . . . yakka yakka yakka, proving McInnes isn't making up what he's telling the cops. Suddenly the world knows for *sure* there's someone else involved. But then a high-ranking member of the security operation commits suicide inside a police station and *voilà*: the world has its mysterious background figure. A few people get jumpy about the

114

fact that he popped a cyanide capsule rather than hung himself, but apart from the hyper-paranoid UFO-spotting brigade, everyone forgets about it after a while, because there's no hard evidence to suggest anyone further was involved. Cops won't go a-hunting when everyone's satisfied that all the questions have already been answered. Bad guys live happily ever after. End of story again.

"Situation number three: as before, but this time lawyer is in possession of information suggesting that whoever was behind it had sufficient resources to blackmail McInnes with faked security stills. Lawyer wonders aloud whether this was maybe a bit too impressive for a one-man show, and suddenly it's not just the UFO-spotters who are looking beyond Donald Lafferty for the source. However, if bad guys steal evidence and kill lawyer, or as it turns out, lawyers, before they can produce it and do the wondering aloud bit, then we revert to situation number two, in which, you may remember, the bad guys live happily ever after."

Nicole nodded, sighing.

"So who are they?"

"Bollocks," he said, patting his pockets. "I've lost their business card. That would have been really handy, too."

"You know what I mean. Terrorists? Organised crime?"

"Well, whoever they are, they're very well organised and extremely well connected. Enough to plan and execute the burglary of your offices in a matter of hours and leave so little trace that no-one noticed. Enough to find out the registration of your car and booby-trap it."

"So how did *you* find out which car was mine?"

"Friends in the police. Same as them."

"The *police*?"

"Like I said, well organised and well connected. Enough to acquire security shots of burglaries-in-progress and drop Tam McInnes's face on to them. Enough to murder Finlay Campbell in broad daylight and make it look like a mugging. And enough to murder Donald Lafferty in a room inside the headquarters of a major regional police force."

115

The feeling of grasping, hopeless exasperation returned. Another encore in the interminable Jack Parlabane Contradictions and Impossibilities Showcase.

"Donald Lafferty committed suicide. I thought even you had just mentioned *that*."

He burned into her eyes with a look of such darkness that she suspected his previous glowers had been his idea of a sunny demeanour to put her at ease in this time of stress and anxiety. The idea of nipping out to meet the unseen assassins supposedly waiting in a car in the street acquired a fleeting allure.

"Donald Lafferty," he said, very quietly, in low rumbling tones she could feel in her own diaphragm, "is the reason I'm here. And by extension, the reason you're still alive. The fact that they murdered him was what made me realise they might also murder you, get it?"

She nodded solemnly, waiting until he had acknowledged her acquiescence to add, appealingly, "But how?"

"Well, what's the official story?" he asked agitatedly. "What's been on the news all day? Someone – some cop who 'can't be identified for security purposes' – walks into a room and sees Donald Lafferty swallow something, next thing he's dead? Bloke's supposed to have attempted to make him cough it up but he was fought off. Presumably there's signs of struggle to verify this. Maybe the bloke's got a couple of bruises and so has Donald. Maybe a few marks on the furniture, a knackered chair. So why am I the only person in the fucking universe who thinks this suggests that the struggle was Donald trying to *prevent* someone forcing a cyanide capsule down his throat?"

He closed his eyes and turned his head away briefly, letting the swell of emotion subside. There was a beguiling but sad and even pained smile in his eyes.

"Let me tell you a wee secret about Donald Lafferty," he said, "although it won't be secret for long, unless I'm way off the mark. He used to be a cop. That's not the secret. But get this: he was the cop who arrested Tam McInnes for the Robbin' Hoods burglaries.

116

It's not common knowledge. He was just a plod at the time, and the credit officially went to the guy leading the investigation, but it was Donald who made the big breakthrough and it was Donald who physically put the cuffs on McInnes. *I* know this because he was also my friend. And the whole world will know it soon enough because somebody is about to use it to establish his guilt, posthumously, now that he isn't around to answer back."

Parlabane had a sour look, regret and anger.

"Cops at the time were totally stumped. They had few clues, little evidence and the MO just didn't fit any of the usual suspects, or even any of the wilder cards. To cut a very long story short, Donald sussed that the reason they couldn't match up the methods was because the culprits were new to the game – previously, everyone assumed it was a gang coming in from another part of the country, or some bunch of housebreakers moving up the social scale. As a result he looked a bit harder at the details of the first place to get tanned, and from the fact that the items stolen there were fewer and on the whole more personal than in later robberies, worked out that there might be an element of grudge involved."

"And given that the house belonged to Sir Michael Halworth, the police concentrated their suspicions on recently laid-off car workers," Nicole said, happy to demonstrate that there was part of this she *could* follow.

"Indeed. Now, do you want to hear what I think is really going on?"

"I think it would be grossly negligent not to, given my circumstances."

"Donald Lafferty was murdered because he had worked out that they were setting him up. They were setting him up as the criminal fucking mastermind, just like they set up McInnes and associates as the killers. He's the ex-cop working on the security at Craigurquhart, who knew the place inside out, knew who was going to be staying there, dates, times, advance itineraries, the whole show.

"What the world was supposed to believe is this: Lafferty hatched the cunning and dastardly plan but needed someone to

117

carry it out, so he enlisted the services of some gentlemen he knew for a fact had considerable experience in the field, keeping his own identity secret from them. But it all goes wrong on opening night: the hired help get caught in the act, and whether it was in Lafferty's original script or not, they've left four stiffs at their backs. Robbers tell the cops there's another party pulling the strings, and the hunt begins for the shadowy figure behind the curtain. Someone somewhere makes the crucial and timely 'discovery' that Lafferty was once instrumental in putting McInnes and Hannah away for a string of country-house break-ins, and Lafferty commits suicide after his terrible secret is revealed."

Nicole's face was a study in concentration, suddenly broken by a flaw in the logic.

"But that fact hadn't *been* discovered when he died. Unless it just hasn't been given to the media yet."

"No, it hadn't been 'discovered'. And cyanide wasn't part of the plan. Hear me out. According to my contact, and contrary to the bollocks the spokesman told the TV cameras, Donald Lafferty was summoned to police HQ *specifically* in response to what you produced. You buggered up the agenda. He wasn't supposed to be there right then – he was meant to be in Perthshire, where he had been all night, and from where he should have gone home. And my guess is he was supposed to 'commit suicide' at his house later on, by more conventional means, after 'realising' or 'being told' that his secret was out. But instead he shows up at police HQ, knowing now that McInnes and Hannah – to whom he has a connection – are among the men in custody, and that inside knowledge is suspected. On the way into the building he gives a brief, nervous and extremely weird interview to a TV reporter. The interview is broadcast at 6:20. Donald Lafferty is dead before seven.

"Someone who saw that interview feared Lafferty had clocked he was being set up, or at least that he knew *something*, so his 'suicide' had to be brought forward before he did or said anything that might blow the gaffe. Any money you like, they'll wait until the

118

hysteria has died down over the use of cyanide and the possibility of the fucking martians being behind it all – then they'll leak the Lafferty–Hoods connection and use it to put a firm lid on the whole thing."

"Okay, okay," she said, holding a hand up, eyes narrowed in concentration. "I understand. And it sounds logical, if not entirely plausible – although I'm beginning to lose my grasp on the meaning of that word. But, well, how can I put this? I realise that this Donald Lafferty was a friend of yours, and I mean no offence, but could your friendship possibly be clouding your judgment?"

He creased his brow, looking more quizzical than annoyed, his silence beckoning her to elaborate.

"It's just that you seem very convinced he had no part in it whatsoever. Obviously, in light of recent developments I'm aware that Donald Lafferty wasn't where the buck stopped, but I've got to ask this: if he's the ex-cop with all the information, de-blah de-blah de-blah, and the men in custody are . . . who they are, is it possible that Lafferty was being leaned on to set this thing up in just the same way as McInnes et al were leaned on to carry it out?"

"No," he said blankly.

"And why not?"

"Because it would be pointless, an unnecessary extra remove. If you're setting some guys up to be in the wrong place at the wrong time, you just do it – yourself. You make as few people party to a conspiracy as possible, and you certainly don't *force* someone else to do it, because he could double-cross you, tip off the patsies, tip off the cops."

"But what if he was party to the conspiracy – or thought he was – and it's *he* who was double-crossed later on?"

He gave a little dry laugh and shook his head.

"All right, fair enough," he said, "although he was my friend, I'll admit that nobody can say for certain whether someone is capable of murder – but I *can* say that he wasn't fucking stupid. If he was setting up somebody to take the fall, he'd hardly pick guys with a traceable connection to himself. Do you see? Contrary to how the world is supposed to read it, it's the fact that McInnes and Hannah are involved that tells me Donald had *nothing* to do with it."

"So how long had you known him?" Nicole asked, sitting on the edge of her armchair, unable to prevent her eyes straying occasionally towards the close-curtained windows, out of which Parlabane had expressly forbidden her to peek. He had a shattered look about him almost every time he mentioned Lafferty's name, and she sensed it was bothering him to talk about him only in this painful context. Her resentment of him was subsiding in the sight of his own hurt; before that she had felt angry that he was removed and immune from the anarchy he was unveiling.

They had moved back to the living room upon his suggestion, on the dual grounds that firstly, to their outside observers, Nicole had spent an awful lot longer in the kitchen than was normal for dinner for one, and that secondly, the wooden chairs were becoming literally a pain in the arse.

"Since adolescence, really," he said. "I was a 'budding young hack' – actually office dogsbody on the newsdesk – and he was your actual rookie polisman. I got talking to him at the scene of a major crime incident: couple of teenagers had hijacked an ice-cream van and gone joyriding through a scheme in Nitshill, firing balls of it at the windscreens of passing cars. When they ran out of soft scoop they moved on to oysters and nougat wafers. It wasn't a pretty sight."

His eyes glinted with a symbiotic combination of pleasure and sadness at the memory.

"Misunderstood youth. A cry for help," Nicole offered with a smile, pleased and relieved that her facial muscles still remembered the drill.

"Well, they were certainly crying for help when the drivers started turning round and giving chase. This was Nitshill. Ice-cream scoops are notoriously difficult to retrieve from the lower intestine. Anyway, I bumped into him a couple of nights later at the Apollo."

120

"A club?"

"No, the erstwhile greatest music venue in the world. The Skids were playing and I was reviewing it. As I was getting paid to be there, I was probably supposed to be sitting in the circle, scribbling contemplatively in my notebook. Instead I was down the front – although not that near; the stage was about twelve feet high so you had to stand back to see anything – engaging in activities known in the modern parlance, I believe, as 'moshing'. There was the usual tangle of bodies – you just grabbed on to someone in the crowd and burled around for a bit. At the end of *Into The Valley* I found that I was hanging on to Donald. We went for a few after the show and it kind of started from there.

"We weren't bosom buddies, like. We just met up every so often, usually for gigs, occasionally just for a few beers. I never knew much about his personal life; I know you're probably condemning this as a guy thing, but there are some pals you meet up with and discuss anything, and others with whom you stick to . . . I don't know, established common ground. We talked rock'n'roll, work and a bit of football. We stayed kind of in touch as we got older; despite climbing the ranks and having to be generally respectable, Donald could still occasionally be tempted along to a show, usually some bunch from the old days that really should have chucked it by then. Irresistible allure of nostalgia for the aging male who's pining for lost youth. How the hell else could SLF and The Buzzcocks sell out venues in the late 1980s?"

He leaned back on the settee, running a hand through his unco-operative locks.

"I went to work in London for a few years and then Los Angeles for a couple more, and I guess we had probably forgotten about each other. It's a bit difficult after all that time to just call up like it's been a fortnight, even on the off-chance that you do have the phone number. Then a few months back I met him in Edinburgh out of the blue, outside the Usher Hall – Big Country had been playing; Skids connection. We went to a pub nearby and caught up a wee bit. He told me he was no longer in the police; he was working as a security adviser on some kind of government project. He wouldn't say what or where; and to be honest, I'd have been the last person he would tell, if he was doing his job properly."

"I can't think why."

"I got his address and phone number. I was kind of in the middle of moving into a new place with my girlfriend at the time and we didn't have a phone number yet, so I said I'd forward it when I knew. Of course I didn't, but I had his, and when you see someone after more than five years, it's pretty easy to wait six months before ringing them up again."

Nicole looked disapprovingly at him.

"Look," he said defensively. "Wait until you're at least ten years older before you start getting judgmental about this kind of thing. Anyway, the next time I saw him was on the TV last night."

"On the six o'clock news?"

"No. The morbid action replay on *Newsnight* after he was dead."

"God, that's how you found out? I'm sorry."

"Ach," he said, dismissing the need for any ministrations of sympathy.

"No, that must have been a horrible shock. Believe me, I'm becoming something of an authority. And I'm sorry for pressing the idea that he might have been in on the Voss thing."

"It was a fair point at the time."

"Still sorry. It was just that when you mentioned his appearance on the news, I thought . . . well, he said some rather odd things, and I wondered if what he said might have been some kind of message or code after all. That the . . . bad guys . . . knew what he meant because he had been, I don't know, somehow one of them."

Parlabane sat up, that sad smile on his lips and in his eyes again, like when he had spoken about first meeting Lafferty.

"'I haven't had time to catch up on developments at this end of the arena'," he recited. "'It's not as if I've been sitting around listening to my favourite music, although a lot more people should.'"

"Yes, that was it, that was what he said."

"It *was* a message," he stated firmly, causing her to sit up and

122

even to hold her breath. "Donald would have been trying to work out what the fuck happened all night. Examining the scene, the grounds, talking to the cops . . . all that stuff. Trying to explain how someone so successfully circumvented all of his security systems, trying to deduce what failure had allowed four people to be slaughtered in cold blood. At some point he'd have found out who was being held, and we can only guess at what else he might have discovered. But whatever he suspected, he could see that he was being manoeuvred into the frame, and unlike McInnes he couldn't preempt the accusation. He knew they had him done up like the proverbial kipper, and very possibly that the culprits had heavyweight police connections. I doubt if even *he* suspected they would kill him, but he knew he was going down, alongside the four stooges.

"He needed an advocate, someone on the outside. He needed someone to start searching for what really happened at Craigurquhart House before the conspirators had covered their tracks and completed the job of framing up their scapegoats. Someone he could trust, someone who would believe him. Someone with a track record for tenacious, exhaustive and frequently illegal methods of investigation."

"Someone in black, perhaps?"

"These are just my working clothes. Try breaking into someplace in faded denims and a white T-shirt and you'll be counting the seconds before you hear sirens. But yes, you're right."

"And someone whose phone number he didn't have."

"Correct. So he got a message across the only way he could, a message he knew only I would understand – though he probably knew he was also inviting the bad guys to burgle his flat and rifle through his record collection."

"So what does it mean? What was his favourite music?"

"Lately? No idea. Once upon a time, I don't know, The Skids, The Boomtown Rats, The Police, Undertones."

She felt the pain returning behind her eyes. He was regressing once more into inscrutability.

He reached for his duffel bag and rummaged inside it, then produced a battered and aged-looking white cassette, minus cover, which he threw to her.

"Clue was in what he said beforehand. 'At this end of the arena'," Parlabane explained. "Skids had a song called *Arena*. Donald loved it. We both did. Well, not the whole song. Verses and chorus were ploddingly awful, and the lyrics were among the most excruciatingly pompous, pretentious and downright stupid that Richard Jobson ever wrote – and believe me, that's saying something."

"Richard Jobson?"

"Yes. For it was he. Self-styled Aryan-Olympian-Dunfermlian post-punk poet, fashion model, ubiquitous TV star etcetera etcetera. Like I said, most of the song is absolute bollocks. But after the second chorus, it gets interesting. Play it."

Nicole put the tape into the hefty but purportedly portable cassette and CD player on the mantelpiece, momentarily nervous that Parlabane's geriatric tape would give it the audio equivalent of a sexually transmitted disease. He had cued it up at the right place, and she pushed up the volume as the sound began to break through.

She glanced briefly at him, but he was staring fixedly at the machine, either urging her attention or aware of the awkwardness of not knowing where to look when two people are concentrating on simply listening to something.

The recently abused chorus was ending, and the song broke down to just a synth sound and a tentative, creeping bass for a few bars. The synth riff was repeated as a rhythm guitar surfaced somewhere, a dry sound like helicopter blades chopping overhead. Then a lead guitar entered quietly, snaking around the synth and growing gradually louder in the mix as the hypnotic melody circled again and again and drums began to pulse in the distance, getting ever clearer, ever nearer.

She felt a thrilling sense of anticipation as the orchestration expanded and each of the instruments grew louder, her desire for the song to reveal its hidden secret enhanced by the dramatic and teasing build-up. The tension reached breaking point and the toms suddenly gave way to snare, the lead guitar screaming in, full-blooded, to take up the riff introduced by the synth, a crashing wave of sound and emotion. Somewhere she could see the man in black, younger than her, swaying and waving in a bacchae of sweating bodies beneath the swelter of stage lights.

There was a voice, somewhere, lost amidst the storm. She was about to reach for the volume control again when she realised that, like what had gone before it, the voice would grow stronger and louder in passing cycles. Other voices joined it on each pass, their tune now defined but the lyrics still agonisingly obscured.

With the next repetition, she *thought* she had made out what was being said, and it was a possibility that stopped her breath until the next pass confirmed it.

The voices were singing the same words over and over.

Over and over.

"All the boys are innocent."

"Well, if this isn't what he meant, it's a hell of a coincidence," Nicole admitted.

"Yeah. Either that or I've picked the wrong song and someone called Albert Tatlock is getting away with murder."

"What?"

"Never mind. Skids joke. Let's get going."

Nicole shifted in her seat, straining momentarily against the belt to glance up at the buildings as the car passed beneath them, the looming glass towers slalomed by the motorway incongruously futuristic amidst the dignified age of the terraces, domes and spires. The night was crisply still and clear, the waters of the Clyde black, motionless and reflective as the vehicle crossed a hundred feet above.

She felt sharply awake despite the late hour and the unusual rigours of a long and unprecedentedly distressing day, brightly alive to the beauty of the city by night. As they passed through the

125

centre of it, she felt they had the place to themselves, so deserted were the roads, pavements, buildings and even the motorway.

She looked across at Parlabane, his profile composed and determined as he held the wheel and fixed his eyes upon the road, occasionally glancing down at the speedometer. He had maintained a steady thirty until reaching the motorway, and once upon it stuck rigidly to the fluctuating limits despite the inviting emptiness of the highways. She had wondered for a while whether he compensated for his repertoire of recklessness by being the world's most boring driver, then remembered the importance of avoiding the attentions of the law. If people with major police connections were going to be out looking for her, it probably wouldn't help to have some traffic cop say her description matched the passenger of a guy he booked for speeding the other night. Hey, here's his name and address.

There was a cool reality about her situation now, a feeling that it was actually happening, made less frightening by the sense that it was now something she was doing, rather than something that was being done to her. It was the travelling that did it. The discussions, the devices, the revelations had all been enclosed in the cocoon of that absurdly twee flat, just words and stories about events going on elsewhere. In there it was disturbing, certainly, but somehow removed; like she could go to bed, get up tomorrow, walk out the front door and get on with her life, while all that nastiness happened to someone else. But the moment she took action was the moment she accepted it, the moment she became part of it, and when she left the flat, the feeling that her old life was gone hit her hard in that first breath of cold wind as they emerged from the close into the back court.

The grass underfoot; the steam of his breath in the half-light; the sudden, stupidly startling noise of water down a drainpipe above them; the smell of the old Sirocco's interior.

This was not a dream.

He had slung her bag in the boot and then opened the passenger door for her, pushing the seat forward and telling her to lie along the back, out of sight. Once they were well clear of her neighbourhood he had stopped the car and allowed her to move up front. The radio had been burbling away since they drove off, but she had barely been aware of the songs, jingles and ads, as it wasn't on loud enough to compete for attention with the raging current-affairs debate going on inside her head.

Parlabane turned the volume up, obviously recognising a cheaply dramatic burst of brass as heralding a news bulletin.

" . . . with Graham Forbes.

"The main story tonight, of course, the brutal and bloody escape of the four men accused of murdering Roland Voss, during which two police officers and a driver were killed. Thomas McInnes, his son Paul, Robert Hannah . . ."

Nicole turned to Parlabane. He said nothing, his face poker-set, only a small swallow in his throat betraying any reaction. The radio newscaster's smooth tones were replaced by a highland accent speaking over a crackly phone line from nearer the scene.

"The men were being transported from Edinburgh to Peterhead Prison, where, ironically, they were being taken for security reasons. Details are sketchy at this stage, but it is believed that their prison bus went out of control and turned on its side near the village of Strathgair, after colliding with an abandoned car. Police believe that the four men took advantage of the accident to overpower their armed guards, stealing their weapons before making their escape. It is suspected that one officer may have died from injuries sustained during the crash, but police say that the bodies of the second officer and the driver were found handcuffed to the bus, having been shot through the head in a manner chillingly similar to the murders of Roland Voss's bodyguards on Sunday.

"It is believed the fugitives are now in possession of several firearms, and police are warning the public that these men are extremely dangerous and must not be approached at any cost. With discovery of the escape coming at such a late hour, officers have been sent door-to-door in the surrounding area to warn local residents who may have gone to bed before the news broke."

"Reaction to the escape has been extreme," rejoined the newsreader, "from police and government officials still shell-shocked by Sunday night's atrocities. There have been calls for the army to be brought in to hunt the men down, and a pledge from Scottish Secretary Alastair Dalgleish that no resource shall be spared in bringing the four to justice."

"I will be insisting on a full inquiry into how this atrocity was allowed to happen," began a rasping, upper-class voice, the sound of film winding in press cameras wheezing loudly in the background. "But for now the priority is the apprehension of these . . . *animals*," the voice spat. "For that is all they are. And like animals they will be hunted down – by all means available and by all means necessary."

The Sirocco coasted on into the night, the lights of Glasgow fading behind. Parlabane said nothing, his face still stone-set, Nicole guessing at the babbling frenzy of calculation, projection and conjecture going on behind those locked and focused eyes.

She stared ahead at the dotted white lines being gobbled up by the car, emotional voices echoing through her head, the hum of the engine and the burr of tyres on tarmac somehow silenced by their own constancy.

Someone tried to kill you today.

He's dead. Aw hen, aw pet.

Like animals they will be hunted down.

Scum four must die.

All the boys are innocent.

128

II

This is Iron Age,
Steel blue Medusa eyes,
If I could scratch a name,
That would outlive hers,
That would make me feel that I belong here,
To everything and not a fraction,
To everything and not an age.

– Billy Franks, *Age*

SIX

Of course, he *had* to go.

There really was no choice in the matter, and the sadly ironic thing was that it had been Voss who saw to that. He had them by the balls, there was no denying it, demanding that they fall on their swords or he would run them through.

Some might say that they were biting the hand that fed them, but that would be to make the same mistake as the deluded and arrogant Dutch fool. Men like Voss, intoxicated by the self-made mythology of their own success, seemed to think that they were beneficently visiting prosperity upon a country, the choice of which nation to honour in their gift. They believed they were the engine of their own achievements, and that the era, location and political climate were incidental, a painted landscape in the background of their magnificent portrait.

In truth they were merely actors. There were roles that needed to be played, but it was up to men like himself to decide who should play them. "The part of the arch-conservative media tycoon will tonight be performed by a stand-in, as Mr Roland Voss is indisposed."

It was *we* who had made *him*, thought Alastair Dalgleish bitterly, still smarting from the stinging gauntlet-lash of betrayal. He winced at the fiery taste as he sipped at his whisky and stood, staring from the window of his study, the chair at his desk uncomfortable during such moments of agitated reflection. The brown liquid glinted tauntingly in the crystal glass, its volume militantly refusing to deplete itself no matter how many drops he braced himself to swallow. And it was nothing to do with it being early morning; the stuff was undrinkable night and day. Damn the image-makers. He longed for the soothing cool of a nice, long G&T.

We made him.

There was a limited amount of success to go round. A finite number of major roles. Voss didn't take, Voss didn't demand, Voss didn't earn. Voss was given. Voss was *allowed*. They didn't need *him*, they just needed someone to fill the role, perform a function. Someone.

Anyone.

Voss thought that his editorial support of the Conservatives was what ensured him special consideration, allowed him to expand his media interests so unhindered. What he failed to understand was that those newspapers were going to be saying very much what the Party wanted them to, whoever owned them, as that was always going to be a condition of being green-lighted to buy them. What Voss's monstrous ego had obscured from his view was simply that if it hadn't been him, it would have been someone else.

The arrogance of the man.

That was what had really upset them. If it had simply been greed it would have been different. Wanting an even bigger slice of the pie when you've already vomited from over-eating was ideologically understandable. Perhaps a compromise could have been reached, some sop to acknowledge that the rattle of Voss's sabre had been heard and duly noted.

But it hadn't been about money, business or politics. It had been about power. Voss had known exactly the consequences of what he was asking them to do; not only for themselves, but for the party. For the two of them it was electoral poison – in the highly unlikely event that their constituency branches didn't de-select them anyway. And far worse, the poison would be all the more bitter as the lethal draught was transmuted from the elixir that was ready to revive the party in the polls.

If they did not comply, Voss would destroy them anyway. His revelations would demand their resignations from the cabinet, amid a scandal that would be the coup de grace for the government's scarred and wounded credibility. Damage limitation was a negligible concept; even a repeat of the Scott spin tactics would be futile. "They acted in good faith" wasn't going to cut it on this one. And there would be no finite period of penitence on the backbenches before rising phoenix-like into the cabinet again. They would not be forgiven for the devastation caused.

Things had changed since the glorious Thatcher era. The free-spirited philosophy of "anything goes" that came with a massive majority was but a cherished and distant memory. And it was nothing to do with Nolan. In the Conservative Party in the Nineties, there was only one rule on "standards in public life": don't get caught.

Consequently, they couldn't even *tell* the boss about the threat.

Voss didn't really need what he was asking from them. The Dutchman wasn't the only one well-placed to carve out a share of the new market, and Dalgleish had wondered what impact it might have on the reputation of his newspaper group, given that its sales pitch was from a prominent kiosk on the moral high ground. Dalgleish of all people knew that Voss had always kept that aspect of his European interests conspicuously quiet.

So what had enraged him was the realisation that Voss might not particularly *want* what he was demanding of them. The realisation that *that* wasn't the issue. He just wanted the satisfaction of exer-cising power. Of arbitrarily deciding to destroy a career or bring down a government, as if they were gladiators whose life or death depended upon the whim that turned Caesar's thumb up or down.

Voss was merely amusing himself by playing a game, and the game was called God. He cared nothing for the real people whose lives were affected by his power-mongering and political masturbation. People like Michael Swan. People like Alastair Dalgleish.

So what did he think, that they were impotent little pawns on his board? That they were his creatures, to do with as he pleased?

Yes, indeed, it was about power. And by God they had shown him the true meaning of the word.

It was rather a shame about the wife, of course, but the embarrassing little Eurotrash trollop did insist on following him around, always managing to make several hundred thousand pounds' worth of clothing look like mismatched items from a particularly insalubrious jumble sale. Unfortunately they didn't have a lot of time to play with, and there simply hadn't been an opportunity to get the bugger alone.

The bodyguards he felt no remorse about whatsoever. Bloody gorillas, the pair of them. Just because someone had taught them to walk upright when in public didn't mean they were actually sentient beings. He had always hated the way they still eyed him up when they knew exactly who he was, and had never forgiven them for the time they pinned him to a wall at that dinner in Paris, within six feet of about twenty bloody photographers. They claimed that he had approached Voss a little hastily and suggested that they feared he might be reaching for a weapon as he put his hand inside his jacket. He was actually reaching for a cheque made out to the charity Voss was hosting the dinner in aid of, having decided that if he was going to chuck money away on some bunch of foreign parasites, he might as well try and get a half-decent photo-op out of it.

Two years on, the "Mugger Dalgleish" tag was still following him around.

From his town-house window he looked across the gardens of Drummond Place and considered with a smile that its concave terrace reminded him a little of Bath. However, the memory of the real thing served to sadden him once more, as thoughts of England always did while he was stuck up here.

There was no getting away from it, he hated the place. Hated the whole bloody country. Getting back to London felt like coming up for air after any prolonged stay, an oasis after days in the parched desert of this remote and detached wasteland. Summer had been the worst, with so little parliamentary business to take him back south. An endless ordeal of flesh-pressing in shoddy factories and smelly community centres, under perennially grey skies. Where the sun don't shine, indeed.

And what really stuck in the craw, what burnt and was as hard to swallow as the bloody whisky, was being thought of as *Scottish*, as one of them. He had never even been to the bloody place until about three years ago, and that was an overnight visit to the Scottish party conference as the token senior minister. He was an Englishman, through and through, and damn proud of it. His father, admittedly, had been a Scot, but for goodness' sake, no-one considered Portillo Spanish, did they?

But he had needed to be Scottish, or at least to put on a show of displaying his credentials, because of the ridiculous fuss made over the idea of an Englishman being Secretary of State for Scotland. And it *was* ridiculous. Who, for instance, was the last Welsh secretary who was actually bloody Welsh? Or Northern Ireland secretary who was from the province? In Dalgleish's opinion, it was precisely this sort of pandering and indulgence that was responsible for the party's poor showings north of the border – if you let a child have its way every time it whinges or whines about something, you end up with an indisciplined brat, don't you? He simply couldn't understand the inconsistency of it all. To put it bluntly, if you're not worried about whether having only ten MPs out of seventy-two constitutes a mandate to govern, why start getting mealy-mouthed about the nationality of the man in charge?

There were plenty of Scottish MPs whose constituencies were in England, weren't there, and the English didn't make a fuss about that, did they?

But no, bloody Scotland had to have a bloody native son. His own suggested strategy was to accuse the dissenters of racism, talk about their "sinister insistence upon ethnic purity", chucking in some overtones about Bosnia, and topple them from their self-righteous PC perches.

Disappointingly, the party spin-doctors wouldn't wear it. Not right now, anyway, they said, although he could tell they would be considering its viability for the future. Chances were they would soon have to. That was part of the reason he had been made Scottish Secretary in the first place: there were just no Scots left to choose from. Between the aforementioned ten and the dribs and drabs representing seats in England, it had been a rather meagre selection to begin with. And out of those you could discount a couple who had too firm a grip on their current portfolios to step down into this regionalised (and marginalised) role, several more who had been picked off by various scandals involving everything from pick-axes to bedroom slippers, and a few of the remainder who were either too autonomous or too sporran-swingingly barmy to be entrusted with ministerial duties.

Of course, the bloody stupid thing was that many of those who had fallen through scandal had actually been stitched up by each other's manoeuvrings as they vied for position in the Scottish party. He had found it rather pathetic, such mediocre, medium-sized fish battling for supremacy in a small pond, and only having the opportunity to do so because of the scarcity of their own numbers – absolutely none of them would have any chance of rising above eternal back-bench obscurity had they been down south. The abject lack of competition in Scotland would have ensured most of them a half-decent job just by default, if they hadn't buggered up their own chances with their parochial disputes.

So that rather much left his good self.

He hadn't exactly been delighted at the appointment (although under the circumstances it was better than the proverbial poke in the eye with a sharp stick). He saw it as an isolated post, keeping you out of the cut and thrust of the parliamentary party by whisking you up north to quell the uncivilised and ceaselessly hostile natives. It cast his mind back to the Thatcher days, when the favoured punitive sanction of TBW against dissenting cabinet ministers was banishment to Gulag Ulster to face Dr Paisleystein and the three Bs (Bogtrotting Bastards in Balaclavas).

It was no secret he and Swan had been doing a bit of posturing and jockeying in '95 – the odd fringe meeting or keynote speech – just to see where the land lay with the backbenchers, but as everyone else was at it, it would have been silly not to buy a ticket for that particular raffle. However, only Redwood had been either deluded or crazy enough to ask the boss to step outside, and he had paid the price. Dalgleish and Swan hadn't directly spoken out against the PM and had given their backing loyally in that summer's scrap behind the bikesheds, but the boss (wisely) still didn't trust them. However, he had clearly been wary of alienating the considerable support they carried, which was why he hadn't bounced them altogether. Party unity could be a strange and wonderful thing.

Dalgleish saw the PM's famous balancing tricks at work in Swan's new appointment. The younger man was made Heritage Secretary, which could be seen as a comparatively light ride for a first senior ministerial post, a place to train for bigger things; but it was also a rather difficult job to shine in, fielding endless gripes about the Lottery, and with few opportunities to "get tough" with anything or anyone. Swan's being a good little boy would therefore be his only ticket upwards.

There seemed a similar ambiguity in giving Dalgleish the Scottish job: it would keep him at arm's length for a spell, while allowing him the chance to prosper as an ally, should he choose to toe the line. However, he suspected a great element of serendipity had saved him from being given something more obviously retributive – a poisoned chalice like Health, for instance – by a PM who would have liked to be rid of him without being seen to *get* rid of him.

It was the only time in his life he had felt reason to be glad of his father's nationality.

137

It was not a job he had wanted, but then it had never been a job he had even considered. It was Scottish business, parochial politics, nothing to do with him. However, once he was forced to start thinking about it, he saw in it a great deal of potential. For a start, you could play a hand in several games at once; you could be Home Secretary one minute, Employment Secretary the next, Chancellor, Health Secretary . . . a chance to audition for any number of big future roles. And in playing the statesman, you had the chance to show that if you were able to run one part of the country, then you just might have what it takes to run the whole boiling.

A huge bonus was the level of party support he had to be given right from the off. The tenuousness of his Scottish connection was inevitably going to be seized upon by the Opposition, who would drone on tediously about colonialism and the Tories not being able to find a Scot to govern Scotland, but the flak was always going to be aimed at the man who had made the appointment. By protecting Dalgleish, the party were protecting the boss, and to make the boss look good, Dalgleish had to look good.

An early hurdle was the fact that his constituency was – rather obviously – not in Scotland; in fact it was a comfortable and satisfying 300 miles from the wretched place. So with much distaste and greater regret, he agreed to proclaim an abiding love for his "homeland", and to declare that he would stand in a Scottish constituency at the next election. The latter part was agreed with party bosses on the tacit understanding that he would be in a new job by that time and therefore relieved of this unthinkable obligation.

But then next had come this bloody Scottishness business, a pantomime of tartanry and shortbread as the PR people flailingly over-compensated for his understandable ignorance (and, he would have loved to be able to admit, indifference) about the country.

Learning to drink whisky was only the tip of the iceberg. He had suggested that he could just pose for the odd photo-op drinking cold tea, like they do on stage or on television. However, they insisted that he would have to drink it at dinners and other social events, and apart from the impracticality of supplying him with phony stuff on such occasions, the threat of being found out – and the ensuing tartan-media gloating frenzy – was considered too great.

The biggest disaster, however, was the football match.

It had been decided that his public profile needed to be boosted, and the ideal opportunity, the PR man said, was a sporting event, where he could be seen to be actively supporting his "beloved" country. Dalgleish was nervous about the idea from the start, and his concern over straying into dangerous, uncharted territory grew when his suggestion of a cricket match was rejected.

"No, no, a *public* event," the PR man said.

Dalgleish looked quizzically at him, wondering where the breakdown in logic had occurred.

Bill Mason, the rotund and hygienically challenged editor of the Scottish edition of one of Voss's tabloids, had been present at the meeting, during which they were also discussing press strategies to discredit Labour-controlled unified councils. Mason more helpfully explained that "the average attendance at a Scottish cricket match is usually about thirty – and that's including both teams, the umpire, stray dogs and any tramps who happen to be sleeping off the Special Brew in that particular park that day".

This had made things a little clearer but also served to make him feel even more lost and further from home. Who could imagine a land where cricket meant nothing?

Unfortunately, Mason was not present at the meeting during which a bloody football match was decided upon. He was a gruff and rather ill-bred character, but Dalgleish suspected he might have been able to offer sufficient local insight to abort the public relations catastrophe conceived that day.

A rugby international had been suggested first, and sounded absolutely ideal. Being seen on national TV waving his little plastic saltire next to Princess Anne would do his profile no harm whatsoever – on both sides of the border. And he remembered one of the Scottish cabinet members telling him that Murrayfield was always a sell-out despite the paltry attendances at club rugby matches, "because it's the biggest public-school reunion in the world", which suggested that he would be seen by and among the right people. However, the PR man had muttered something about preaching to the converted, and any further debate on this had anyway been curtailed when his assistant consulted the fixture calendar: the Five Nations had not long passed, and there weren't any more internationals scheduled for six months. There was, however, a big game coming up at Hampden Park in Glasgow in a few weeks, and it was being screened live on BBC1 . . .

It was the longest, most humiliating and thoroughly miserable night of his life.

His first torment came when he went to take his seat, emerging from the stairwell as the bloody awful pipers marched up and down the pitch, bathed in the brilliant glare of the floodlights. The blast of freezing air hit him in the chest, and as he struggled for breath he noticed that all of the SFA representatives in the VIP party had suddenly acquired long, heavy coats over their suits. Within moments of sitting down he feared he would develop hypothermia. And within ten minutes of that, he wished he had died of it.

It looked a full house, an imposing mass on long, sloping concourses, alive with a riot of swirling flags – none of which, he was concerned to note, were Union Jacks. He was sure there had been plenty of those when he saw a clip of a Scottish football match on TV a couple of weeks before, and indeed had felt reassured about the prospect of the international after learning how much Conservative support there was from the board of the biggest club, Glasgow Rangers.

Then it began. Not the match, the disaster.

"Welcome to Hampden Park for tonight's European Championship warm-up friendly between Scotland and Norway," announced a disembodied voice crisply over the PA system. "And the National Stadium welcomes as its guest tonight, the Secretary of State for Scotland, the Right Honourable Alastair Dalgleish."

As a cricket man, prior to that moment he hadn't known what thirty-five thousand people furiously booing sounded like. He did now, as indeed did anyone who happened to tune in for the live television and radio transmissions.

It reverberated terrifyingly around the stadium, amplified by the sweeping roof that covered the grandstands, which he suspected had been partly designed for that specific purpose. The blast of baying voices was dotted with piercing whistles, the overall effect like an angry titan with asthma. He felt momentarily in fear of his life, his mind filling with images of spontaneous mob eruption and his corpse swinging from a noose tied to one of the crossbars. Then, as the fear passed, he felt his cheeks begin to burn with a mixture of humiliation and utter fury, no doubt captured in glorious Technicolor for posterity.

When the booing subsided, the air was filled with concerted chanting.

"DURTY ENGLISH BASTARD. DURTY ENGLISH BASTARD."

"ALLY DALGLEISH, YOU'RE A WANKER, YOU'RE A WANKER – ALLY DALGLEISH, YOU'RE A DONKEY'S ARSE."

And "DALGLEISH, DALGLEISH, GET TAE FUCK, DALGLEISH, GET TAE FUCK," upon which someone behind him rather obscurely commented, "Well, I never thought I'd hear those words here."

He thought his ordeal was finished when the teams took the field and the crowd turned their attention to the match, but as the game turned out to be a dispassionately drab affair, the neanderthals in the stands chose to amuse themselves every so often by striking up another chorus of this gratuitous and foul-mouthed abuse, every word of which was heard across the land.

But the nightmare didn't end there. It turned out some malignant and no doubt pinko director at the BBC had chosen to zoom in on his face during the pre-match playing of the national anthems, and of course after the first roll on the drums he had launched full-throated into "God save our gra . . ." before stopping as he realised that everyone else was singing "Oh flower of Scotland". To compound the gaffe, he didn't know any of the words to the stupid bloody dirge, and the cameras had returned a couple of times to show him close-mouthed and blushing as those all around him strove to burst a lung.

The lefty press had a bloody party with the whole affair, and just to complete the fun, he later learned that there was a special "sporting What Happened Next" round on that *Have I Got News For You* nonsense the following Friday, in which they had shown footage of him taking his seat at Hampden and then stopped the film.

He demanded to know who the PA announcer had been, so that he could insist on him being sacked on the spot, as the bastard must have known he was giving the animals in the crowd their cue. However, the PR man advised that this would be further bad publicity, as whether the announcer had ulterior motives or not, it was a hard thing to prove; besides, it was best to show that he was above reacting to such disgraceful behaviour. He agreed with this, and comforted himself by sacking the PR man instead.

Dalgleish glanced down to the street below, his attention caught by the manoeuvring of a black Ford Scorpio as it slotted itself smoothly into a parking space. Knight was at the controls, his broad shoulders and bullet head recognisable from thirty feet above. He had one hand on the wheel and the other holding that scrambled-frequency carphone to his ear, his head twitching as he spoke, probably talking as forcefully and deliberately as he did everything else.

Knight was possessed of many admirable qualities, as far as Dalgleish was concerned, but the most valuable – and certainly these days the most rare – was that he knew his place. Knight knew the measure of remarkable men and was not too proud to serve. He knew what he did well and was content to do it, without ambitions beyond his station in life. There are men born to command and men born to obey, and it was a tribute to Knight's strength of character that he knew his role. Certainly, he also knew he would be well rewarded, as loyalty always is, and that he would enjoy his own measure of power as his dividend from Dalgleish's success, but he had no illusions as to who was in charge.

That was why Dalgleish trusted him, and Knight clearly understood the value of such a man's trust.

Knight was MI5. They had got to know each other some years back when Dalgleish had a fairly junior Home Office post, and both had recognised the potential benefits of reciprocal cooperation. At the time Dalgleish was liaising with Knight over a standard dirty tricks campaign, setting up a few opposition frontbenchers and the odd union leader for nasty and very public falls. Knight was working on, you could say, the practical side, and Dalgleish was involved for the valuable links he had with Voss, whose newspapers would have their own vital contribution to make.

Dalgleish found it rather wryly amusing that in later years – a good way down the road for both of them – they had found themselves doing much the same thing, except that it was now Conservatives they were setting up, as he and Swan pursued their *Kind Hearts And Coronets* strategy within the parliamentary party. But that, of course, was a more clandestine affair, only possible thanks to the way his and Knight's relationship had developed.

For a time, like all the other young and ambitious spooks, Knight had kept a foot in many camps, playing MPs and civil servants off one another, and like a magpie took what he could from each of them. But Dalgleish had let him know that there came a stage when you had to bet on one horse, and that he was, if not the favourite, at least offering the biggest potential payout.

Knight had been a promising and already resourceful figure, but with Dalgleish's sponsorship he had progressed apace, and the higher he climbed, the more useful he was to Dalgleish, who in turn could use his growing influence to open more doors for Knight, and so on.

Knight had become extraordinarily well-connected. The length and breadth of the land there were senior policemen and military officers whose cooperation and confidence he could rely upon; influence that could, with just a phone call, get things done which might otherwise require a great deal of legal wrangling and conspicuously traceable paperwork. And of course, the occasional document of permission or request from a government minister could be rather helpful from time to time.

But the deadliest ace up Knight's sleeve was his team of "little helpers", whose services were quite definitely *not* officially engaged by anyone, but who had proven useful to variously the government, MI5 and Alastair Dalgleish on a number of occasions. Knight paid them a retainer himself, while their operations fees and expenses came from "the client". They were bloody expensive, but as they say, if you pay peanuts . . . There was also the consideration – of which Knight was patently aware – that if your predicament or even intentions were such that the little helpers' involvement was required, then you probably needed *them* a lot more than you needed the money.

But what the hell, they got the job done, and nobody ever knew a dashed thing.

He had called in Knight when he realised the full magnitude of the consequences of what Voss was demanding. He had been confident Knight would have no reservations; apart from the fact that he was hitched to Dalgleish's gravy train and would suffer greatly from its derailment, Knight was entirely professional when it came to such things. The stature of the man who had to be removed would mean nothing: he thought only of logistics, practicalities, contingencies. The hunter does not stop to consider the social position within the herd of the beast in his sights, only where best to put the bullet, which position to take for the clearest shot.

Knight had been as steady and emotionless as ever, talking immediately of the how, when and where, his invaluable experience in the political arena coming into evidence as he even

discussed how they might best "play" the murder. Only the furthest glint in Knight's eye perhaps betrayed a reaction to the
audacity and ruthlessness of what Dalgleish wished to under-
take – and that reaction, he was sure, was one of delight and
admiration.

For Dalgleish had walked through fire in making this commission, been cleansed by the flames, galvanised by the
experience. There had been political comings of age, rites of passage, milestones and watersheds, but this was a door through
which he could never go back (and talk about being hung for a
sheep . . .).

Dalgleish had destroyed a few lives, wrecked careers, companies even, but this was an entirely new domain. He had known
that once he entered it he would be a changed man; he had never
anticipated what it would change him into. He had feared he
might become a haunted creature, forever running as the Furies
flew about him, too distracted by their torments to pursue his
agendas, hold down jobs . . . would Voss's ghost pursue him until
his murder had destroyed not only the Dutchman, but himself
too?

But instead he was a greater man, a more resolute man, a more
powerful man, and it had been that man he saw reflected in the
glint in Knight's eye. He felt, like some mystic ancient warrior,
that he had absorbed the stature of the man he had slain, and felt
a near-convulsive rush of power as the news broke that Voss was
dead. He was no longer some cabinet hopeful, jostling for position
with the rest as the PM dangled favours above their heads to buy
their obedience. He was a man who could order the death of
Roland Voss, for the good of himself and the good of the country;
a man of strength, determination and resolution.

And such men are born to rule.

For a long time his and Swan's had been an uneasy alliance.
Each understood not only the use the other could be to his own
aims, but that they could travel further together than individually.
Dalgleish carried more experience, more years, and ties in more

places. Older places. Dalgleish had the breeding, the ancestry, the tradition. His mother's family name had carried weight in the party for centuries – there were many who thought it gravely amiss that a fellow of the Waldemere line had never been PM – and his father's name represented land and business that went back to the first seeds of Empire.

Swan, on the other hand, understood well how the game was played nowadays. He traded on a success built upon *no* foundation of ancestry or tradition, portraying himself as living evidence of the achievements of the Thatcherite revolution. He was steeped in the victor's hatred of the defeated, despising those whose ineptitude left them foundering at the foot of a system he had negotiated triumphantly with vision, sweat and nerve. He regarded it as a direct insult to his accomplishments that those whose efforts (or lack of) had brought them less should be in any way subsidised to compensate for their own shortcomings. "Hunger was man's first motivator, and remains his strongest," was Swan's defining sound-bite, trumpeted joyously by party and press ever since that ebullient fringe meeting at the Conference in '91.

He was the darling of the thuggish new right: first-generation Conservatives who had cleaned up in the Eighties and were desperately looking for someone to lead them back to that lost paradise, that new Jerusalem of glass towers, red Porsches, champagne and satisfyingly over-priced sandwich bars.

So Swan brought the new right, Dalgleish the old, and together this unusual but powerful alliance made the boss very nervous indeed. Truth be told, each made the other nervous, as their mutual respect for each other's abilities, connections and resources had meant neither ever tried to pitch himself as the senior partner. What remained unspoken but understood was that one day they might have to stand toe-to-toe, and neither was particularly looking forward to it.

But Voss had changed that.

It had been Swan that he leaned on first. Swan was the one he really needed; Dalgleish was thrown in as an added bargaining tool. It was Swan's department – Heritage – and therefore it would have been Swan's call, but the wily Dutch bastard had hooks in Dalgleish too, and had decided to give the lines a little tweak. If it had just been Swan and he said no – if Swan chose to martyr himself – then it would just have been one resignation by a promising but comparatively junior cabinet member; damage could be limited and Swan was young enough to bide his time until he was rewarded for his selfless act by being allowed back on board. Throwing Dalgleish into the equation not only made the harakiri option too catastrophic to contemplate, but was intended to strengthen Swan's hand in asking the boss for what Voss wanted from the government.

Swan had been lost. He had been a man dithering over the choice of method for his own political execution, the last real decision he would have any power to make. It had been Dalgleish who came up with the solution, Dalgleish who resolved to carry it through, and Dalgleish who had command of the appropriate manpower. For a while he had thought about not telling Swan, as the fewer people who knew the truth the better. But he *wanted* him to know. Not just because the little shit ought to be shouldering his share of the worry, but because it would let him know the difference between them. Swan had flapped and despaired while Dalgleish had acted, and acted with a power and a ruthlessness that would take Swan's breath away.

The matter of who was the senior partner was no longer in question. And he could rest assured Swan would never break their alliance in search of the main chance elsewhere. They were tied forever by this act, and true, each had the power to instigate mutually assured destruction. But Swan owed him. Admittedly, in a man like Swan's world view, that might not count for much or for long, but Dalgleish still found it unlikely the younger man would ever try to deceive, disobey or betray him.

He had friends, you see. Friends in very high places.

And friends in some very, very low ones too.

*

Dalgleish sat at his desk as Knight stood opposite, shoulders back and hands clasped behind him. He had been a soldier once, Dalgleish knew, and seemed to slip back into the role during these debriefings. Dalgleish liked that. It showed respect, and it also kept both men focused on matters at hand. There was a time for drinks and armchairs, and this wasn't it.

"The prisoners made their escape exactly according to plan, sir," he said, traces of a Somerset burr nudging the ordered ranks of his firm, unemotional delivery. "Right on schedule."

Dalgleish nodded, looking down as if taking a mental note, trying to appear as detached and dispassionate as if Knight was telling him his itinerary for the week.

"And do you know where they are now?" he asked, clasping his hands on the polished hardwood surface.

"Oh yes, sir. We have men tracking their movements from a close distance. I will be kept informed of their position at all times, and I will be using this information to direct police operations away from the fugitives. Sir?"

Dalgleish's brow was furrowed, a hand raised six inches above the desk, wavering in sympathy with his thoughts.

"There have been calls for me to bring in the army, George," he said ponderingly. "I didn't actually agree to anything on air, but I'm not sure whether it might look more impressive. Only trouble is that they might do too good a job and actually find the buggers."

"Sir, I have been monitoring the media's coverage of events as closely as the events themselves, and I had anticipated this eventuality, particularly given the number of army bases located in the region. I can arrange for a unit to engage cooperatively in the search today."

"When you say cooperatively . . ."

Knight smiled thinly. "They will diligently hunt down all TV cameras in the vicinity and, with extreme prejudice, walk past them purposefully and impressively in full camouflage gear."

"The finest soldiers in the world. Thank you, George. Now,

we'll need a bit of time for all this. No-one knew they had escaped until rather late last night, and most of the country were in their beds when I was talking about it on television, so I could really do with the hunt continuing through the early evening slots, up to at least *News at Ten* and past the morning dailies' deadlines if possible. I need to get it across to the nation that this is *my* operation while it is still in progress, rather than look like I'm taking credit for it after the fact."

"Of course, sir. As I say, I have the fugitives under constant surveillance. Not only can we move in at any time, but we can make sure that they remain safe from the search until you give the signal to end it. However, my men must reserve the right to act independently if they fear a development that we cannot control."

Dalgleish nodded, lips pursed. "I trust your judgment and that of your men as implicitly as ever," he said.

"Thank you, sir. Was there anything else?" he asked, noticing Dalgleish's scrutiny of the desktop, a characteristic symptom of a concern that he was reluctant to broach.

"Well . . ." he said, almost apologetically. "This business with the cyanide. It wasn't what we discussed."

Knight breathed in through his nose, pulled his head up as if reined.

"No, sir," he stated. "It was a field decision. I had reason to believe Mr Lafferty suspected foul play and could not take the chance that he might impart some information which would detract from the plausibility of his later planned suicide. I appreciate that it was not ideal, but we were all a little surprised by the lawyer's revelations. In an undertaking of this scale, as I explained, it is impossible to anticipate all the rogue elements, but what we *can* do is lock them down quickly and effectively when they do arise."

"Indeed," said Dalgleish. "You acted swiftly and decisively. I can't ask for any more than that. And have you 'locked down' the other problem?"

"We acquired the documents McInnes submitted with his

lawyers two nights ago. They contained nothing intrinsically substantial but they did have the potential to encourage speculation, so we destroyed them."

"And the lawyer?"

"We believed two lawyers posed potential difficulties. We have eliminated one but an equipment malfunction temporarily obstructed our neutralisation of the second."

"Which one is that? The girl?"

"Yes, sir. But we have her under surveillance and expect her to be out of the equation by close of play today."

"Very good."

Knight shifted his stance, the slightest impatience creeping in. Dalgleish appreciated that he had things to attend to.

"Will there be anything else, sir?" he asked.

"Just one final thing, George. The contents of the safe. Any joy yet?"

"Nothing, sir. I have good reason to be confident that they didn't manage to open it; and I believe it was empty simply because Voss never hid anything in it in the first place. The police have been combing the area looking for the murder weapons; obviously they're not going to turn those up, but they would certainly have come across anything that was stolen by now. It would have been nice to have a few diamond earrings or a necklace to produce as evidence of what the robbers were up to, once the terrorist motive has been eliminated, but the story of them murdering four people only for the cupboard to be bare has rather a neat tone of tragic irony to it, don't you think?"

Dalgleish smiled.

"Quite."

Knight trotted briskly back down the stairs, all the time concentrating on resisting the urge to shake his head in case Dalgleish or any of his entourage saw it. He had heard nothing during their conversation to conflict with his long-held opinion that the man was among the biggest arseholes ever to walk the earth.

He had to stop himself sniggering at the thought of his own "soldier at attention" routine, which Dalgleish lapped up every time. He wished the pompous sod hadn't been behind the desk so that he could have seen the bulge in his trousers.

"You acted swiftly and decisively," he thought.

Sad pratt.

Dalgleish was often referred to as being one of the "old guard" in his party, as if he had some rare and precious attributes that were all but forgotten these days. Maybe he did, Knight thought, but he also knew that self-deluding snobs were one species in no imminent danger of extinction.

It was ever thus with blokes like that. It was so simple it was almost laughable, to maintain the illusion that it was *they* who were in charge, *they* who were running things. It was easy to convince someone of what they desperately wanted to believe. Dalgleish thought Knight's colours were tied to his mast, and that Knight's fortunes would rise or fall, live or die with his, as Dalgleish chased after the fool's gold that he thought was power. What did he expect ultimately to get? A post near the head of a waning and increasingly ragged political party? Maybe a few years in the limelight before fading back into obscurity as the party or even the country decides it's time for new faces?

Dalgleish would be a forgotten has-been sitting on useless subcommittees and giving bitter interviews while Knight was exercising the real power he had built, the power to destroy politicians, businessmen and even monarchs. Power that you didn't need to be re-elected to.

What he always found so eye-poppingly incredible about Dalgleish, as indeed about most of them, was that he never suspected a thing. In all the little commissions, all the dirty tricks, the set-ups, the surveillances, it never occurred to the stupid cunt that Knight would be gathering the dirt on him too, filing it away for when it might come in handy like he did on so many others.

The videotapes of Dalgleish and the embassy "secretary" (Knight's plant) in Singapore typified it. The way he had let her manoeuvre them around the bed as they fucked away, doggy-style, so that both of them faced the two-way mirror.

They were all the same – probably a class thing, a public school thing; they were so busy worrying about the threat from each other that they never suspected where the real danger would be coming from. It just never occurred to them that they had anything to fear from someone who was not one of them, who was not part of their game, and not on what they so arrogantly perceived to be their level.

Dalgleish was far sharper than most, Knight had to admit – that was why he had chosen to hitch a ride on his back all those years ago. Dalgleish had an honest understanding of the depths to which he could stoop, and had not vainly convinced himself that no-one else could be so cunning or so ruthless, which was why he had survived so long and so well. He anticipated the traps his rivals *could* set for him, even if most of the time they weren't smart enough to have laid them.

And, he had to admit, only Dalgleish could have had the balls to suggest the Voss thing. Truth be told, if anyone else *had* suggested it, Knight would have said no, because Dalgleish was probably the only one with the nerve to carry his part of it right through. He wouldn't have considered anything as risky as this if he didn't think the man at the top could be trusted not to give the game away through guilt or fear-induced stupidity. So far he was doing fine, but the acid test would be if something got loose that they really couldn't nail back down.

As Knight approached his car he could hear the *breeeep* of the phone inside it. He removed a parking ticket from the windscreen, scrunching it up and dropping it to the tarmac as if it was a flyer for a car-boot sale. When the meter-maid keyed the reg into the system she'd quickly know not to pursue the matter. He climbed into the car, grabbing the receiver as he pulled the door closed at his side.

"Knight. What."

"Morgan, sir. Look, I think we might have a big fucking problem."

"Speak to me."

"It's the lawyer. I checked under her car and the cable-cutters have gone."

"Yes, I think we had established that they were knackered last night when they didn't work. I ordered Addison to get you some new ones. Why are you telling me this?"

"No, sir, I mean they were *gone*. As in, no longer attached."

Knight swallowed, took a moment to digest the news.

"Could they have fallen off?" he asked.

"No chance. She must have removed them. She's on to us, sir."

Christ.

He couldn't afford to even think of the ramifications.

"Kill her," he said, quietly but firmly. "Immediately. Where is she now, her office?"

There was a pause, a short intake of breath on the other end of the line.

"Well, that's the big fucking problem I meant, sir," Morgan finally said, a dread reluctance in his voice. "She's disappeared. We watched the place last night, saw her go to bed and . . ."

Fucking hell.

"Look, Morgan," Knight said, with the sort of hollow calm that precedes a typhoon, "I don't want to know the details of how you fucked up. They are not relevant. All I want to know from you is that she is dead and that so is anyone she might have spoken to, and I don't want to hear your fucking voice again to tell me anything else. Understood?"

"Yes, sir. But how will I find . . .?"

"If she knows something, she'll want to tell people. If she wants to tell people, she'll have to surface. When she surfaces, you kill her. However, wherever. Clear?"

"Yes, sir."

SEVEN

The sunlight was piercing and impatient, as if angry that it had needed to climb this high in the sky to get their attention. The smell of cold sweat, stale breath and arboreal mulches had an incongruous freshness about it as a chill-edged breeze diluted the congested air. Wisps of steam spiralled balletically in the broken shards of sunlight, Tam watching their graceful dance for a suspended moment while somewhere in his head he knew he was about to switch on again, stretch mind and body against the rack of their predicament. It was a moment of freedom, of uncomplicated pleasure, the sweeter for its briefest finity.

Some long-sealed chamber of dormant memory released its captive and caused him to think of a fragment of a poem he had been made to learn in school. He couldn't remember its name or that of the poet, but the threat of six of the belt had apparently ingrained the words on his mind not only long enough to recite them before Mrs Dornoch the next day, but long enough for them to return on a cool September morning in the highlands, nearly half a century later.

"Him whose strenuous tongue can burst joy's grape against his palate fine – his soul shall taste the sadness of her might."

Tam wasn't sure how well it reflected upon the Renfrewshire education department of the time that it had taken him two hours to learn it but forty-odd years to understand it. Still, at least he hadn't been a Catholic. All Bob could remember was bloody prayers.

He blinked, and when he opened his eyes he was no longer lost in the motes of breath, but back under a pile of logs, off a footpath in a forest. His eyes flitted around and noticed that Spammy was also awake, lying back but hunched up a little, supported by the spiny stanchions of his gangly elbows. He was staring out of the opening, eyes squinting against the stabs of the sun through the gaps in their shelter, steam billowing out from his nose like he was a shaggy-headed and drug-addled dragon.

"You been awake for long?" Tam inquired as Spammy caught his eye.

"Aye."

"Well why did you no waken us?"

"Yous were sleepin'."

Conversations with Spammy were frequently like this. He seemed somehow able to circumvent logic, or alter its nature so that it behaved differently in his hands.

Tam had learned not to tread further into the labyrinth.

He nudged Paul and Bob to life, then crawled into the daylight as they yawned and groaned behind him, dragged back into confrontation with their seemingly omnipotent foe.

Tam climbed to his feet and stretched, a dozen strains and aches responding to his reveille from posts around his anatomy. He edged forward tentatively, moving up the incline of the mound at whose foot they had made their camp, and taking position behind a large pine. Slowly he leaned around it, looking for he didn't know what – police, soldiers, Jeremy fucking Beadle (in which case he hoped he'd lubricated his microphone) – and saw a valley bathed in the crisp sunlight from behind him, its angrily craggy mountains cruelly beautiful as they loomed inquisitively over their dominions below. The river glinted with an icy sparkle, winking in defiance.

The sight delighted his eyes but wounded his soul. It was a place of breathtaking dramatic spectacle, but he now saw the harshness, the mercilessness that must always have existed behind the picture-postcard splendour. He saw the rain-lashed shepherds in the cold damp of the clachans, the punishment of the outcast, and the gauntlet run by the pursued.

Funny how such places didn't fill your heart with quite so much joy when you couldn't get back into your car and drive the fuck away from them.

Tam looked back, down at the lean-to where Paul and Spammy were helping Bob to his feet, and glanced with relief at the surroundings. The base of the mound protruded into a low hollow, a tributary path of brown needles leading up to the main trail on the opposite side from where he stood, with trees huddling protectively around the entire area. They had arrived there in darkness, and he had half-expected morning to reveal that their improvised refuge was on the edge of a main road or some other such staringly conspicuous site.

In fact it had been the encroaching darkness that had cast the deciding vote the night before on whether to run; or if not cast a vote it had at least forced the election.

"Heh, do you think we might be gettin' set up again here?" Spammy had asked as they stood, dazed, beside the two dead men in front of the bus. No-one answered, even Bob having grasped that feigned obtuseness was Spammy's equivalent of a rhetorical question. Tam had already made the further leap of deducing that the sloth-like fuzzball's occasional deeply obvious comments were a caustic means of taking the piss out of anyone who thought he was slow-witted, a misconception he had probably endured for years.

"They're gaunny do us for this along with the other two," Bob offered, shaking his head at the gruesome sight.

"Four," Tam reminded him. "There were bodyguards, sure."

"Oh aye."

They hadn't even seen the bodyguards. The first any of them

knew about the two other victims had been during their interrogations.

"They were shot as well," Bob replied.

"So I heard. The question is, what do we do aboot it?"

"Well that's obvious," said Paul. "We run. It's the only chance we've got."

"Aye, but if we run we look mair guilty," Bob offered.

"What," said Spammy in a slow monotone, "do you mean it's actually possible for us to look mair guilty than we do already?"

"Ach, you know what I mean," Bob retorted, irritated. "Whoever it is is playin' us like a cheap fuckin' moothie, and I'm sure us runnin' is the next bar on the music sheet. I say we just sit and wait for the polis. Maybe noo they'll start believin' that there's somebody else at work on this."

"Bob," said Paul, gritting his teeth to keep his temper in check, "the excuse that a big boy done it and ran away didnae work the last time. What makes you think it'll be any different noo? I say we take our chances. As far as I can see, there's nothin' gaunny convince the polis aboot what really happened at Craigurquhart. You know what kinna papers that bastart Voss owned, so you can imagine what kinna picture the public's got of us. We're never gaunny get a fair trial and we're never gaunny clear our names. If we run for a day or a week or we manage to run for the rest of our lives, that's as much time ootside a prison as we're gaunny get. Once we're back in custody, it's forever."

Inevitably, Bob sought mediation.

"What do you say, Tam?"

Tam looked at the sky for a few seconds, then back at the corpses, then at his friends.

"I say we keep our options open. This looks like the maist lonely and desolate road in the world. Naebody's gaunny know we're missin' until whenever this bus was supposed to arrive, and there's no exactly a queue of motors goin' past. It could be hours before anybody shows up here. Plus it's gettin' dark and it's gettin' cauld.

"I say we move on, find some shelter. Somewhere oot o' sight, where we can hide and bed doon for the night. Then in the mornin' we'll see how it looks. If we decide to run, we'll have a start, and we'll have had a bit o' kip. If we decide to gie up, or we get caught anyway, for what it's worth we can say we werenae runnin', just takin' shelter for the night. Naebody'd want to sleep in the back of a bus with a deid body. Either way, we can sleep on it."

Tam suggested they walk on the road, partly so as not to leave tracks, and partly to avoid the ankle-snapping treachery of the clumpy fields on either side. He walked in front at first, before relieving Paul who was helping Bob limp along on his one good leg. Spammy straggled along at the rear, having earlier dismayed them by kneeling over the dead driver and rifling his pockets. He held up a lighter by way of explanation.

"I saw him havin' a fag. We might want to light a fire."

They came to where a dry, hard-earth track met the roadside on the left, the chevrons of mucky tractor tyre-tracks arcing out across the tarmacadam in both directions. There was little light left, just a low glow playing off the underside of the sparse cloud cover in the distance. Tam looked up the slope, where the track followed a drystone dike towards the edge of a wood, into which the dusty trail disappeared.

"That'll do," he said. "Right. Naebody stand on these tyre marks. Try an' move fae stone to stone," he instructed, indicating the sunken boulders that jutted out of the track like acne. He sent Paul ahead first, while he and Spammy carried Bob – legs and arms – over the chevrons and as many yards along the trail as they could manage.

By the time they reached the edge of the forest the sunlight was completely exhausted, but the clouds were shuffling disgruntledly out of the way of a bright and insistent moon, and the trail remained enticingly visible before them. They came to a clearing where the track ended, a circular area occupied by three large piles of felled and stripped tree trunks and a small hillock of gravel and pebbles, which looked like it was being either gradually built up or gradually depleted by the attentions of the small dump vehicle that sat motionless in front of it, its metal scoop resting on the ground like it was a grazing brontosaurus.

There were three exits: the track, leading back down to the road, and two paths. One led downwards in roughly the opposite direction, continuing to skirt the edge of the pines, and the other led up, higher into the hill and deeper into the woodland.

"Decisions, decisions," said Spammy as they stood motionless in the clearing.

Bob hopped over to one of the timber piles and fished out a sturdy length of wood to serve him as a walking staff.

"Ach, fuck it," Bob said. "If we're gaunny run an' hide, let's dae it properly."

Their gradual progress along the path was made to the slow, thudding rhythm of Bob's stick as he thrusted it down to bear his weight on alternate steps. Everyone was tired and sore but no-one would admit it when any of his companions enquired. For each of them, the feeling of walking, of moving, of once again – to whatever extent – controlling their own fates urged them forwards despite the pain. Eventually, however, they came to a small hollow as the clouds returned with their big brothers to chuck the moon back out of the swingpark.

All the time they had been passing small piles of trunks by the edge of the path, awaiting collection and transportation, and near to those were carpets of discarded boughs and branches. They worked silently and quickly to build the lean-to, Tam, Paul and Spammy dragging and placing the trunks against the needle-strewn mound that jutted into the hollow, Bob laying branches across the top for insulation.

Spammy's suggestion of lighting a fire for added heat was vetoed on the grounds that in the unlikely event that they didn't burn themselves and the whole fucking forest down, it might act as a homing beacon for any pursuers, as they couldn't be sure how close they were to roads or houses.

"I'll be pickin' skelfs oot ma hands all night," Paul moaned as they lay down side by side and huddled together for warmth. "That's when I'm finished pickin' bits of glass oot ma shoulder."

"Ach, shoosh," Bob muttered. "I've had hauf a tree through ma leg the night, an' you're talkin' aboot skelfs."

"Aye, but they say size doesnae matter," Paul countered.

Bob farted loudly in lieu of a rejoinder.

"Aw for fuck's sake," Paul protested.

"Jesus, Bob, that's a liberty," added Tam. "This is a confined space."

"I hope they've nae sniffer dugs," mumbled Spammy.

They all laughed. Wee boays at scout camp.

Tam suspected none of them would actually sleep, but he reckoned without the effects of having barely done so in several days, combined with the exertion of their hike and the sheer mental, physical and emotional exhaustion from all they had been through. He had felt the power drain languidly from his limbs as soon as he took the weight from his feet and lay down, and realised they had been running on fumes for several miles. Within minutes they were sleeping like . . .

Unlike some, Tam McInnes never found himself looking back upon his life and wondering where it all went wrong, because he knew exactly, to the year, month and day. It all went wrong when some prick in a suit who had never lifted a shovel in anger decided that record productivity and decades of loyalty counted for less than the fact that you could get cheaper labour in Mexico.

Well, that wasn't the whole truth, really, but it was easier to put a face on your need to blame. There was a political agenda that none of them had known about; in fact that no-one was ever supposed to know about, but for some documents being leaked to a journalist a few years later. Tam had read all about it in jail, which seemed cruelly ironic. He was serving his sentence for the burglaries that had started as an act of revenge for what Sir Michael Halworth had done, when he discovered that Sir Michael Halworth was really just a willing cog in a far bigger machine.

160

It was about ideology, about politics, about power. The big bosses in the States had probably been toying with the idea for years, and to people of that mentality it must have been tantalisingly tempting. But they were never going to do it in America – well, not in those days. In the battle with the Japanese for domestic sales, waving the stars and stripes was about all they could do in the face of an increasingly superior product. Shutting down plants in Michigan and fucking off to Guadalajara might just have been misinterpreted by the American public as a less-than-patriotic gesture.

For a long time they couldn't do it in the UK either, despite the fact that the British operation was usually barely in profit. And the only reason it was in profit at all was that it was heavily subsidised – the government trying to keep things ticking over until the recession lightened and people started buying new cars again – which was also the reason the company couldn't pull out. Not only would it be regarded as a hellishly ungrateful breach of trust, but it wouldn't have done a fuck of a lot for Anglo–American relations.

Enter the Thatcher administration.

On the surface, Tam remembered, it appeared that the Yanks were unilaterally shipping out, muttering about obstructive unions and restrictive industry regulation, amidst crocodile tears of regret from the government and many "you've only got yourselves to blame" speeches. We chased the jobs away, they said. We have to learn our lessons from this: we have to be more competitive, we have to streamline, we have to abolish the restrictions and archaic union practices that have hamstrung not just our car industry but all our industries.

"The lessons of Meiklewood", was the irritating phrase that chimed throughout dogmatic declamations down through the Eighties.

We have to wreck the unions. We have to slash jobs. We have to worry less about health and safety, because it eats into profit. We have to decimate wages, because we're in a global labour market now, and that means we're competing with the Third World.

Never forget the lessons of Meiklewood.

Of course, it was all a fucking stitch-up. What had later been discovered by this investigative hack was that the government instigated the whole thing. They had very quietly decided to pull the plug on the subsidies, and tipped the wink to the Americans, assuring them that there would be no public blame, and that there was no potential for damage to "the special relationship".

Why?

Christ, why not?

The government had nothing to lose. The money that would have gone into subsidising Meiklewood could be spent on something useful instead, like nuclear submarines, or tax cuts. And the loss of a few thousand jobs wasn't a drawback, it was a bonus.

Mass unemployment wasn't a government failure, it was a government strategy – as everyone well knew. It was the weapon they used to break unions, force down wages, dictate conditions. But it was more sophisticated than that. It wasn't merely a question of finding any three or four million people to haunt the thoughts and weaken the resolve of every disgruntled employee. It was a specific three or four million people, Tam knew.

It was three or four million people like him.

They hadn't been out just to break their strength – they had been out to break their spirit. To do is to be; the Tories took away what they did. They took away what they were, took away what their fathers had been, took away their past and their legacy, and left them not just without means, but without purpose. And a man without purpose offers little resistance as a foe. He has nothing to fight for, and no comrades in arms.

Steel. Coal. Ships. Cars.

They closed whole industries.

Scotland had to change, the Tories insisted. Its days of heavy industry were gone, and its future, as envisaged by Thatcher, was as a "service economy". Tam would have found the idea hilarious if the reality hadn't been so fucking painful.

Picture it.

The Fegie Park Public Relations Agency – "We'll make sure they get the message". Get your point across with force. Lethal force if necessary.

The Barrhead Advertising Bureau. Guaranteed, to get your name seen, with prime-site positioning: railway bridges, bus shelters, derelict buildings and more. Previous campaigns and slogans include: "Fuck the Pope", "Up the Ra", "Priesty Young Team ya bass" and "Ulster Says No".

Glenburn Financial Services – sound investment advice for when you fancy playing the futures market with your next giro.

A service economy. Gie's a brek.

Tam couldn't believe it. Then with more pain and anger it gradually sank in that the Tories had never really believed it either. It was just an excuse. Disembowelling the country's industries, breaking its backbone and bringing the unruly northern colony to its knees was the primary objective.

Sure, they could vote *en masse* against the Tories at every opportunity – and they did – but the bastards were probably laughing up their sleeves about it back in London, like adults at the tantrum of a petulant but powerless wean: "You can whine about it all you like, but we're not changing our minds. Now stop crying or we'll really give you something to cry for."

Meiklewood had been quite a nice district. Not exactly affluent, but certainly respectable. Tam's had been a modern wee council scheme, built in the Seventies, and it had looked fairly pleasant – although admittedly people's tolerance for bad taste in those days extended to architecture as well as clothing and hairstyles. But colour-schemes and exterior wallcovering materials notwithstanding, it was always neat, always clean. People looked after the place because they had known a lot worse. They had jobs and they had self-respect, two things that could make stray chip pokes and lager cans fill the mind with a far greater dismay than if you actually had something serious to worry about.

They had been happy there, him and Sadie, and the wee yin. He had been a man of modest dreams, he knew, and had felt a degree of pride at where he was, what his family had, and what he might realistically hope to bring them. He had left school at fourteen, as had two of his brothers. Only Greig, the youngest of them, was allowed to stay on, with the other three helping his da bring money home. Greig went to university, up in Glasgow. These days he was *teaching* in a university, down south, a professor of physics.

There were brains in the family, he definitely knew that, and he had felt a sense of progress and achievement that Paul would get the chance to use his. Tam hadn't sat at night and wondered what if, bitterly reflecting on missed potential and chances denied him, but he did feel a dull ache of regret at times, and that was soothed by the thought of his son being able to spread his wings. Sibling strife and petty jealousies aside, when it came right down they had all felt pride in Greig, and in the part they had played, but that would be nothing compared to the pride Tam would have in Paul, and in himself for having got his son that far.

Then the plant closed.

Certain powers had made the law jump through hoops to keep him inside for almost the full seven years, but it was only when he got out of prison that Tam realised the full extent of the price to be paid. He had walked, like bloody Rip van Winkle, unsteadily and in weeping disbelief, from the bus stop and through the scheme to the old house. That was when he realised that jail had just been where they kept him while they got his real punishment ready.

He had known about it, heard the tearful and increasingly blameful bulletins from Sadie in letters and visits. Pressure, strain, and inevitably, disintegration. But when he heard it, it was just news from the other world, the one he'd been banished from. His world stayed the same, and with his emotions frozen and anaesthetised, the only meaning the other world had existed purely in the words from Sadie's mouth and the letters on the page. Just stories.

What he had shut out, what he couldn't afford to face during all those years inside, was that the world Sadie's words created was the world he would have to live in later. The one he used to live in hadn't been taken away for a time decided by the judge. It was gone forever.

The scheme looked like Sarajevo without the tanks. Chipboard seemed to have become a popular alternative to glass in a great many of the window frames, enjoying the same insulation qualities at a lower price, but perhaps sacrificing a certain degree of transparency. However, glass itself had not gone out of fashion; rather it was now employed as a road surface material, making the streets glisten and sparkle, kaleidoscopically reflecting the blue flashing lights of the patrol cars and ambulances. Stray dogs snapped angrily at each other in the overgrown gardens, where the balding and broken hedges slumped above walls daubed with slogans uniformly promising violence and retribution against various groups or individuals for unspecified transgressions.

Burnt-out or just knackered domestic items and appliances lay abandoned on front greens and once-grassy squares, like the fallen in a war of the furniture. And across the road from the house, like a sneering epitaph to the life Tam had lost, was the burnt-out metallic husk of a car. It was so many years since he had seen one, and the thing was charred and mangled, but he could still recognise the make and the model: built in Meiklewood.

There was no emotional scene when he chapped the door and Sadie opened it to let him in. No big hugs, no tears, no smiles. There was barely eye contact. He had stepped into the hall, his nose recognising immediately the smell of the place, but its very familiarity was disconcerting, seeming only to remind him of the fact that he didn't belong any more. He felt unsure where to go, which room to head for, as if he needed to be shown, invited, permitted. It wasn't his house. It wasn't their house. It was Sadie's house. The woman he had left behind, the woman he had failed. He had long ago ceased to think of her as his wife, of himself as a husband or father. Prison didn't let him. His marriage, their relationship, was something else he had been forced to forfeit as part of his penalty.

He could feel only humble in her sight, the only emotions pre-cipitated being regret for what he had done to her and gratitude that she was charitable enough to take him in.

It had been a self-indulgence, really. A boys' thing. All of them feeling rightly sorry for themselves over what had happened to them, betrayed, sold out and chucked on the scrapheap at an age when it was getting a wee bit late to be learning a new trade. They were feeling vengeful and reckless, wanting to strike out at someone to demonstrate their anger and frustration, too worked up to worry about the consequences. That self-deceiving logic of self-pitying abandon: what could happen to me that's worse than what already has?

Big wean. It was one thing not to care what happened to him-self, but his sin was in not caring what happened to Sadie and Paul. His indulgence – the indulgence of all the so-called Robbin' Hoods – was to think that what had happened had only happened to him. To forget that it had happened to Sadie too, that it had hap-pened to a family. But Sadie didn't retreat into herself for days and weeks; Sadie didn't go out drinking with her fellow sufferers and bemoan her lot before collapsing in a puddle of spew and pish; and Sadie didn't try and kid herself on that she could feel like a man again by breaking into somebody else's house in the middle of the night and stealing a few fucking baubles.

Sadie just got on with it. The women always just got on with it.

She hadn't known about the burglaries, and it hadn't been hard keeping it from her. They didn't make a great deal of money from the stuff, not even later on when they knew what to go after, and Tam hid what he did make from Sadie by secretly topping up the account with his redundancy in it each time they made a withdrawal.

They had no idea what the first stuff was worth when they decided to flog it after accepting that the cops weren't coming for them. The plan had been to hold on to what they took from Halworth, all of it, until they were collared, then give the whole lot back untouched to show that it had just been an angry act of protest. None of them had convictions for anything before, so

166

they had hoped that between that fact and playing the whole thing as a political stunt, they would get off with probation or suspended sentences at the worst.

They didn't know any handlers, any fences. Well, there were a couple of dodgy characters drank in The Meikle that were always trying to offload the odd video or hi-fi, but certainly no-one who could deal with fine art and jewellry. Eventually Bob Hannah got in touch with some pal of a pal's dug's owner's brother's cousin's mate who gave them some cash – a few hundred – for the Halworth gear, probably an utter fraction of what it was worth, but what the hell would they know? However, it was the guy this bloke passed the gear on to next who came back with a message to say he'd be on the lookout for more. He told them what sort of gear he was specifically interested in, and what kind of figures he was prepared to pay.

Maybe, they told themselves, it was the promise of the money that made them go back; maybe the need to provide for the family now the plant was shut and they were on the dole. But Tam knew what really did it: it was the buzz. It was the hyper-awareness, the vitality, the excitement you felt in the shadows of those grandiose rooms, where every nerve-ending felt electrified as the thin torch beams slashed across lacquered tables, chaise longues and paintings. The planning, the talk, the recce drives in Bob's Hillman Hunter, leaving a trail of empty Export cans all the way back to Paisley.

The secrecy. The companionship. The brotherhood.

Christ, maybe they should have all just joined the masons and saved everyone a load of bother.

But they had all felt so useless, worthless and impotent after the plant closed, and the feeling of purpose – so intensified and dynamic in those circumstances – gave them back what they had lost. It was a *job*. And of course when the headlines started appearing . . .

Jimmy Bell was the first to suggest they chuck it. There had been a close scrape on the last job, down near Stobo, with some wee au pair lassie coming up the stairs in the middle of the night to investigate whatever she had heard. Dinger had looked through a keyhole out of the big dining room and seen her heading down the corridor towards them. They had to leg it out the window and down a drainpipe, and Frank Docherty broke his ankle when he hit the ground. With the story all over the papers in recent weeks, not only was every cop in Scotland champing at the bit to come flying out in response to a call from one of these joints, but the householders were on their guard like never before.

Frank's injury aside, they had been really lucky that night, and they knew it. They were only a floor up, and they had been able to get out a different way from the one they came in, a route they hadn't planned or checked. They might not be so jammy in future. It was Dinger who came out and said that he didn't want to be in a situation where the only means of escape would involve violence, but it was something they had all come to contemplate. They could have walloped the au pair lassie, no bother. Capability wasn't the issue. They could even have hidden and jumped her from behind, made sure they weren't seen, then blindfolded her and tied her up or locked her in a cupboard while they escaped. Minimum force, the lassie's worst injury would have been the fright she got. But that wasn't the issue either. There was a line to cross.

They talked about one last job, one meticulously planned and executed operation, some place where there would be no-one home, guaranteed. One last job where they would get hold of some really valuable gear, to make it all worthwhile, and where they would leave a note to announce the Robbin' Hoods' retirement. Then they'd pool what they made and what each of them still had left from before, and start their own business – a repairs and bodywork shop, where they could work honestly, and which could never be sold out and shut down.

But it was a dream Tam couldn't believe in, and he suspected it was a unanimous conspiracy of false faith. It was something to talk about over pints, some hazy fantasy of putting yesterday into tomorrow, just a less painful way of mourning what was gone. And if you ever admitted that to anyone else, its comfort was ruined for all of you.

There was no last job, not even a plan or a target, when the cops came for them. Somehow they had deluded themselves into thinking that if you didn't get caught in the act, you were in den one-two-three. Keys up. They had never formally decided upon their "retirement", still talking about that mythical final robbery because it kept them in touch with the excitement of what they had experienced to pretend to themselves that it wasn't over. But it was. So after months of Tam feeling his heart leap every time someone chapped the door or the phone rang, the police were the last thing on his mind the morning they arrested him. He was so surprised that he felt as if they were making an absurd cock-up, like he was being taken prisoner by enemy soldiers who hadn't heard that the war was over.

It was when Sadie was allowed to come in and see him that the truth and its enormity hit him. When he saw the confusion, fear and disbelief in her face and he couldn't tell her it was a mistake. When he had to admit to her what he had done, how he had deceived her, and admit to himself what the cost for both of them would be. He didn't feel angry and he didn't feel hurt and he didn't feel defiant and he didn't feel wronged.

He felt like a stupit wee boy.

A stupit wee boy.

And he didn't believe Sadie would ever see him as anything else.

But Paul . . . Jesus Christ, Paul.

What he had done to Paul.

He had kidded himself on for a while that it was because he was inside, because he couldn't be there to keep him in hand and to offer him paternal support. But he knew that the real damage had been done by his crime, not his incarceration.

The wee fella had always believed his dad would be there for him, always believed his dad was his best pal, and always believed what he told him. What was right and what was wrong. What was on and what was not.

"Stealing is the worst kind of cheating. It's cheating at life, son. It's for folk that arenae any good at life, so they have to cheat."

Remember that?

He had left Paul, at fourteen, not only without a father, but without anything to believe in, at an age when kids can be self-destructive enough under the best circumstances.

Hearing Sadie's episodic chronicle of Paul's deterioration was more a process of confirmation than disappointment. Exams he hadn't got, exams he hadn't even sat, trouble with the polis, drinking, fighting. Inside, it was like listening to the football results. You never saw any of it, you just heard the outcome, and you knew fine the news would be bad because you had long lost any positive expectations. St Mirren always got fucked. The Huns always won. Paul always screwed up in a new and worse way.

Stealing motors. Joyriding, they called it now. Didn't even have the sense to sell the bloody things. Just drove them about at speed, and then when the petrol started to run out, took them out of town and set them ablaze. Tam couldn't understand the kick. You had to walk home, for a start.

Paul was in and out of a load of duff jobs. Shops and offices. Fast-food dives. Crap hours, crap money, crap prospects. Sadie would tell Tam about each new start with a mother's dutiful optimism, and his heart would sink as he knew that she'd be back in front of him in a couple of months, looking that bit more shattered by the blackness following another false dawn.

Occasionally she would urge Tam to "have a word with him" on one of the blue moons when he turned up for a visit. But there was absolutely nothing that Tam felt he was in any position to say. What authority did he have to chastise Paul for letting his mother down or making a mess of his life?

None. And he couldn't face hearing Paul point that out.

In the first couple of years after Tam was released, he saw his

170

son barely more than when he was inside, even though he only lived a couple of miles away, in that flat he shared with some other waster. Paul came to see Sadie when he knew Tam would be out. He never acknowledged it, but he knew it. Sometimes it hurt and sometimes he was grateful. When they did see each other, there was an uncomfortable latent atmosphere of blame and disappointment, unspoken wounds and grudges. They were two people who could no longer respect themselves and could no longer respect each other, and it hurt more because they regretted it.

Tam lay face down, the dry grass under his chest, his sleeves rolled up and one foot curled around a tree stump behind him. He could feel the growing strength of the sun on the back of his neck, its light playing up on to his face, reflected by the unbroken surface of the water. The heat of it would soon take the chill off the wind; by midday it would feel more like late summer than your usual Scottish September.

The stream was about twelve feet across, the eighteen inches from the surface to the bed translucently visible in a light copper gel. The movement of the water was languid, grown lazy over the summer and as yet awaiting the invigoration of cold winter rains. Tam watched the hair-like legs and feet of insects dimple the surface tension like it was cling-film, the motion of the water itself evidenced only in the fragments of submerged weed, pulled along underneath by the invisible threads of the current.

He reacted a fraction of a second too late to the brief disturbances, the movements stilled by the time his eyes had picked out the area of their source. He had to concentrate on focusing not on the vivid light and activity above the surface, the play of the sun and the reflections of the trees, but below, into the slow-time haze of shapes – boulders, dead branches, silt. Like looking out of a window at night with the light on in your room.

The shadow of a cloud drifted over the stream, and in its brief passing revealed them; more, he could still make them out when the shadow cleared. Dozens, lazy wee bastards. Lounging underneath and sometimes lying on top of the rocks, sunning themselves like they might be about to get the paper out at any minute.

Trout.

And once he could see them, it seemed impossible that they had remained camouflaged before. He strained and leaned out a little further, feeling his stomach muscles stretch and tense as he held his right hand about an inch and a half from the surface. He slowly, gradually, delicately penetrated the surface with his fingers, edging his hand underneath millimetre by millimetre. Then another shadow suddenly loomed across his field of vision.

"Have you been sick?" asked a low, droning voice, causing Tam to quiver in a moment of startlement, brief but enough to ripple the surface and cause several fish to reach frantically for their beach towels and disappear indoors.

Tam turned his head around slowly to look up at Spammy, who was standing over him, chewing on some kind of stem, perhaps in search of hitherto undiscovered natural opiate sources.

"Whit?" he asked, with unconcealed irritation.

"You're lyin' doon. I thought you were mibbe bein' sick in the watter."

"I'm tryin', Spammy," he said with an obvious effort of restraint, "to sort us oot wi' some breakfast. Noo staun oot the way an' let us get on wi' it."

"Aye. Nae bother. Cool," Spammy said, shifting to one side with his hands in his pockets.

Tam concentrated on the stream once more. The surface was restoring its dignified expressionlessness, and the trout were slapping on the Nivea again. Tam's fingers were teasing their way back into the cool liquid when he sensed more movement to his side.

"Throat's as dry as an arab's sanny," Spammy declared hoarsely, crouching down at the water's edge.

"Downstream," Tam hissed.

"Whit?"

"Downstream. Downstream of me, if you're gaunny start skid-dlin' aboot."

"Sorry."

Tam once more resumed his attempt to guddle a trout, trying to shut out the slurping and grunting sounds to the left of him, where it sounded like Spammy and a Vietnamese pot-bellied pig were attempting to drown each other. He eventually got his fingers underneath a biggish one, and drew them tantalisingly along its belly with a deft and reflexive sensitivity that his hands seemed to remember better than his mind.

"Spammy," he whispered as the big yin wandered back over to observe his prostrate industry, "you used tae play in goals, didn't you?"

"Aye. How?"

Tam felt himself giggle in the sudden action of flipping the fish out of the water and into the air behind him, where Spammy flapped and flailed at it in surprise, the wet and slimy thing bounc-ing off his thigh before landing, gasping on the grass.

"Wow," Spammy said, genuinely impressed. "How'd you manage that?"

Tam looked up from the waterside, right arm dripping from the open-palmed hand he held up.

"Kinda thing we had to amuse oorsels with years ago, when we didnae have access to mind-altering chemicals."

They made their way back up to the hollow with Tam's catch, Spammy protestingly carrying two of the fish, expressing his con-cern at his hands "mingin' like a cat's arse" as a result. Paul was completing the task of hauling the logs back under the trees to remove the evidence of their camp. He had a look of intense con-centration on his face as he manoeuvred a large trunk up on to his shoulder, Tam guessing he was trying to lose himself a little in everything he did. Easier just to think that you're shifting some wood than that you're shifting some wood to cover your tracks because there's a manhunt on and etc etc.

Tam crouched down and picked among the scattered twigs on the dry carpet of pine needles beneath the woven green canopy.

"Small, dry and clean bits of wood," he told Spammy. "Nothing with bark on it, unless you can get the bark off. And definitely no leaves."

Spammy crouched in a familiarly ungainly cluster of jutting and jagged knees, shoulders and elbows, long shaggy hair tumbling from around his face as he bent his neck to scrutinise the forest floor.

"Zat so there's nae smoke?"

"Aye."

"Cool."

Bob sat on a fallen tree, holding his staff in his left hand, a strained look of pain contorting his features and ruddying his cheeks. He glanced down glumly at his damaged ankle, moving it slightly and wincing, shaking his head.

"Ma leg's fucked," he declared with regret and ominous portent.

Tam looked at it, swollen and discoloured, an angry riot of bruising and inflammation under the streaks of dried blood. A combination of desperation, determination and pure adrenalin had allowed Bob to continue the night before, but once his system had been given time to rest and react, it had reached a condemnatory verdict on the abused limb.

"I cannae go on, Tam," he said, looking his old friend firmly in the eye.

Their gazes remained in silent intercourse for a few moments, as a burdensome inevitability closed in upon them.

Tam nodded. "I know," he said softly.

The trout tasted of charcoal in the places where the sticks had pierced them – near each end – for holding them in the heat. Other mouthfuls had a bland, chewy consistency that betrayed where the flames had been a little tentative in their ministrations. However, the flavour, warmth and solidity of it in Tam's mouth and going down his throat, together with the smells and the muted

174

crackle of the small fire, made it the most satisfying meal he had eaten in ages. It could have been some primal sense of fulfilment that did it, of having hunted or caught the meat you ate, but Tam suspected it was probably the even more primal matter of being absolutely fucking starving.

They sat on the ground or on logs, gnawing at their fish on sticks, surreally reminiscent of kids working away at big ice lollies. It was unlikely to catch on, though, Tam thought. Definitely not at the pictures, anyway.

"Have you tasted the finest of trou-out," Spammy sang, inexplicably, to no-one (of course). "In the woods pickin' skelfs oot your mou-outh."

"I never knew you could cook, Dad," Paul said, gesticulating with his skewered breakfast. "Why'd you never bother at hame?"

"Ach, your mother wouldnae have it," he said."

"What? Have you offered?"

"Aye. But she'll no let me build a fire on the kitchen flair."

"So what's the plan?" Paul asked. They had disposed of the sticks and fish skeletons by burying them a few yards into the trees, then kicked away the ashes of the fire and covered the site of it with handfuls of pine needles.

Bob looked over at Tam, then at the ground.

Tam sighed with resignation. "Bob's no comin'," he announced.

"Whit?" asked Paul.

"Ma leg's totally knackered, son," Bob explained regretfully. "I cannae go on."

"Aye, but we could cairry you, couldn't we, Spammy?"

"Sure. We could make a stretcher wi' jaickets an' a coupla logs."

Bob smiled, laughed a little, and shook his head.

"I'll bet you could as well," he agreed. "But I think it's the end o' the line for me on this wan."

"Bob needs treatment," Tam explained. "His leg's in some state, and Christ knows what infections he might be gettin' in thon cut."

Bob nodded affirmation. "There' nothin' else you can dae aboot it, boys. I'll have to take ma chances wi' the polis again."

"But, Bob," Paul protested. They had come a long way together. A hell of a long way.

"But nothin', Paul," he interrupted. "Never bother aboot me. I'll be in a nice, comfy, warm hospital bed the night, while you're under another fuckin' tree wi' eariwigs crawlin' up your arse."

Paul smiled sadly in reluctant acceptance.

"I'll tell them everythin' that happened," he said. "I'll tell them all aboot the crash an' aboot how it was that wee shite an' his china that kill't the polismen. An' this time they'll already have proof that there was somebody else there – that there was somebody else on that bus wi' us, and that it was him took the guns. And mibbe by the time they catch up wi' you I'll have sewn a wee bit o' doubt aboot what happened at Craigurquhart."

"Fuck, let's hope so," Paul breathed. "So what are *we* gaunny dae?"

"Well, we're no just leavin' Bob here," Tam stated. "There's the off-chance that we've actually done this runnin' cairry-on quite well, and that nae bugger'll come along here to find him for a wee while. We don't want him sittin' here freezin' his baws aff an' starvin' to death. We also don't want it to be too obvious what way we've gone when they do find him. So I'm gaunny help Bob back doon the hill a wee bit. I've done a bit of a recce this mornin', an' there's a road on the other side o' this hill, runnin' through part o' the forest in places. I'll get Bob doon as far as that, then I'll catch up wi' you pair."

"Where are we gaun, then?" Paul asked.

"Onwards and upwards," Tam stated, looking along the trail. "This forest sits on these hills like a big green blanket. It goes ower the ridges, doon the sides, into the valleys. Just acres an' acres, miles an' miles of pines or firs or whatever they are. I want you pair to head upwards to the ridge an' wait for me there. Fae that kinna vantage point you'll be able to see me comin' nae bother, but mair importantly, you'll be able to see anybody else

176

comin'. If you see polis or sodgers before you see me, then just get aff your marks an' let me worry aboot maself. And while you wait for me, you can keep yoursels amused by findin' water sources an' anythin' that's edible."

"Like what?" asked Paul?

"Mushrooms," said Spammy with a grin.

"All right, correction," said Tam. "Edible and non-hallucinogenic."

"So where are we gaun after that?" Paul enquired.

"Doesnae matter," Tam said curiously. "We're no headin' any-where specific. We're just stayin' hidden. Like I says, this is a big forest. If the weather stays mild, and we've got food, water and shelter, we can lie low here for days."

"Days?" Paul exclaimed. It was as much a protest against cir-cumstance as against his dad's judgment.

Spammy just gave a low giggle. "Mental," he gurgled.

"They'll have roadblocks all over the place, Paul," Tam explained. "They'll be watchin' towns and villages, railways, everythin'. There's naewhere we can go."

"What, so are we gaunny all turn into fuckin' Grizzly Adams?"

"Naw. But if we can stay oota sight for a wee while, they might start to think we've got past them somehow, and they'll relax the search aroon' here. They'll be expectin' us to turn up in a hijacked motor or somethin', headin' for Glesca or somewhere they think we might have pals."

"Ferr enough. But then what?"

"Then . . . we'll see."

There was comfortingly little sound as they made their progress along the forest floor, the soft cushion of needles and moss muffling the whump of Bob's makeshift staff and his lopsidedly heavy footfalls. Bob had his left arm thrown around Tam's broad shoulders and gripped the wooden shaft with his right hand, his injured left leg dragging uselessly beneath the multi-limbed and two-headed arboreal creature they had formed.

177

"Will thae two be aw right?" Bob asked in a gasping whisper, resting breathlessly against a staunchly straight-climbing trunk, a tree so formidably solid and strapping that it looked like further up it ought to have its arms folded.

"Aye," nodded Tam. "They'll no dae anythin' stupit. And there's mair to that Spammy wan than he lets on."

"Aye, you're tootin' there," Bob concurred, with a wee grin and a shake of the head at some memory of the lanky zombie's inexhaustibly bizarre behaviour.

"You know, he could be the wan that saves us in court," Bob added.

Tam furrowed his brow, curious but suspicious.

"See, the prosecution'll describe everythin' we're meant to have done. Then the defence'll put Spammy on the witness stand, then the jury'll clock 'im and just go: 'Naaaah. You've got to be fuckin' kiddin'. He doesnae look like he could brek intae a run, never mind a mansion.'"

Tam laughed, finding a pleasure in the return of the once so-familiar sparkle in his old pal's eye, and a sadness in the prospect of its impending loss.

"You realise, Bob, we're all probably famous by noo," he observed, opting not to expel the two of them from the comfort and shelter of their patter. It was very cold beyond it, and there was no need to go out there just yet.

"We were famous before," Bob replied.

"Naw, back then the Robbin' Hoods were famous. Naebody knew who they were, that was the point. But you can bet just aboot every person in Britain knows oor names right this minute."

"Probably got nicknames as well," Bob added. "To make us sound mair authentically criminal. Tam 'mad dog' McInnes."

"Bob 'the bastard' Hannah."

"Cameron 'where am I?' Scott."

They laughed together for a few moments before setting off once more.

"I think infamous is mair likely the word, actually," Tam

178

reflected. "I don't imagine we've been portrayed in a very flatterin' light by the media. Specially as that Voss bastart *owned* hauf the media."

"Aye, true enough. But at the same time, we're probably no public enemy nummer wan for everybody. I know what happened to him was terrible, an' I'm no sayin' it was right or he deserved it, but he was a bad, bad man, Tam. There'd have been plenty queuein' up to kill that bastart. An' there'll have been a few havin' a fly wee drink tae oor names this week."

"Aye. Not least whoever it was that actually fuckin' kill't him."

"Well," Bob sighed, shaking his head, "I wouldnae be wastin' brain cells wonderin' aboot that wan, cause we're never gaunny fin' oot."

"Naw, you're right."

They came to a tiny stream, just a couple of inches of water spilling over gravel and rocks, but going at a splashing, cascading pace, so they stooped for a few mouthfuls.

"Aw, that tastes guid," Bob declared with a growling approval. He bent to the flow again and slurped up another couple of handfuls.

"Keep at it," Tam suggested. "Could be a wee while before you get the chance o' mair."

"You as well," Bob replied. "Specially wi' that pair on watter-divinin' duty."

Tam laughed.

"What are you gaunny dae, Tam?" Bob asked, his tones suddenly low and serious.

Tam looked up from where he knelt by the stream.

"Don't know, Bob," he admitted. "Couldnae tell the young yins that, obviously, but . . ." He looked away, turning his head.

"You're just buyin' time, aren't you?"

Tam nodded, saying nothing, still looking away into the trees.

"I'll do what I can," Bob said. "Tell somebody that'll believe us. They cannae keep up this terrorist shite any mair, so sooner or later they'll have to let us talk to a lawyer."

"It's no a lawyer we need, Bob, it's a fuckin' miracle."

"Noo, less o' that, big yin," he said, reaching out a hand and grabbing Tam's shoulder. Tam looked back at him.

"Don't you be lossin' the place at this stage," Bob chided him. "You dae what you *can* dae. Stay hidden, lie low. This isnae aw as cut an' dried as you think. Mind how fucked-aff the polis were gettin' back in Embra, just before we got huckled intae the bus. They were gettin' frustrated, cause aw they had was us. They'd nae murder weapons and nae witnesses. Just circumstantial evidence, an' that might no look quite as fuckin' dramatic when everybody's had a wee while to calm doon an' look at the picture again in the cauld light of day.

"You stay doon, Tam. Bide your time. Keep thae boys safe. An' don't gie up. *Never* gie up."

Paul watched Spammy's progress a few yards ahead of him, struggling to think of a word to describe his curious gait, reminded as ever of images from wildlife documentaries featuring baby deer taking their first steps. Lolloping seemed to cover the long-limbed stride, but carried utterly inappropriate connotations of haste and energy. Equally, it would have been unfair to say he was slow, because Spammy somehow covered a lot of ground underneath those uncoordinated legs, but there was a lethargy about his motion sufficient to belie the fact that he was moving at all. In that respect, Paul reflected, the appropriate metaphor was a corporation bus.

They were able to walk along the forest floor in the daylight, the limited visibility of their moonlit trek having restricted them to the path the night before. There was a fresh, clean and wonderfully pure smell, sharpened by the slightest chill in the air. Paul breathed it in in greedy snorts and gulps, filling himself with it like he was quenching a thirst. Every sound they made was muffled by the trees and the springy ground underfoot, the clear but softened tones of their voices not carrying more than a few feet, like they were in a recording studio.

Spammy had gone through a brief fixation with stamping on loose sticks and twigs to try and make them snap.

"See in the films nawrat, some daft bastart ayeways gives himsel away by staunin' on a stick," he had mumbled. "It goes KE-RACK, like a fuckin' gun gaun aff. It reverberates for fuckin' miles, as well. Folk in Alpine villages comin' oot their doors to see what the noise was aw aboot. Fuckin' avalanches startin' fae the earth-shakin' impact of this mighty stick gettin' stood on by some skelly bastart, or a fuckin' deer.

"But it's pish. I've been staunin' on sticks aw fuckin' day, an' they don't even brek, never mind snap. They just sink intae the grun, or they just bend or kinna roll roon. You've really got to put some effort intae it to get the fuckin' things tae brek, you know? Like, you've got to fuckin' *concentrate*. If your mind's else-where – like the daft bastart's ayeways is in the films – then you've absolutely nae chance of a result. And see when you do actually get wan tae brek? Listen."

He placed a stick against the protruding root of a tree and trod purposefully upon it. There was a a dull, unobtrusive crunching sound.

"See? Snap? Mair like a fuckin' click. Like brekkin' the lead aff a pencil. Piece o' nonsense, so it is."

Paul just shook his head and followed on. This was quintessential Spammy. He'd say bog-all about anything for hours, no matter what or how important the conversation around him was. Then he'd rant on passionately about something that would re-define the extremities covered by the term "inconsequential".

Their journey had proceeded to an intermittent soundtrack of clicks and (dare he say it) snaps, amidst many thuds of failure, until Paul got fed up and told him to chuck it.

"I accept your point, Spammy, but eh, nonetheless, like, we are still technically on the run from the law. You know, meant to be hidin', like? Keepin' quiet?"

"But that's what I'm sayin'. I am bein' quiet. Naebody can hear us."

Paul stopped, looking up into the branches above for a moment to stem the building charge of exasperation.

"Fine, Spammy," he sighed. "But think how sadly ironic it would be, havin' so vividly demonstrated your argument, if the sound of you staunin' on a stick did give us away."

"Aye but it . . ."

"Well how about the sound of a stick gettin' shoved up your arse?"

Paul still wasn't sure why Spammy had become involved.

It wasn't the kind of thing you asked him, either. You *could* ask, but the answer would be perplexingly nonsensical, and he'd give you that amused look that said he couldn't believe you were stupid enough not to anticipate the consequences of such a foolhardy enquiry.

But what was in it for him? Oh, they all thought they might make some money, sure – at least it was what they kept telling themselves to help them get through the Kafkaesque nightmare – but it seemed absurd that that could be it. Spammy didn't seem to bother much about money. When he had any to spare he never fucking bought anything, except extra hash "for a rainy day" (and given the West of Scotland's prevailing levels of precipitation, opportunities for its consumption tended to present themselves fairly quickly). If someone gave him several grand for nothing Spammy wouldn't say no, Paul was fairly sure, *fairly*, but whatever dreams or aspirations he wasn't talking about, cash didn't seem to be something he lusted after. And the word career was quite definitely not in Spammy's lexicon. He did wee odd jobs, fixing videos and tellies for people, occasionally doing maintenance stints at local recording studios, but he seemed more motivated by an obligation to help out whoever needed his services than for the payment they handed over. It was almost incidental, like he needed to be reminded to take it. Look, Spammy, money. Remember? Stuff you buy drugs with. – Oh right!

See, ironically, out of the four of them in this sad wee fiasco, Spammy was the one who had skills and knowledge that would be considered viable in today's labour market, or whatever you wanted to call it. Paul's dad and Bob's abilities were long redundant, and his own were, eh, "not vocationally defined". No-one had use for what they could do, whatever they could do. Plenty of people could use what Spammy could do, though, but the applications they had in mind were, in Spammy's view, "not sufficiently inspirational or satisfying", which roughly translated to a complete fucking waste of time. There was also the potential obstacle of no-one in their right mind giving him a job after they saw what he looked like, but Paul wasn't sure that hurdle had ever even been reached.

Spammy liked to portray himself as the classic college dropout, but was extremely vague and cagey about the details of his dalliances with Paisley Tech, like it was not so much an *alma mater* as a bit of a loose tart that he didn't want people to know he had shagged. Paul had got drunk in the flat one night with one of Spammy's dangerous girlfriends, the man himself missing in action since a trip that afternoon to Cappielow, lair of the Inverclyde Shite (sorry, Greenock Morton, and formerly just Morton, a calculated name-change like Windscale to Sellafield). Such tangential associates were the best (if not often the only) sources of information about what was or had been going on in his flatmate's life.

Her name was Fiona, an equally spidery creature with scary hair and make-up like something out of a silent movie, most of which looked like it had been applied in the dark. She was becoming increasingly dischuffed with Spammy's evasive or just plain bewildering behaviour, acutely so that evening. This wasn't because he had failed to show up at the pub. That usually happened. She would then arrive at the flat, shout at him for five minutes as he came round from his slumbers or continued tinkering with some pile of exposed and worryingly sparking electronic circuitry, and then fail to talk him into leaving the building. After

183

that they'd get pissed or stoned and retire to Spammy's room. Half an hour later there'd be more shouting as she protested about his preferred response to her undressing and turning the light off – sleeping – and then finally huffy silence or Fiona's breathy orgasmic noises, depending on how much Spammy had smoked.

But that evening Spammy hadn't even been at the flat, negotiating the return bus journey to Greenock having apparently proven too much of a challenge. Paul had been slightly worried that his flatmate might have fallen prey to some of the local wildlife, the *Mortonsupporterus vulgaris extremis*, but either Fiona didn't share his concern or the thought of it was not entirely disagreeable. She seemed happy enough for Paul to be a substitute companion in her familiar Saturday-night routine, and they had made inroads into a bottle of Grouse together, watching shite telly because Spammy had left the stereo partially dismantled. Paul had eased off his own consumption as his suspicion grew that Fiona intended to use him as a stand-in for all four acts, so to speak, and had turned the conversation to the subject of Spammy in an attempt to cool her ardour. This worked, in as much as it put her in an extremely bad mood, and set her off into drunken and incoherent stream-of-consciousness Spam-hate, certain snippets of which shed a stroboscopic light on the man in question.

"Drop-out? First bloke to drop out of Paisley Tech with a degree in electronic engineering." . . . "Bloody waster would have companies queuin' up to give him a job if he'd just get his act together. Have a haircut. Have a bloody *bath*." . . . "Classic student that never grew up. Got used to dossin' aboot, livin' aff tins of beans an' haggis suppers, lookin' like an advert for Man at Oxfam. I know Spammy's not easily bored, but he's got to get fed up with this eventually. You cannae do it your whole life."

Well, maybe you couldn't, Paul had thought, but if anyone was ever born to have a crack at testing the theory, it was Spammy.

"Remember, I'm no gaun doon there as their prisoner, Tam. I'm gaun there as your emissary."

He had needed to be physically pushed by Bob to begin his retreat into the woods. Tam felt more like he was abandoning his friend than just taking a different path, but he knew the guilt was really just anger and frustration in a guise of humility. It was still hard to leave, nonetheless, knowing what awaited Bob, lame and isolated on a grey roadway, with the ire and retribution of a vengeful nation out looking for its stray scapegoats.

It was a strange kind of parting, a parting very like death. Like Tam was at Bob's bedside as he slipped away. Bob was going now, and although Tam knew it wouldn't, couldn't be too long before the same happened to him, the point of the exercise was still to put that off for as long as possible. Knowing capture was inevitable was like knowing death was inevitable. It made no difference. If it did, they all might as well commit sidey-ways on the spot.

And much as he would miss him, he couldn't tell Bob he hoped to see him again soon, as they both knew that quite the opposite was true. It was a regretful farewell that both parties nonetheless hoped was final.

Tam paused against a tree, taking some of the weight from his legs and regaining his breath after a swift and strenuous ascent. He had no idea when Bob would be found, but he needed to get as far away from him as possible in the time before it happened. He had told himself not to look back, because if he glanced once, he'd be glancing every ten yards, and he had to keep his eyes on the ground before him, and on the trees and bushes ahead.

However, he couldn't resist one last look, just to see whether Bob had made it to the road yet. He leaned around the tree and strained his vision, but he had stopped on a part of the slope where a veinous spur rose to one side of him, obscuring his view down into the valley. Tam took another few breaths and set off again at a light jog, veering his course to the right to reach the brow of the spur another hundred yards on. He dropped to his knees and crept forward, keeping his body close to a tree and his movements slow. He could see the road in two places, either side of a bend where it skirted a rocky hillock like a big toe sticking out from the green sleeping bag of the mountain.

Jesus.

This was it.

He could see Bob, sitting patiently by the roadside on a fence-post, his now familiar stick still present in his hand. Calm and relaxed, like he was just out enjoying the unexpected gift of autumn sunshine. And out of Bob's sight, heading his way in swift, purposeful strides, were two figures in camouflage fatigues, breaking into a run as they approached the bend. Tam wanted to close his eyes, told himself he should be using these vital moments to get deeper, further, higher, but he couldn't move any more than he could stop looking.

The figures were out of sight now, obscured from Tam's line of vision for a few seconds as they rounded the outcrop. Bob was able to see them before Tam. He shuffled down off the fencepost and hobbled out into the road, holding on to the stick with one hand, his other raised in surrender.

Then as the figures drew nearer, now visible to Tam again, Bob's free hand slowly dropped, as if in uncertainty, and he gripped the staff with it also. Bob turned and began desperately to run, the hard thumps of the staff hitting the road rising to Tam's ears after a few moments' delay, as Bob lurched and stumbled erratically away from the approaching men.

Tam watched in confusion as the pursuers broke into a sprint and, rather than seize Bob as they reached him, passed on the outside and continued ahead a couple of yards. They stopped and turned to face him as he staggered helplessly towards them, carried forward by the momentum of his last lunging, hopping pace. The smaller of the two held something out at arm's length.

Tam saw Bob's head whip backwards as if suddenly pulled by a rope.

The report of the shot reached his ears a second later.

EIGHT

Ken leaned over the desk to peer closer at the computer screen, where the same graphic appeared three times: once in colour, once in black and white and once in miniature. He took his glasses off and focused on the images again, feeling the first heralds of a headache that would be marching in mob-handed and boisterous as the day wore on. He hated bloody computers, and had ample evidence of reciprocation. Put simply, he resented their presence in the building – nay, the business – and they in turn had been campaigning concertedly for years to get him sacked.

Once upon a time the backbench had very much the final say on what actually appeared in the paper. Now it was these wee plastic bastards, which seemed to decide for themselves whether they were going to follow your suggestions for what should be on each page, and tended to change their minds or chuck in idiosyncratic alterations *after* you had pushed the button to send the plates to film. Swapping pictures was a big favourite, and not just ones on the same page. With all of the scans swimming around in the same digital-electronic tank, the DTP system had a terrifying tendency to fish out the wrong one when you went to press, and as the on-screen preview picture was a separate file, What You See was not necessarily What You Get. Ken would have written off the fuck-ups as pure technological accidents if they hadn't evidenced a suspiciously consistent sense of humour.

Caption: "EVIL AND DEPRAVED – Rosemary West was told she would never leave prison after being found guilty on ten counts of murder."

Picture: The Queen Mother.

Caption: "SACRED VOWS – Father Shaw insists there *are* practical alternatives to divorce."

Picture: OJ Simpson.

Caption: "NATIONAL EMBARRASSMENT – The country's reputation on the world stage suffered further due to an appalling lack of self-control from Ferguson." As in Duncan.

Picture: Sarah.

Bastards.

He rubbed his eyes and sighed as the pony-tailed graphic artist, Keith, magnified the four-colour version of the image until it filled the screen on its own. This was the second time he had found himself staring dumbfoundedly at it.

"Look, can I not just get a picture of it on a bit of fuckin' paper?" he had asked earlier, after the pixels had glared back angrily at his strained and complaining retinas.

"No problem," Keith said, and proceeded to print out a colour laser-copy of his creation, which he handed to Ken after it was excreted from the fag-burnt, moulded fibreglass anus of the printer-cum-photocopier.

On it there was a blurry and smudged stramash of colours, visible only when the sheet was tilted at an angle that didn't reflect the strip-lighting off its glossy sheen and into the lenses of his specs.

"Bugger it," he had declared, scrunching up the print-out and bouncing it off the head of Keith's assistant, an exasperatingly sloth-like creature whose name he couldn't remember as he had only ever heard him referred to around the newsdesk as Lump.

Lump didn't move, didn't even react. Lump evidently didn't have reflexes. And possibly not a spinal cord either.

"Ach, give us another wee look at it on-screen," he sighed.

This was bloody hopeless. Apart from the fact that the graphic was presented in a colour-scheme Quentin Crisp would have said no to, there was a rather inappropriate Fred Quimby kind of feel to the icons within it, and he half-expected to see little birds tweeting around the heads of the figures lying in front of the upturned prison bus.

What was even worse was that the manhunt could end at any time, and it was at least eight hours before the first edition of this shite went to bed; eighteen hours before most folk were looking at it next to the coffee and toast. He had said as much in protest, when that pompous fanny of an assistant editor suggested the graphic in the first place, but had been over-ruled with a pile of mince about "reader accessibility" and "leading the eye into the story".

"If they want to look at cartoons they can buy the fuckin' *Beano*," he consumingly wanted to say, but had to bite his tongue, as his jacket was already on a shaky nail, and that skinny wee shite was dying to be the one who gave it the decisive shoogle.

The whole Voss thing had been such an awkward beast to wrestle, and this latest twist was threatening to throw off his grip altogether. Some might have imagined a story like this was a newspaperman's dream, especially with it growing and running on so expansively, but Ken wasn't enjoying it one bit. Oh sure, it meant you didn't have to waste much time deciding what to lead with on the front, and with it all happening up here there was no room for the usual debate over the comparative merits of some local brouhaha against a "national" story that the London papers would be going big on. But the downer with something as toweringly huge as this was that it was never quite yours. You had to queue up with everyone else to get your share, and although there was plenty to go round, well, that in itself was the problem. You sent a couple of hacks to go and collect your wee slice of what the polis were handing out, but tasty as it was, everyone else had got the same, and the cops weren't letting anyone near the pie itself. So you sold your dish to the punter on the strength of your trimmings, rather than the meat. Big background pieces on page two, life of Voss, facts about the four suspects. Sidebar on reaction to events, local angle, national angle, quotes both from political heid bummers and ground level – maybe some wee wummin whose daughter's a cleaner at Craigurquhart. Comment pieces from the picture-byline-status columnists. Plus the obligatory what's-the-world-coming-to hand-wringing article to satisfy the Presbyterian and Catholic needs for assurance that society is indeed gathering speed on its plummet into irreversible moral decline.

And the sad thing was that it worked. It sold papers. Even this fucking stupid bus-crash graphic would do exactly what that hand-knitted plamff had said. It would catch the eye. It would attract readers, because they'd have already seen the pictures on TV, and if the other papers carried agency shots of the wreck, *The Saltire* would stand out because it was offering something colourful and new.

Ken took a seat between Keith and Lump and stared blankly at the screen, stroking his beard with one hand to give the impression that he was pondering the image, when in fact he was blurring his vision and letting his mind wander.

Ken had been at *The Saltire* for nearly forty years, from a fourteen-year-old copy boy to news editor, a position he had held – more or less – for over a decade. There had been an interruption to that tenure when he was appointed deputy editor six years back, at a time when his full editorship seemed inevitable. However, widespread realisation of the haplessness of his replacement on the newsdesk coincided with a realisation of his own. People had always said that if you cut Ken, he would bleed ink, and in those short months away from the coalface, he discovered that it was true. The power, the prestige, the kudos and the cash had always seemed so attractive from below, but once they were within his grasp he understood that what really mattered was doing what you were best at and what you enjoyed.

He returned to the newsdesk on the deputy editor's salary,

giving him what seemed for a while like the best of both worlds – until the paper was sold and the new management began to salivate at the prospect of Ken's removal and replacement with someone younger and cheaper.

But that wasn't what was depressing him.

He was lonely in his dissatisfaction with the paper's coverage of the Voss affair. The young reporters were wetting their pants the whole time about getting their bylines on the story of the decade, walking around full of energy and self-importance, like they had just broken fucking Watergate. But none of them had got their hands dirty; not unless the phones hadn't been cleaned for a while. Ken was reminded of a few pompous sports hacks who seemed to think it reflected on their careers and abilities that they had covered Real Madrid v Eintracht Frankfurt at Hampden. Christ, all you needed was eyes and a fucking typewriter.

The circulation department was equally pleased, Monday morning's edition selling more than any other since the Sixties, and Tuesday's a decade record for that day of the week. The boss was happy, and so, reportedly, were the suits upstairs. And given the, er, uncertainty over his position of late, Ken should have been on his knees thanking the heavens for this godsend, making a show of his own efforts and enthusiasm, and reminding a few people that the compliments should be passed to the same place the buck usually was.

Ach, he didn't really think so harshly of the young yins. He didn't harbour any sentimental notions that they didn't make hacks like they used to, or that these kids couldn't have handled it back in the [insert personally preferred golden decade]. Hacks never changed much, in any generation. You always got the same complement of trojans, skivers, flakes, whizzkids and bampots. If there was anything different about this crop it was that – probably as a consequence of high unemployment and hence gratitude for not just a job but a job they liked – they maybe worked a bit too hard and drank a bit too little for his liking. But they'd grow out of that in time.

He shouldn't begrudge them their day in the sun with the Voss thing, either. What was bothering him, he knew, was just another bout of the periodic crisis of purpose and identity that afflicted every print news editor in the latter third of the twentieth century, usually precipitated by a big, world-scale event such as this: dealing with a stark reminder that your job wasn't to break the story any more. That lay in the domain of the TV and radio boys. Sure, he knew that when it came to actual coverage, to intelligent, insightful rendering of the facts and details, his paper pissed all over the broadcasters – and from an increasing height since the Beeb and (particularly) ITN started interpreting the news for the sentiently challenged, assuming the comprehensive faculties of a four-year-old viewer. But in a way, that made the reality of it even more painful. These fucking morons told you *first*. No-one had picked up *The Saltire* on Monday morning and learned with a jolt that the Grim Reaper had shown up at Craigurquhart the night before and said "taxi for Voss". No-one bought it on Tuesday because they wanted to find out the latest developments in the investigation. But still they bought it.

Ken knew the game had changed for the print boys, and he wasn't some anachronistic fossil who couldn't deal with it – in fact it was his proven ability to deal with it that had put him where he was now. But the hack's most primal instinct did growl every so often: to be the first to know, first to tell. No – the *only* one to tell. For your paper to be the only place someone could "read all about it".

But that was just a self-torturing pipe-dream, a practical impossibility, even when you did get something ahead of the competition, like some local scandal or even just a new angle. First edition was on the streets for the back of ten at night. Anything you ran that the others didn't have would be quickly shoehorned into their pages within the hour, with some half-redundant new quote added so that they could tag their version of *your* fucking story with "Exclusive". And by that time it was hardly relevant anyway, because the public already knew the juice before *any* paper hit their doormat, having heard it on the morning radio or caught it at the arse-end of *Newsnight*.

There was barely such a thing as an exclusive any more, not really. Not a big one. What passed as a poor substitute these days was when some scheming politico chose one particular paper to leak some hopefully damaging document to. Or when some star-fucker signed up to one or other of the sleaze sheets to exaggerate the sexual content of his or her fifteen minutes. And the success of that tabloid in netting such stories was much like the success of the Rangers in netting league titles: there was little merit to admire when it was simply a matter of having the biggest chequebook.

All of which he could live with – most of the time. See, despite the sales, the quality and the accolades, the Voss affair depressed him because none of it was exclusively his. And for the most part he could live with that too. But as John Cleese had once said in tortured agony: it's not the despair, it's the hope. Every so often something *did* come along that no-one else had, something that even on TV and radio would initially be prefixed with the phrase "revelations in *The Saltire*". So despite putting all his efforts and abilities into making his paper's coverage and analysis of second-hand news the most fresh, incisive and downright fucking *sharp*, a part of him was not only hoping, but indeed had to be alert and ready, for someone to walk in the door and tell him they had an exclusive on the Voss story that would not only blow the competition away, but would rock the whole country.

He shook his head, bringing himself back from his reverie, focusing again on the bus-crash graphic as Keith hovered and Lump vegetated.

Then Jack Parlabane walked in the door and told him he had an exclusive on the Voss story that would not only blow the competition away, but would rock the whole country.

"This one comes with fries and salad, Fraz," he said. "Let's go somewhere quiet."

*

"So what the devil is that?" Ken asked, staring quizzically at the metal contraption Parlabane had dumped on a table in the art office, which was where Keith and Lump lurked when they weren't demonstrating their creations to the appropriate desk.

"That's what was supposed to kill Nicole Carrow, McInnes's lawyer. Fitted under the car, triggered by a remote, takes out the brake cables, then it's down to that law of physics which says two objects can't occupy the same space simultaneously."

"Jesus. Who's trying to kill her?"

"Whoever killed Voss."

Ken leaned back against an old paste-up board, a relic of the lamented pre-DTP days, apparently saved from the skip by Keith, although as he did all his work on computers too, Ken couldn't figure what it was used for.

"Wait a minute, Jack. You're saying they didn't . . . McInnes, Hannah . . . they didn't do it?"

"It's a set-up, Fraz. They didn't kill Voss and I'd take short odds that they didn't kill anyone last night either. They're the fall guys. Carrow was showing every intention of pointing that out, so she had to be silenced. So did her boss, but I didn't know that in time, and now he's dead."

"Her boss?"

"Finlay Campbell. Murdered yesterday in Glasgow by – reportedly – two muggers. You interested yet?"

This was familiarly bleak Parlabane humour. Ken knew he looked anaemic.

"And the lassie?" he asked stumblingly.

"She's safe for the time being."

"Have you told the polis? I mean, have you shown them this *thing*?"

"Not yet. Whoever's behind this has family-size cop connections. This is the only hard evidence I have right now, and I don't want it going 'missing'. Neither do I want to answer any questions about where Nicole Carrow is, or advertise my own involvement in this thing."

"Fair enough," Ken reflected, folding his arms. "So what does the lassie know that's so dangerous?"

"Tam McInnes and amigos weren't being assisted from the inside, they were being blackmailed. They were being forced into carrying out a burglary – a burglary, note – basically to put them in the right place at the right time to pick up the tab for Mr Voss's sudden demise."

"Any proof?"

"Not any more. What there was took a walk from the Manson & Boyd offices in Glasgow, probably overnight on Monday."

"Fuck's sake. You've got them comin' oot the woodwork, Jack."

Parlabane nodded.

"And polis connections? How do you know that?"

Parlabane paused.

"They killed my friend, Fraz," he said after a few seconds, looking him in the eye and then looking away, in his face a hurt and uncertainty Ken had never witnessed before. He didn't follow the logic, but it could wait.

"Jesus, I'm sorry Jack. Who . . .?"

"Lafferty. Donald . . ." Parlabane shook his head. "It wasn't a suicide. Don't ask me how I know, but believe me, I know."

"But why? I mean, I thought . . ."

"They're killing anybody who knows anything, anybody who can pick a hole in the case against the Voss Four. This is someone very powerful but very desperate, and that's a fucking dangerous combination. That's why I'm here."

"What do you mean?"

"I need you to run this."

Ken laughed. "Christ, Jack, if the Queen suddenly confessed to killing Kennedy it wouldn't bump this story off my front page."

Parlabane smiled a little, at last. "I know, Fraz. But what I mean is I need to lead on the angle that someone tried very surreptitiously to kill Nicole Carrow, and that by a remarkable coincidence her boss was murdered the same day. I don't have anything solid on the other stuff; for instance, Nicole and I are the

195

only people who know anything went missing from her office, and the reasons I have for believing Donald Lafferty was murdered would get the paper laughed off the news stands. But I need the world to know that someone is trying to kill Nicole, because that could be the only way to protect her and protect anyone else tied into this."

"How would that protect her? If these blokes are so powerful, surely they can still top her and leave us all wondering in vain who they are."

"It would change the game," Parlabane stated, leaning his elbow on top of a Mac monitor. "Right now they don't want anyone playing join-the-dots with the bodies they've left behind. They don't want people to know that these victims were specifically targeted. Lafferty's a guilt-ridden suicide, Campbell's murdered in a mugging, Carrow's supposed to die in a car-crash. These guys don't want anybody to know they *exist*, never mind that they're trying to stop anyone poking their nose into the Voss murders, because knowledge of their existence, their activities, their *agenda*, in itself casts doubt on the guilt of the current suspects. If we let them know we're on to them, let the world know Carrow is a target, then they can't kill her – or anyone else, such as my good self – without it turning the whole Voss affair on its head."

"And won't running this story do that anyway?"

"To an extent. And yeah, they could just decide to proceed with wiping out anyone in the know and hoping they don't get caught before they slink off back to the shadows. But I'm hoping it makes them change their strategy. Cover their tracks some other way and let the mystery of these unsolicited improvements to Carrow's car fade from the public's short-attention-span interest."

"What'll you do then?"

"I'll keep breathing, and so will Nicole, and I'll take it from there."

Ken took a seat on the high stool that had been tucked under the tall paste-up board, while Parlabane slumped into a swivel-chair in front of a big Mac monitor that was aswirl with multicoloured screen-saver patterns.

"So your friend," Ken began tentatively, "did you manage to speak to him at all after the Voss murders?"

"I hadn't spoken to him in months. I knew him from back when he was a cop in Glasgow. I didn't find out he was working at Craigurquhart until after he was dead."

"Right."

"Incredible, isn't it? Would have been a hell of a source, and I didn't even know that's what he was up to."

Ken gave a regretful little laugh. "It's funny," he said. "It keeps cropping up."

"What does?"

"Craigurquhart House. Been a great source of stories on its own in recent years." Ken reached down to beside another of the Macs and lifted a fat and tattered brown folder, dog-eared sheets of paper jutting untidily from its three open edges. He offered it to Parlabane.

Parlabane placed it on the table and began leafing through, glancing at the headlines on the clippings and the captions on the pictures. It was a well-worn and much-accessed library file, corroborating what Ken had just said. There were yellowed newsprint sheets dating back to the Twenties, when the place suffered a blaze which claimed five lives, through its restoration in the Thirties, visits by several Hollywood stars and starlets in the Fifties, when its owner was something of a playboy, and on until the political storms of recent years.

"The real fun went on while you'd have been living in the States a few years back," Ken explained. "The place was under the ownership of Lord Wainscroft, a Tory peer, whose freight and shipping business collapsed, you might remember, after the company finally lost an extremely distasteful negligence and compensation claim in Singapore."

"I remember the incident," Parlabane said. "Ship went down somewhere off Malaysia, didn't it? Lost about fifty crew and polluted the fuck out of some nearby islands. Set new standards in the cheerful contravention of safety procedures in pursuit of driving down operating costs. I think *Private Eye* started calling the proprietor 'Lord Wainscroft of Kuan Lan' afterwards. But that must have been way back in about '87."

"It was," Ken confirmed. "But Wainscroft's lawyers played a blinder at stalling every inquest, inquiry and report, as well as the court case itself. And the book of legal dirty tricks came out in a revised edition after some of the moves they pulled to avoid paying a wooden thrupenny to the widows and the islanders. Smear campaigns, intimidation, you name it. I think they were maybe hoping the plaintiffs would give up or even die so that they could walk away from it. But a verdict was eventually reached about four years ago, then upheld after the inevitable appeal which dragged the saga on for the best part of another year, and Wainscroft got it hard up the jacksie to the tune of about thirty mill."

"I wish I'd known at the time," Parlabane reflected. "I'd have drunk to that."

"Aye, it was fairly entertaining. Especially when the Singapore courts seized all of Pole Star's assets before Wainscroft could siphon the cash away and claim the company was skint. He didn't have the thirty mill, but at least they fleeced him of what there was. So back in Blighty, Lord W is on his uppers with a wife and six racehorses to support, and needs to liquidise some assets. He decides to sell Craigurquhart, as he only goes there for the odd shooting weekend now and again anyway, and happily finds a buyer."

"A company called HMG, by any chance?"

"The very same. They paid two mill of public money for the estate, cash which I'm sure came in very handy for Lord W at such a *difficult* time. Justification was the same line as for when they bailed out that Churchill tit with Lottery dosh, that it would be in public ownership, a fine country estate, invaluable part of Perthshire's heritage staying in the nation's hands, blah blah blah."

There was an inquisitive and expectant glint in Parlabane's eye, something Ken welcomed greatly after the shock of seeing him so unusually grave. "So what was the juice?" he asked.

"Guy from Leith phones me here, a chartered surveyor down in

Bernard Street, which is CS central. Says he surveyed the place seven or eight months before, for revised insurance purposes. He put it at seven hundred K, and he's got the documentation to prove it."

"Olé," said Parlabane.

"Indeed. It was a happy couple of days round here, I can tell you. But like everything else with these unconscionable fuckers, they just rode it out, brassnecked it. Got the Voss papers to rubbish the evaluation, dug some dirt on the CS, full overkill, and by the time they're through, the establishment version is that the government stiffed Wainscroft by taking advantage of his urgent need for cash to snatch this incredible estate for a song."

Parlabane flicked further through the clippings file. "But the fun didn't stop there, I see."

"Far from it. They spent a further fortune doing the place up, then waited until the next royal extra-marital shaggarama was hogging the front pages to let slip that they're not opening the joint to Joe Punter. It's to become a facility for 'entertaining' civic guests, VIPs, and foreign businessmen considering major investments in the UK."

"By which you mean Beanoland Holiday Camp for major Conservative Party contributors and supporters."

"You're a harsh and cynical man, Jack. And absolutely correct. I've got a contact up there, a chef. Pal of my son's from college."

"You've got someone on the inside?" Parlabane asked, suddenly sitting up in his chair.

Ken shook his head, waving down his excitement. "I know what you're thinking, but it was a non-starter. He was the first guy I phoned when I heard, but he knows nothing. He wasn't even there. Voss and his wife weren't eating in Craigurquhart on Sunday night, they were supposed to be going to some party fund-raising shindig in Perth. Kitchen and waiting staff had the night off, as did half the folk who worked there."

"Which whoever killed Voss must have known. Fewer potential witnesses."

Ken nodded. "Plausible enough. Anyway, this chef – Davie Evans is his name – has always kept us informed of who the taxpayer's hospitality is being extended to at Craigurquhart."

"In advance?"

"No, no. He just lets us know who's been, and it's served us quite well. A sort of 'running embarrassment', 'on-going scandal' kind of thing. I mean, there *are* people entertained at Craigurquhart who are on diplomatic business or might well be planning to start an electronics firm in Livingston or whatever, but the number of free-loading wankers who are up there as gratitude for political or financial services rendered is astronomically greater.

"We waited until it had been up and running for a few months before we broke the story. We ran a wee table of who had been there, weighing up the legit against the liggers to emphasise the point. And every so often after that we'd update it, mainly for mischief value, as the Scottish Office never gave the slightest indication that they cared a fuck what anyone thought of the situation. These days we only dig it up if somebody that the average lefty reader finds particularly loathsome has been hunting, fishing and guzzling at public expense. There would probably have been mention in the paper this week of Roland Voss's stay there, if circumstances hadn't cut it short the way they did."

Parlabane gave a dry laugh. "Yeah," he said. "Cannae quite see the VIPs queuing up for a weekend there now."

He put the folder down on top of the computer's keyboard, open at the maligned CS's report. Ken rubbed at his beard in a manner so familiar that it often irritated himself when he realised he was doing it.

"Don't suppose you've got any theories about who actually did it, Mr P?"

Parlabane exhaled slowly, opening his bloodshot and tired eyes wide. "Not a scoob, Fraz." His hand strayed idly to the folder, fingers toying with the edges of pages without actually turning any. "It's obviously someone very powerful, very connected and very ruthless, but that doesn't really narrow the field much, as that kinna profile fits a lot of people in the circles Voss moved in. Think about it. Voss owned people – politicians, cops, Intelligence – not only in this country, but probably every country in Europe and quite a few beyond. His friends and enemies would too. I mean, we're not just talking about media magnates or international businessmen here, Fraz. We're talking about arms dealers, arms manufacturers, people who make, buy and sell fighter jets and fucking tanks. The big media moguls get such a high profile simply because it comes with the business they're in, and maybe it's a business that attracts a fairly extrovert personality, but Voss was in partnerships – and rivalries – with guys whose names few ordinary people have heard, but who have a sight more money and clout than any newspaper baron."

"The old military-industrial complex chestnut?"

Parlabane smiled. "Well, not exactly. I know how that sounds. But what I'm saying is that we'll probably never know what this was really about, what Voss did to deserve it, never mind who actually called in the hit. Even if we did catch who pulled the trigger or wielded the blade, they're not going to talk – that's if they live long enough to be asked any questions."

"Aye, true enough," said Ken. "We'd never know the real story. But I don't imagine those four poor bastards up in the hills would be worrying about that. If you found out who did pull the trigger, then at least it would prove it wasnae *them*."

Parlabane gripped one arm of the swivel-chair, rolling his eyes to the ceiling. "I know, I know, *Christ*," he said. "But I've nothing to go on. If I knew a wee bit about what was found, what evidence there is, it would at least be a start. Working out how is usually a big help in working out who. But it's not like the polis are gaunny let us have a wee traipse round the murder scene. In fact, the cops are wrapped so tight about this one that my own contact is giving me heavy vibes that I should keep my head down for both our sakes. Let me tell you, it's a hell of a trick discrediting the evidence against someone if they won't tell you what the evidence is."

Parlabane reached for a couple of the many old newspapers that were scattered about the small room liberally enough to cause a fire safety officer to torch the place himself just to get it over with. He placed a copy of *The Times* on the desk first, then slapped a *Saltire* down on top of it.

"I mean, look at this," he complained, indicating the two front pages. "This is as much as anyone's got. Same details, same quotes, even the same fucking stupid graphic."

"Well, Keith was working on our own," Ken explained in half-hearted defence, "but Lump crashed the system, so we had to just pull that one off the wire at the last minute. It's from NewsGraph or Infographics or somebody."

The graphic was an extremely simplified detail of the layout of Craigurquhart House – Voss's room and part of the hallway outside – showing where each of the four bodies were discovered; the two VIPs side-by-side in the bedroom, and the two bodyguards just outside the door. The little black silhouette figures each had their arms around their heads and their right legs bent at the knee. From a certain angle they looked like they were performing a Highland Fling.

"Christ, it's pathetic," Parlabane spat. "Folk are actually happy to accept this sort of pish as a substitute for news. Maybe they think the easy-to-understand wee diagram makes up for the fact that none of it is telling them anything. I mean, what does this graphic actually say?"

Ken laughed wryly as he watched Parlabane stand up and lean over the desk to scrutinise the two front pages, wishing the acerbic wee bugger could have been an ally in his recent discussions with the assistant editor.

"The copy tells us four bodies were found," Parlabane continued. "Two in the bedroom and two in the hall. You don't really need a diagram to get your head round that concept, wouldn't you agree?"

"With all of my heart, Jack."

Parlabane shook his head, stopping himself from ranting further, his eye drifting momentarily away from the two newspapers and over the open folder. He was about to sit down again when he apparently realised what he had just been looking at, and had another glance to confirm it.

"So Jack," Ken said, "do you . . .?"

Parlabane raised a palm to request Ken wait a moment. He continued to look at the open folder, but now far more intently.

"This is your genuine 'fishell architectural floorplan for Craigurquhart, yeah?" he asked.

"Aye. Part of the CS's report. We didn't need it, but we kept all his stuff together."

"Master Bedroom. That would be the VIP suite now, wouldn't it?"

"Aye. One of the English Sunday supplements did a big photo spread on it when it had just been done up. What's the deal?"

Parlabane lifted the photocopied plan from the folder and placed it and *The Saltire* on the tilted and scalpel-scarred paste-up board.

"Right. Forget Voss and Mrs Voss," he said, drawing a couple of matchstick men on the plan to represent the corpses of the bodyguards. "What's wrong with this picture?"

Ken rubbed at his face-fuzz in consternation, then suddenly stopped himself. He was doubly self-conscious about doing it around Parlabane, as he had once said Ken's beard "looks like a squirrel's shagging your mouth".

"I'm afraid you've lost me, Jack," he confessed, placing his hands in his pockets.

Parlabane took his pencil and pointed at the plan.

"These were highly trained bodyguards, Fraz." He put the point of the pencil between the two matchstick men and began slowly tracing a line down the long corridor that led away from the door of the Master Bedroom to the top of a spiral staircase. "This hallway is about fifteen yards long," he said as he drew.

"And?"

"There's no *doors*. Look at this. There's an outside wall on this side, and on the other side, the rooms that back on to this passage are accessed via another hallway, another staircase, *here*," he indicated, jabbing the pencil into a different part of the plan. "Do you know why there's no doors, Fraz?"

203

"Well, I read something about it keeping the master's quarters separate . . ."

Parlabane was shaking his head, the gas turned up a notch in those Stygian flames in his eye. "Security purposes," he said. "This place was built back in pretty rough times, remember. Never mind privacy or any bollocks like that, the purpose of this big long approach to the master's room was so that no-one could get to it without being seen by the master's guards, who would have been positioned – then as now – right outside the fuckin' door.

"The bad guys couldn't have come in the window of the bedroom because Voss and his wife were in there and they'd have called for help – the guards would have come storming in in a second, not wait to be gunned down in the hallway. And if by some chance the killers were able to get into the room and do their thing without Voss raising the alarm, then why bother offing the bodyguards if they don't know anything's amiss? No. Whoever took out these two had to come up *this* staircase and into this hallway to do it. These men were shot, what was it, once each through the forehead? Between the eyes?"

"Something like that." Ken nodded, smiling. "I see what you're saying. If someone who's not supposed to be there comes into that hallway, he – or they – have got about half a second to get their shots in before the bodyguards draw their own weapons and ask what they want. Less than half a second, because if the bodyguards see guns, they're going to react as trained – do all that 'smallest possible target' shite. So from fifteen yards, that's bloody sharp shooting. They'd have to be serious pros, not some ex carworkers or spaced-out druggies."

Parlabane was shaking his head again, intriguingly. "They were pros, certainly," he said. "But that's not the point. The point is they didn't *need* to spring out suddenly and shoot these blokes through the forehead from that distance, even if they were capable of it. The point is they were able to walk right up to them. The point is the bodyguards *knew* them. It was someone who was supposed to be there, whose presence wouldn't trigger any reaction. 'Oh hi guys, how you doing.' Blam."

"Someone on the inside. But why didn't the cops suss this out?"

"There was no need. If they had just come across the four bodies, it's the sort of thing they'd have clocked right away, to help work out who they should be looking for. But they didn't need to go looking for anyone. They already had four guys caught running away, one of them resembling an extra from a Peckinpah picture."

"Maybe this is what your pal was on to," Ken said quietly after a moment.

Parlabane nodded, solemnly. He closed the folder and handed it to Ken. "Right," he said. "Give us the number of this chef bloke."

"I already told you Jack, he wasn't there on Sunday night."

"I know. But he might be able to tell us who was."

Sarah sat on the settee in her dressing gown, hair still damp, nestling a coffee in her lap, and glancing through the gap between the door and the frame where she could see Nicole standing by the telephone table in the hall. She looked very small and very tired, standing on uneasy legs and staring blankly into space with eyes that were feeling the strain of having been open far too long. She held the receiver to her ear but didn't speak.

Nicole was an awkward person for Sarah to meet.

Was that unfair?

She thought of Jack on Monday night, shattered and crying, dropping to the floor as if shot, a hamstrung version of himself that she had never seen before. Buckled with grief, tortured by the thought of phone calls he never made, ways he might have made things different. Some might find it odd that he could be so hurt by the death of someone he seldom saw, someone he wasn't even that close to any more, but emotion has a long memory. He and Donald had been very close once, and that's how close you feel when the loss hits home.

She was also wise enough to know it's a sentimental heart that beats in the chest of the cynic.

She had held him so tight, and for so long.

She knew he'd have to get involved now, and she wouldn't ask him to sacrifice doing so "for her", because it would really only be for some insecure and selfish part of her. She knew that people's lives were in danger, and that Jack might be able to help them. And she knew that despite his grief and anger, he'd be careful; that he loved her too much to give in to the self-indulgence of any nihilistic recklessness. But still she had wished she could stop him, and had clung on to him in bed as if she might be able to prevent him ever leaving her grasp.

They had made love as words and tears spilled into kissing and entangling; the proximity of death is so often curiously aphrodisiac. How she had gripped and squeezed him, so possessively, with every part of herself.

Now here she was, looking at a young woman using her telephone who – had it not been for Jack – would have died last night. Scared, exhausted, confused and disorientated, but still alive. And Sarah understood that with his instincts, his insight, his skills and his abilities, whether he liked it or not, there was a great responsibility attached to being Jack Parlabane.

Female doctors had the highest divorce rate in the country, and many of those marriages broke up because the husbands couldn't take what their wives brought home. It wasn't so easy to blame them. Sarah dealt with so much suffering, so much pain, so much grief, and so, so much death. You couldn't just hang it up along with your hat and jacket when you came home at night. Jack had appreciated that. He listened to her cathartic rants, talked her through the periodic depressions, forced her into the pub when he had decided nothing but a skinful would clear her head of it all. And he had told her that he knew this would always be the price of being married to her.

Now she understood her side of the bargain.

"I couldnae believe it, like. I *cannae* believe it."

"Don't. It's bollocks. It's a set-up."

"I mean, Donald. No Donald. Donald was cool, ken?"

"I know."

"Aye brightened the place up. He was never miserable, ken? No like some o' the dour-faced bastarts he was in charge o'. Took his job serious, but he never took himsel too serious, ken?"

"I know."

"It's no like he'd somethin' on his mind. It's no like you'd have got the impression he wasnae – I dinnae ken – content, much as any of us are. Like he was . . . fuckin' . . . lookin' for a way oot, or a way up. Christ, if Donald had wanted tae screw somebody in the place for money, he coulda done it himsel' wi' a lot less bother, ken?"

"I know."

Parlabane was patient, despite his pressing need for what Evans could tell him. He of all people understood the young man's need to give vent to his exasperating incredulity, his perplexing frustration at what he had been asked to accept. Yet another soul tortured a thousand ways by the loneliness of one single thought: it doesn't make sense. At least he wasn't having to run for his life or his liberty at the same time.

"Used to talk music to him. Man, he knew so much stuff, ken? Fuckin' saw The Clash at The Apollo. Never had a ticket. Got helped in a back windae aff Joe Strummer."

Parlabane couldn't help but smile. It was a well-known story, the hall full to bursting because the band had been operating an unofficial open-door (or open-window) policy from their dressing-room. Everyone you met who had been there that night claimed they were one of the fortunate freeloaders. There had actually only been about forty of them, and four thousand liars. Donald was one of the latter, and apparently still persisting when he should have been too grown-up to fib. Parlabane knew this because he personally had queued all fucking night in Renfield Street in a pish-smelling doorway to get tickets for both of them. And if Parlabane had wanted to break in free through a window, he wouldn't have needed Joe fucking Strummer to help him.

"He was sharp, tae," Evans continued. "Ken't everythin' that was goin' on."

"Apart from who was telling *The Saltire* about who was visiting."

"Naw, he ken't that fine. He turned a blind eye partly because he didnae have much love for the Tories, ken? But mainly 'cause I was just tellin' them who had *been*. If somebody was leakin' who was due to be comin', that would have been a different story."

"So tell me, Davie, apart from Donald, who else was working on security for the Voss visit?"

"Eh, let me think . . . there'd have been Tony Cowan, Grant Crossland, Jimmy Mc . . ."

"Is this Donald's guys you're talking about?"

"Aye."

"That's not what I meant. Who else, who was involved that wasn't part of the regular Craigurquhart set-up?"

"Oh, I see. Well, there were Voss's two bodyguards, obviously. And there were the government guys."

"Government?"

"Ken, like fuckin' secret service or somethin'. We usually only get them when there's some foreign politician or ambassador or somethin'. They're, like, overseein' the whole visit, ken? So if it's, say, likes o' the prime minister of somewhere or other, he might be at Craigie for a coupla days, then doon tae Embra, then London, ken? And these guys are checkin' oot aw the arrangements right doon the line. So I suppose at Craigie they come in an' check what Donald's set-up's like – *was* like – then gie it the thumbs-up or ask for their ain wee alterations.

"As I says, but, this is usually only for real big noises. If it's just the high heid-yin of some company, then it would just be up to Donald. But this Voss gadge got the full bhoona; he wasnae part o' any European government, but I suppose it was because he owns hauf the European governments."

"So these 'secret service' guys. Did you see much of them?"

"Aye. I couldnae tell you how many there were, 'cause some o' them keep an awfy low-profile, ken. Just kinna blend into the background, which is their job, I suppose. Only ones I saw much of were the under-cover guy and the boss man."

"Under-cover?"

"Aye. That's what we called him. They'd a guy brought in, posin' as a waiter. Happens with quite a lot o' the high-security visits. They think we're fuckin' stupit, an' we'll no notice anythin' strange aboot a new waiter startin' work a week before a big visit, always some big clumsy fucker wi' hauns mair used to haudin' necks than dinner plates. I think they dae it to check we're no spittin' in the Tory bastarts' dinners. This wan was actually all right. He knew we had clocked him, so he came clean fairly soon and we all got on okay."

"And the boss?"

"Built like a brick shitehoose. I wouldnae have fuckin' messed wi' him, believe me. He came into the kitchen a coupla times, looked around then started sayin' move this, shift that. Made fuck-all difference, but it happens all the time. I think they dae it to let you know they're in charge."

"What was his name?"

"Never heard. They tend no to say. Even the under-cover gadge, he says *his* name was Billy, but he wouldnae tell us his surname. Never answered to Billy a few times, either. All I remember aboot the bossman was that he liked to come across as Mr Control, ken? Really calm and soft-spoken. But it was funny, like, 'cause you could tell he was wan o' these guys that only does it 'cause he's permanently wan fuck-up away fae losin' the place awthegether. I heard him crackin' up at Grant Crossland wan time, and shoutin' at his own guys, tae. When he lost his temper he dropped the posh accent and started soundin' like, fuck, I don't know, a country bumpkin, ken? Some fuckin' yokel wi' a big daud o' straw stickin' oot his mooth."

"And do you remember anything about any of the other guys, anything at all?"

209

"Naw. They aw look much the same after a while. Torn-faced bastarts in suits, tryin' to look hard. To be honest, I couldnae even tell you how many of them there were that weekend. Could have been four, could have been six. They just float aboot tryin' to look intense to disguise the fact that they're bored oot their trees. Every now and then wan'll stop you an' ask where you're gaun wi' that steak pie, like there might be a fuckin' bomb hidden inside it. Or a very wee assassin. Fuckin' wanks."

Quite, thought Parlabane.

The phone rang, again. It had been like a mewling bairn, girning away for attention all morning, never satisfied by any amount of delicate handling and soft words, wearyingly restless in its cradle. The handle was uncomfortably warm, the earpiece more so and sticky with it, and the mouthpiece was starting to bounce back last night's garlic.

"Hello, D . . ."

"You know who this is," interrupted a quiet but insistent voice.

"Uh-huh."

"Usual. Twenty minutes."

"I can't do that," she said flatly. "I'm in the middle of . . ."

"Nothing as important as this."

Click.

The bastard. The *bastard*. The arrogant, egotistical, self-important wee shite. Irritating, cock-sure, obnoxious, presumptuous little toley.

He had something.

Jenny jammed the file she was looking through back into a forbiddingly messy drawer, grabbed her car keys and left.

The Cask was busy with the lunchtime pie-and-a-pint crowd, the loud hubbub of mixed conversation hitting her as she came through the double doors. It was standing room only, drinkers ringing the horseshoe-shaped bar and leaning against pillars across the wooden floor. She peered between gaps in the throng and saw him, sitting alone at a small table, his bag slung proprietorially across the empty chair opposite, which was attracting disapproving glances from some leg-weary bystanders. She went towards the bar, catching the landlord's eye from behind a few fiver-clutching punters. He gestured hello with a raised brow, then indicated one of the pumps to request confirmation that she'd like the usual. She replied with a gesture indicating that a half would do, and he set about pulling it.

"Cheers, Mac," she said, lifting the drink and handing him payment.

"Welcome, Jen," he said, then nodded to one side. "Sherlock's over there."

Jenny placed her drink on the table with one hand and whipped Parlabane's bag off the chair with the other, sitting down and staring him confrontationally in the eye.

"This better be fucking front-page news, Scoop. What the hell's going on?"

He took an annoyingly long pull at his own pint, then placed it very slowly and precisely down on the ring of liquid it had previously left on the table-top. Then he sighed.

Jenny was about to grab him by the throat and tell him to get on with it when he began speaking.

"All right, Jen, I appreciate the inconvenience and the short notice and so on, so I'll do you the courtesy of giving it to you straight. Here's the facts. Tell me if there's anything you don't follow."

He glanced down at the table for a second as if he had notes written there.

"Sunday night, an evil, Machiavellian, right-wing, scheming, worthless piece of shit called Roland Voss finally gets what's long been coming to him. I don't care. His wife gets it too, which is a bit of a shame, but to tell you the truth, I'm not too broken up about that either. Maybe she didn't deserve to die, but then again, neither did any of the thousands of civilians killed in Angola and various other war-torn African hell-holes by the anti-personnel mines that helped pay for her rocks and frocks. I don't know. Call it compassion fatigue.

"Two bodyguards also die. Again, I'm not squirting too many tears. To paraphrase the late great JC, live by the automatic, die by the automatic.

"Monday afternoon, well that's different. Monday afternoon a friend of mine dies inside *your* police station, reportedly by his own hand. That one I care about."

"You knew Lafferty? I'm sorry, Jack . . ."

"Hear me out," he interrupted, calmly but firmly. "The song ain't finished. Tuesday afternoon someone walks into an underground car park in Glasgow and attaches a remote-controlled device to the bottom of Nicole Carrow's car – that's McInnes's lawyer, by the way. It's supposed to take out her brakes at a rather inopportune moment on her way home from work. Fortunately, it gets removed by an intrepid, intelligent and devilishly handsome journalist . . ."

"Any relation to a paranoid, short-arsed soap-dodger?"

". . . And the attempt on her life fails. Also on Tuesday afternoon, Carrow's boss is stabbed to death in Partick by two alleged muggers. Tuesday evening, the bus transporting the Voss accused to Peterhead mysteriously crashes somewhere in the hills. The four prisoners escape. One guard is apparently killed in the accident, and the other cop and the driver are shot dead. Now, maybe it's just paranoid old me, but is the word 'conspiracy' entering your mind here at all?"

"Well, when you say . . ."

"Not sure? Fair enough. Let me continue. Wednesday morning, said short-arsed soapdodger is looking at a floorplan of Craigurquhart House when he notices that the two unfortunate bodyguards were shot through the forehead at one end of a fifteen-yard-long corridor with no doors off it. Now, either they were taken out from that distance by Martin fucking Riggs – and I haven't seen Mel Gibson round these parts since *Braveheart* opened – or they were shot from close range by one or two persons they thought they

212

had no reason to be suspicious of. Either way, it couldn't have been any of the four men hiding in the hills with acorns up their arses. So you tell me, Jenny, what the hell's going on?"

"Why you asking me, Scoop?" she said huffily. He could get very smug when he was on to something. "Sounds like you're the one with all the answers."

"Somebody killed my friend, Jenny. Who was it?"

She sighed, staring down into her drink. "I'm sorry, Jack, I really am. I don't mean to be moody, but, well, things haven't exactly been a barrel of laughs lately. The station's felt like a terrorist siege, between the media camped outside and the arrogant wankers shouting orders inside. As for Lafferty . . ."

"He didn't kill himself, Jenny. He tried to get a message through to me just before he died. Whoever claims to have 'found' him taking cyanide must have been the one who force-fed him the stuff. Who was it?"

If anyone else had suggested this, Jenny would have fallen off her chair. Coming from Parlabane, it was just in context. She knew it was too late now. He was involved. Call was right. The whole thing was now a Parlabane situation. Fasten your seatbelts.

"I don't know," she said, weary and worrying. "Seems like no-one knows anything about this whole disaster-opera, including the cops investigating it. Place is crawling with MI5, giving everyone suspicious looks the whole time, as if to say 'fuck off, you're no gettin' a game'. There's cops from L&B and Tayside on the case, but it sounds like the suits are really running the show. When the Lafferty thing happened, they just seemed to come out of the woodwork, running past you to get to the interview rooms. They wouldn't let anyone else near the area. Can't say I was suspicious about the fact that they're not talking much about the incident. It represents a Class A fuck-up for all concerned, and controlling what the media knows about shite like this is paramount."

She shook her head and took a quick sup of her beer. "I don't know, Jack. You say you don't think he topped himself . . . I've learnt not to question your instincts – too much. But the other stuff you're saying, well, Christ, I suppose it would explain a few things."

"What?" he said insistently.

This was probably a bad idea, but as the genie was already out of the bottle . . .

"Well, like I said, the suits are trying to keep the whole deal strictly within their own domain, but you know what cop-shops are like. Biggest gossip-parlours and rumour-mills on the planet, so if someone tells them to mind their own business, it sends them into overdrive. It's like telling a kid not to look over there. But the word is that the investigation was running into the proverbial brick wall. I mean, obviously they've caught these guys literally red-handed, and they've been dubiously given Prevention of Terrorism powers, a real licence to lean. So they're off to a flier, then bang." She slapped her palms together, left on top of right.

"I think on Sunday night/Monday morning they must have thought they'd have a confession before first light, but they get fuck-all. All four of these guys are telling the same story, and the full repertoire of psychological trip-up tricks fails to get one of them to contradict another, or to make an inconsistency in repeating his own story. Even lying doesn't work, telling them one of their pals has cracked and confessed. None of them changed his tune by a note. Actually, strictly speaking, we're talking about three of them here. This Cameron Scott character apparently had his two interviewers threatening to resign if someone else didn't relieve them. And according to one of the Tayside boys, the next bloke to try it broke three of his own fingers punching the wall after a couple of hours with the guy."

"And what were the other three saying?"

"That they didn't kill anyone. That they were being forced, blackmailed into carrying out a robbery."

"No shit. And it didn't occur to anyone after about thirty hours of questioning that they might be telling the truth?"

"Look, Jack, we're not fucking idiots up there. We pull in guys we've caught red-handed all the time, and trust me, contrary to what you might think, on the whole they tend not to put their hands up and say 'it's a fair cop – you've got me bang to rights, guv'nor'. Added to that, in this case there's a plethora of rumours buzzing around about everything from terrorism to mafia to arms dealers, you name it. So no, under the circumstances, after thirty hours or more, a good cop would have every right to think not that they were telling the truth, but that they were fucking good at lying. That they were pros. That they knew what they were doing."

"Okay, okay," Parlabane said, holding his hands up in surrender and apology. Which was just as well.

"But the interviews were only half of it," she continued, calming down. She might as well tell him. If there's a load of weird shit flying around your head, doing nothing but confusing you, you might as well give it to someone who'll appreciate it.

"What else?"

"Nothing else. That's the point. No murder weapon. No guns, no knives, no witnesses, no fingerprints. Fuck all. Hundreds of people combing the area, and all they've found's a laptop, some wire-cutters and a wee contraption for carving holes in windows, which obviously wasn't used to cut any throats as it was blood-free and still had glass fragments all over it. This time yesterday, the whisper was that if the cops went to court with what they had at that stage, it would be a far from foregone conclusion. Without a confession, they're relying more on the public's moral outrage to convict them than on hard evidence. So the detectives are all geared up for one more big push, when the word comes through from on high that the prisoners are to be moved. Cops are incandescent with rage, but the suits are listening to none of it. Someone somewhere has decreed. They're talking about growing security risks following the Lafferty death, saying they're uncomfortable having the whole world know where these men are being held, 'don't know what we could be dealing with here', that sort of thing. Plus, I think, concern over the travelling fair outside on the front steps, as well as louder and louder grumblings from the lawyers in Glasgow.

"They were being moved to Peterhead," she told him, "except no-one was supposed to know."

"What, without being charged?"

"Wasn't the first time it's been done. If they were charged, the lawyers could move in, which tends to make confessions harder to extract. The idea, I'm told, was to resume hostilities up there, where – ironically enough – security would be tighter and the lawyers would be as inconvenienced as possible."

"So whose call was this?"

"Chief suit, presumably. There was certainly no consultation with our guys, who naturally freaked, but they had to live with it, and the prisoners all got bundled into a bus yesterday afternoon."

"After which the story took a radical new turn."

"Hmm," she said, arching her eyebrows. In for a penny. "So you want to hear this morning's wee rumour?"

"Is the Pope a misogynist?"

"A few cops over at Crammond station got their knickers in a twist, claiming they had seen a bus pick up a prisoner from the back of their nick yesterday evening. Some guy who's been sitting handcuffed in a big Rover with two suits keeping guard on him. Bus comes in, they chuck him out of the Rover and into it, bus fucks off again, and so do they. Cops were told it was très hush-hush. But one of them says he's sure it's the same bus that he saw on TV and in the papers, claims he remembers the last three letters of the plate because when it pulled into Crammond he thought it would do his wife for a personalised reg."

Parlabane's eyes looked like they were being inflated from the back.

"Now before you get too excited, Scoop, the suits have reined this in tight, because they don't want conspiracy theorists like your good self coming in their jeans. Patted the cops on the head for being observant, but assured everyone that it was a different bus, that they've got documentation for both vehicles' schedules, and that according to the paperwork, the Voss prisoners' bus didn't stop at Crammond. It just crossed the Forth and went on into the sweet by-and-by."

"So they're saying this guy's wrong about the registration?" Parlabane said incredulously. "About his own wife's initials?"

"No. He only remembered the last three letters. It wouldn't be such a huge coincidence, because if the prison service bought a few vehicles from the same manufacturer at once, they *would* have the same last three letters. So yes, there could have been two identical buses with near-identical plates driving out of Edinburgh last night."

"But there could also have been only the one, with a fifth prisoner on board that nobody's supposed to know about."

"Yes, Jack. Theoretically. But if you're speculating about a conspiracy to frame McInnes and his mates on the kind of scale that could facilitate all this . . . I mean, why don't we have a planted murder weapon, why don't we have a bloody knife or a smoking gun? And why would there be a fifth prisoner smuggled aboard the bus?"

"Why else? To cause the crash. To carry out the killings, same as at Craigurquhart," he said, as if astonished she didn't recognise it as the most screamingly obvious thing in the world. "To murder the driver and the guards then fuck off, leaving the four mugs to take the blame. Again."

Jenny looked away momentarily, calming herself in a fashion much practised in conversations with Parlabane.

"Well, tell me this, Scoop," she said, voice trembling slightly with latent frustrated rage. "Just why the hell would they want the guards and the driver dead? And why would these evil conspirators want their whipping boys to escape?"

"You've just told me," he said quietly, unsurely, as if answering the question for himself rather than for her. Bad sign. Lightbulb-above-the-head moment.

"What?"

He was quickly losing the colour that his excitement and indignation had stoked up. She was witnessing the bizarre Parlabane thought-process in full, insane, runaway-train-with-a-madman-at-the-controls tilt.

217

She braced herself.

"You don't have enough," he said, somehow to the air in front of Jenny than to her face directly. "The cops don't have enough. But the public already think these guys are guilty and are crying out for blood. If they escape and kill a few more people, then go on the run with a bunch of stolen guns, it pisses all over any confession you could squeeze out of them in an interview room."

"Aye, but this time they can actually point a finger at someone else when it gets to court."

Parlabane shook his head gravely, swallowing nervously.

"There won't be a court case if the suspects are all dead."

Jenny started to get up. "You're out of your fucking mind, this time," she said.

"They're seen to kill Voss, they're seen to kill the policemen . . ."

"You've got a personal involvement, Jack. Your pal died. Your judgment's doo-lally."

". . . they go on the run, a danger to the public, they're hunted down and killed, there's an inquiry but no real investigation . . ."

"You're losing it, Jack. Take a holiday. Get Sarah to prescribe you something."

". . . and the bad guys live happily ever after."

"I've got to go."

Jenny was still fizzing as she got into her car and drove off. He was insane. This time he was totally, eye-bogglingly, twisty-head bonkers. His friend had died, and that was upsetting, but he was over the edge, in a way that perhaps only Parlabane could be.

She sped out of Broughton Street and across Queen Street, cutting off some toss in a Probe, which was either the most or least self-consciously named car in automotive history; she could never decide which.

No wonder she had walked out. It was ludicrous. If Parlabane's mind was usually like a Gary Larson cartoon, then today it must look like the one with all the cows, dinosaurs, snakes and horn-rim-bespectacled matrons piled shamblingly on top of one another in the cluttered frame, the words "Out of order" tacked across the picture.

Then the thought began, and she wanted to scream and shout it down; it was something she wanted to blot out, pretend she hadn't heard, but inside, in the place of painful honesty and self-knowledge, she knew it was like a cancer whose development was inexorable once it had started. And it *had* started. She could fight it, but somehow fighting it always became a stimulant part of the process of its growth.

She had walked out on him, something she had never done. But then he had never come out with something quite so outrageous – it was a time for new precedents.

So why didn't she argue the case? Why didn't she laugh him down or agree to disagree? Why did she up and leave, and why so suddenly? Because his case was too irrational to argue against. Because he had equally suddenly postulated an idea that was insulting to her intelligence and her sense of reality. Or something.

But did she walk out . . .

shut up shut up shut up shut up

. . . or was she running away?

Was the reason she had reacted so dismissively to Parlabane's theory – to the extent of leaving so that she didn't have to listen to it any more (like a big wean holding her ears and shouting) – not because she didn't think it could be true, but because she didn't think she could handle it if it was? That if he was right, she would have to deal with it? That she was part of it?

She thought of the atmosphere around the station this week, the suspicion, the secrecy, the feelings of impotence and imposition. The suits, the spooks. The contradictions. The rumours. The inconsistencies. The fear. So if Parlabane was right, then her world was suddenly a very scary place.

But still. How could he be right? Maybe these four guys didn't kill Voss, and maybe whoever did would have a reason to try and kill the lawyers because it would ruin their frame-up. But Lafferty? Murdered rather than suicide, in the station, in HQ? And the bus crash? Christ, how high would this thing have to go for them to pull off what he was suggesting? It would be ludicrous, ridiculous, it would be . . .

Terrifying.

She thought of the dead-eyed bastard, MI5 big-noise that was calling the shots. Knight was his name. Bomber, the cops in the station had nicknamed him. Whose call was the prisoner transfer, Parlabane had asked.

His.

What was it Callaghan heard from Crammond? Two suits, English, unknown to anyone local. Very hush-hush. No-one knew where they had come from or who the prisoner was, or where he was being taken. And no-one was supposed to ask. Didn't come inside, just waited for the bus in their big black car.

MI5. ID, authority . . . documentation.

Christ.

She had to take a deep breath before walking back into the station, fearing that her mind could be read, hoping she didn't look too pale or that God forbid she was trembling. But when she got to her desk, there was a comfort and security about the familiarity of it all, and her own chair would be a more stable position from which to put what she had heard – and thought – into perspective.

Then Callaghan came over and told her that Robert Hannah had been shot dead by detectives late this morning, having come at them with a pistol.

It took less than ten minutes for the phone to ring.

"You know who this is."

"Cunt."

"I take it you've heard, then."

"You know, one day you're going to be wrong, Scoop, and I'm going to enjoy it *so* much."

"Who killed my friend, Jenny?"

"Working on it."

220

NINE

Tam sniffed back tears and catarrh, sighed and took another drink from the receptacle proffered patiently by Spammy. Spammy had found the Irn-Bru can lying discarded at the bottom of a wide tree-stump, which jutted out of the ground to a height of about three feet, and had either been used as a stool or a table by the vessel's previous owner. He had explained to Paul that the small metal item had profound ideological significance.

Oh Christ, Paul had thought.

It was proof, Spammy said, that those bobble-hatted rambler wankers aren't quite as self-righteously green and eco-friendly when they're halfway up a mountain and nobody can see them. To Paul's immense relief, he left it at that and went off in search of a burn so that he could fill it.

Paul heard his dad's approach before he saw him. They had found a spot high on the ridge, as instructed, which afforded a good view of all approach routes, but he hadn't been on the look-out at the time, not really expecting Tam to have made it this far yet. He heard a panting – heaving, hurried breaths – and the regular but rapid thud of running feet. Crouching low behind a tree, he looked down the slope and saw Tam clambering towards him, driving forward desperately, erratically, the protest of his exhaustion seemingly silenced by the need to keep moving.

Paul saw the tears as his dad drew closer, thinking at first that they were the drawings of the crisp, cool breeze from wide, uncovered eyes.

Tam now sat on Spammy's tree-stump, holding Spammy's ideologically significant can. When he had finally stopped running, the cumulative anger of his abused limbs had dropped him to his knees, and then to prostration, gasping and moaning, lacking the breath to voice what was wrong.

Tam handed Spammy back the can and stared at the ground. No-one had spoken since his staccato splutterings, the horrifying facts delivered in wheezy, one-word issues. Neither Paul nor Spammy seemed to know whether they should say anything before Tam broke his own silence, if they could actually find anything to say.

It was the bleakest, coldest silence Paul had ever known, leaving each of them alone with the torment of their thoughts and imaginings.

"He started to run," Tam eventually said, eyes gazing forward, into the shadows and the trees. His voice was low and slightly questioning, as if he was having difficulty understanding his own words. "He couldnae run, no really. That's what was even queerer. He was walkin' towards them, givin' himself up, then he started to run. Hauf-bouncin' on that big pole he had. Why did he run?"

"Mibbe he saw they had guns," Paul offered.

Tam grimaced, shaking his head. "Mibbe. But I never saw them pull a gun until the last minute. Besides, he'd have been expectin' guns – he'd have known *they* suspect *we* might have guns fae the bus, unless they've found that wee shite an' his pal. Ach, fuck knows. Whatever, he saw somethin' that scared the hell oot him, an' . . ."

He shook his head, wiped at his bloodshot eyes again. Tam clamped his lips together, and though he said nothing, Paul knew he was thinking about Bob dying in fear. Right now he could imagine no worse way to go.

"So they just shot him in the back?" Paul asked, maybe wanting to think Bob was spared . . . he didn't know, *something*.

"No. They ran after him. They went ahead of him, turned around and . . ."

"Sick bastards," Paul said.

"Smart bastards," Spammy interjected.

"Whit?" Paul demanded, angry and confused.

"Cannae shoot him in the back. Too much explainin' to do. If they shoot him head-on, they can say he was attackin' them or somethin'. Probably put a gun in his hand once he was down."

Paul looked to Tam for a reaction to Spammy's words, fearing he might, in his distressed state, finally flip out at the insensitivity of this matter-of-fact theorising.

"He's right enough," Tam said quietly. "After they . . . after they . . ." He swallowed. "I knew I had to run. I knew I had to get away, get up here, warn yous. But I was frozen for a few seconds. Ma brain was screamin' 'run, run', but ma body, well, ma eyes, couldnae leave. I was stunned. I couldnae look away. Mibbe it was because I couldnae believe what I'd seen, but . . . They bent ower Bob, while he was . . . lyin' there. They might well have been puttin' somethin' in his hand, I couldnae make it oot fae that distance.

"Aw Christ," he said mournfully, his shoulders slumping as if some weight had been burdened upon them, or some power inside him extinguished. "Aw Jesus fuckin' Christ. Spammy's right. Jesus Christ, Spammy's right."

"What do you mean?" Paul asked, but that wasn't what he wanted to be told. He knew exactly what his dad meant. What he was asking was to be told it wasn't so, to deny it for a last moment of hope, a last second of options and possibilities before he faced this unmerciful truth.

"They're gaunny kill us all," Tam said, his voice descending into the dry, barren tones of a frightened whisper. It was as if the words imparted their meaning to Tam only as he heard them from his own lips, as if the thought that formed them had required this translation to be understood. Or maybe just accepted.

"That's what the crash was for," Tam continued. "We were *supposed* to escape. The crash wasnae aboot springin' that wee shite, it was aboot springin' us. Now we're dangerous men on the run. Kill't that Voss wan, and his wife. Kill't the polisman an' the driver. Then we aw get shot tryin' to fight off whoever tries to, whatchamacallit, apprehend us. We cannae even give oorsels up. Bob walked oot wi' his hauns in the air."

"How could they spring us?" Paul pleaded. "How could anyone know we were on that bus, or where it was headed?"

"It's a government conspiracy," said Spammy.

Paul wasn't sure if this over-familiar Spammy joke was his attempt to lighten the atmosphere or just another instance of his bizarre penchant for amusing himself with deeply inappropriate humour. "It's a government conspiracy" was Spammy's stock explanation for any kind of anomaly that someone was imprudent enough to point out in his company, from the over-complication of the bus route between Meiklewood and Paisley Gilmour Street to the fact that you never saw white eggs any more, only brown. Roughly translated, it was Spam-speak for "please stop talking about this, you're boring the arse off me".

"I mean, who could have pulled that kind of thing off?" Paul continued, ignoring him.

"The same buggers that set us up to rob Craigurquhart in the first place," Tam replied. "The MM, and his chinas. This Voss character – we're talkin' aboot *bloody* powerful people here. Powerful friends, powerful enemies. Christ knows what kinna cairry-on there is among these billionaire bastarts. The wee games they play wi' each other. But whoever was organised enough to have him killed in the first place and set us up to take the blame – that level, that kinna calibre – who could say *what* they're capable of? If they can kill a man as rich, influential and protected as that, then I'm sure organ-isin' a wee road accident wouldnae have stretched their resources.

"We're just the Lee Harvey Oswalds here. Just the fuckin'

mugs. It could have been anybody, but it was us. They kill their man, serve us up as scapegoats, then spring us so we can be hunted doon. Once we're deid, naebody's gaunny start lookin' into what happened in Perthshire. It's end of story."

Paul felt full of questions, as if by picking holes in the credibility of what was going on he could render it untrue. "But once we were on the run, how could they be sure we wouldnae just be captured? How could they be sure that the polis or whoever would go ahead an' . . . an' . . ." He couldn't say it.

"It's a government conspiracy."

"Fuck's sake, shut up, Spammy," Paul hissed, wanting to burst a lung screaming in frustration, but now even more aware of the need for quiet.

"I wasnae bein' facetious, Paul," Spammy stated evenly. "It *is* a government conspiracy."

"How could it . . .?"

"Naebody else could manage this. Aye, sure, some – I don't know – billionaire or gangster or 'criminal mastermind' could get somebody into that mansion gaffe an' top Voss. Could mibbe even set us up wi' the blackmail an' the photies an' that. And they could have found oot we were gaunny be on that bus – bent polis contacts, inside information or whatever. But what they couldnae have done was put that wee shite on board. That was, like, official. And the whole point of him was so's we'd run. So's we'd believe it was him that was bein' sprung. We might have been a wee bit suspicious if they had just stopped the bus in the middle o' naewhere an' says, 'Right, oot yous get. We're it. Yous've got fifty to get away. Nae keys.'

"Plus, as you said, how would they know we wouldnae just get rounded up again? Well, they'd know if they were givin' the fuckin' orders. Armed fugitives. Shoot on sight. Shoot to kill. But don't shoot them in the back because we have to make oot they were a danger. Tell me I'm wrang."

Paul stared furiously at Spammy, hating him for what he was saying. Shooting the messenger.

"But if it was the government," he groped, looking for the absurdity, the piece that wouldn't fit and could therefore work like a talisman to ward off the truth of what was being outlined, "if it was the government, why go to all this bother? Why not just get us convicted, send us doon and then everyone forgets aboot it?"

"Because they willnae want another Guildford Four or Birmingham Six or Carl Bridgewater case. Even if we're in jail forever, the story willnae go away. Somebody's gaunny believe us. That lawyer lassie, for instance. Aw the wee inconsistencies would gradually come oot, an' eventually folk would be startin' to demand to know what really happened at Craigurquhart Hoose. But if we're deid, who *gives* a fuck?"

"But why kill us up here?" Paul couldn't believe he was discussing what he was discussing, but at this conjectural level it seemed comfortingly removed. Like he was talking about someone else. His dad was staring blankly into the trees once more, saying nothing. Tam wasn't seeing events on a conjectural level, and he knew who they were talking about. He had seen one of the men they were talking about die on a roadside with a bullet in his head.

"The government could have us . . . you know, in jail or somethin'," Paul argued. "They wouldnae need to do it away up . . ."

"Aye they would. If the four blokes accused of – but persistently denying – the murder of Voss all snuffed it in jail or in some other mysterious circumstances, that would just advertise the fact that somethin' dodgy was goin' on," Spammy said. "This way, we've practically signed a confession before they get us. We kill't the guards and ran away. We were guilty. Naebody starts shoutin' aboot miscarriages of justice – we got what we deserved. You saw that fuckin' newspaper the polis were windin' us up with. What did it say?"

Paul refused to reply, staring away from Spammy.

"What did it say?" he demanded again. "It said 'scum four must die'. What would it be sayin' noo? Wan doon, three to go, mibbe?"

"But . . . why would the government kill Voss?" Paul asked, the strain of fighting off this growing, dawning truth telling in his broken voice as he found one last stick to beat it with. "Voss was the biggest Tory bastard in the world. The government fuckin' loved him."

"I don't know," Spammy spat, an unfamiliar anger in his eyes. "But fuck's sake, does it matter?"

Paul's own silence told him that it did not.

He had persisted with the argument despite knowing he was losing it, because the consequences of its conclusions wouldn't have to be faced until it was over. It was like you were seven-nil down with five minutes left, but you weren't out of the cup until the final whistle blew. In his head he tried to outline alternative scenarios, explanations that might save them. There was some other reason they had shot Bob, something Tam couldn't have seen from his distant vantage point. It couldn't be some huge conspiracy, that was daft. You couldn't just order polismen and soldiers to shoot men who were giving themselves up. How could you be sure they would go through with it? How could you be sure one of them wouldn't blab? It was totally implausible. It made no sense.

But, like why the government would kill their own benefactor and propagandist, it didn't matter.

Billionaires, gangsters, conspiracies. That stuff didn't matter either. It didn't make a difference whose finger was on the trigger. What mattered was that *they* were in the cross-hairs. The rules had changed. They were no longer running from capture. They were running from death.

He looked at his father, drained and pale, and saw that Tam had understood this the moment Bob was murdered. What Spammy understood was normally a matter of extremely futile speculation, but right then Paul appreciated the source of the anger in his friend's eyes. It had been a rebuke, an impatience with Paul's self-indulgent, self-deluding procrastination, saying the sooner he grew up and accepted the situation, the sooner they could try and do something about it.

Paul felt a fear unlike any he had ever experienced, and Christ knew he had made acquaintance with a wide variety in recent weeks. It was a hollow, desolate, paralysing fear; not the nerve-stretching terror of horrible possibilities, but an enveloping hopeless dread of an approaching inevitability.

There had been shock, fright, terror, anger, horror, revulsion and pain. But apart from those eardrum-bursting, vicious moments as the bus turned over, he had not been in fear for his life. What set the pulse racing and the stomach tightening – the stake, if you like – until now had been freedom, or the danger of losing it. Getting away with it. Or just getting away. The risk to life had always been around somewhere – the threat of falling from the building, of being shot during or after the break-in, of violence by the police, of violence in prison, of falling over a bloody cliff as they scrambled around in these dark forests – but either it seemed unlikely, undefined and remote, or he had simply expelled it to get himself through.

Now it was survival that seemed remote, a scenario both un-defined and unlikely. They had been running because they didn't know what else to do, knowing capture was inevitable, but ready to savour the liberty of each moment they could postpone it. Now these moments were the last of their lives, not of their freedom. Death was here, on this hillside. A brutal death, slaughtered like some beast of the forest.

No-one was going to save him. No-one was going to pull the rifle away from the sniper's shoulder and say, "Stop! That young man is innocent! It's all right, kid, we know the truth. We've sussed the plot and Jean-Claude is kicking fuck out the bad guys even as we speak." No-one was going to know the truth. He was going to be shot dead on a mountain and forgotten.

He looked to his father again. Somewhere inside, a wee boy was wanting his daddy to stand up and tell him it was going to be okay. Tell him Daddy would look after him. Daddy wouldn't let any bad men or big dugs hurt him. But Tam was still slumped, as if the life, the energy had gone from his body, drained away by

228

exhaustion and resignation. Then he turned and looked at Paul, tears forming in his eyes, and behind the beads of water a look of . . . apology.

He looked broken and defeated, the way he had looked, Christ, the way he had looked in that horrible visiting room all those years ago. Broken, defeated and . . . *weak*. Sorry for his own weakness. Sorry for failing his son. And Paul had hated him so much. Hated that image of him, that version of him. Hated him for being that man and not the man he had grown up with.

He had blamed his dad for what he did back then, back when he was a kid with so many ideals and hopes and expectations, and fair enough. But Paul knew he had managed his own fair share of fuck-ups since then, and there comes a time when you realise that you can't trace all your own failures back to someone else's Big Mistake.

He hadn't really been looking to his dad to save him, to rescue him. It was just another way of wishing someone else would come along and sort it all out for him. But now it was growing-up time.

He knew his dad wasn't weak when no amount of strength could have fought off the forces that assaulted them, and he hated whoever had made Tam see himself that way. Back then, back in that visiting room, with the fag-burnt, moulded orange seats and the peeling-plastic tables, he had hated the man who took away someone he loved, admired and respected and turned him into a sorrowful, apologetic wreck. In recent months, maybe even years, he had grown to understand that he still loved his father, and over these insane weeks, he had once more added admiration and respect. Now someone had taken that man away again, and Paul hated whoever it was with a far greater rage.

He drew on the hatred, sucked it in, let it fill him. Let it invigorate him, stimulate him, chase the cold shadows of dread from within.

The despair had been at his own loss; his, Tam and Spammy's loss. Defeat, and the unseen but inexorable approach of death. The hatred refocused Paul's vision. Liberty was written off. Escape was written off. They had regarded their own survival as the final

229

thing they could hope for, the final thing they could want, and therefore the final thing they had to lose.

They needed something to win.

"Fuck them."

Paul stood up, brushing the needles and moss from the backs of his legs, both Tam and Spammy suddenly looking on in surprise at his unexpected deliberateness.

"We're lookin' at this all wrong," he said. "If they want us deid so much, then what they really fuckin' *don't* want is us back in custody, alive and talkin'. We know we cannae give oorsels up to the polis or the soldiers oot here in the hills. But if we can make it to civilisation, that's a different story."

Tam looked at Paul with a mixture of confusion and anticipation, and maybe even a splinter of hope.

"Now, we've managed to evade capture so far, so who's to say we cannae show up in the nearest town or village – anywhere there's civilian witnesses – wi' oor hauns in the air. We're seen surrenderin'. Unarmed. Alive. They cannae shoot us then."

"We do go to jail, though," Spammy added.

"Aye, but what aboot all those reasons they want us deid and the case closed? If what you were sayin' is true, then us makin' it to court is their worst fuckin' nightmare."

Tam stood up, seeming to grow and expand as he rose to his full standing height. He nodded his head, a look of powerful determination on his face.

"You're right, son. Fuck them."

Spammy untangled his limbs, like one of HR Giger's aliens uncurling from slumber, and somehow assembled himself into a sedentary position.

"Well," he said, "I suppose it's that or leadin' a pastoral existence, livin' aff the fruits an' berries of the forest. An' I don't fancy that, to be honest. Sooner or later we'd aw get terrible diarrhoea."

Would it have been different, Paul wondered, feet padding softly along the forest floor, eyes scanning the periphery, ears searching beyond their footfalls and breathing for the sounds that might herald the end. Could it have been different? If Spammy had slept in, as usual, that morning. If he hadn't risen at the unaccustomed hour of, well, daylight, bringing the post into the kitchen and slapping it down on the table as Paul devoured the reheated remains of last night's take-away curry.

If the big yin hadn't been there when he opened the envelope and the contents spilled on to the table, on top of the *Daily Ranger* and Spammy's *TAG*. Grainy, blurry, poorly lit black-and-white pictures, date and time in a cheesy digital read-out on the bottom right-hand corner of each frame. Shapes that could be desks, computers, tills, melting into the background due to the low contrast of the image. But recognisable, unmistakable, in every shot, his dad's face atop the figure that had been captured by the security camera. On the back of each picture was the name and address of the premises, and a list of articles, presumably those stolen.

"It's your da," Spammy had said, as Paul looked on, too stunned to speak.

Paul reached into the envelope and dislodged the last of its contents, a sheet of paper.

"Dear Paul," it read, halfway down the page in very small type, one tiny line of print. "Stay by the telephone."

They sat in silence, staring at the photographs, Paul speechless and Spammy just Spammy.

It couldn't be true. He knew it couldn't be true. Christ, one of the dates was just a week last Friday, and he had been at his parents' house that night. Admittedly at the time stated on the photo, he was fast asleep on the couch, well stuffed with steak pie and Export, but he couldn't quite envisage his dad getting up quietly in the middle of the night to go out to Paisley and screw some office in New Street. It was a wind-up. It had to be a wind-up.

"Was this you, ya lanky bastard?" he asked. "Fartin' aboot wi' the computers at Arlene's work?"

Arlene was Spammy's latest relationship-cataclysm-in-progress, a nerve-frazzled neurotic who worked as a copy-setter at a graphics bureau in Glasgow. Spammy looked back at him blankly, an almost unprecedented hint of worry in his eyes telling Paul he wasn't lying. "I swear to God, Paul. I know fuck-all aboot this."

The phone started ringing.

Paul and Spammy looked at each other for a second of shared trepidation, then Paul shot up from his chair and headed for the living room to answer it. Spammy grabbed at his shirt from behind as he reached the living-room doorway, forcing himself in ahead of Paul and gesturing to him to let it ring as he fidgeted with the partially dismantled answering machine so that it would record the conversation.

"Hello?"

"Mr McInnes," they heard, metallic, voice-disguiser tones emanating from the small speaker next to the rotating spools of the cassette, which seemed to be operational in spite of the contraption's lack of casing and generally disembowelled appearance. "You got the envelope?"

"Yes. What's this . . .?"

"Just shut up and listen," it said, the mystery caller's breath crackling electronically as he paused. Despite the disguiser, they could make out that the voice was male, and there was enough tone in the accent for them to reckon he was English. Or from Edinburgh.

"There was another article stolen in each of the robberies," he continued. "The security videotape. Consequently, the police have found it very difficult to proceed with their enquiries. If you do not do exactly as I say, copies of the pictures you have seen will fall rather serendipitously into their hands. I am also in the position to provide witnesses."

"But, how . . .? My dad didn't . . ."

"No, indeed, your father didn't. You didn't sell any smack to fourteen-year-olds in Glenburn, either, but I can supply pictures and evidence of that, too. But let's not make this complicated. Here are your orders. Pay attention. You will go directly from here

232

right now, to lot 12b, Gourlay Street, Renfrew. In there you will meet someone who will provide you with further information. If you go to the police, so do the photographs. And if you deviate from your instructions . . . well, as I'm sure you appreciate, if I can make things like these pictures happen, Paul, I can make other things happen. And I can make people die, too."

The line went dead and the dialling tone trilled loudly out of the speaker a few seconds later.

Paul's relationship with Spammy was one of the great mysteries in his life, constantly baffling him as to what each really got from the other's company. Spammy often gave the impression that he wouldn't exactly be daunted by the prospect of not having a conversation with another human being ever again, and when Spammy *was* feeling expansive, Paul often felt he wouldn't exactly be daunted by the prospect of not having a conversation with Spammy ever again.

There's always one weird kid in every neighbourhood, every school. Meiklewood had Spammy. Paul first remembered him from Meiklewood Primary, singled out for having singled himself out, ostracised for being a loner, and of course persecuted for the social sin of being a bit quiet. He was always awkward of appearance, even as a child looking as though he had been assembled from limbs and appendages intended for several other bodies of varied size and build. However, there were a few kids as quiet as Cameron Scott, and plenty more who could make him look a graceful exemplar of deportment by comparison. What made the difference, what sealed his categorisation, what turned Cammy into Spammy, was that he was "wan o' the mental Scotts".

In today's parlance the Scotts would be described as a dysfunctional family, but as far as Paul could remember, as a family the Scotts functioned routinely and efficiently. Every morning, Mr Scott went out to his work, the weans went out to school, Mrs Scott stayed home, and in the evening they all returned, ate their tea and then knocked fuck out each other until bedtime.

There were three forms of communication in the Scott house-hold: silence, screaming and physical assault. Spammy told Paul that the kitchen was a lot like Beirut, such was the tension between each of the potentially warring parties sharing the place, any two of which could escalate hostilities at any moment. Spammy had come along some years after his two brothers and his sister, not so much a late bonus for his parents as a consolation goal when they were already three down.

Spammy's brothers weren't really feared as hard cases around town because they seemed to expend so much of their aggression on each other that there was seldom much left for anyone else. It was as though the complex history of resentfully recorded Scott politics that sparked or fuelled their frequent inter-sibling atroci-ties made the notion of extra-familial violence seem a pointless frivolity, like casual sex when you're in a consumingly passionate long-term relationship.

Spammy's sister, Lizzy, was a far scarier prospect. Paul's abid-ing impression of her was formed at the age of nine, having scaled the swingpark climbing frame and noticed with some distress that "Belter" Burns, a weasel-eyed and nasal-toned hard-ticket from the big school, was heading his way, past the see-saw, smoking as demonstratively as possible for the instruction and edification of junior on-lookers. Paul hadn't noticed that Lizzy was among the crowd of "big lassies" standing near the roundabout, until she sprang from the group and assaulted Belter with a ferocity that Paul had never witnessed before, and seldom again. Not since Roy Aitken retired, anyway.

The ex-hard-ticket had staggered away, his T-shirt covered in blood from his nose, mouth and several cuts about his face, as three of her pals restrained Lizzy from committing further damage. Little as Paul understood it, he heard in school the next day that Lizzy was exacting punishment for Belter "puttin' it aboot that he'd shagged her".

Tales of further acts of retributive – or equally often, random – violence by Lizzy were legion. Unlike her brothers, Lizzy didn't need that intimate, personal aspect to her brutality. This was because she was a psychopath.

Spammy, therefore, was less a product of his environment than a by-product of it. He had been afforded some degree of protection amidst the Elderslie Crescent theatre of war by his parents' indulgence of their wee yin and by the fact that they and his siblings regarded him as having nothing to do with their battles, a cross between a neutral state and a defenceless refugee. This didn't stop him being a civilian casualty now and again, though.

Paul and Spammy had become pals at primary school, sort of. He could remember things they had done together, could remember being in the same classes, but couldn't remember anything they had said to each other. Which was natural enough – that's how kids get on. They strike up an unspoken rapport and can be happy to be around each other, even if not much is being said. What naggingly disturbed Paul was that their adult relationship seemed to work on much the same basis.

Spammy had taken Paul round to his house once when they were about ten, which was when he was shocked – and indeed, at first, horrified – to learn that Spammy lived in a cupboard. It was basically an alcove with a door on it off the upstairs hall, with room enough inside for Spammy's single mattress and precious little else. Paul was only slightly relieved to learn that this had been Spammy's decision, and not some parental cruelty or deprivation. There were three bedrooms in the wee council semi: Mr and Mrs Scott had one; "the boys" occupied another; and Lizzy had one to herself, ostensibly on the grounds that she was a girl, politely avoiding the reality that no-one of either sex would want to share close quarters with someone so terrifyingly unstable anyway. When he had grown too big to sleep in a cot in his parents' room, Spammy had been moved in with "the boys". And as soon as he was big enough to lift his mattress, he had moved into the cupboard. This seemed to suit everyone, particularly Spammy. His clothes and toys and stuff remained in The Lebanon, but the cupboard – with its shelves five feet up and its bare bulb hanging from the ceiling – was his sleeping quarters and, most importantly, his retreat.

Spammy had taken Paul there right away, to just sit and look through annuals and swap football cards. It had been okay. Weird, but okay. Then they had gone downstairs for a piece and jam, and the cupboard had suddenly revealed its sanctuary qualities. Paul often wondered, later in life, if his own fears and knowledge of the family's reputation maybe projected something, but the tension in the fragile-ceasefire atmosphere of mutual suspicion, resentment and latent hostility as they walked through the living room and into that kitchen was like nothing he had ever imagined.

Paul didn't see so much of Spammy at secondary, and saw even less of him after his dad went to jail. That was when Paul started running about with that bunch of, well, arseholes. Stealing motors, getting into barnies.

Paul's Wild Years.

Pathetic, really.

He had been pretty angry, right enough. Angry and confused and fragile, and a teenager, which was a volatile enough state under the best conditions. The shock and the loss hit him pretty hard, but it was the abuse that triggered off the anger. He had been one of the "good boys", see. Got his sums right, read books, did what he was told. So that lent a truly malicious joy to the relentless slagging, as if he had been knocked off some perch he had never even bloody attempted to occupy.

"Watch, hide your gear boys, here comes McInnes."

"Lock the windies, it's the burglar's boy."

"Heh McInnes, your da been fucked up the arse yet?"

And so on.

And it was all his dad's fault. Not just for being a criminal, not just for going to prison, but for everything. For making him work so hard at school. For drilling it into his head to be respectful and obedient towards the teachers. And for going on and on and fucking on about fucking Uncle Greig and his fucking physics professorship and how there were fucking brains in the fucking family.

Paul was shite at physics. Maths too. He had tried, Christ knew he had tried, especially as his dad was so bloody married to the idea that he had genetically inherited a genius-like aptitude for the sciences that would show in time if he worked hard enough. But he didn't even *like* science. He liked history. He quite liked English, apart from interpretations. He liked to read. And he liked plays. The class had been taken to the Citizens Theatre in the Gorbals once, and he had expected it to be the most tedious evening since Hibs were last at Love Street. But it was wild, this ancient Greek thing. The language was a bit pompous, and everybody seemed to be English, but there was so much action. There was fucking blood everywhere and by the end there were only about three folk left alive. No monsters, but it pissed on *Clash Of The Titans*.

The first of the trouble, the first evidence of Paul becoming a bad boy, had been the fights. Finally snapping at one robber or burglar or prisoner jibe too many, and going in in a storm of fists, feet and forehead. Then the full-on delinquency had set in: the *attitude*. Dogging school, doing close to fuck-all when he did show up, failing exams, winding up the teachers, running with the gang. He thought he was doing it because he didn't care about nothing no more, because nothing matters, man, what's the point of anything in this world etcetera etcetera snore snore. But really he was doing it because of who it would hurt. Who it would punish.

Christ, the psychoanalysts would have fucking loved it. He might as well have shagged his ma as well, taken it to its logical conclusion. Oedipus McInnes.

He ran into Spammy again a few years later, one Friday night at Paisley Tech Union when he got signed in by a mate, Kev, who had subsequently run into the girl he was there to get pished to "get over". Paul had seen this sort of thing before. He stood a few polite metres away from them at the bar when the relationship-dissection process began, biding his time as he expected it to get acceleratingly acrimonious before concluding – within five-to-seven minutes, on average – in shouted insults, highly judgmental analysis of sexual technique, and finally tears on the girl's face and a red slap-mark on the guy's. This one didn't quite run to form. Within three minutes Kev and the girl he "never wanted to see again" were attempting to eat each other alive in front of Paul, before stumbling off to some chairs nearby, where their rediscovery-of-lost-love-please-forgive-me-you're-the-only-one-I've-ever-wanted snog continued for the rest of the night.

Paul had been left standing at the bar like a prick at a dyke wedding, holding his plastic pint-pot and feeling conspicuously abandoned. He wandered over to a nearby table where he could rest his drink and keep an eye on whether Kev and "that fuckin' two-faced bitch, fuck knows what I ever saw in her" had come up for air at all.

Spammy had plonked his pint down next to Paul's and collapsed himself on to the bench opposite without a word. Ordinarily, this encounter would have been well off the end of the awkward scale, the pair barely having exchanged a dozen words in more than ten years, but it just didn't happen like that. And within three pints it felt to Paul like each of them had actually just been waiting for the other to get back from the bog, even though ten years was a hell of a long time for a slash.

Seven or eight months later, Spammy's flatmate had got a life and moved out, and Paul was sucked in by the vacuum.

Paradoxically, living with Spammy had actually given Paul a sense of dynamism about his life. He had considered himself a bit of a waster before this, moving from crap job to crap job with periodic bouts of dole-somnambulance to punctuate it. It was an existence that flitted between boredom, numbness and depression, with a constant sense of guilt and regret filling in the corners. And he thought that was how it was always going to be.

Then he saw how Spammy lived, and realised that some people truly are born for sloth. Spammy was signally unbothered by thoughts of what he could or should be doing with his life (or his degree, or his knowledge). Spammy was perfectly happy to arse about the flat all day, smoking hash, regularly electrocuting himself as he carried out experimental surgery on various electronic appliances, occasionally going down the studio or fixing a telly for someone. Paul had previously thought all wasters were haunted by the same vague sense of time slipping away, by boredom, guilt, against a constant ambient hum of dissatisfaction.

He knew then that he was in the wrong line, so to speak. Finger had to be removed from arse. Said arse had to be got into gear. But Christ, that didn't mean he was going to polish up his shoes and set about climbing the Comet career ladder. His great regret – to the point of embarrassment – was chucking it away at school. And at the time he *had* been aware he was chucking it away; that was the point – he was chucking away his dad's dreams, not his own. Missing out on the chance to study physics or whatever had not seemed a great loss, and it still didn't. But at twenty-four, having spent a few years out in the so-called "real world" (you know, that place of rich and vivid experience that taught you a lot more about life than books or colleges ever could – i.e. Paisley) he figured taking time out to get inside far greater minds than his own was unlikely to leave him any further behind in life's great race than he was right now.

A few conversations with some of Spammy's old college mates soon told him he had already read more ancient history, drama and literature than most of the folk they had known to have graduated in the subjects, although one did warn him of the dangers of actually being interested in what you were studying.

Paul enrolled for night classes to get his Highers, and resolved to cut down on the take-aways and six-packs as he saved his cash to support his future academic pursuits. The conditional offers had come through a couple of weeks before the photographs.

So. Paul and Spammy, sitting by the phone.

Everyone kept wondering why Spammy had got involved, signed himself up for this mess. The truth was, Spammy had just been there. He had got sucked in at the start, before anyone knew what it was all about, and by the time they did know the story, he was already in too deep to back out.

Christ, what else was he going to do? Say "wow, tough break, man. Hope it goes all right. I'll see you when it's all over, and if you don't come through, I'll visit you inside"? Not Spammy. And if it had been the other way round, Paul liked to think he'd have done the same thing.

Spammy had come with him to Renfrew on the bus, bringing along an ancient camera that looked like it was only about three models on from the Box Brownie. He was going to keep an eye on the place from round the corner, snap the mystery man on his way in or out.

Gourlay Street was on a light industrial estate, a cul-de-sac with two rows of "units", basically garages with a paint job and a logo from some development agency. 12b was at the end, next to the rusted mesh fence which was being gradually worn down by the advance of grass, weeds, empty superlager cans and chip pokes on the other side. Across the street he could see 13b, its "To Let" sign mirroring its neighbour opposite, as did the graffiti, broken glass and kicked-in door. Paul wished he could write the ad copy: "Workspace Unit to let in busy industrial estate. 100 square feet. Fence-side location ensures regular nocturnal visitors. Petty vandalism and regular spray-tagging included in rent."

He pushed nervously at the door, which sat slightly ajar from its wood-splintered frame, his stomach feeling like the inside of a washing machine. Somewhere he felt the fear that he was about to be set upon, but he chased the thought, blocked it out before his imagination could embellish it. He didn't have any idea what to expect. He didn't even have much of an idea what to dread.

He edged past some empty cardboard boxes and wooden palettes in the darkened passage, pushing through the tacky translucent-plastic strips that hung over the interior doorway, and found himself in a dank, musty, rubbish-strewn chamber, lit dimly

240

by the sun through the small part of one grimy window that wasn't boarded over.

His dad was sitting on a wooden crate in the middle of the room.

They looked at each other, and Paul saw his own reaction mirrored in his dad's face. Not you, please not you. Shock, disbelief, and anguished resignation as the picture suddenly came into sickening focus. His dad put his head in his hands, elbows on his knees. Paul pulled another crate on to its side and took a seat opposite.

"What's goin' on, Dad?"

His dad looked up. He was tired and pale, older.

"Aw, Jesus, Paul," he said, shaking his head.

"I got pictures, Dad. Pictures of you . . . in burglaries. And a phone call. Tellin' me to come here . . ."

Tam nodded. "I was told to wait here for . . . Ach, fuck's sake."

"You saw these photos as well?" Paul pulled them out from his jacket.

Tam's eyes filled up. "Naw . . . it was . . ."

"Me? Dealin' drugs?"

He shook his head. "The guy mentioned that. But . . . it was . . . your mother." He swallowed, a couple of tears escaping as he fought to keep his voice steady. "In the bath . . . in the . . . bedroom, I don't know how they . . ." Tam sobbed a few times, then sniffed loudly, wiping his eyes and nose with a hanky. "I burnt them oot the back in case she saw them. But they were tellin' me they could get to her," he said.

Paul nodded.

"They can get to any of us, son."

"So what's it aboot?"

Tam took a couple of deep breaths. "They want us to rob a place. The guy's got . . . inside information, but he wants someone else to pull it aff. He's gaunny give me the details as and when."

"But why you?"

"Reckons I might have an aptitude. Said it's the kinna place we used to do before."

241

"So why me?"

"I didnae know it was gaunny be you until you walked in the noo. He said I'd to work wi' somebody specific. I'm allowed whoever else I need, but I've also got to work wi' this guy, and I'd to wait for him here."

"But I've never broken intae anywhere, except a few motors when I was aboot fifteen."

Tam nodded sagely. "I know, I know. But I knew why you as soon as I saw you."

"What d'you mean?"

"It's so I'll do it right. So I'll try ma best to pull it aff successfully an' no get caught. So I'll no gie it some hauf-arsed attempt an' then go blabbin' to the polis when it fucks up. It's a means of ensurin' commitment. Whoever this bastart is, or whoever these bastarts are – an' there cannae be just the wan o' them – they're afraid I might no gie a fuck if I end up in the jile again. But they know I'll no want ma boy goin' doon with me."

They edged forward on their stomachs, to the rock outcrop that jutted from the ridge "like Kirk Douglas's chin", Tam said, a landmark they had been heading towards for about an hour. They saw a small farmhouse below, next to a barn and the standard but nonetheless inexplicable mound of old tyres. A little cloud-cover had assembled as the afternoon wore on, but the light was crisp enough to afford them a long view of the valley. There were no other houses in sight, and the road that led snakingly to the farm from beyond the spur of another adjutting hill a few miles off looked too narrow to suggest that there were any settlements nearby, out of sight.

They decided that nothing less than a village would do. They needed witnesses, plural, not some old farmer who could be paid off or lied to – or who knew what – if he saw them gunned down on their way towards him.

"I know they had their arms in the air, sir, but it was a ploy. They would surely have killed you. That's how they did it with

242

that poor bus driver, didn't you hear the news? Oh, you're not convinced? Eat this."

They were shuffling back from the edge when Paul heard the low, distant sound and crawled forward once more.

"Christ."

There were two helicopters swooping out from behind that spur, banking to turn and head up the valley towards them.

"Helicopters."

"Anybody remember *Whirlybirds*?" Spammy asked vacantly, watching the McInneses scramble down from the rocks on their hands and knees.

They ran back under the cover of the trees, it occurring fleetingly to Paul that such blind charging around might run them straight into a search party, and spent a frantic, breathless few moments looking for camouflage as the sound of the helicopters grew insistently louder with each second.

"*Two riders were approachayn'*," he heard Spammy sing to himself, as the big eejit calmly lay down under some bushes and pulled several discarded branches over himself as if they were a duvet. Paul curled himself up in the foetal position, huddled against the trunk of some conifer with low-hanging branches, on the opposite side to where the helicopters would arrive from. His dad did likewise a few yards away.

Paul felt the thumping in his chest grow more and more violent, like his heart was angrily slamming itself against his ribcage, as the noise of the blades increased and the wind tossed the dust and dead needles briefly into the air six inches above the forest floor. He wanted to close his eyes tight, bite his bottom lip and clutch himself in paralysed terror, but he knew he had to look up, had to know if they had been seen. He saw the underbelly of one copter head away from them, passing above at speed. Too high and too fast. They were on their way somewhere rather than combing the area. He exhaled slowly and rolled over on to his back, his heart still head-butting his chest wall like it had a pogo-stick and a crash helmet.

*

There was a kind of freedom in it. An *abandon*.

Once Paul had swallowed it down, once he had accepted that there was no choice, no alternatives, no options. A liberty. A freedom from responsibility.

They weren't burdened with the morality of it, the right and the wrong. That had been taken out of the equation. They didn't have to think about whether they should be doing it, as they didn't have the option not to; all they had to worry about was *how* they were going to do it.

Getting in.

Getting out.

Getting away with it.

Nothing else mattered. Nothing. The rest of their lives, the rest of their *world*, was on hold. All their thoughts, all their energies, all their concentration was focused on the job.

Paul didn't feel a victim, didn't feel persecuted. He felt important, powerful, excited, ten feet tall. Those first days, walking through Paisley, he had looked at the passers-by, jealous of their freedom, that they were not struggling under this burden, resentful of their carefree fortune. The old *you think you've got problems* line of self-pity. Once he had accepted it, once the process had begun and the plans were underway, he looked down upon them as nobodies, scurrying about their mundane business, oblivious of the giants who walked among them. Relieved of his own conscience, he was able to – no, he *had* to – think of himself as some kind of international-class criminal, part of an elite team planning a daring and ingenious heist, a meticulous operation. Something out of *Die Hard* or *The Usual Suspects*.

And it was a ride. He understood now why his dad had done it, so many times, back when he would otherwise have been just an unemployed car-worker. Going up to Craigurquhart on a reconnaissance mission, dressing up in chunky jumpers and ridiculous bobble-hats to look like ramblers as they staked the place out. Standing next to Spammy, his dad and Bob walking about twenty yards ahead, staring over the wall and through the fence at the white building, taking notes. An incredible feeling of power, of the things they were going to do and that no-one suspected.

They all shared it. He saw that glint in his dad's eye a few times, a determination, a self-confidence and a pride as they put their plans together. Bob too. Maybe especially Bob. Paul had marvelled at the ease with which his dad recruited Bob's assistance, even though they were best friends, as it wasn't quite like ringing up and asking if he fancied giving him a hand papering the living room. But Bob had been one of the Hoods (in fact, the only one around: Frank Docherty was dead and Dinger Bell was back inside, having failed to find a market for his less famous work skills), and who knew what bonds were forged and promises were made back then; Paul himself had never felt so close to anyone before as he did to his three partners-in-crime.

Bob's wife was dead now, and he had little to fill his day between shifts as a lollipop man, a job he had taken as a sad wee consolation to himself. He loved kids, and they loved him, but he'd missed the best part of his own grandweans' childhoods while he was inside. He didn't feel he had much to lose if he ended up back in the jail. When Tam called, he came running. And the years fell off him as the job approached.

Paul saw his dad in a new light, him and his old pal the respected pros, assessing the situation, calling the shots, anticipating the pitfalls. He was strong, authoritative, knowledgeable, in his element. And there were the tales. A sign of initiation and acceptance, that he and Spammy were imparted the stories of the Hoods' glory days. Or maybe a sign that his dad felt close enough to and respected enough by Paul to open up that part of himself like it was a trophy cabinet rather than a locked cupboard full of shame.

Paul had chucked his job right away. He knew that either he would be unavailable for work after the Craigurquhart robbery or – just maybe – he'd have some cash in his hands. Aye, right. They talked about the money jokily, like a shared conspiracy of false faith. Pretending it was an incentive. "What'll you do with

your share?" they'd ask each other. It was being a spoilsport not
to join in. But no-one believed they'd see any, even if they did
pull off the job, despite the mystery man's assurances that he'd
make it well worth their while. It was hard to retain an optimistic
hope for any reward when they didn't know what they were stealing, just being told to blag whatever was in the safe, which the
MM himself claimed not to be able to anticipate.

There was no arrangement for a handover, the arrogant bastard
nonchalantly saying that he had "faith" they wouldn't try and
make off with the loot on their own, and not just because he could
fence it more lucratively than them. Photographic faith.

Cunt.

There was a stillness amidst the trees that Paul just knew he didn't
like. He was aware that the wind, gentle breeze that it had been,
had dropped, and that the background noise of twittering birds and
rustling branches had all but silenced. Like an air-conditioning
system or a convection heater, a sound you only become aware of
when it ceases. It was one of those moments when he felt like he
was standing on the planet, not just on the ground. Accidents of
nature on a rock spinning through the void. What he didn't like
was the feeling of the day winding down, clocking off. The
relaxed quiet of late afternoon, the busy industry and activity of
the day – from the creatures to the weather – having come and
gone, looked at the time and thought, fuck it, we can pick this up
again tomorrow.

Standing on the planet. Lonely on the planet.

The feeling that it was too late. That they hadn't made it.

Their progress had to be slow, cautious, observant, quiet. After
seeing the view from the outcrop they knew they had to continue
along the mountain, hoping the next valley wasn't too many miles
on, and that more than about three people bloody lived there. He
sensed the lengthening of the shadows and the frustrated disappointment that they hadn't reached another valley, never mind sight
of a village. But worse, he sensed a drawing to a close. A dying.

246

This was a day that had to last, had to keep going. Why was it abandoning them? Why couldn't it have still been summer?

They weren't going to reach safety, they weren't even going to reach sight of it. Night was going to fall. And this was a night he couldn't face, a night that it seemed no morning could follow. The prospect of his own fear chilled him, the inescapable ordeal of either progressing, hunted, in the darkness, a million imagined weapons ranged against him unseen; or of crouching, still, hiding, the hours, the minutes, the seconds an eternal, silent scream of insane suspense as he waited, helpless, to see whether the dawn would outrun the gunmen.

"I think if we take it as read that there's gaunny be a double-cross at some stage, we can put oor minds towards anticipatin' it," Tam had said.

No-one was comfortable with the way terms were being dictated by the MM in his voice-disguised phone calls to Tam, which Spammy was taping with another answering machine that looked like it had been salvaged from a domestic gas explosion.

Specific date, because that's when the unnamed rich guest would be staying there. Specific time – very specific – of 7:20 p.m. because that's when the rich guest would be out *and* when the MM's man on the inside could temporarily shut off the electric fence, security video cameras, laser trips, alarm system and so on.

Tam came up with the idea of depositing the envelope with the lawyer as a kind of insurance policy, or more a damage limitation exercise. They put in photocopies of all their "evidence": the faked burglary pics, the diagrams and plans Tam had been sent, and a letter explaining as much as they could. They held on to the tapes, Spammy stashing them – with the original shots and diagrams – under a floorboard in the flat, on the grounds that they didn't want to put all their eggs in one basket in case the lawyer screwed them or anything happened to the envelope. Paul had to point out to Spammy that – even though under the loose board in the airing cupboard *was* a good hiding place – he might want to remove his hash from it after depositing the tapes, because if it came to that, it might be the polis who were under instruction to retrieve them.

On the Friday before the job, Paul had come back to the flat to find Spammy watching a small cardboard box move erratically around the kitchen floor on its own, giggling to himself. This was it, Paul decided: Spammy's chronic drug-taking had altered his mind so much that he could now project his trips into someone else's consciousness. But weirder still, Spammy had to be tripping without gear, as he was off all but late-night whisky since becoming involved in the robbery plans.

Paul looked again, after briefly closing his eyes, wondering if maybe the pressure was getting to him. But the blue box was indeed moving, in short, speedy bursts, frequently changing direction as it glided back and forth across the grotty lino. Spammy was leaning back against the sink, wide-eyed, big dopey grin on his face visible between straggly strands of over-hanging hair. He wasn't holding any strings or anything, and no radio-control device either.

Paul knew he would regret it, but was nonetheless helpless to resist asking what in the name of arse was going on, when the blue object did a ninety-degree turn and caught a table-leg a glancing blow. The box turned over on to one side and a wee white mouse scampered away from it, through Paul's legs and out the kitchen door.

"Aw fuck, get it!" Spammy said with a laugh, and took off down the hall after the thing.

They cornered the mouse in the living room, cowering beside the small safe Spammy had mysteriously acquired, and coaxed it into an old budgie cage that had been gathering dust in a cupboard since Paul moved in. The safe was in that familiar state of mid-surgery, the cover having been wedged off the plastic keypad and the LED read-out. Wires led to a complicated junction arrangement, and thence to laptop that Paul suspected neither Arlene's employers nor Arlene knew had been borrowed from Pixagraph Limited. The MM had told Tam he would only give them the master over-ride code for the electronic safe on the Sunday, as it was changed regularly, so Spammy decided to have a crack at developing his own over-ride facility. "The less we're reliant on the MM, the less chances he's got to double-cross us."

The mouse, Spammy explained, was the fifth member of the team, and his name was Sparky. "Sparky will warn us of danger," he said, crumbling – of course – cheese through the bars of the budgie cage. "Sparky's got EFP."

"Extra-sensory perception?" Paul asked, thinking he had mis-heard.

"Somethin' like that, aye."

They were walking faster, and the pace was accelerating still. An urgency hauling against the restraint of caution.

Paul could feel it, they all must feel it. The strain of the tension, of quieting their fears and not screaming because it would give them away, of steadying frayed nerves to retain their discipline, while all the time they wanted to run. They wanted to run for the end, sprint for the finish line, throw it all into one last life-or-death effort, make or break, do or die. But there was no end, no finish line. Just the forest and the mountain, going on and on as the sun paled and slid and the light grew more selective in its castings.

No looks, no gestures. Just the strides, longer, quicker. And quicker.

Paul wondered how little it would take – what sound or half-glimpsed sight – to cause the snap and set them running blindly forward towards God knew what, driven mad by the unknowing.

The other reason for the buzz, the excitement, of course, was that he didn't really believe it was going to happen. A secure, anchoring thought. They weren't actually going to have to go through with it. It wouldn't get that far. Something would intervene. Someone would stop it.

They hadn't told his mum. Talked about it, plenty, but never told her. If they got away with it, if they came through it, then she never had to know anything. And if they didn't, well, it wasn't going to help her or them if she was worried sick before her worst fears were realised.

Tam wrote her a letter; so did Paul. Put it in the Craigurquhart envelope as they set off on the Sunday. Told her as much as they could, plus instructions.

Jesus, Sunday. That was when it became real, that was when the feeling of freedom from choice and responsibility turned into something else entirely, something poisonous within that no amount of gut-mangled puking could purge. Paul hadn't expected to sleep on Saturday night, but the sanctuary of unconsciousness had quickly tempted him in and traitorously brought the morning to him all the sooner.

He didn't think he could go through with it, sitting disconsolate and ill on the bathroom floor, spew trickling down the outside of the bowl, failing in his attempts not to cry. Terrified.

Why him?

But it was why Dad, too, and why Spammy, and why Bob. Threats, photographs, phone calls. He had no choice, and he owed it to the others to dry his eyes, blow his nose, and don the mask of the Brave Face Club.

He sat in the back seat of Bob's car beside Spammy, a tense silence between the four of them, the sounds of the engine and the tyres against the road emphasising the quiet. He hated Bob for driving them there, for not turning the car 180 degrees and heading back to Paisley, or all the way south and through the fucking Channel tunnel.

Tam turned his head round at one point, attracted by Spammy's back-seat fidgetings as he popped some morsel of food into the household-size matchbox he had put Sparky in.

"Christ, he never brought the fuckin' moose?" he asked Paul, having learnt not to ask questions of Spammy himself.

*

250

And then there were three, again, Paul thought, just him, his dad and Spammy. Moving swiftly and quietly through the undergrowth, keeping their heads down, chests thumping, wishing they could block out the fear, but knowing they had to listen to it for what it might tell them. Same as before. Even the same clothes, apart from the sweatshirt that policewoman had given him after they took his own bloodstained one away as evidence. It was what, Wednesday? He had been in the same underpants since Sunday, a thought that might have amused or horrified him in some other world where it mattered.

Just the three of them.

Bob had been the driver. He dropped them at the side of the road and they took off into the trees as he pulled away, before any traffic happened along. Speed wasn't the getaway vehicle's strong suit, but it did have the advantage of supporting an insanity plea in the event that they got caught. Nobody in their right mind would drive to or from a robbery in a 1978 Hillman Hunter.

Potential double-cross number one: security cameras still on and recording. They had looked at it logically. The MM did want them to get in – there was no point in going to all this bother only for them to get caught scurrying through the grounds because some security guard had clocked them on a monitor. However, the MM could potentially fix it so that no-one saw the monitors – allowing them to get inside and do the job – but that the action was still recorded, so they got the blame and he pocketed the loot. Who knew. It paid to be paranoid. They pulled on their ski-masks.

Masks help. No-one can recognise you, most importantly yourself.

"Ayah, this is jaggy," Spammy said, reminding them all for a nostalgic moment of the concept of humour.

Potential double-cross number two: electrified fence still operational. Again, defeated the purpose from the MM's point of view. But no-one particularly wanted to find out that despite having

251

genuine intentions, the MM had somehow failed to hit the switch. Tam pulled the long-handled wirecutters from a black polythene bin bag, eyeing the fence apprehensively. Spammy put a hand on his shoulder.

"Hang on, Mr McInnes," he said.

Tam rolled his eyes as Spammy produced his matchbox and upturned it. He cradled the mouse delicately in his hand, before suddenly tossing it against the fence. It bounced off the mesh, fell to the floor in a ball, stayed still for an unsure second, then scuttled away out of sight.

"Sparky says it's safe," Spammy declared triumphantly. "EFP."

"E*F*P?" asked Paul.

"Aye. Electric-Fence-ory Perception."

Tam cut quickly through the wires, pulling open a flap for them to crawl through. They were in the compound, on the west side near the back of the house.

While out at the front, unseen, unheard, the limo was still waiting, engine idling, watches being glanced at again.

Paul was the agile one. He was supposed to climb up to the window on the first floor, by scaling a drainpipe a few yards along to a ledge that ran above it. From there he was to edge back and dreep down. But there was no need. Maybe the MM, maybe just luck. There was a paint-spattered wooden ladder lying sideways against the wall of the stables, just across the gravel and loose-chip behind the house. He gripped it to pick it up, pulling his hand sharply back as a splinter pierced his index finger, which served to remind him he hadn't put on his gloves.

He'd have to move the thing first, though. No point in wearing them if the skelfs cut them to shreds. Paul took more careful hold of the ladder this time and lifted it across the gravel, manoeuvring it to rest its top against the ledge of the Master Bedroom's window. Then he climbed up the rungs and pulled on his latex-smelling surgical gloves, peering into the darkness beyond the glass.

He took Bob's home-made gizmo from his back pocket, a pair of compasses with a rubber sucker at the end of one leg and a stiff,

252

sharp blade at the end of the other. Of course, it had to be bloody double-glazed. He was reminded of the end of his short career as a DG sales rep, when he had explained to some biddy in Renfrew about the vacuum between the panes. She asked him what happened if one pane broke. "Well it's like on an aeroplane," he told her. "You and your family get sucked out the living room . . ."

He stuck the sucker to the glass and cut a saucer-sized hole just below the top of the lower pane of the window, then pulled the gizmo back, removing a disc of glass. He squeezed the sucker to make it give up its grip, placing the disc carefully on the ledge by his feet. Then he repeated the operation on the inner pane, before reaching in delicately and disengaging the window-lock.

He held his breath. Potential double-cross number three: burglar alarm systems still on. Ach, fuck it. Sentence for getting caught breaking in must be less than for getting caught making off with the big bag marked "SWAG". He slid the window up smoothly and quietly, and was greeted by a welcoming absence of flashing lights and electric bells. He signalled to the others to follow.

The silence was desolate. Callous. The world turning its back, looking away. Abandonment. No birds, no creatures, no animals, no people, no witnesses. Just them and . . . whoever. Not the hunted and the hunters, more the condemned and the executioners.

The tread of their feet, the rubbing of their clothes against their skin, it all got louder and louder. Their breathing was becoming the crashing of waves, the roar of a crowd. The forest had ceased to absorb their sounds, the channels between the trees seeming to open up and carry the noises to alert, predatory ears.

Shadows lengthening still.

Light, time, *something*, running out.

Paul stood at the back (or was it the front?) of the room, furthest spot from the windows anyway, before the double doors, watching

Spammy in the half-light crouching on the other side of the four-poster. The safe was built into the hardwood base that ran from below the mattress to the floor, the hinged panel that hid it disguised as a drawer like the big one next to it. Spammy had thrown the valance back over the bedclothes and was working concentratedly and quickly. Paul should have had a camera.

Urgent looks had been exchanged when the MM's over-ride code drew a blank. The denial, the thumb-sucking thought that the whole job was never going to happen, had been replaced by the unfounded faith that Everything Was Going To Be All Right. They had anticipated being double-crossed, expected to be deceived, but clearly, inside, they all still wanted to believe that they wouldn't be. And so far it had been smooth. But when the code didn't deliver, another hope died. A little bit more of their fear became a reality they were having to deal with.

The MM *was* fucking them over.

Because they were never supposed to open the safe. Because the MM wasn't interested in the safe. Because the safe was only there, was only mentioned, to make them believe in it all, to make them believe in the job. Because the safe was *the double-cross.*

Spammy's fingers worked the laptop frantically. He held two of them up and crossed them, then hit the return key with his other hand. No-one breathed. It had worked on the wee safe in the flat, a simple programme that convinced the electronic lock that four-digit codes were being keyed into it. All of them. From 0000 to 9999, one after another, more than a thousand per second. The tricky part was getting the safe to understand the laptop. The worrying part was that it might have a security contingent that set a time-lock after a limited number of wrong attempts. Spammy hadn't been able to come up with anything that could circumvent that; if he had, he explained, no cashcard in the world would be secure.

There was a sudden, high-pitched whine and a metallic whirr from the safe, before its steel door was swung open by its own weight. Paul was about to step forward, to come around the bed and see finally what this was all about. Then he heard the noise, and discovered *exactly* what it was all about.

A scraping at the door behind him, fingernails, then the thump of knuckles. A gasp, a choked, gurgling splutter. Paul turned around, twisted one of the handles on the double doors, pulling it open, the moonlight through the big open window spilling into the ante-room, with its chairs, its coat-rack, and its secret.

Its punchline, to the sickest joke in the world.

Snap.

Without, within.

Maybe they *all* thought it was a gunshot. Maybe they were running before they looked, before they saw. The order the information arrived in was lost in their heads.

Off to the right, up the slope, they saw him. The figure, in camouflage gear, holding up two halves of the stick he had just broken, waving at them and staring.

Desperate, careering panic, all thoughts jettisoned but the need to run. Paul saw the man begin to run too, and lost his own footing beneath him as his body's momentum pulled him further around the next tree than his feet were ready for. He rattled his knees off the exposed roots, scrambling on all fours for a few yards until he could right himself again, his dad and Spammy charging blindly ahead of him.

No more caution, no more thought, no more options. Just flight. Each footfall the last before the bullet. Just running. No target, no destination, no finish line, no sanctuary. Just . . .

Running running running running running run . . .

The woman's face was turned away. The man reached out to Paul, dying, the act of rapping the door having almost finished him. Paul held him in his arms, kneeling on the floor with the man's torso in his lap. The man gasped, unable to speak, a look of incomprehension, such lost incomprehension in his eyes, so full of tears. He reached out a hand towards Paul's head, pulling at the material of the ski-mask. He wanted to see a face, a last human face.

Paul pulled the mask off and let the man look into the mirror-image of bewildered fear, pain, horror and sorrow.

"Oh God, oh Jesus God," Tam said, looking down upon them. "Oh Jesus Christ."

Then a woman's voice outside. "Oh NO! OH NO!"

A hammering at the door. "Oh God, Mr Voss? Mr Voss? Oh no. HELP! SOMEBODY HELP ME!"

Tam pulled at Paul, urging him to let go. Paul couldn't.

"Come on, son, come on."

Tam handed Spammy the padded envelope, thrusting it into his hands, the useless, pointless thing they had found in the safe secreted inside. Tam didn't know why he went ahead and put it in there, in with the letters to Sadie. But somehow he needed to do it, needed to achieve what he had come there for, even in the face of what was happening. Maybe especially in the face of what was happening.

"Go, Cameron, son," he said. "Go."

Spammy glanced back at Paul before climbing out of the window.

"Come on, Paul. Come on," Tam said.

He held Paul's shoulders, helped him to his feet after Paul had gently laid the man's head on the floor.

"Come on, son."

Tam took Paul's hand, leading him to the window. Paul could only look back, into the man's dying eyes.

Tam climbed down the ladder, looking up to make sure Paul was following. The security guards were already charging towards him as his feet hit the gravel.

Bob pulled manfully at the steering wheel, struggling against the skid, but with the Hillman in fourth going round that corner, he got no cooperation from the accelerator and the car veered across into the (thankfully empty) on-coming lane, slamming side-on into a pair of telephone boxes outside a Spar mini-market.

Spammy had come crashing out from the hedges, his eyes wide, nostrils flaring, possessed by an energy Bob had never seen in him before, and Bob had guessed immediately that it wasn't a good sign. Spammy had climbed into the passenger seat and just babbled – more words, spilling out of him like an upturned skip, than Bob had heard him utter cumulatively before.

"Just drive, just drive, got to drive," he said, before Bob discovered what had taken place, picking up the facts amid the jumble, like the black box recorder amid the debris.

Spammy had insisted manically that they head into the village of Craigurquhart rather than away from it. Bob had protested until Spammy pulled up his sweatshirt to reveal the envelope tucked into his jeans.

"They'll catch us anyway," Spammy said.

The Hillman had been tearing down the village's main street when Bob saw the flashing lights coming towards them, about three or four hundred yards away. He reacted before he was aware of what he was doing, jumping momentarily on the brakes and hauling at the steering wheel to take the car around into an adjoining road.

Spammy released his seatbelt and opened the door, clambering out of the ancient vehicle.

"Just drive, Bob. Just go."

Bob understood.

Spammy took off on foot across the road and up a lane between two buildings as Bob managed to coax enough enthusiasm from the Hillman to pull it away from the shattered phone boxes and head on up the street. The police car rounded the corner, swaying slightly as it righted itself after the sharp turn, and accelerated.

A second police car appeared further up the sloping road that headed past a trickle of small shops – knitted jumpers and tartan dolls in plastic tubes – to a row of cottages and then out of town. The big Senator slewed itself across Bob's path, causing him to swerve up on to the pavement. He put the Hillman into reverse, with thoughts of some swift doubling-back manoeuvre, but the

257

engine cut out with a scornful splutter, as if to say "in your dreams".

Spammy edged out from the lane, peering up and down the street that ran parallel to the one he had left Bob on, looking with frantic hope. There had to be one somewhere. He dashed across the road, spotting another connecting lane, but it turned out to be a dead end.

He had to do this, he knew. Not simply for Paul's mum, or for Paul or for Tam. For all of them. It had to be worth something, even if they didn't know how. They were never supposed to get into that safe, but even if the MM never had designs on what was inside it himself, well . . . Well, whatever the fuck it was, it wouldn't have been in the safe if it wasn't valuable. Somehow.

He edged towards the corner, at the junction with the main drag, and saw it, through the side and front windows of a darkened, closed bakery. It was up a street on the other side of the road, about ten yards along. He took a deep breath and charged, spotting from the corner of his vision the police car sitting further up the main street, men climbing out of it and breaking into a run as they saw him. He didn't pull it out until he was out of their sight, as he couldn't afford for them to see.

He folded the envelope in half and gripped it tightly, then rammed it into the open mouth of the postbox as he passed, and kept on running. He heard them round the corner behind him, several feet in an applauding clatter of heavy soles on the pavement. He knew he had nowhere to go, no way of evading them, no hope of outrunning them, but some instinct wouldn't let him stop.

Legs aching, lungs bursting, throat rasping, hopes abandoned, just running, still running . . .

Still running, pursuit behind, panting, footfalls, still running. Driven by instinct, nothing else left. Still running. Until the figure loomed ahead, standing on the protruding root of a vast, ancient pine, the figure they had been swept towards, guided towards.

Smiling, pointing a gun.

And they saw, and they understood. Understood the truth, the sickening truth. Understood Spammy was right. Understood why Bob ran, despite his fucked leg, despite being there to give himself up. They saw it all in the face of the man before them.

The Wee Shite.

TEN

Careful what you wish for 2.2.

Nicole lay on Parlabane and Sarah's sofa, resting her unshod feet on a cushion and leaning back against one arm. She glanced out of the window, where the late afternoon sunshine seemed tauntingly inappropriate. "Where were you last week when I was bored but comparatively carefree in Glasgow," she wanted to ask it. "Don't you know, I don't *do* Glasgow," she imagined it replying, "you ignorant English bitch."

Parlabane had come back in from his travels, and she was aware of him and Sarah out in the hall, hearing indistinct whispers, the brushing together of clothes, the soft sound of a kiss. She reckoned she might have found them an irritatingly tactile couple had the circumstances not made her cry out for signs of humanity and affection in a world gone very recently, very suddenly and very frighteningly insane.

She had felt a short second of relief when she saw Sarah's jackets on the coathooks last night, and a photograph of her and Parlabane on the wall (in which they wore, rather curiously, matching Elastoplasts on their cheeks). It had struck her – amidst

260

the cacophony of panic and confusion inside her head – that she was walking into a close with a complete stranger, and no-one knew she was there. Parlabane saw the look of apprehension in her eyes as he reached for his keys outside the door of the flat, read the scenes of kidnapping, sexual ordeal and murder that were playing behind them, and sighed impatiently. He gave her a stare that said "you know, we really can't afford this", before adding vocally, "Look, you're going to have to start trusting me a bit more. I know it's not easy, but well, tell you what: try thinking up some helpful images, I don't know, maybe charred flesh, mangled wreckage, car exploding in a plume of flames, that kinna thing. I'm not the bad guy, Nicole."

She didn't know the woman's name, hadn't heard him mention her, but there was evidence that she lived here, and it somehow calmed Nicole to see Parlabane rendered more normal, that he had a life outside of car booby-traps, hired assassins and murderous conspiracies. The feeling only lasted until she realised that those two worlds weren't separate, and that she was standing at the proverbial crossroads where they met.

1.1 summarised: "I want to help real people with real problems."
Enter Mrs McGrotty and Mr McCandlish.
2.2: "I'm bored. When does it get more exciting?"
Enter Jack Parlabane.

What a picture the three of them would have made, sitting around the flat that afternoon, matching luggage under the eyes, tired but restless. Nicole felt exhausted but too edgy to contemplate sleep; who needs caffeine when They are out to get you. Parlabane retained an energy about himself, a drive that animated a knackered-looking face and body; like a cross between a marionette and a zombie. Sarah had been up all night trying to figure out what was obstructing the breathing of a 25-year-old RTA victim (Harley Davidson meets Eddie Stobart), before his aorta ruptured and he exsanguinated spectacularly, mouth pouring blood like a burst fire hydrant, and died shortly before six a.m. In between worrying about him she would have been worrying about Parlabane, so altogether she didn't look entirely peachy either.

Nobody was treating Nicole like a victim, which was not only good for her self-respect but made it feel less like there was nothing she could do. In fact, both Parlabane and Sarah (perhaps rather worryingly) gave the impression of having had sufficient experience of this kind of thing as to give the air of experts who would not work with amateurs. She had got the impression the night before that Parlabane couldn't afford to carry passengers, but had felt then that he only expected her to pull her weight and do as she was told. Sarah let her know that her contribution would have to be greater.

It was while Parlabane was out, during that awkward time when they were first alone in the flat without him, urgent circumstance having truncated introductions to the most cursory of details. She had been trying to press Sarah for information on what sort of person Parlabane really was, without sounding too much like she was saying: "What, you actually *live* with this maniac? Are you out of your fucking mind?"

"He thinks you're very sharp, very perceptive," Sarah had told her, in that surprisingly (and right then comfortingly) English accent. "He was singing your praises after your TV performance. I know you must be feeling like the little girl that's lost in the department store right now, being led around by the hand, but believe me, if Jack didn't think you had something he could use, he wouldn't have brought you here. He'd have dumped you with some babysitter – Jenny, probably – and picked you up again when the coast was clear."

"Who's Jenny?"

"Oh, I'm sure you'll probably find out. But believe me, Nicole, when he comes back you'd better be wide awake."

Nicole felt momentarily distanced from herself as Parlabane spelled out what he had done and what he had discovered, suddenly catching a glimpse of where she was, what she was doing, what she was part of. Part of – not on the fringes, not spectating, not along for the ride. In on it. Working to crack a conspiracy of unknowable proportions, staying frosty to evade the assassins, discussing options and scenarios, her opinions sought and considered. Despite the fear, the fatigue and the disorientation, it was an image of herself she wished she could frame. If only they could see me now.

If only who? Her father? No. With the best will in the world, he'd still only be able to see his little girl in danger, and the thought of his concerned face brought the little girl within that bit closer to the surface, training the fear upon where she was most sensitive to it. She blocked his image from her mind.

Rob.

Yes. If fucking *Rob* could see her now. Rob who saw her as a different little girl, a little girl with cute little tits who he liked to screw, and a little girl whose triviality got on his nerves after he came. Rob of the standard-issue scrawny goatee and ever-present pack of "Marley Lights" sticking out of his shirt pocket, that triangle on the lid like the attention-seeking pride badge of a love that can't help but speak its name: narcisexuality. Rob of a thousand lefty causes, each one more earnest than the last, providing moral reasons to disapprove of just about every nation, state, organisation and individual on Earth. Rob the sensitive feminist, who used his disgusted-deconstruction-of-aggressive-male-sexuality routine to get women into bed. And Rob, whose habit of saying "come to Papa" as he rolled on a condom and she took her knickers off, might keep psychoanalysts busy for a very long time.

Parlabane wasn't really expecting Michael Swan to appear on national television and admit that he had murdered Roland Voss. Mind you, he hadn't been expecting a dead man to appear on television a few nights before and tell him that there was a massive cover-up going on, either. But while each revelation came in a form that was understood by Parlabane alone, the difference was that Swan didn't know he was telling him.

"So can't you find out who was up at Craigurquhart, who these MI5 guys were?" Nicole asked, with a restless impatience Parlabane would only tolerate in someone whose life was under threat.

"Not today I can't," he stated, leaning back in his chair, Sarah sitting on the arm of it, absently stroking his hand. The six o' clock TV news was burbling quietly in the background, the volume down since the latest Voss manhunt item ended, but the VCR still whirring, Parlabane now obsessively recording every broadcast on the matter. "I've learned in this line of work that you have to be careful who you're asking questions about, and who knows you're asking. And on this case, I think we only have to look to the late Messrs Lafferty, Campbell and now Hannah to appreciate that discretion is definitely the better part of valour."

"So what are you going to do?"

"Right now? Lock all the doors and windows and sit tight until *The Saltire* comes out. By which time I expect to be sound asleep. Tomorrow, things will look a lot different. I know it doesn't help these poor sods on the run, but there's nothing we can do until that paper hits the streets, and we certainly can't do them any good if we're dead. *The Saltire*'s running the booby-trap story plus pictures, which should buy you a little insurance. It's also running the floorplan and my contention that the Voss Four couldn't have done it."

"This is running under the false byline, right?" Sarah said, concern on her face.

"Yeah, the usual," Parlabane confirmed. "John Lapsley. Anyway, once all this stuff's public, we can stand back and watch where everybody jumps. *Then* we can start asking who else was on that grassy knoll and other such awkward questions. Because then *everyone* is going to be demanding to know what really went on up there."

A silence fell among them, the absence of their voices letting the sounds from the TV fill the gap, their re-awareness of it in the corner once more drawing their eyes. Michael Swan was standing at a lectern in a low-ceilinged room, temporary lightstands visible on one side of the small stage, which was partitioned off by pale blue hoardings. Michael was talking but it was not his words that provided the soundtrack; whatever his speech had said, it was being summarised for the viewer by Roger Oakham, the Conservative Central Office press officer who had long been masquerading as the BBC's political correspondent.

"Bring back John Cole," Sarah muttered.

"Hondootedly," agreed Parlabane.

Then Michael's voice did break in, the snippet that had been selected for direct consumption.

"We will not let Europe impose its so-called standards on Britain, when by 'standards' it means dragging us down to its level," he said, all bad suit and rehearsed histrionics. "We will not let filth flood into this Christian country, filth that will corrupt young minds, filth that will degrade women . . . and filth that will cause sexual violence figures to soaaar."

Very onomatopoeic, Parlabane thought.

"For let anyone who doubts the power of this filth listen to these words: 'We are your sons, and we are your husbands, and we grew up in normal families. I had a wonderful Christian home. But pornography can reach out and snatch a child from any house today.' These are not the words of a moralist, or a campaigner. These were the words of Ted Bundy, the American serial murderer, who confessed that pornography drove him to kill and to kill and to kill and to kill. And this same pornography is what Brussels wants to bring into *our homes*. *British* homes."

"Jesus, not this shite again," moaned Parlabane. If the Voss story was this week's orchestra, Swan and his crusade had been the kazoo player in the background, more irritation than distraction, and Parlabane had been a wee bit too busy to pay attention to it. It had started on Monday with a few radio soundbites, fairly off-the-cuff, but now Swan had obviously progressed to the full-on press conference, doubtless including glossy info-packs for the assembled hacks, and probably a homepage on the fucking Internet: http://www.tory.wanker.co.uk.

"Quoting Ted Bundy," Parlabane said, shaking his head. "He'd sound more credible quoting *Al* Bundy. 'Hey, Peg,'" he mimicked, "'vote Conservative.'"

The Bundy shite was familiar to Parlabane from his LA days, when he had heard it trooped out regularly by Republican equivalents of Swan to support a worryingly fundamentalist "family" agenda. Christian Reactionaries Against Pornography. Bundy was a serial sex killer sentenced to death in the US, who was approached by the pro-censorship Meese Commission and told that if he linked porn to his crimes, they might be able to get the sentence commuted to life. So despite never having blamed it before, and despite the police finding none on him, Bundy suddenly decided Porn made me do it. (Cf: God made me do it; see also: A big boy done it and ran away.)

What Bundy didn't tell the Meese Commision was that from the age of three he was raised by his grandfather, an exceptionally violent man who regularly beat up his family and tortured animals. Neither did he mention that his own mother was a wee bit concerned at occasionally finding this normal wee boy stabbing his own bed with butcher's knives. But hey, that kind of shit didn't work so well in a soundbite.

"So what's this about?" asked Sarah, whose routine of alternate working/sleeping often meant major news developments passed her by.

"It's the FILM Accord," said Parlabane. "All caps, but it's not an acronym. It's an EC body; they'd need a different name or acronym for each member-state's language, so instead they come up with something everyone understands and then cap it up so that it sounds important. They used to have MEDIA 92 and MEDIA 95, before the funding plug got pulled."

"So what's FILM?"

"Glorified policy and consultative committee. They sat down with the movie and TV industries to see what they could do to make Europe less of a maze in terms of rights, ownership, copy-right, legislation etcetera. They came up with the FILM Accord. Everyone's ratified it except us, surprise, surprise."

"And what does it actually do?" asked Nicole, who like most other people in the UK had only heard about it since the start of the week, and then only in relation to Michael Swan and "filth".

"Well, lots of itty-bitty boring things to do with 'satellite foot-prints' and 'domestic production quotas', and some bigger things, like a new, EC-wide co-production treaty, which does away with the old treaties' pain-in-the-arse obligations to employ a certain amount of cast and crew from each participating country, which resulted in what you call Euro-puddings – dreadful movies full of B-list actors from three different countries with tortuous plot devices to explain away the clash of accents."

"Cut to the chase, Jack," said Sarah.

"Okay. The FILM Accord would also standardise film and video censorship across the EC. That's the big one, controversy-wise. At the moment, the distributors have to submit *every* movie to *every* country's censors, then have to re-edit to that censor's standards to get a certificate, because what gets the equivalent of an 18 in France might still need further trimming for the UK or Belgium or wherever. So it wastes a lot of time and costs an unnecessary fortune; apart from re-cut costs, censors themselves charge by the second. And obviously in some countries – some extremely sad and repressed countries not a million miles away from where we sit – there are things you can't show at all. So par-ticularly at the 18-certificate end of the spectrum, you can end up with oodles of different cuts of a film floating around. And to do all that re-editing and resubmitting, obviously you're spending time and cash that might better be used to make more films and therefore more jobs for actors and technicians.

"The FILM Accord would mean that what's allowed in one country is allowed in all. So the distributor just submits the one cut of a film across the EC, and each country can say 'we give that an 18', or 'we give that a 15', but they can't say 'we're banning this' or 'we won't classify it unless you remove such-and-such'. Each nation retains the right to *classify* a film as they see fit, but what they can't do is cut bits out. So in this country, the name British Board of Film Classification would no longer be an Orwellian euphemism. It would cease to censor."

"But the bottom line is that hard-core porn would be legal in the UK?" said Nicole.

"The legalisation of images explicitly depicting sex between consenting adults would be a by-product of the legislation, yes," he said with a wryly false importance. "And that's something Mr Swan appears to have 'just noticed', even though his government – indeed his department – was represented on the FILM committee that drafted the proposals."

"What are you getting at?" asked Nicole, aware of Parlabane's arch look.

"I mean I wouldn't be surprised if it was his fucking idea in the first place. Or if not, that he was aware of this ramification early enough to have done something about it before now."

"And why would he do that, why would he wait?"

"Because this is the Tories' last roll of the dice. This is where he raises the banner one last time and hopes the troops stop fighting amongst themselves long enough to rally round before the election. All this Euro-rebel and Euro-sceptic nonsense . . . The reason it did so much damage wasn't just because it caused rifts in the party, but because it confused and thus bored the arse off the voters. Your Tory-voting *Sun*-reader doesn't have a bloody scoob about whether he's in favour of monetary union or a single European currency; probably thinks the ECU's that blue and yellow thing Rod Hull used to cart around. The only issue the Tories were able to get them remotely interested in was whether Lizzie's head would still appear on the notes and coins. So it doesn't do any good to pose around objecting to Brussels if the average voter doesn't understand what you're objecting to."

"Well," said Nicole, "it strikes me that what most of them were really objecting to was the idea of Johnny Foreigner telling

Blighty how to steer its own ship. 'Bloody cheek, don't they know we used to run this planet' and so on."

"Yeah, but they couldn't actually come out and say that. But *now*, now Michael's giving the punters something they can really get their teeth into. Jesus, forget cows. That was obviously desperation, any excuse, no matter how embarrassingly ridiculous – I mean *cows* for Christ's sake – to unite us glorious Brits against a common foe. Mooo! And it was an own-goal of Terry Butcher proportions, because even the fucking tabloid-readers knew the whole farce was Britain's fault. But this? This is manna from heaven. Dirty foreigners trying to force filth into decent, British, Christian homes. This way he's calling in the xenophobic vote, the moral-majority vote and the religious vote. Thus giving the disillusioned Tories out in the shires a common enemy to struggle against, a real cause to fight for."

Sarah was shaking her head. "Sneaky bastard."

"He's also giving himself the role of champion," continued Parlabane, "plus a stoater of an aunt sally to be seen battering."

The term rang a bell for Nicole, her dad talking about his own disillusionment with the current state of the party. An aunt sally: a dummy to throw things at, so that you can vent spleen and act the hard case without actually taking on a real opponent who can hit back. Her father had been muttering about Michael Howard.

"All this talk of longer sentences and harsher regimes," he had said. "The man knows perfectly well it's unlikely to change anything. Probably knows it'll never be implemented, either – too bloody expensive. But he gets to look like a man of purpose, gets to do some *tough talking*, and I'm sure it does impress certain people. But that's what's depressing me about the way the party's going, Pepper. We used to be about *ideas*, not waving big sticks. We used to go after the ABC vote. Now it seems we're relying on the LCD vote."

Single mothers. Asylum seekers. Aunt sallies all. Punch-bags to bash, a threat to exaggerate, with the correct sexual, moral and

269

ethnic make-up to fit the demonology that would elicit maximum response in the Tory heartlands.

But pornography, thought Nicole, *hard-core* pornography, well that was one threat that wasn't exaggerated.

"It's not exactly an aunt sally, though, is it?" she said.

Parlabane gave her the sort of grin that would scare psychiatrists.

"I understand your reservations, Nicole, but believe me, it's the biggest one there is. It's the queen of aunt sallies. It's a cheap politician's wet dream. Christ, these days, nobody in government wants to suggest or implement a policy that won't deliver a return before the next election – or even before the next opinion poll. But this? It's video nasties all over again. Not just something you can blame, but something you can *ban*. So that you can show the electorate that you're Getting Something Done. Thatcher's lot did it back in '83, to distract attention from the fact that crime was going through the roof and there was rioting on the streets. They brought in the Video Recordings Act, which blamed it all on a few cheesy B-movies and banned, among other things, hard porn.

"Then in '92, after the Jamie Bulger killing, you had another uproar. David Alton, for whom the irony of being nominally a 'Liberal' never quite chimed in, sniffing for votes by Getting Something Done, demanding that video censors be given powers that they . . . er, already had, since the Video Recordings Act in 1984."

"But this isn't *Child's Play 3* or *Reservoir Dogs*, Jack, this is hard porn," Nicole protested.

"Wooooh! It's the bogeyman, isn't it. All dark and scary. At least that's what Mikey-boy's relying on. But think about it, Nicole. Rape, sexual violence, misogyny, these things have been around since we came down from the trees. Pornography happens along at the arse-end of the twentieth century and it's suddenly the cause of it all? What, does it work retroactively? Do wank-mags travel through time? Perhaps Stephen Hawking could investigate."

270

Nicole felt unsteady. The feeling of erosion of a trusted foundation was unpleasantly reminiscent of certain discussions with Rob, but the difference was that Parlabane wasn't trying to replace it with anything. In fact, it felt less like he was eroding the rock she stood on than that he was revealing it to be a hologram. Either way, though, it wasn't comfortable. She needed to balance herself.

"But you've still got to admit," she said, "we're talking about some material that is highly offensive to women."

"No," he insisted. "We're talking about material that some women find highly offensive. There's a difference. But bollocks to all this liberal introspective navel-gazing. You want to retire to a quiet room with a VCR and a box of hankies, fine with me. I'll even recommend an optician. That's not your scene, cool with me too. The moral debate is not relevant here. What we've got to concentrate on is Swan's con-trick, because it's one of the best there is."

"And what's that?"

"It's simple. Right," Parlabane now sat forward in his chair, eyes shining through their bloodshot tiredness. He was clearly impressed with Swan's cleverness, and therefore more impressed with his own for sussing it. "When asked whether sexually explicit material should be legal in the UK, most people say yes it should. Ask the same people if hard-core pornography should be legal, and they all say no. So you ask them to define pornography, and they say: sexual material that is perverse, depraved, corrupting, Offensive To Women, yakka yakka yakka. Who the fuck's going to say yes, let's legalise *that*? Nobody. But it's completely meaningless. There's no imperial scale of depravity, no universal standard of what is Offensive To Women or to men for that matter. It's entirely subjective. And this is Swan's coup. That's why pornography, like it or loathe it, is the greatest aunt sally in politics. Back Swan, vote against porn, and you're voting against whatever you individually disapprove of, your own personal sexual demon. Nobody knows what they're really objecting to, because nobody's ever going to *see* what this material is that they're banning. But in the voters' minds it's whatever they don't like. This fine upstanding man is fighting *for them*, against whatever they don't like."

"The LCD vote," said Nicole quietly, mainly to herself. "So they don't just rally to the Tory banner, they rally to a man and a party who are once more saying exactly what they want to hear. Or think they want to hear."

"Yes," said Parlabane, laughing. "And never mind uniting the Tories, it'll wreak havoc on the Left. Labour won't know where to stand, with Clare Short and her sisters on one side, and the anti-censorship, civil liberties lobby on the other. And while they're dithering, Swan is hoping all those dischuffed voters who were pondering whether it might be time for a change will come flooding back, because only the Tories are going to Get Tough on Porn."

Nicole rolled her eyes. "The *Guardian* leader-writers won't have a clue *what* to say," she said. "I suppose it's a liberal-lefty nightmare. When does censorship become PC."

"Yeah, but the right-wing press will be a bit more resolute," Parlabane mused. "*The Sun* will of course condemn this filth in the strongest possible language, next to Kurvy Kathy and an advert for an 'adult products' catalogue. While the why-oh-why lot on the *Daily Mail* might actually die from their collective apoplexy. At least, let's fucking hope so."

"I thought they were all dead already," offered Sarah.

"Of course, the Voss papers will be interesting," he added with cheerful malice. "It's always fun to watch them tiptoe round the subject. Their silence is usually deafening."

"Why?" asked Nicole.

"Well, because . . ." Parlabane's eyes seemed to glaze over. He seemed to be staring, unfocused for a moment, like his surroundings had disappeared and he was alone somewhere. He looked back at Nicole, as if she had suddenly appeared in the room, or he had.

"Because what his papers were always conspicuously reticent

about was that Roland Voss was one of the biggest publishers and distributors of hard-core pornography in Europe," he said, voice barely above a whisper. "It's hardly common knowledge in this country, but it's true. That's how he made his money back in Holland in the Seventies, with wank-magazines. It was his first publishing interest. He got into newspapers once he had the cash, but the jazz-mags were what really stoked the fire, and what bailed out a few of the fuck-ups he made at first, too. When home video came along in the early Eighties, he was well placed to move into that. And nobody would have been better placed to expand into the UK if the FILM Accord legalised hard-core over here.

"Jesus Christ," he said, eyes wide in realisation. "Ladies and gentlemen, I think we have a motive."

"Swan?" gaped Sarah.

"Voss *owned* Swan," he said. "Christ, he owned half the government, but Swan was one of those closest to him. Swan always got big licks in the Voss papers, otherwise the wee nonentity would still be on the back-benches, throwing paper aeroplanes. It's all very cosy. Then the FILM Accord comes along, and Swan is Heritage Secretary. Voss sees the Accord as yet another licence to print tenners. The soft-core market in this country is astronomical, and Voss has never made a move on it, ostensibly because his hypocritical *British* image is to disapprove, but really because Raymond and Sullivan have it already sliced up between them. However, he knew fine that the punters really want a bit more than striptease. I'm sure he was aware that the competition would also be quickly ready to deliver a harder product. But Voss had fucking *warehouses* of the stuff, ready to roll. He'd have the jump on them; he'd be in first. And so what if it's in Dutch or German, nobody's buying it for the dialogue."

"So he could have leaned on Swan to ratify the Accord?" said Nicole. "Swan being his man at the heritage ministry. But it would be political suicide, wouldn't it? To be the man who legalised – or failed to stop – hard-core pornography. It would be a vote-loser of unprecedented effect. Never mind his cabinet career, there wouldn't be a constituency party in the country that would re-select him. How could Voss force him to go through with something like that?"

"Voss made him," said Parlabane. "Who knows what juice he might have on Swan, what control he could exercise. But there's a huge conflict of interest. Voss stands to make yet another fortune if Swan does as he's told, but to do that, Swan wouldn't just be giving up what he's already got, but what is so close to his grasp. By opposing the Accord that would further enrich Voss, Swan's got the chance to be the man who turns the tide back in his party's favour. To be the hero of the hour and the new darling of the Right. And who knows, maybe even to be the one who leads them into an election, now that he's the one who made it winnable.

"It's an old, old story. Voss is Mephistopheles, Swan is Faust. He gives him his heart's desire and then asks for his political soul. Except there's a twist to the tale this time that Goethe never anticipated: Faust murders Mephistopheles before he can collect."

"Is she okay?" Parlabane asked, lifting his head from the pillow as Sarah came back into the room and took off her T-shirt.

"Yeah, I just had a look," she said, pulling a thick handful of long, red hair out through the neck of the nightie she had slipped on. "She was asleep already. Must have gone out right away. I suppose she's less used to sleep deprivation than us junior doctors and paranoid hacks."

"Well, it's not every day you crack a major government conspiracy. I'm sure she was very tired."

Sarah climbed under the duvet and wrapped both arms and one leg around Parlabane, resting her head on his warm chest.

"Jack," she said quietly, "are you sure about this? This government thing, I mean. It's just that, well, I'd have thought if the government wanted someone out of the picture, they'd have just done it and no-one would ever hear about it. You know, that it would be less . . . I don't know, complicated."

274

"Are you kidding?" he said with a quiet whisper of a laugh. "Just because it's a total farce and they've left smoking guns lying everywhere, you think it wasn't the government? Come on, they've made a complete arse of absolutely everything else they've turned their hands to. The health service, education, transport – what makes you think assassination would be any different? In fact I'm feeling a bit stupid myself that, with all the mess, fuck-ups and general incompetence, I didn't recognise it as their MO earlier."

Sarah giggled. "Yes, I suppose the only thing they've ever been any good at is lining their own pockets."

"Hmm," he muttered. "I'd bet they're not even particularly efficient at that, either. It's just the only thing they've really been committed to, but that doesn't mean they're necessarily good at it. I mean, I bet the Germans would be much more organised and industrious at skimming the public till. The Japanese would manage it seven days a week, 24 hours a day on a shift system. And I'm sure Alex Salmond would insist that in an independent Scotland, the opportunities for governmental corruption and scamming would be far greater than as part of the Union. That's if he can find an irritatingly couthy Scots phrase to crowbar into his soundbite, of course . . ."

Sarah placed a hand over his mouth.

"Go to sleep, Jack," she whispered, and gave him a soft kiss.

Ken Frazer sat back in a chair and watched the slight, bespectacled figure of Angus Gilmore pour two large measures of Springbank 21-Year-Old from a bottle on his desk. Through the large windows of the editor's spacious office he could see across Princes Street Gardens to the Scott Monument and the empty shops on the other side, along to the Mound and the museums, little movement to catch the eye but taxis buzzing occasionally back or forth. They said it was the most delicious whisky in the world, but he knew it could as well be a shot of some cheap blend and it would still taste like nectar, because it was the moment that was so sweet.

The editor handed him his drink and raised his own.

"Fuck 'em all," Gilmore said with a grin, and they chimed their glasses together.

Ken looked at the proof on the desk in front of him, Jack Parlabane's shattering stories screaming out at the reader under *The Saltire*'s distinctive, page-wide banner. The crisp, sharp photograph of the remote-controlled booby-trap, and the colourful graphic showing the positions of the bodyguards and the hallway, with arrows emphatically denoting the distance to the staircase. Keith and Lump had really come through on that one.

Among the many grateful compliments Gilmore had paid him, he had perhaps most enjoyed being applauded for his judgment in retaining the sometimes problematic services of Jack Parlabane. This was because the plaudit was delivered in front of the assistant editor and acted as a pretty hefty slap in the face to the pompous prick, who had (as Gilmore knew) only recently clashed with Ken over precisely this subject. The assistant editor had been peering through the books and questioned the amounts of cash Ken sent Parlabane's way, by way of a retainer and in payment for individual stories.

"Jack Parlabane works for as long as it takes to get a story," Ken had stated. "Days, weeks or months. He frequently risks life, limb and the jail to find out what he's after, and he gets stories no-one else would find in a million fuckin' years. Do you think I should pay him wordage?" Ken had toyed with telling him to phone Jack about the matter, but it would have been very ugly and he didn't want complicity in such an atrocity on his conscience.

He glanced at the other front-page proof lying next to it, then at Gilmore, and smiled again. He'd had his reservations about the new man. He was a Scot by birth, apparently, but had worked most of his career in Canada, and Ken had thought he might be another glorified accountant brought in by the proprietors. But when he'd agreed to this, Ken knew he was a true newspaperman like himself. In fact, the bugger was as excited about it as he was.

Gilmore hadn't just agreed, he'd pulled out all the stops. Ensured maximum cooperation from the printing and distribution people, got in all the top men, regardless of what shifts they should have been on. This kind of chance didn't come along to a newspaper too often, and they couldn't afford to waste it. They couldn't let all the competition see it and re-hash it for their own later editions. Couldn't let them reproduce the sensational photo from *The Saltire*'s front page and cover the plagiarism with a tiny boxed paragraph from their pics editor about how great the shot was, legally claiming they were "appraising the photograph".

This was to be an exclusive, in the true, old-fashioned sense of the word. If you want to "read all about it", buy the fucking *Saltire*.

They had run a dummy front page, with a few tales promoted from page two below a wire lead about the Voss manhunt and the death of Robert Hannah. The dummy went to press on a limited print-run for the first edition, the one the competition would receive and quickly glance through to see what they had. The rest of the distribution staff had been briefed not to panic when their usual first-edition bundles didn't show. First edition, they were told, had effectively been cancelled.

The edition that arrived a wee bit later, the edition that they chucked into their vans, that rolled up to the Highlands and down to London overnight on trains, that sat in wrapped bundles on the doorsteps of newsagents waiting for dawn, and that would make the country choke on its Rice Krispies, led with something a bit more tasty.

The people of the UK would have to wait just that bit longer than usual for a look at *The Saltire*'s real front page, that was all, Ken thought with satisfaction, sipping his Springbank. It was just a wee delay. A delay that would earn them record-breaking sales. A delay that would boost the paper's reputation through the roof. A delay that would win them every journalism award going.

And a delay that would sign Jack Parlabane's death warrant.

*

Among those people of the UK not yet alerted to the exposition of the plot to murder Nicole Carrow were three men on a rooftop on East London Street, who coincidentally were there for precisely that purpose. Also among that number was their boss, who had given the green light for the operation and had therefore seen no reason to call it off.

Morgan signalled to his two companions as they pulled on their balaclavas: silence now. The entire op would be silent. No radios, no phones, no whispers. And no fuck-ups. He had briefed the other pair sternly, and they knew it wasn't just him who had to redeem himself. Knight had been ape-shit over the car thing, and they had *all* been keeping their fingers crossed that they'd get a second chance to put it right. Now that it had presented itself, they were on full concentration to make the most of it.

She had phoned her own flat, stupid bitch. She had one of those remote-controllable answering machines, and had rung up to listen to her messages – mummy, daddy, auntie, sister and office, all wondering where the blazes she had got to – staying on long enough for them to run a trace. Some pad in Edinburgh, a bloke named Parlabane.

Morgan had reluctantly called Knight. He knew Knight had said he didn't want to hear from him until the girl was dead, but he thought the big man might want a say over what they should do next. He did.

The girl was to be taken from the place alive, but anyone else who had the poor judgment to be there was to join the ranks of the mystery slain. They needed to find out what she knew and who she had spoken to, but not at the flat. She had vanished; no-one knew where she was – except this Parlabane bloke, and his missus if he had one – so no-one would know she had ever been there once the witnesses were eliminated. Knight didn't want any connection traceable between her and whoever happened to die in this place. And the girl's body was not to be found. She would just be someone who disappeared one night and was never seen – living or dead – again.

Morgan was point man. He abseiled down the short drop to the kitchen window of the top-floor flat, placing his feet on the sturdy wide stone of the ledge. He shone a small but powerful torch inside, below the bar where the top and bottom halves of the window met, and all around the frame. The guy was either very paranoid or had bought the place from someone very paranoid. The frame was wired; if he opened the window, the alarm would trip. Not that he could have got the window open anyway – not without a bit more noise than he could afford. There was a very solid-looking lock on the bar, a key-operated number, too, so he couldn't just cut a hand-hole and reach in. Where it broke down, though, was the window itself. Ancient but no doubt trendy and attractive stripped wood, old as the building, surrounded on the interior by pine panelling. Way too beautiful to haul out and replace with dull, clinical, functional and secure PVC double-glazing. And as for the glass! It was so old, warped and bevelled that the inside of the room looked like it had been painted by that mad Spanish cunt with the moustache.

He took a knife from a pouch on his trouser-leg and sliced quietly and easily around the crumbling putty of the bottom left-hand panel, then tipped the loose glass towards himself. He gripped it tightly in one gloved hand, then held it up for Harcourt to lift on to the roof.

And in they went.

He and Addison got the girl. She was asleep on the sofa in the living room. He had the gag in her mouth and the gun between her eyes almost before she could open them.

He was something of a connoisseur of terror. He knew how to recognise all breeds and variations of it in those wide pools, in the moments of surprise, of panic, of sudden realisation. The bewilderment, the horror, the anger, the astonishment. And in hers he could see they still had work to do. This wasn't the realisation of any wild nightmare; this was the realisation of a specific nightmare.

She knew why they were here.

279

He slugged her between the eyes with the handle of the gun, knocking her cold. Blood began trickling from the wound as Addison lifted her, his arms under her knees and shoulders. Addison nodded to indicate the bleed, and Morgan dabbed at her forehead with his sleeve as they moved stealthily back into the hall.

Harcourt was standing outside the bedroom, waiting for his signal. To Harcourt's surprise, Morgan didn't give it, instead beckoning him towards the living room. He pointed at the bedding on the sofa, Harcourt taking a look at it for a moment and then nodding. He was to put it away before he left, as even the cops might think it suggested someone else had been staying.

Morgan carefully unlocked the front door, slowly sliding back the bolts centimetre by centimetre, and turned the knob. He swung the door inwards slightly, and glanced at the brass nameplate: two names, one above the other. He held up two fingers to Harcourt, then mouthed the word "remember", and made a few short up-and-down motions with a closed fist.

Frenzied stabbing. That was Knight's order. Nothing too slick, nothing too professional. Nothing too painless, either, Morgan thought. Knight didn't much appreciate people sticking their oar in.

He gave Harcourt his signal as Addison carried the girl out into the close, watching him draw his long, serrated knife and grip the bedroom door with his other hand. Morgan backed out of the flat, glancing again at the brass plate as he pulled the front door to, now able to make out the actual names in the brighter light of the close.

PARLABANE
SLAUGHTER

He smiled to himself and walked swiftly down the stairs.

"All governments are lying cocksuckers."

– Bill Hicks

ELEVEN

Bowman looked at the four figures standing among the trees and fingered the handle of his automatic in its holster, just touching it for reassurance of where it was. The way Paterson wanted to do this made him uncomfortable. Three against two at close quarters was unnecessary risk, even if they were unarmed, and even if you'd done this shit a thousand times. Percentages. They were desperate men with absolutely nothing to lose; what would it matter if they went down lunging at their executioners if they were about to be shot anyway? The oldest one, McInnes Senior, he might be tired but he was a big man and he looked like it might take a few bullets to put him down, especially if he dived for you and you couldn't make the headshot. The kid had fear to the point of madness in his eyes; he was unstable enough to just lose it and precipitate something ahead of Paterson. And then there was the weirdo druggie; he wasn't going to be a threat, but the pessimistic side of Bowman thought that if it all went haywire, it would be just too ironic if the only one left standing was the one who looked least like he knew he was alive in the first place.

Actually, truth be told, it wasn't only how Paterson wanted to do it that made him uncomfortable; it was working with Paterson full stop. Bowman had suggested they scatter the three of them, split them up and take them out one at a time. The light was failing but that wouldn't matter as he figured they could finish it in fifteen minutes. Twenty max. One each then whoever catches up with number three first.

But that was the problem. Paterson wanted to do them all himself. Round them up, all in one place, bang bang bang, let loose a few rounds from the semis they took from the bus and place them in the corpses' hands, make it look like there had been a fire-fight. That way, Paterson explained, on the off-chance one of them did manage to run for it, they could shoot him in the back, as long as they added a few rounds to the face and body as well – in a five-way shoot-out, there's bullets everywhere.

It was true, Bowman had conceded. Plus there was the overall advantage of greater plausibility – taking out all of them in what would look like a last stand would elicit fewer questions than three more single bodies. But the logic of it was merely convenient. The real motive was that Paterson liked to kill Jocks and he didn't want to share. It wasn't that he had ever said it, just something you couldn't help but notice after a while. He liked to hear the accent, liked to know where they were from. Pretty strange considering the short-arsed little bastard was Scottish himself, but fuck knew what was behind it. They said serial killers tended to hunt inside their own ethnic groups; maybe there was an element of that. Or maybe it was some anthropological, hyper-macho, dominant male monkey trip, and the psychotic cunt thought that it made him master of his own race. Add all that to the obvious Napoleon complex and you had a well-volatile mix.

Problem was, it wasn't volatile enough for Paterson to be a liability, something Bowman regretted any time he had to work with him. A psychiatrist might get lost wading through the mess inside the little bastard's skull, but, however much it looked like he might, he never fucked up on the job. If he was a liability, Knight would have disappeared him ages ago, like that mental

Welsh fucker, Davis, a few years back. Almost blew the whole show down in Cornwall because he couldn't resist raping that girl before they torched the place. He vanished after that. Morgan said it had been contracted outside, but Bowman was pretty sure Knight had done it himself. Knight didn't tolerate screw-ups much, and he certainly didn't tolerate loose cannons on the staff.

If you fucked up because the job went sour, that was one thing. But if you fucked up because you were a flake, you got erased. Because flakes don't simply fuck up, flakes talk. Especially if they've got a grievance.

The penalty for just plain blowing it was simple and understood. If you could still put it right, then you moved heaven and earth. If you got caught, you were on your own. The suits wiped all trace of you, all connections. You took the heat and you kept your mouth shut. And Knight made it worth your while, in as much as you stayed alive. The same went if you wanted out. If you didn't fancy it any more, you said so right away and you didn't do one more job. You didn't wait for someone to notice that your heart wasn't in it or your mind was somewhere else. Knight might be pissed off to lose you, but he wanted one hundred per cent or nothing at all. You just handed in your notice and you fucked off, and you developed acute amnesia, which ensured that neither you nor your family got a late-night visit from Harcourt and his stainless-steel collection.

Knight's Little Helpers. It sounded so fucking stupid. But then the CIA equivalent was "wet boys", which made you sound like a bloody poof, so maybe they should be thankful for small mercies. Ex-army, ex-cops, sometimes ex-cons. The line-up had been the same for a while now, which had its good points and bad points. They all knew each other's strengths and abilities, knew who could handle what. But sometimes Bowman feared it could get a little cosy. Sometimes you needed fresh blood, a new face, someone you didn't know – someone you didn't yet trust – to keep everyone that bit sharper. Christ, you only had to look at what had happened in Glasgow to see the problems seeping in. He was trailing round the fucking hills and glens playing hide-and-seek with Paterson, while those stupid cunts down there had the easy end of it, yet they'd still managed to miss one of their targets.

Booby-trap malfunction, last he heard. Addison must have been at the fucking vodka again when he was putting the gadget together. They didn't see as much of Knight these days, mainly just talked on the phone, and that was probably a good thing too. He'd blow a gasket if he found out some of the things that had been going on in recent jobs. Bloody complacency, that's what it was. Addison and Morgan had often turned up looking too hung-over to walk properly, never mind work an op, and none of them was quite as fit as he used to be, except maybe Harcourt. A certain chauvinism made Bowman like to think it was the ex-cops who hadn't quite retained their discipline – or never had sufficient discipline to begin with – but Morgan was ex-army like himself, and the strain at Bowman's own belt reminded him he wasn't quite at fighting trim either.

Fuck, even Harcourt had only been off the sauce and shaping up because he was partnering Knight at Craigurquhart, and the thought of carving a world-famous billionaire had proven sufficiently intoxicating on its own. But if it hadn't been that Knight decided he needed a blademan, Harcourt wouldn't have bothered doing the first press-up. Bowman couldn't see why they didn't just shoot Voss and his missus, but Harcourt told him it was to do with apparent motive or some other bollocks. The wanker had been trying to come across like it was just another job to a pro like him, but Bowman could tell the guy's cock was like granite at the thought of it.

Killing a billionaire didn't make you any richer, he had wanted to tell him, except that it wasn't strictly true. They all stood to clean up on this job: fifty per man, but close to seventy K once all the exes were added on. The government stuff never paid like this. It was Knight's independent ops – "homers", as they jokingly called them – that really laid down a purse, and this was the biggest ever. The client was going to be shelling out close to half a mill, he reckoned, once everything was totalled up, and no wonder, as it was a hell of an ambitious show.

Maybe the money was making him nervous as much as Paterson. Suddenly there was a lot to lose. It wasn't the answer to his prayers or anything. Fuck, he wasn't exactly going to retire on it. But he was getting too old for this nonsense, and it was losing its appeal. They said you could never give it up, never go and do something ordinary, but with what he had already banked plus seventy K, he could at least *try* and do something else. Fucking hell. Short-timer's itch after all these years and all this experience. All right, he wasn't exactly quaking in his boots but he wasn't quite laid-back and whistling while he worked either.

As usual, only Knight knew who the client was. From some of the arrangements and some of the considerations, Bowman had felt fairly sure it was someone in government, someone high up, but with Knight going on about TV coverage and news deadlines, he was starting to think it might be bloody Trevor McDonald.

He had been glad when they noticed the fugitives pick up pace, heading faster and more deliberately in one direction instead of just moving about, trying to stay hidden. It was a good bet they had sussed they would be shot on sight like the first guy, and were making for somewhere with civvy witnesses. Even if they hadn't worked that out, they certainly looked like they were on their way to give themselves up; more concerned with getting somewhere than staying out of sight.

This meant he could end it at will, as he had orders not to let the fugitives be seen. He had still called it in to Knight, though. Technically, Bowman had the authority to kill them any time if he thought there was a risk of exposure, but as he had a bit of leeway on it, it was worth giving the boss his say.

Knight had been chatty, which meant he was feeling upbeat, mainly because Morgan had got a new location on the girl and matters were back under control. Knight said the client was delighted with their progress, especially in taking out the first one earlier today. It had "played" so well, as Knight put it, that the client requested the hunt continue overnight again, because the first kill had really whetted the public's appetite for the chase.

Knight had told the client he wasn't on (thank Christ). The boss had enlisted the cooperation of his big-noise mates in the cops and the army, but it was nonetheless too delicate to push, he said. These guys were happy to have their men wandering around and looking in the wrong places for a *while*, as long as they had Knight's assurance that his own agents had a bead on the fugitives at all times – and that these agents would disappear and leave them to divide up the credit for the collar when the show was over. They'd suspect there was some kind of political motive for the pantomime they were helping to stage, but they wouldn't ask questions; it wasn't the done thing. However, Knight had told the client the cops wouldn't go for a second night without a result because it questioned their competence, while the army needed their men back on exercises – running around a different mountain, blowing up large quantities of tax-payers' money in a glorified, large-scale game of tag. Ah, the nostalgia.

"Yeah, finish it," Knight had said. "I told the client that if he wants it to run on a bit longer, we can delay breaking the news that they're dead. But it would be bloody negligent to let these fuckers continue scurrying around in the woods. Take them out, clean and quick."

Bowman took his hand away from the gun, placed it back on his hip. Basic crowd control. If he had his weapon drawn, one of the targets might do something hysterical. But with him standing by, as it were, it defused the sense of critical urgency, created a deflated and less explosive air of, well, anti-climax. A bit of chat would be next. It relaxes them, for want of a better word. When they've not been shot straight away, they start to wonder what might be going on, and in that state of despair, the poor bastards are open to imagining any alternative scenario that carries a trace of hope. You don't need to spin them a line, just talk. Maybe ask a few questions. Names and stuff. Then while they're confused, wondering what's going to happen if you're *not* going to shoot them, you plug them quickly, bang bang bang.

Too sudden for panic, too fast for reaction.

Bowman looked across and saw Paterson flip down the safety.

Paul never knew violence could be so sudden, so unheralded, so *fast*, and yet on some other screen in his mind's eye, the scene played out in simultaneous slow motion.

Amidst the tortured seconds that were stretching because they would be his last, but which he didn't want anyway.

Lethal force, so shockingly brutal, so merciless, so remorseless, and strangely quieter than he had imagined.

Spammy, God help him. In that small clearing, surrounded by the unheedful trees, a few feet from the bump, the rise where the Wee Shite had been standing when they ran into the trap. Spammy. He was the one standing nearest to the gunmen. Christ, was it as arbitrary as that?

A moment suspended, a moment when Paul's faculties could not or would not make sense of the image. The image, the moment, when Spammy's knees seemed to buckle, just the start, the hint of the slightest bend in those familiar spindly legs; and when his shoulders began to fall backwards.

Then his elbows jerked sharply as his left foot flew up and forward with a ferocity that shattered the Wee Shite's wrist and sent the pistol spinning fifteen feet through the air. Before it landed Spammy had sidestepped and thrown his right arm into a solid, straight blow, power travelling from behind his shoulder to the outstretched tips of his long fingers as they connected with the throat of the Wee Shite's comrade and collapsed his windpipe. The man dropped as if hamstrung, clutching at his neck and making a strangled, rasping, guttural noise as his knees hit the dirt.

By that time Spammy had blocked a wild swing from the Wee Shite, sending his left instep crunching into his would-be assassin's groin, then bringing the outside of the same foot down on to the

Wee Shite's straight-locked right knee, which twisted to an angle evolution had unfortunately not anticipated. As he fell, Spammy pirouetted and caught him on the temple with a bone-jarring kick, his foot describing a long, swift arc, and the Wee Shite's head snapped back, seeming to drag his torso round with it.

At this point, the clock would have been reading less than two seconds.

Spammy sprang back towards the gasping man, leaning down and gripping a hand that had been reaching for a gun. He twisted the wrist, pulling the arm straight and pinning his man to the floor, face-down, then drove his left foot against the up-reaching elbow, which was wrecked with a sharply audible SNAP.

"Heh, just like a twig," Spammy muttered as his victim began to scream and howl in pain. Spammy grabbed his ears from behind, the man's head inches from the ground.

"Shut it," he spat, and knocked him out by smashing his face into a protruding tree root.

Spammy got up again, panting a little, brushing some tangled and sweaty locks from his forehead. Paul and Tam stood, transfixed, eyes bulging, jaws matchingly agape, utterly, utterly speechless.

"What," said Spammy, "did you think I grew up in *that* hoose an' never learnt a few things?"

When Paul's brain kicked in again, its first attempt to comprehend what had just happened was to revise some of his own personal history, reaching an understanding, a realisation that Spammy would later confirm. The reason none of the hard cases around Meiklewood ever bothered him was that they were fucking terrified of him. When Spammy was fourteen, he revealed, when he had suddenly sprouted into an elongated and oddly proportioned shape that most males normally recover from, and when his feared older siblings had flown the nest, a bunch of chancers had set about him, their big opportunity to "waste a Scott". They were all older than him, by two, three, even four years. Four on one. He put all of them in hospital.

"I was very humane," he said. "I called the ambulance maself when I was finished."

"But I cannae see how *your* way's gaunny work," argued Tam. Mortal danger having evidently passed, normal service had been resumed. Spammy was being enthusiastically strange.

"I'm no sure it'll work maself," Spammy admitted, "but for your way, we'll have to hang aboot until that wee shite comes round, which could be a while. The other yin's startin' to moan a bit the noo. Let me see what I can get fae him while we're waitin'."

Tam rolled his eyes. "Aye, fair enough. Gaun yersel'."

They had been sitting around a small fire, too little to be seen from a distance, the smoke swallowed up by the darkness above. The failed killers lay slumped against two tree trunks a few feet away, hands tied at the wrists behind their backs, various parts of their features and anatomies beginning to swell and discolour. The Wee Shite's knee, in particular, looked irreparably damaged.

Suffer ya bastard, thought Paul.

They had found the Wee Shite's pack near the bump he had been standing on, and proceeded to make their way through the provisions they found among the guns taken from the prison bus and the ropes they used to tie up their captives. The spare magazines, knives, walkie-talkies and maps they had removed from their prisoners' persons lay in a small pile beside the fire. Paul was toying with the high-tech but oddly bulky phone he had discovered in a pouch in the Wee Shite's bag. It was a kind of cross between a portable and a field telephone, Spammy opined, working off a local relay somewhere, as they were a bit removed from normal network reception.

Spammy held the pistol he had taken from the bigger man, ejecting the magazine for a moment as he examined the sliding action that fed the chamber. He shuffled it back and forth a few times, pulling the hammer with his thumb and locking it on a hair trigger, then squeezed and listened to the click.

"You know, if we have to shoot one o' these bastards – you know, if it comes to it, like – I'm gaunny empty every last round intae his heid."

"Have you no fucked them up enough?" Paul asked.

"Naw, it's no that," Spammy explained, with that "being reasonable" tone of voice that warned "reason" was about to become a redundant term. "It's you know, like in the films. I fuckin' hate it when the baddie comes back again, like when he's been shot the wance an' everybody thinks he's deid, but he's no. Every last fuckin' bullet. Let's see the cunt come back efter that."

The game had changed once again, thought Tam. The scale of what they were up against had suddenly been reduced. Yes, whoever framed them and killed Voss was high enough placed to manage all that *and* organise the bus escape, but when the "sprung prisoner" showed up to hunt them down, it suggested that their enemy's personnel were considerably fewer than suspected.

The other guy must have been the driver, the man who rigged the crash. He and the Wee Shite had driven off in front of them, then presumably dumped the car and doubled back, stalking their movements all along. So why wait to kill them? Because they had to be "on the run", dangerous fugitives that the public wanted dead. But once these guys killed Bob, they couldn't just leave him there, could they? The authorities – someone for fuck's sake – would need to know what happened, who shot him. Same would go for himself, Paul and Spammy, even if they were found lying dead with those stolen guns in their hands. Still too many mysteries, too many contradictions.

They needed answers, and now they had someone to ask.

"Where did you get this stuff?" Tam asked as Spammy transferred the boiled-mushroom concoction to a second, cooler can, gripping the one that he had sat over the fire with a bunched-up sleeve.

"This forest's hoachin' wi' them, if you know what you're lookin' for. It's autumn. They're in season."

"But you're tellin' me you went to the bother of collectin' them earlier on? While you two were on your own? Did you think they'd let you take them intae the jile?"

"Naw. It was in case I was gaunny get interrogated again. I think I'd have come up wi' some brilliant answers if I'd chewed doon a couple."

"An' what d'you think they'll do tae him?"

"Should be mildly hallucinogenic. But for somebody in physical and mental distress like your man there, it could be a very bad trip. Might make him a bit mair expansive when you ask him questions."

Tam stared at him blankly.

"You're aff your fuckin' heid. Totally fuckin' bananas. He'll tell us nothin'."

"Naw, naw, we'll definitely learn wan thing," Spammy insisted.

"Whit?" Tam asked.

"Whether this strain's toxic."

"You mean you don't know?"

Spammy shrugged his shoulders. "Perfect way tae fin' oot."

Paul held the man's nose with one hand and opened his mouth with the other as Spammy poured the contents of the can down his throat. Paul held his mouth shut as he convulsed, the captive having groggily started to regain consciousness as they force-fed him. He spluttered when Paul took his hands away, some of the dark liquid spilling over his chin. He opened his eyes momentarily, then closed them again, then reopened them, his head jiggling woozily on his shoulders like a baby's.

They stepped away and waited.

Paul stood holding the portable phone, glancing occasionally at the lifeless figure of the Wee Shite slumped against a different tree. Tam crouched on the ground next to the other prisoner as Spammy knelt by the fire, looking his captive closely in the face.

The man made an involuntary gasping noise, upon which Spammy's eyes lit up.

"We're away," he said delightedly, and began to dance spastically in front of him, waving his arms and legs and making "wooooo" noises.

Tam closed his eyes and shook his head.

Bowman watched the shapes swim, the light and darkness weave before him, the figures draw in and out of not-quite focus. He felt pain, nausea, asphyxia, disorientation. The haze, the amorphous mass seemed to pull together, sounds warped and stretching, his thoughts and memories returning, but in an equally contorted form.

Then fear.

He remembered what had done this to him, saw it loom before him. It had been the octopus-thing. It had reached out and crushed his neck, lashed at him with its self-elongating tentacles. It was floating there, those long protuberances feeling their way towards him, extending out from its body, and its body was made of fire. The fire blinked and flickered in its middle as the octopus-thing swam in the air, while beside it the telephone man stood and stared, and the question master demanded answers.

But he couldn't answer. He couldn't talk. You never talk. If you talk, they'll send Harcourt for you. Harcourt and his knives, the stainless steel. Never talk. Can't talk. But if you don't, the octopus-thing will put its tentacle through your neck and down your throat and open your stomach and burn its fire into your guts and the octopus-thing is here and is moving and is coming and . . .

The man's eyes widened and bulged and he started hyperventilating, trembling and sweating.

"Who are you? Who sent you?" Tam asked.

"Don't know," he said, throat wheezing. "Don't know. Can't talk. Can't tell."

"Who's behind this?" Tam said, louder, more aggressive. "Who are you working for? Tell me."

294

"Don't know. Won't tell." His eyes flitted randomly around, never seeming to focus. "Don't know. No-one ever knows . . . client."

"Client? Who's the client? Who are you working for?"

"Never know . . . client's name . . . never know . . . someone . . . government."

"Who killed Voss? Who killed Voss?" Tam grabbed him by the lapels, shaking him, growling the questions. "Did you kill Voss?"

The man gasped again, as if surfacing after having his head forced underwater.

"No . . . not me . . . Knight killed Voss . . . White Knight . . . Chaaarge!" He giggled, then wheezed again. "Knight kill Voss . . . Knight takes Voss . . . Check . . . Knight and Harcourt . . . Harcourt . . . big hard-on . . . killing a billion . . . billionaire . . . doesn't make you any . . . any richer . . . fucking cunt . . . cock like gra . . . granite."

"RIGHT!" came a voice from behind, suddenly shaking and silencing them all. "Party's over, cunts."

It was the Wee Shite, standing unsteadily, untied, supporting his injured knee with one hand, pointing a gun at them with the other.

Paterson had come round quietly, without any moaning and groaning, and when he opened one eye, he had surveyed what was before him and quickly remembered, despite his throbbing skull, why and how he had got there. Fortunately, they were all busy looking at Bowman at the time, so he closed his eye again and tested his bonds. They were tight, and the pressure ached against his right wrist, the one knackered by the lanky cunt, fucking jammy lanky cunt and his fucking lucky kick. But these guys were no experts, and he could already feel his pinky finding its way into a loop and working a section of the rope loose.

Then he had rocked back slightly – slowly and gently to avoid detection, partially opening one eye to check they were still look-ing elsewhere – so that he could get more purchase to strain against the knots. And that was when he felt it. The hard wee lump, pressing insistently into his back where it rested against the tree. His spare gun, still taped there. His back-up.

He redoubled his efforts to loosen the ropes, summoning all his will-power not to grimace or wince too obviously as he twisted his wrists and the right one screamed its howl of protest around his nervous system. Then he was free.

He pointed the gun at the lanky cunt, who was nearest, while the others stood by, unable to take their eyes off him for the space of a blink. Aye. They weren't fucking smiling now. He backed away a few more feet from Lanky and his elastic legs, unlatching the safety catch and glancing down at the pistol tucked into the skinny bastard's belt.

"Drap that," he ordered. "Slowly. An' haud it by the barrel."

Elastic man delicately withdrew the gun from his belt and let it fall to the ground at his side. Paterson smiled.

"Thought you were so fuckin' smart, ya cunt," he said. "Well we'll see how smart you are in a minute. Yous are aw fuckin' deid. All o' yous. But you, Skinnymalinky, I'm gaunny make *you* fuckin' suffer before I finish you."

"Aye, you're a real hard man wi' a gun in your haun," said the old cunt, McInnes. The other boy just stood there, frozen, holding on to the portable phone like he could use it to ask Scotty to beam him up. He'd be fucking lucky.

"Why don't you put it doon, then you an' Spammy here can have a square go," the old cunt continued.

"Save it, Faither," Paterson spat. "This isnae the fuckin' movies. I don't need to prove to masel' that I can waste any o' yous cunts." He shook his head derisively. "You think this gangly yin wasnae just lucky back there? Yous think yous were fuckin' geniuses 'cause the polis never found you? Listen, Faither, an' you listen as well, Daddy Long Legs. The only reason yous cunts made it this far is because they were followin' orders to look in the wrang places, an' because they knew *we* had yous in oor sights the whole fuckin' time. Wan phone call, wan order, and yous three were dropped. And the phone call's came, by the way."

With that thought he looked again at the other one, McInnes Junior, holding *his* phone.

"Put that doon. On the floor. Gently," he ordered. He didn't want it to smash when he shot him, and he certainly didn't want to put a slug in the phone by accident.

As Junior bent down, he noticed Faither had his hand in his pocket. Wary of the danger of attack from different sides, especially with Bowman in some fucking psychedelic trance, he shouted "EVERY CUNT FREEZE" and pointed the gun at the oldest of the fugitives.

"Whit you daein'? Take your haun oot your pocket. Slowly."

The old cunt's hand withdrew from his trousers, his fist balled tight around something.

Paterson was getting nervous. He should have dropped them a minute ago. He should drop them now, but he had to check what Faither had in case it meant trouble.

"Drap it. Open your haun," he commanded.

He glanced cautiously at Skinnymalink to make sure he wasn't planning anything, cast a brief eye over Junior, still crouched on the floor by the phone, and looked at the fist. Faither's hand rotated gently so that his forearm faced upwards, and his fingers opened out.

Paterson saw a glint of something gold, reflecting the flames of the small fire, then saw a brief cascade of metal objects falling from the old man's palm to the ground.

Bullets.

Fuck.

He pulled frantically at the trigger, again and again and again, only to hear the hollow, impotent click of the hammer against an empty barrel.

"What, have you never seen *Die Hard*, ya stupit prick?" said Junior with a withering look.

The old cunt smiled. "Well," he said. "Looks like it's gaunny be a square go after all. Get him, Spammy."

*

297

"I've got to hand it to you, Spammy," said Tam. "I had ma doubts, but we got mair information daein' it your way."

Spammy was crouched behind the Wee Shite, who was on his knees, tears leaking from his eyes after a second assault on his testicles. Spammy was tying him up – properly this time – fastening his wrists together behind his back and then looping the rope around his ankles.

"Aye," he said, "but I've got to admit, your way was fun too."

Tam stared. Fun? Spammy still wasn't getting this.

"Yous've got fuck-all," grunted the Wee Shite.

"I'm no so sure aboot that," countered Paul. "Polis lookin' in the wrang places, was that it? And eh . . . Knight and Harker, Harcourt, somethin' like that. They killed Voss, I believe the man said."

The Wee Shite snorted, a mixture of indignation, tears and snotters.

"Dream on. As if any cunt's gaunny believe yous."

Paul allowed himself a smile. "True enough," he said. "But they might believe you."

"Whit?"

"Oh, nothing."

Paul glanced down with satisfaction at the portable phone, with which he had dialled his flat, where Spammy's answering machine had recorded every word the Wee Shite and Mushroom Man said.

Spammy stood away from the Wee Shite, who was secured in a kneeling position, eyeing his captors with contempt and spitting occasionally. He moved across to check the bonds restraining the Mushroom Man, who had vomited and then passed out a few moments previously.

Tam stood a few feet away from the Wee Shite, staring him intently in the face.

"What's your name, son?" he asked.

"Fuck off."

"Is that Russian?" Tam continued, but there was no humour in his voice.

298

"I'll be back for you cunts," the Wee Shite snarled.

"Aye, very good, look forward tae it," said Tam, almost absently. He walked forward until he was standing over their prisoner. "Listen, ya wee wank," he said quietly. "You killed ma friend today. Friend I've known since before those two there were born. Friend I worked with, drank with, did *time* with. Friend that stood by me all the way, even when I got sucked into this shite. An' you just kill't him, shot him in cold blood like he was nothin'."

"I'm really fuckin' sorry," said the Wee Shite. "In fact I'm cryin' ma fuckin' eyes oot here."

"Let me tell you a wee bit aboot this man you killed," Tam continued, ignoring him. "This man that was worth a million o' you. Just so you know who you murdered. His name was Bob. Bob Hannah."

"I know aw your names, *McInnes*," he sneered.

"You see, I was workin' alongside Bob before I knew it. We only fun' oot we baith worked thegether when we got talkin' after a match. We played in the same fitba team, you see. Baith played for Renfrew Juniors back in the Seventies."

The Wee Shite made great play of yawning.

"Bob was a winger. Wee and fast; nippy, cheeky player. The boys nicknamed him Jinky, after Jinky Johnstone that played wi' the Celtic. Me? I played up front. I was less subtle, but I knew where the goals were. And I'd a nickname as well."

The Wee Shite looked up, realising that the next revelation might have a significance for himself.

"They called me Lorimer," Tam stated, purposefully pacing backwards away from the kneeling figure.

The rapid drain of all colour from the Wee Shite's face assured Tam that he was familiar with the reputation of the former Leeds and Scotland striker, renowned for being the hardest kicker of a football in the world.

Sergeant Shearer had another gulp of his tea and turned back to the typewriter. Paperwork like this could sometimes have him climbing the walls and swinging his size tens at the station cat – criminal damage to a rabbit hutch, for heaven's sake; right up there with that joker last year who kept attaching rubber handle-bar grips to the ends of the horns on all Dougal McGunnigle's highland cows – but this evening it was actually helping him stay calm. If he concentrated on the report, sipped away at his brew and turned up the radio, he could ward his thoughts away from the murderous intentions he was harbouring towards just about every-one connected with this bloody manhunt.

They had rolled into Strathgair *en masse* last night, like the bloody Trenchcoat Roadshow, lots of jumped-up nobodies from Edinburgh and London who had seen a few too many FBI movies. Waving all sorts of supposedly impressive IDs and orders from the Scottish Office, and letting him know, basically, that it was in the hands of the professionals now, so he could get back to mind-ing the cornershop like a good little sheep-shagger.

Then there had been that arrogant heid-the-baw from MI5 or whatever, Knight. Flew in in a helicopter, barked a load of orders, pointed his finger a lot and then buggered off again, no doubt sat-isfied with his brief but invaluable contribution. And after that came the Portakabins, turning the south end of Dingwall Street into what looked like a site-office.

Run along now, they had told him. We're sure you've got lots of important teuchter things to be getting on with. "Someone's still got to maintain law and order down in the village while there's all this excitement in the hills," one of them said. Patronising wee jobbie.

They didn't want to make any use of his local knowledge, his familiarity with every blade of grass for umpteen square miles, in the hills he had known since boyhood. Didn't want to hear where he thought the fugitives might end up if they needed water, or where the best vantage points were. Oh no, they obviously didn't need any assistance from some mutton-molesting village bobby.

Well sod them, he had thought. Neither, presumably, would

they need to know where the most treacherous bogs lay, or that where they had parked their Portakabins was about ten yards downwind of Duncan Sutherland's slurry pit.

They hadn't even wanted to use the station once their wee mobile HQ was set up, and the nearest he had got to any involvement had been around lunchtime, when the bastards towed in the wrecked bus and dumped it on the shinty pitch behind his office window.

"Keep an eye on it, Sergeant. We'll be moving it down to Edinburgh later."

Aye. Like somebody's going to steal it.

He sighed, still simmering, and tapped again at the keyboard. Then Morag put her head around the door, knocking on the frame to get his attention.

"Sarge, can you take this call? It's some bloke asking to talk to the desk sergeant on duty. Says it's 'a local matter'."

A local matter. He growled to himself, lifted the receiver and pressed the blinking pink light.

"Hello, Sergeant John Shearer speaking," he said tiredly. "Fit can I do for you?"

"Are you the desk sergeant on duty?" asked a male voice. Sounded like a Glasgow accent. Definitely not local.

"I'm the *only* sergeant in a radius of aboot forty miles . . . well, usually." He thought of the trenchcoated legions. Grrr.

"Right," said the man. "So are you anythin' to do with this, eh, manhunt cairry-on?"

"*Don't* talk aboot that," he couldn't help but mutter. "Dinnae get me started. Just tell me what I can help you with. Fit's your name?"

"You're definitely not involved, then?"

"No, I think it would be pretty bloody safe to say I'm *not* bloody involved," he replied, starting to lose it.

"Good," said the man.

"Weeeyyyaaaiiiaaaaw," said the cat, propelled through the doorway by Shearer's boot.

301

"What was that?"

"Nothing. Stress-relieving office toy. Look, fit is it that you want, sir? I believe you said it was a local matter."

"Aye, sort of," said the man. "Would you be interested in knowin' where you could find two of the gang that killed Roland Voss?"

"Are you trying to take the piss?"

"Not at all. I know where they are, and I also know that they're not in much shape to resist arrest. They'd a wee accident, I think."

"Who is this? You'll have to give me your name."

"I cannae give you ma name. This is kinna an anonymous tip, you know. But it's legit. I swear it."

"That's okay," said Shearer, reaching for a pen. "So where are they?"

"I need your word that you'll come alone."

"I'm afraid I couldn't possibly come alone. For procedural reasons I'd need to bring at least two of my men."

"Aye, fair enough," agreed the man. "But can you give me your word you won't tell the other cops, the folk on the manhunt, until you've made the arrests?"

Shearer grinned, beaming until the corners of his mouth felt the strain.

"Oh, I can certainly promise you that. How many members of my extended family would you like me to swear on the lives of?"

It took almost two hours to reach the spot. Shearer had listened to the description of the place and been sure of where the man was talking about right away. His "two men" had been Morag (WPC McLeod) and her brother, Andrew, who wasn't actually on the force, but needs must and all that. Andrew was a solicitor, so that almost counted, even if he was usually in the station to represent the toerags Shearer arrested. The only other candidate who lived locally was PC Ross, but he was still suffering from the flu that had kept him off for a couple of days, so he was only fit to mind the station while the rest of them were out in the hills.

"Keep a close eye on that bus," Shearer said to him before leaving, to Ross's obvious and entertaining puzzlement.

Shearer wasn't able to drive the Land Rover as near as he would have liked, which was why it took so long to get there. The moon was bright enough, and there were few clouds, but he still couldn't risk leaving the roads and tracks in such poor light. Buggered axles and squashed sheep were but two of the potential hazards.

"Over 'ere!" Shearer heard, as the beams of their torches thrust ahead of them through the trees and bushes, swinging to and fro as if slicing through the vegetation.

"Oi! Over 'ere!" came the shout again. Shearer picked out the waving shape first, and led his company into the wee clearing, a quarter of a mile down from the ridge. He indicated to Morag and Andrew to stay behind him as he surveyed the situation. Shearer swept the torchlight around the scene, taking in its constituent parts and quickly building up a very interesting picture. He beckoned his assistants forward.

"Thank fuck for that. Get us out of this, mate. Thought we was gonna be here all night," said one of the men. They were both lying against trees, thoroughly trussed, like you could put a pole through the ropes and carry the pair of them home swinging. Even in the darkness, Shearer could tell that the man who was speaking didn't look at all well, while the other one was inert, doing little more than breathing and moaning. He shone his torch over the moaning man's face and noticed with a start that it didn't quite fit together the way faces normally do. It looked like it had been jaw versus train, and the clash had run to form. All the king's horses and all the king's men couldn't put this numpty together again.

Morag made to move towards the man who was doing the talking. Shearer put out a hand to her arm, stopping her. He gestured with his head and swung his torchbeam towards a pile of shapes on the ground, past the ashes and embers of a recent-looking fire. Morag's eyes bulged. Then he pointed it above the moaning man, six feet up the tree trunk. Morag craned her neck, directing her own beam at it and staring. Golly gosh.

"I was told I could find two of the men who killed Roland Voss up here," Shearer announced loudly. "An anonymous tip."

The man shook his head. "That's who got us, mate. That's who did this to us. They're still on the run. They're armed and dangerous. We're on the search team. I don't even know why they let us live."

"No," said Shearer, "that does seem inconsistent with their recent record. But I wonder if you could tell me why these armed and dangerous men would leave a big pile of guns just lying on the ground here?"

The man gawped for a moment, then shook his head. "It's a set-up. These bastards have set us up, and they're settin' you up as well. They took our portable phone. Probably them that gave you the tip."

"Probably," said Shearer, reflectively.

"Look, mate, this isn't exactly comfortable. My fuckin' arm's broken. And me mate's in a right mess. Are you gonna untie us then, or what."

"No. I think I'm going to place you under arrest, actually."

"*What?* What for?"

Shearer walked over to the tree where the moaning man lay, then reached up and removed the large sheet of paper that was fixed above, out of both the restrained men's sights. Training his torch on it, he turned the sheet around so that the man could read what it said, the Ordnance Survey map it was scrawled on the reverse of facing towards himself.

WE ARE INNOCENT.
THE GUNS ON THE GROUND ARE THE ONES TAKEN
FROM THE BUS.
THESE MEN KILLED THE POLICEMAN AND THE
DRIVER.
THIS WEE SHITE WAS ON THE BUS DISGUISED AS A
PRISONER.

304

YOU'LL FIND HIS FINGERPRINTS ALL OVER THE
HANDRAILS ON THE LEFT-HAND BACK SEAT.
WE KNOW WHO REALLY KILLED VOSS.

"Sorry," said Shearer, mock-absently. "Fit was that you were saying a wee minute ago, aboot a set-up?"

Tam looked back once more, and this time ordered them to stop. Turning around, they could all see the headlights in the glen, a motile glow at first, occasionally splitting into distinct shafts as the vehicle negotiated twists in its course. Tam felt himself hold his breath, as if the sound could carry so far. He breathed out again, finding comfort in their distance from the lights, impressed that they had made such progress. It was dark and they were dog-tired and sore, but hope had granted them purpose, and purpose had granted them one more extension on their energy overdrafts. It was another mercifully clear night – well for fuck's sake, they were due *one* break – which not only assisted their journey, but now allowed them to measure it.

He couldn't be sure yet if this was *the* vehicle, and not some farmer perhaps. But what it wasn't was a parade of vehicles, of dozens of polismen and soldiers hurriedly pursuing their quarry. So for that moment it was still in the balance. The vehicle stopped, and the headlamps went out. Then they could see separate beams, bobbing individually, progressing slowly away from where the headlights had disappeared and moving towards the trees. Soon afterwards, the beams became intermittent, broken up as the torchbearers moved into the forest.

Tam exhaled slowly with relief, and Paul couldn't help but laugh as his own tension eased.

They'd *had* to give it a go. Obviously, if the information had fallen into the wrong hands, not only would what they had revealed be covered up, but the MM would have a good idea of where to send his next seek-and-destroy party. But that was why Tam had rung directories and got the number of the local station

305

in Strathgair, not just dialled 999 and asked for the police – especially as someone with a lot to hide might recognise the number the caller was ringing from. The man had given his word, for what that might be worth, but Tam's real trust had been placed in the accent, and in the attitude. He was local – Christ, with a name like Shearer – which meant he wasn't up from Edinburgh or Perth or London, and he sounded genuinely hacked off with those who were. If he acted on the information, went to the clearing, he'd pursue the matter properly, not just report it to someone further up the chain then keep his mouth shut as they wiped the Wee Shite's prints from the bus.

Because this wasn't just about survival and freedom any more. This was about evening the score.

This was about vengeance.

Someone had killed Voss and gone to a lot of bother to frame them for it. There could be no greater revenge, then, than seeing the bastard's efforts thwarted, watching his face as the judge sent him down. Back at the clearing they had left proof that they didn't murder the driver and the polisman. And on a wee cassette in Paul and Spammy's flat, they had proof that they didn't kill Roland Voss either – plus the names of who did.

The tape was too precious to take a chance on. What they had left to be found at the clearing was a card that was only useful if you played it. A first legible message to the world that they were innocent, sowing doubts and taking the fingers off a few triggers. But the stakes would have to go a sight higher before they let the table see what they were holding. And they weren't going to trust *any* polisman with the location of the one piece of evidence that would not only wreck the case against them, but point the finger at – among others – the cops themselves.

So the plan had changed again. They weren't going to give themselves up and sit in a jail cell waiting for justice hopefully to prevail and prove them innocent. They were going to stay hidden, stay free, as long as they could, how ever they could. And if the world figured out for itself what had really happened and decided to apologise, fine. But in the meantime they were going to get word about the tape to their lawyer.

"They'll have a tap on her phone, remember," Spammy warned. "It's a government conspiracy."

Spammy had issued the same note of caution at the suggestion they phone Sadie to let them know they were still safe. Paul had looked crestfallen, but Tam's first thought had been of those photographs, his wife naked and oblivious in her bath, and decided any action that reminded these bastards of her existence was not an option. Chances were they now knew he had a portable phone. The last thing he needed was them calling him up and saying they would kill her if the three of them didn't surrender to their executioners.

"It's all right," Tam said. "We can phone the lassie at her work and get her to ring us back from a call box, tell her aboot the tape and where to find it that way."

Then she could play their ace.

It was Paul who spotted it, and just as well, as they were running out of trees. Not the wee loch – they could hardly have missed that, as it was the reason the forest was coming to an end – but the pier and its attached row of canoes. It looked like the loch had been created – or at least shaped – artificially. From their vantage point at the edge of the woods, maybe half a mile above, they could all see where two small rivers fed it from the north, flooding east and west towards unnaturally straight banks and shores, but it was Paul who appreciated the significance of the waterway that ran back out of it to the south, continuing below the looming hills as far as they could make out its moonlit glint.

There was a compound of low, one-storey buildings on the shore the pier extended from, which Paul guessed was an outdoor activities centre; the sort of place they used to send deprived city kids for a horizon-broadening holiday, but which these days was more given over to character-building and leadership courses for making executives more robustly disposed to sacking people.

307

"Can you both go a canoe?" Paul asked.

"Whit?"

"Look where that river goes," he said.

"I cannae *see* where it goes," Tam replied.

"Exactly. Could be miles. We could travel a lot faster an' a lot quieter than on foot, and naebody's gaunny be lookin' for us in the water." Paul glanced at his watch. "It's aboot two. By the time dawn breaks we could be miles from here. An' I mean miles from where everybody thinks we are, miles from where they're searchin'."

"That'll do me," Tam agreed.

"Merrily, merrily, merrily, merrily," mumbled Spammy, which Paul took to be an affirmative.

They had seen no cars around the compound, but they nonetheless remained stealthy and noiseless in their approach to the pier. Paul untied three of the canoes and prodded them to shore with a paddle. Tam took hold of each boat in turn, dragging it slightly aground to ensure that it didn't float away. He and Paul were about to climb into their craft when they noticed that Spammy was scuttling around the pier on all fours like some giant mutant crustacean, bending over and untying the remaining dozen or so canoes and making every effort to ensure that they *did* float away.

Spammy launched the last of the canoes and then walked softly back to where Paul and Tam were staring in familiar, what-the-fuck-are-you-doing incomprehension. He rolled his eyes indignantly.

"When they show up for work here the morra," he whispered, "how long do you think it'll take them to work oot the score if precisely three canoes are missin'? This way, they'll not know *what's* happened. These things'll have floated all over the place by mornin'. They'll no have a clue how many are away or how many's just stuck in the rushes an' shallows somewhere."

"Aye, fair enough," shrugged Paul, and pushed off into the water.

The river to the south was about twenty feet across, the smooth calm of its surface hinting at its depth, but belying the speed of its current. It wasn't swift, by any means, but it did pull them along steadily, eliminating the need for more paddling than was required to negotiate the bends and to keep pace with one another.

Paul had been right. They were well hidden down below the banks, they were moving faster (for considerably less effort), and noise would not betray them. There was little to disturb the night other than the soft lap of water against their fibreglass vessels and the occasional gentle splash of a navigational paddlestroke. And the loud, shrill, electronic shriek of a portable phone.

Paul almost capsized. It rang a second time before he could reach between his legs to where it was sitting, but he was lost for a moment as to what to do.

"Fuck's sake, answer the thing," Tam hissed from the canoe in front, turning his head. "Before the whole country hears us."

"B-but what . . . who . . .?" stumbled Paul, looking alternately from the phone to his father as it rang a third time.

"Just *answer* it!"

Paul pressed the Receive button and cut off the fourth shriek, thoughts cascading rapidly through his head as to who the caller would be expecting to answer, and therefore who might be on the other end. He swallowed and cleared his throat.

"Hello," he said sheepishly.

Tam turned his head around again, even in the moonlight able to read the bewildered incredulity on his son's face, a look he had seen too many times of late.

Oh Christ.

Paul held up the phone.

"Dad," he breathed, as if he couldn't believe his own words. "It's for you."

309

TWELVE

It made a sort of sklumpfing sound, going in so suddenly, so without warning, and so lightning fast, metal forcing its way forward, flesh and cloth giving way painfully and bloodily to sharp, cold steel.

Harcourt had edged the door open with a practised delicacy. He tucked his gun into the back of his belt with his left hand, gripping the knife in his right. He placed the gloved fingers of his left hand loosely on the door, spread and curved like a spindly insect with a black leather exoskeleton, his hand working as a suspension system to smooth and temper the force of his arm as he pushed forward. The door, then, didn't so much swing open as slide away from him like a smooth-rolling drawer.

He had stepped inside and out of his shoes, fearing the rubber soles would squeak on the polished floorboards. The lightweight curtains over the casement window glowed with orange streetlight from outside, the assassin's equivalent of a bomber's moon. There was no sound but the breathing of the two bodies, lying there motionless, obliviously unaware that they would be staying that way. She was on the right, lying on her side, face turned away from the doorway, her hair spilling out over the quilt. He was the nearer, lying face up, one arm by his side, the other tucked under the pillow to help support his head.

He'd get the bloke out of the way first, quick blow straight through the throat. There'd be time later to make it look frenzied. That way he could have some fun with the woman before he did her too. Make the scenario more authentic; in fact it would be negligently suspicious not to. What kind of knife-wielding crazed maniac breaks into a bedroom and murders two people without shagging the tart?

Harcourt paced forward slowly, concentrating on the face of the man, but staying aware of what was in his peripheral vision. He was standing over him by the side of the bed when he became worryingly aware of a sniffing sound amidst the breathing, and realised with relief that it was himself. Wasn't the first time. You could be so intent on what you were doing, so focused on the victim or victims, and upon what you could see, that you kind of forgot you were there in the flesh, as if you were watching it on closed circuit.

He placed his left foot on the wooden base of the bed, like it was a stirrup, and swung his right leg over the sleeping man, touching his foot down lightly on the quilt, then lowered his frame, sliding his right knee into the space between the bodies. He was straddling the man, but without resting his weight on him – yet. He heard his own sniffing noise again and thought for a second he saw the man's eyeball move behind the lid. He switched his breathing to his mouth instead, which was quieter, but made a slight sucking sound. Harcourt knew he tended to breathe in sharply as he brought the knife up, just before that first precipitous moment of attack, so, checking his weight balance and raising the knife above his shoulder, he breathed in silently by opening his mouth wide.

Upon which the man stuck a gun in it.

Sklumpf.

*

311

Parlabane was, to be frank, completely fucking sick of this.

There was an infuriatingly egocentric arrogance to the fact that they probably all thought they were the first bastard to have a go at it. He wouldn't even dignify this particular loser's attempt by saying he had been face-to-face with death. Death wasn't even in *town* that night, and if he had been, he wouldn't have been seen – well, you know – in the company of this fucking arsehole.

Parlabane was not, on the whole, a light sleeper. When the gods had been smiling, when Sarah had been smiling, when the story broke or the cheque cleared, when Celtic and Rangers both lost, several pints down and feeling no pain, he was a hard man to rouse. But when pondlife like Michael Swan had been doing away with billionaires and had a party of hitmen out on clean-up duty, looking to tie up a loose end that was asleep in his living room, a bird farting outside on the telephone wire would have startled him. The scratching of a blade effecting criminal damage to his kitchen window was more than enough.

He had shaken Sarah, placing a hand over her mouth and explaining the situation with a few brief gestures and whispers. Sounded like three of them coming in over the kitchen sink, unquestionably armed. He told her to lie back and pretend to be asleep until he said otherwise, no matter what she saw or heard. She nodded nervously but unquestioning; he wouldn't tell her how to give an anaesthetic.

Parlabane reached under the bed on his side, padding his hand quietly along the boards until he touched it: a nine-millimetre Beretta, held in place by masking tape. He pulled it loose with one hand while his other located the magazine, then drew both of them under the quilt. He slid the magazine into place and smoothly, quietly gripped the top of the shaft and pulled it back to chamber the round, heart-wallopingly grateful to himself for keeping the mechanism clean and oiled. What noise there was was muffled by the covers.

Parlabane swallowed hard, contemplating what he could do. He had the element of surprise in his favour, plus the fact that he was a prodigiously accurate shot, something to do with his "mutant middle-ear and short-assed low centre of gravity", according to his friend Larry, who had once taken him to an LAPD practice range. Larry had been admiring but enviously acerbic, talking distastefully like it was some kind of deformity. Parlabane had been even less pleased with his new-found talent. It had scared the hell out of him and he'd resolved never to touch another firearm. Circumstance had subsequently over-ruled that resolution.

He knew from experience that the level of resistance these testosterone-overloaded fuckwits expected from innocent victims seldom extended to close-range ballistic weapons fire, but at three against one there was nonetheless something unmistakably suicidal about it. He looked across to Sarah, lying with her face away from the door, trembling very slightly, and thought then of Nicole, their principal target, asleep and defenceless in the living room, where he had heard them go.

Christ.

Conscience, morality and sheer logistics tortuously tangled the paths before him.

But in the time it had taken him to warn Sarah and prepare his weapon, he realised the decision had been made for him, as he heard his front door being unlocked. Whatever had happened in the living room was over – one way or the other. Through the wall he could hear footsteps in the close. He had lain back with the gun gripped in his right hand, under the pillow, and fractionally opened his right eye, watching the door.

Then the latest candidate for the post of Jack Parlabane's Assassin had walked in to receive his Dear John letter.

The hard, sharp triangular sight on top of the barrel had snagged for a fraction of a second on the wool around the top of the balaclava's mouth-slot, before its momentum snapped it free and drove the muzzle viciously into the back of the failure's throat. Parlabane pulled back the hammer until it locked and forced the sight deeper into the soft flesh of the not-assassin's palate.

313

"Hair trigger and the safety's off," he said, staring furiously into the man's eyes as they peered out through holes in the wool. "And I'm not just talking about the gun, by the way."

Parlabane sat up, peremptorily tugging the weapon up and backwards, gouging excruciatingly with the sight. "Arms out. Wide," he commanded. "Drop the knife. You disobey, you try anything, you rock the bed, you even *look* at me funny and it's gauny be brains tartare served on a culee of loser's blood all over that wall behind you."

The man dropped the knife on to the duvet.

"Sarah," Parlabane instructed. "Get the knife. Pad him down, he'll have a gun somewhere."

Sarah slipped out of the bed and walked quickly round behind him, now trembling again as she stood at his back and ran her hands around the intruder.

"Sarah," Parlabane added with nagging impatience, "I wouldn't stand directly behind him if I were you."

"Oh, sorry," she whispered, ducking so that she was out of the bullet's probable path. She patted her hands down the man's spine and found the gun tucked, muzzle-down, into the back of his trousers. So *that* was what arse cleavage was for. She backed away, training the pistol on the failure, and switched the light on.

Parlabane saw it: the look, the flinch. The light went on in the bedroom and a light went off in the guy's mind; the moment he saw Parlabane's eyes properly and realised there was going to be no bluff to call.

"Yeah, that's right," he said, burning his diabolical stare indelibly into the man's retinas. "And don't think you're the only one here with connections. I'll have someone in here repainting that wall while your weighted carcass is falling off a ferry in the Firth of Forth. And try saying *that* with a gun in your mouth, prick."

Sarah had edged out of the room. Parlabane was momentarily concerned for what she might see, but as they had each witnessed

314

a roughly equal share of mutilated bodies (Sarah's ones frequently still alive – at least temporarily) and as he was otherwise engaged, there was no point in being sexist about who went.

"Nicole's gone," she said loudly, looking through the doorway to the empty settee and discarded quilt. Sarah ran into the living room, to the windows that looked on to East London Street. She saw a black Ford Mondeo driving off at speed, and made out the head of a man in the back window before it disappeared towards Broughton Road.

"Phone Jenny," Parlabane called out. "Get her round here pronto."

Sarah walked briskly back to the hall and speed-dialled the number.

"All right, just let me work this out for myself, and don't interrupt," Parlabane said to the failure, kneeling up on the bed. "Couldn't kill her on the spot because you didn't want anyone to know she was ever here, in this flat where myself and my good lady were to be found murdered. And before you top her, you've got to find out how clued up she is and who she's told, in case you need to add some more names to the death-list, where there are already ticks against Lafferty and Campbell."

The failure's eyes flashed at the mention of the names.

"What, you wondering what else I know? Well I know this. I know one of you fuckers killed my friend by force-feeding him a cyanide capsule. I know that some of your wee balaclava brothers killed Voss and his missus up in Perth. I know that you were going to kill me and then Sarah, and I'm trying to restrain my imagination from speculating what else was on your agenda before you planned to leave here tonight."

Parlabane put a foot on the floor and stepped off the bed, pushing the gun roughly forward until the man gagged, then drawing it back a little and lifting it up, the man's head with it, indicating he should rise to his feet.

"What I don't know," he continued in a slow, breathy tone, "is where your pals have taken Nicole Carrow, but believe me, Jim,

315

right now I'm not sure whether I want to know that quite as badly as I want to pull this trigger."

"Jenny's on her way – *oh shit*," said Sarah, walking into the bedroom as the failure backed out of it, prompted as ever by Parlabane's nine-mill. He wasn't as big as he had seemed, she noticed. He was taller than Parlabane, but then most people were taller than Parlabane, and his build seemed deflated now that he was slouchingly upright. As they edged past her she could see blood beginning to seep into the balaclava amidst the drool from the man's mouth and the tears leaking from the corners of his eyes from the sharp, constant intrusion of the metal into the delicately sensitive tissue in the roof of his mouth. The intruder's gaze occasionally strayed nervously towards his feet as he was forced reluctantly backwards, but Parlabane's never faltered from blazing into his captive's face.

"Get the door, please, Sarah," he said quietly, as they made their four-legged way through the hall.

As she swung the front door in, Parlabane's arm straightened and he angled the gun upwards and more urgently backwards, seeming suddenly to drive at the intruder as his feet picked unsteadily at the floor of the close. It forced him off balance as Parlabane lengthened his own stride, his weight distribution low and solid like he was a bowling ball and the failure was a pin.

Parlabane kicked a foot against the close wall to turn the man as he began falling, the small of his back hitting the banister with a wooden thud and a low hum of vibrating metal. Parlabane shifted his weight on to his front foot and toppled him over the edge, the failure's upper body out in space above the wide spiral, his feet straining to touch the floor on the other side, his coccyx the fulcrum, the banister the pivot. He pushed the gun out, causing the man to gag if he tried to strain back towards safety, and stretching his head backwards so that he could see the cold stone of the close floor, four storeys and forty feet below.

Parlabane stepped a pace to his left, resting his right foot over the failure's insteps as they dangled a couple of inches off the floor. In one movement he yanked the gun out of the man's mouth and pulled backwards at a thick handful of balaclava and hair with his free hand, before jamming the gun between the intruder's eyes and pressing down so that matters remained in the balance, as it were.

"Maybe you can talk or maybe you can fly," Parlabane told him, pulling his securing right foot a few centimetres away from the failure's legs until he gasped in fright, then reapplying the pressure. "But trust me, if you don't demonstrate one ability right now, you'd better be ready to make good with the other. Where is she? WHERE IS SHE?"

The failure looked away, trying to turn his head as if needing confirmation that the ground *was* forty feet down. Parlabane watched his eyes flit back and forth before returning to face his own. The man had glanced at his arms, flailing uselessly against the air as he fought against the conspiracy between gravity and his own upper-bodyweight, still looking for options.

"Murrayfield," he suddenly gasped, generic Home Counties accent. "A place in Murrayfield."

"The address?" said Parlabane, twisting the muzzle of the Beretta. The eyes flitted again.

"Murrayfield Park," he said, with as much of a nod as he could manage, eyeing his interrogator beseechfully.

Parlabane looked down ponderingly at him for a moment, then nodded himself.

"Ach, fuck you," he said, pulling his arms away and easing the cocked hammer safely back, as he switched his right foot from in front of the man's insteps to behind his ankles, and kicked both legs up.

"BARNTON! IT'S BARNTON PARK," the failure yelled at that moment, feeling his body tumble back, a fraction before Parlabane swept his arms across the banister to catch his insteps as his feet shot into the air.

"Number?" he added, while the man dangled, trying somehow to grip the wooden bar between his thighs and his calves.

317

"Thirty," he whispered breathlessly but without hesitation. "Thirty. Thirty. Thirty Barnton Park."

"Thank you."

The failure gripped one of the metal railings at the base and kicked out at Parlabane with both feet, one boot catching him in the mouth as they whipped free of his hold. He swung down, twisting his grip as his weight jolted heavily at his wrist, leaving him hanging by that one hand, dangling above the drop. Then he kicked his legs in the air and swung himself agilely outward, letting go on the return swing, aiming for the landing below Parlabane's. The failure's left leg cleared the downstairs banister cleanly. Unfortunately his right leg didn't.

"Aw, Jim, that's gotta hurt," said Parlabane, looking down. "I felt that from *here*."

The failure struggled to his feet but didn't quite make it, settling at first for all fours, then gripping the handrail for assistance as he hobbled slowly down the staircase.

"You're fucking dead, mate, you hear me? Fucking *dead*," he grunted, gripping the banister tighter and looking up to see Parlabane's less-than-worried expression.

When he turned back and resumed his descent, he found himself face-to-balaclava with Dalziel, who broke his nose with the heel of her palm.

"You're under arrest, Fuzzy," she told him.

"Bitch," he spat defiantly, lying dazed and sore on the grey stone. "What for?"

"I don't know yet, but from experience, if you're fucking with Jack Parlabane, you've *got* to be up to no good."

"I knew that was the neighbourhood gone when you hetero trash moved in round the corner," Jenny said, sitting on the stairs by the now handcuffed failure as the now dressed Parlabane and Sarah descended towards her. "I mean, if you're going to have your S&M friends round," she continued, holding up the balaclava, "you're going to have to make sure they stay indoors."

Sarah held up a plastic bag. "This is his gun and his knife. You're going to find my prints on both, just so that you know."

"Let's shift," said Parlabane urgently, taking one arm of their prisoner as Jenny gripped the other. The failure hobbled like an old man, his spirit broken like his nose, his whole system suffering the aftershock of severe bollock-banister trauma.

"Where are we going?" she asked.

"Barnton. They've got Nicole there."

"How come these bastards have always got such posh digs?"

"Would you rather it was Wester Hailes?"

"Not at this time of night, no."

Sarah unlocked the boot of her Civic coupe, her Honda Sensible, as Parlabane called it, while he retrieved his bag o' tricks from his own car a few yards away. He tossed the bag into the Sensible's back seat as Jenny bundled the prisoner over the tailgate and into the boot. At this point he regained some energy and attempted to climb out again.

"HELP!" he yelled. "HEmmmmmmffffmmm." Jenny kicked his legs back into the boot and stuffed the rolled-up and blood-damp balaclava into his mouth.

"Right. Let's get going," Parlabane announced, gripping the boot and preparing to close it.

"Shouldn't we make some airholes for him or something?" Jenny suggested.

Sarah gave her a reproachful look. "You're not putting any holes in *my* car for this piece of shit."

"There should be enough air for him to reach Barnton," Parlabane said. "So as long as he's not been lying to me again, he should be all right. You got anything else to tell me, Jim?" he asked, pulling the balaclava out.

"Fuck you."

"As you wish."

Parlabane plugged the woollen gag back in and slammed the boot closed, walking around to the driver's door. Sarah jerked a thumb at him, telling him to get over to the other side.

"They're going to kill her, remember," Sarah said. "It's a fucking emergency." She turned to Jenny as she climbed behind the wheel and the policewoman clambered into the backseat. "He drives like a pensioner," she explained. Sarah backed the car out of the space, changed into first and hit the accelerator.

"I can*not* believe you had a gun in our house and never told me about it," said Sarah angrily, rounding the corner into Inverleith Terrace and gunning the engine noisily to wake up all the consultants who lived there.

"I'm sorry, could you say that a bit louder in case the law officer in the back seat didn't quite catch it," Parlabane replied.

"A *gun*?" asked Jenny.

"You're not hearing this," he told her, turning round.

"A gun," confirmed Sarah. "A nine-millimetre automatic. Can you believe this guy?"

"Well, funnily enough," said Parlabane defensively, "I had this outrageous idea that it might come in useful if someone happened to break in and attempt to murder us."

"Yes, but . . ."

"Something, I would remind you, which has happened to me more than once in the past, and which has indeed happened to the both of us together, if you'll cast your mind back to an incident involving your former employer."

"But what if it had gone off by accident? That bed *has* been known to get the odd violent shake. Even you can manage that once in a while."

Parlabane heard Jenny snigger. He thought it highly inappropriate. Bitch.

"It would have been pretty fucking difficult for the gun to go off by accident considering there were no bullets in it. The magazine was taped about a foot away."

"And where did you get it?" Sarah continued indignantly. Parlabane knew she was genuinely upset and not just having a dig at him for its own sake when she sped past the Disney Draws

Gormenghast towers of Fettes College and neglected to give her usual salute in recognition of how many modest, cooperative, considerate, charming and open-minded colleagues had attended it. Parlabane figured she was rechannelling her understandable shock and anger at what had happened on to him, as he was available. He would have tried harder to just sit and take it if he hadn't been so wired by the whole thing himself.

"It was that lunatic pal of yours, wasn't it? Tim. Tim Vale, when he came up to visit you last year. Wasn't it?"

Parlabane sighed. "Yup."

"I *knew* it. He's a menace to society."

Parlabane nodded. He sure was. Tim Vale was a former "intelligence operative" (i.e. spy), one of many left somewhat purposeless by the end of the Cold War. He had been getting too old anyway by the time the Wall fell, but rather than retire to a cottage to pen his memoirs, he had started an endearingly shady freelance surveillance firm, putting old tricks and old contacts to good use. He and Parlabane shared an enthusiasm for unorthodox information-gathering. Their meeting had been almost inevitable. They didn't trust each other a great deal – doing so would have been "a frightfully disrespectful breach of etiquette", as Vale put it – but they did get on.

Vale had given him "a present in gratitude for his hospitality" after coming up to stay a few days, not long after Parlabane moved to Edinburgh. He was still living in that cursed place in Maybury Square, back when he and Sarah had only just started seeing each other. Vale told him not to open the gift until after he was gone. Parlabane knew it would be a gun, but that it was a Beretta nine mill was typical of the bastard, keeping him guessing as to whether it was a coincidence or how Vale could know he had used such a gun in LA – and what for.

Death's Dark Vale, Parlabane called him. He patted the Beretta in his jacket and resolved to write and thank him again.

Sarah took her left hand off the wheel and put it on Parlabane's thigh, giving it a conciliatory squeeze. He placed his right hand on top of it and she smiled, then changed up and floored it as the approaching Quality Street lights turned amber.

"I found out who . . . who was in that interview room with your friend, Jack," said Jenny.

Parlabane turned his head around expectantly.

"It was the big cheese, chief spook, who's apparently in charge of everything in the whole world. Knight's his name."

Parlabane stared beyond her for a moment, then nodded, mouthing the word to himself, storing something away.

"I don't know his first name; it was hard enough finding out his second. Everyone at the station just refers to him as Bomber."

"Why?"

"After that guy in *Auf Wiedersehen, Pet*, remember him?"

"So he's a big fella then? A real bear?"

"Aye, but it's more the accent that got him the name. 'Zounds loik 'e's fram the Wess Con'ree, moi dear'," she mimicked. "Specially when he loses the place."

"Like a country bumpkin?" Parlabane asked anxiously. "A yokel?"

"Well I'm sure they all find *our* accents hilarious too, Scoop."

"No, I mean . . . I talked to a chef at Craigurquhart who said the bloke in charge of security for Voss's visit was a huge guy who spoke 'like a country bumpkin' when he got upset. That would put this Knight character at the scene."

"Why not. He's in charge of fucking everything else. Nobody in the HQ right now is allowed to *fart* without authorisation from him. It would certainly add up that he would be ultimately over-seeing the murder investigation if he was overseeing the visit."

"Then *he* did it," Parlabane stated determinedly. "If he killed Donald, he killed Voss. Even if he didn't draw a blade, he was there, and he knows a man who did. He's a man Voss's body-guards wouldn't have reacted to if he walked down the hall towards them that night. Him and someone else on his fucking spook staff."

"But why would he want to kill Voss?" Jenny asked.

"He's not the man with the motive," Sarah chimed in. "He's just the errand boy. The hitman."

"You pair are telling me you know who's behind the hit?"

"Oh yes, not inconsiderably," said Parlabane, doing a reedy-voiced John Major impression, at which Jenny's eyes bulged.

"You're not saying . . ."

"No, no," he added quickly, realising with a wry smile how she had wrongly interpreted his figure of speech. "But coincidentally, he could be a fringe beneficiary. You're in the right neighbourhood."

"One of his cohorts?"

"Well, I think the word Mr Major used was actually 'bastards'," Parlabane offered. "Personally, I prefer 'cunts'. It's the caring and likable Michael Swan."

"*What?*" She knew better than to ask if he was serious. "But why . . . what motive has he got?"

"Have to tell you later," Sarah said, pulling the car in and switching off the engine. "We're up."

Pain erupted inside Nicole, deafening, shaking, flooding her, enough even to shut out the fear for a moment, before it seeped back in where the agonies were subsiding. She was bent over, head on her knees as she sat on the plastic chair, which had seemed to appear under her as her body was buckled by the blow.

She had been standing before him in just a white T-shirt, in this room with its peeling-paint walls and Blu-tack smudges; its thin grey carpet under her bare feet; its bed where the second man sat, with the off-white candlewick, looking like it had lain undisturbed since the last time anyone actually used a candlewick; its wobbly MFI flatpack bureau; and the plastic chair. Like the lamenting bedroom of a daughter who didn't live there any more, haunted by the ghosts of her presence, where posters once looked down on the bed she slept in and the desk she studied at.

Like a mockery of the place she had felt safest.

She wasn't safe here.

He had put a hand behind her trembling shoulders, her hands

323

cuffed behind her back, her eyes either refusing to focus or too tear-clouded to do so, then he had punched her viciously in the stomach and dropped her on to the chair, where she croaked and gasped, feeling like she had been run through.

Your mind was supposed to blank at times like this. It was supposed to shut out what you couldn't handle, some Mary Whitehouse reflex objecting to the disturbing images and censoring the broadcast. Merciful oblivion, wasn't that what they called it? Taking you elsewhere – maybe above, looking down from one cushioning remove, maybe outside yourself, maybe somewhere deep within.

Or maybe we just hope that's what happens.

She wished she hadn't read all those *Amnesty* articles about torture. About how they weren't necessarily that interested in information, simply wanted to torture you for its own sake, to break and dehumanise you. How it wouldn't do any good to say she'd tell him anything as he'd probably torture her anyway. She wanted the merciful oblivion. Wanted to leave her body, abdicate her consciousness, half in love with easeful death. She wanted to surrender. Resisting was hard. Surrender was easy. Death was easy.

She had been saved from an unknowing end, in a car-crash in Glasgow, and for what? To live another day and a half in fear before the moment came, behind all its heralds, with the fullest complement of pomp and circumstance. There was an irresistibility about it, a demonstration of its power, that it could not be outrun, and that the man who had helped her flee it before was himself now dead, alongside his wife-never-to-be.

But her mind would not release her, the almost inappropriate voice of self-preservation – a voice that didn't understand its own irrelevance here – still babbling its conjecture amidst the screams of pain and the wailing cacophony of fear.

This man *would* ask her questions, did want to hear what she knew. And when he was satisfied she had no more to tell him, then he would certainly kill her. She had known that when he woke her and gagged her on Parlabane's sofa – she hadn't needed to see him

324

take his mask off in the car to work out it was a one-way trip. And she definitely hadn't needed him to tell her, although she was sure that doing so had been mainly for his own benefit.

"You know why you're here, don't you, Nicole," he said quietly, reasonably, crouching down before her as she bent over, paralysed by his blow, and placing his hands on her knees. "I'll make it quick if you're cooperative. And I think you know now what slow's going to feel like."

If she stayed silent, he'd hurt her. If she talked, she died.

Half in love with easeful death.

But only half. The voice told her there was still hope, still a chance. No-one knew she was here, but something could still intervene. It was all going wrong, remember? What she had heard in the car, as she lay pinned on the back seat, the man holding a gun to her head as her face pressed into the upholstery, in his other hand that portable phone, both items now sitting on the desk a few feet behind him. Big problems in . . . Strathgair, was it? And there was the newspaper. People must have seen the newspaper by now. There was still a chance these men would be stopped, somehow, still a chance.

But it was a chance she had to be so brave to believe in, when it entailed facing and forcing herself to comprehend the cold, visceral reality of her predicament, without shutting anything out or giving up. She had to think about what was here and now, stay alert and sharp, not oblivious, not absent and numb. She had to keep herself alive. She had to talk, but she couldn't tell him what he wanted to hear or even what he thought he wanted to hear. And she couldn't let him think she was bluffing or lying. But what could she tell him? Trying to consider what to say, trying to weigh up the plausibilities and project the consequences amidst this pain and panic and fear was like trying work out your rate of vertical acceleration as your engineless aeroplane plummets steeply earthward.

The man pulled out a long, polished and glinting knife and began tapping it lightly on her thigh.

325

"Tell me how . . ."

The dead silence of the house outside the bedroom was suddenly shattered by the sound of a doorbell, ringing long, loud and insistently. Her eyes opened wide in startlement. He saw the hope within them, and laughed.

"That'll be Harcourt," he said, ostensibly to the man sitting on the bed, but really to Nicole. "Go let him in. Tell him to get his gear together for the drive. And ask him if he remembered to put that bedding away. If he didn't, the stupid cunt's going straight back there."

The second man got up and left the room.

"Does this make you feel like a real tough guy?" Nicole said, sniffing and staring hatred at him through her puffy eyes. "Were you bullied at school or something? Daddy interfere with you as a small b . . .?"

He slapped her with the back of his hand; not as hard as he could have, she estimated, but enough to hurt and rattle her jawbone.

"Yes," he said with a cold smile. "All those things. Mummy too and the local scoutmaster and the village vicar. If it makes you feel better I'll tell you I can't get it up and that it's really small anyway. So now I've answered your questions, I'd consider it polite if you answered mine."

He pressed the end of the knife into her thigh and drew it along for a few centimetres, opening a shallow cut around which blood quickly began to collect. Nicole sucked in air as the small wound started to sting, then heard herself moan involuntarily as he pulled slightly at the skin either side of it.

"People don't always respond to pain, Nicole," he said, pushing her head back. "But there are other options." He placed the tip of the blade on the skin above the collar of her T-shirt.

"I'll tell you what you want to know," she said, grudged tears dripping from her eyes, swallowing to steady her voice. "I'll cooperate."

"Oh I'm sure you will, but let's not rush it."

He pressed the stiff metal up a little, forcing her head back, and pulled her thighs a few inches apart with his other hand. She looked upwards and closed her eyes, sniffing and unable to stop herself crying. He pushed his hand in further, slowly, until his fingers were almost touching her underwear, and she opened her eyes again, looking anywhere but at this vile thing before her, looking for imaginary escape, looking for a place to hide within herself, eyes scanning the ceiling . . . the walls . . . then the doorway.

She swallowed again and looked down, reflexively clamping her thighs back together as his fingers brushed the cotton between her legs.

"It's not a very good time to be doing that," she told him.

"Oh that's all right. As I'm sure you've gathered, I don't mind a bit of blood."

"Is that the car you saw?" asked Parlabane, looking at the wheeled slug in the driveway of the detached, two-storey Victorian villa. The garden was cordoned off from the street and its neighbours by a low wall and high firs at the front, towering, unkempt hedges at the sides. There's one in every upmarket neighbourhood. Place that looks like it was all but burnt down some time in the early Seventies, possibly for insurance, and has passed through a succession of anonymous owners who consistently and conspicuously failed to properly restore it, instead just repairing it to basic, well-it's-still-standing functionality. Consequently it had the reclusive and slightly neglected air of a small convent or seat of some other equally fucked-up religious sect.

"I didn't get the reg, but it was definitely a black Mondeo," Sarah confirmed.

"What are these guys, killer sales reps?" asked Jenny.

"No, just killers," Parlabane stated.

"You want me to get us some back-up? I've got my radio here."

"No, Jenny, I quite definitely *don't* want you to radio for back-up. Remember who we're dealing with. You put a call out for assistance at this address and you never know who might hear about it and recognise it. Could have a phone ringing in that house in one minute, letting them know we're coming. They could have Nicole dead and stashed while you and your pals are arsing about trying to get a search warrant. We're on our own."

He released the magazine from the Beretta, racking the barrel to eject the shell he had chambered earlier, then popped the bullet back into the mag. Then he slammed the clip home again. Sarah gestured to Jenny with her head, indicating the gun with a can-you-believe-this-guy roll of the eyes.

"You see a gun here, Detective Dalziel?" he asked.

Jenny covered her eyes, then her ears, then made a zipping motion across her lips. Sarah shook her head. Parlabane leaned over into the back seat for his bag, pulling out ropes, gloves, his lock-picking kit and a small aluminium grappling hook.

"So just how are you planning to do this, *darling*?" Sarah asked acidly.

"I'm going to break in at the back while Jenny causes a distraction at the front. You can ring the bell, flash the badge, say you're looking for a prowler," he told Dalziel.

"What," said Jenny, "then you swing from the chandeliers with the girl under your big manly arm, leap over the baddies and ride off into the sunset? You'll get your fucking head blown off, Scoop. Forget it."

"Well the clock's ticking. You got any better ideas?"

"Yes," she said. "But I'll need your gloves, the knife you took from fumbletrumpet in the boot back there, and an assistant from the audience."

Sarah arched her eyebrows. "You got it."

Parlabane shot her a look of grave concern, and almost began the process of opening his mouth.

"Oh don't you *dare* give me any crap about it being dangerous, Jack Parlabane," Sarah snapped. "I was presumably supposed to sit here and knit while you climbed in like Spiderman, *hoping* you walked out alive again later. What's the plan, Jenny?"

*

Parlabane padded silently off into the shadows, gun in belt and tail between legs. His urgency to get inside before . . . whatever . . . happened to Nicole made an angry partner mingling with his huffiness at being relegated to the sidelines, but he still enjoyed a "that's my girls" moment of satisfaction as he watched Jenny slash the Mondeo's tyres and Sarah smash its windscreen with a dully percussive and surprisingly quiet blow of the policewoman's telescopic baton.

They dusted themselves free of glass fragments then proceeded directly to the front door, where Jenny rang the bell.

After a time, a tall man appeared, well built but just erring on the portly side, dressed uniformly in black but without the balaclava. He pulled the door open and was evidently surprised to see the two women before him, one of them holding up her police identification, the other with her hands behind her back, attention-style.

"Good evening, sir. I'm DS Dalziel and this is DC Jackson. We're sorry to trouble you so late, but at least it seems you weren't in bed, Mr . . ." Jenny scanned the door for a nameplate, but there was none to be found.

"What can I do for you?" he interrupted quickly, in a tone that implied he hoped not much.

"Well, I'm surprised you didn't hear anything, but it was one of your neighbours who called, and luckily we were in the area. It seems someone has been vandalising cars in this street, and unfortunately we suspect your own has been a target. Is this your vehicle in the driveway, here?"

He leaned out on to the porch, looking across to where the Mondeo was slumped like a hamstrung bovine, tyres airless, shattered glass glinting in the gravel round about.

"Fucking *bastard*," he grunted, brushing past them and walking towards the car as if hypnotised.

Sarah whipped out the baton to its full length again and swung it as hard as she could between his legs from behind, both hands, one-wood on a par five, into the wind. Before he could even drop to his knees, Jenny was upon him, forcing his face into the dirt and cuffing his hands behind his back while Sarah patted him down and located the inevitable handgun.

"You'd better fucking pray the girl's alive, pal," Jenny warned, as beside them Parlabane strode purposefully into the house, weapon drawn.

"No, that's not what I meant, prick," continued Nicole, as firmly as she could manage. The man looked up into her bloodshot eyes, slightly concerned to see the fear replaced by anger, and more concerned that it was no longer the anger of the victim, but of the avenger.

"Look," she commanded.

He heard a clicking noise to his right, and turned to notice Parlabane in the doorway, gripping a pistol with both hands, aiming straight at his head.

"Drop the knife, arsepiece," he ordered.

The man instead angled the knife so that it lay across Nicole's throat, pressing it against the skin. "Put the gun down, or I'll kill her," he shouted, his gaze locked on Parlabane.

Parlabane, to Nicole's astonishment, rolled his eyes. "Oh *please*," he said witheringly. "Not the old 'knife to the girl's throat, back, back, I've got a hostage' routine."

"I mean it," said the man, eyes flashing, his arrogant, self-satisfied calm now an incongruous memory.

"Listen, baw-hair," resumed Parlabane more firmly. "In five seconds the knife goes *on* that desk or *up* your arse. It's make-your-mind-up time."

The man turned his head a couple of degrees, straining to look at the bureau, eyeing the gun sitting there, just out of reach.

"I don't know who you think you are, mate," he said, trying to sound confident and relaxed, then lunged for the pistol on the desk with his right hand, the movement of his torso taking the left – and more importantly the knife – a vital few centimetres back from Nicole's neck.

330

Parlabane changed aim and fired with hardly a blink, bullseyeing the automatic on the desk and sending it spinning off the veneer and against the wall six feet away. "No you don't," he said quietly.

The man looked at him with incredulous dismay, then back at Nicole as she kicked out with both feet, tipping herself and the chair backwards on to the floor. He threw himself flat on the floor alongside her, Nicole's body and flailing legs between him and Parlabane, then pressed the knife against her throat once more and knelt up. He couldn't use her as a shield, just her life for a stand-off.

"Look, you've no idea what you're dealing with," he warned Parlabane. "These matters don't concern you. I work for powerful people."

"Yeah, you work for Knight and he works for Swan."

Nicole looked up at the man, watching his Adam's apple bob involuntarily at the mention of the names.

"You're going to be in a lot of trouble, mate," he said. "I'd put the gun down if I were you. I can see to it that your life becomes a fucking nightmare if you don't. I've got powerful connections."

"Yeah, but it'll be hard telling them about me with no head."

"Don't kid yourself, mate, I know you're not going to shoot me."

Parlabane gave a quiet but unmistakably derisive snort. The bullet hit the man in the shoulder, spinning him back and away from Nicole, who rolled herself clear.

Parlabane walked over to where the man lay, kicking the discarded knife towards the door, where Jenny and Sarah soon emerged. Sarah helped Nicole to her feet, hugging her and wrapping her jacket around her.

"Please allow me to introduce myself," Parlabane said to his new captive. "I'm a man of stealth and haste. My name's Jack Parlabane and this is Dr Sarah Slaughter. An associate of yours tried to kill us both tonight. He's now residing in the boot of Dr Slaughter's car. And your other monkey is . . ."

"In the boot of the Mondeo." Jenny explained.

"In the boot of *your* car," he continued. He knelt beside the man, patting him down and removing some keys that were attached to a belt-loop. He threw them to Jenny, who uncuffed Nicole. "DS Dalziel, would you do your thing, read him his rights, etcetera?"

Parlabane stood up and walked over to Nicole as Jenny hand-cuffed the bleeding prisoner. "You have the right to a quality kicking from Ms Carrow here, when she feels up to it," she told him. "You have the right to some extremely slipshod surgery on that wound. You have the right to have Dr Slaughter supervise your anaesthetic management. And afterwards, you have the right to remain in jail for a *very* long time."

Nicole put her arms around Parlabane, sobbing, sniffing, squeezing.

"Thank you," she said throatily. "Thank you."

"De nada," he said.

"I thought you were dead, both of you."

"So did he," Parlabane said with a nod. "You can call for back-up now if you like, Jen."

"Well I'd disappear that gun before they get here, Scoop."

He bent down and picked up the two spent shells from the carpet, sliding them into a pocket in his jeans. Then he retrieved the auto-matic that was lying by the wall and ejected two slugs from it, pocketing them as well. He tucked the Beretta into the back of his jeans, under his polo-neck, and placed the other gun on the desk.

"What gun?" he said. "I don't have a gun. I shot him with his own weapon, but I don't know where the shell-casings have gone, so I'm afraid you won't be able to get a match."

"Aw, that's gonna be too bad," Jenny said, smiling at the man on the floor. "See, we can do conspiracy too."

"Guns," Nicole mumbled, now seated on the bed, Sarah tending to the cut on her thigh with some bandaging she had found in the bathroom, Parlabane leaning on the desk and Jenny frogmarching her arrest down the stairs.

"Huh?"

She jiggled her head briefly, as if shaking herself out of a small trance. "It's what I heard in the car," she explained. "They've got big problems – well obviously – but . . . hang on." She took a few breaths, relaxing herself and ordering her thoughts. "We weren't the only targets tonight. They had two men up north who were supposed to kill Thomas McInnes and the other fugitives. When they were driving me here, the guy you shot kept guard on me in the back seat. Morgan, his name was. The other one drove. Morgan called him Adds, which could be short for something. The guy who was sent to kill you was called Harcourt. Anyway, it looked like Morgan was in charge. He made a phone call to someone – his boss, presumably,"

"Knight," said Parlabane.

"That was it, Knight. Telling him they had me, mission accomplished sort of thing. After that he didn't say much. Knight was doing the talking. When he hung up, Morgan told Adds to pack his bags as he and Harcourt would be going up to Strathgair right away. He said . . . I think 'Paddy and Bowes' . . . had fucked it up. They'd got themselves arrested, which seemed to astonish everyone concerned. In Morgan's words, 'the targets kicked their fucking heads in and left them for the local plods'."

"So it *was* a public execution," said Parlabane. "Staged manhunt and death penalty while the nation wanks, sorry watches. But their hitmen were almost as good as the losers down here."

"Evidently. Adds asked if the targets had taken their guns, but Morgan said no, they'd left those for the plods as well, which meant word would be getting out that the fugitives were no longer armed. Adds said it wouldn't matter, they could still plant something, make out leaving the guns had been a double bluff. But what Morgan said the fugitives *had* taken was their field-phone, as he called it."

Parlabane's eyes widened. He reached behind and picked up the state-of-the-art mobile that had been lying on the desk, flipping the cover open.

"Don't suppose Morgan or his buddies would give us the

number if we asked politely. Maybe if I stood on his bullet-wound. Have you seen *Dirty Harry*?"

"You won't need it," Nicole said. "Morgan only pressed about two buttons to call Knight. A shortcode. If they're operating as a team, then all their portables might be programmed in."

"Very clever, young lady," he said. "And if so, it would constitute hard, electronic proof that they're all working together. Knight and these guys here tonight, Knight and the two goons in Strathgair . . . Let's see." He pressed the memory dial button on the sleek but weighty plastic device, then hit the number 1. The LCD read "1?" Parlabane cancelled, hit M again, then 01. A sequence of numbers arrayed across the LCD panel and a ringing tone purred from the earpiece. It rang once more.

"Yeah, Knight, who is it?" said a voice, irritated, a low, white-noise buzz in the background suggesting he was in a car, and moving.

Parlabane arched his eyebrows, looking across at Sarah and Nicole, then hung up. "Exhibit A, your honour," he said, holding the phone aloft.

He pressed M again, then dialled 02. A few seconds later they heard an electronic chime from somewhere downstairs in the house. He hung up again.

M. 03.

Ring.

Ring.

Ring.

Ri . . . "Hello?" said an uncertain, quiet voice, youthful, Scottish.

"Yes, hello, sorry to disturb you," said Parlabane, "but could I speak to Mr Thomas McInnes, please?"

Parlabane heard what sounded rather bizarrely like splashing noises, then an older voice spoke, defensive, accusatory.

"This is Tam McInnes. Who are you?"

"My name is Jack Parlabane, Mr McInnes. We've got representatives in your area just now and I was wondering if you were interested in any double glazing."

"*Whit?*"

"Knock it off, Jack."

"Perhaps you'd prefer to speak to my associate, Nicole Carrow. I believe you know her."

Ring.

Ring.

Ring.

"Hello? Who's this?"

"It's Jack."

"Fuck's sake, Jack, it's the middle of the night. What is it?"

"Where's the fuckin' story, Fraz? Nobody's read it, nobody's heard it, nobody's even seen it. What's the fuckin' score, here at all?"

"Oh, sorry, Jack, didn't tell you. We ran a decoy first edition so we'd be the only paper with it. Make sure the opposition didn't see it until it's too late."

"A *decoy*? Too late? It was almost too late for *me*, ya fuckin' idiot. Three men who didn't know we were on to them broke into my flat a couple of hours ago and tried to kill me, Sarah and Nicole Carrow. This was kind of the scenario I was trying to avoid when I gave you the fuckin' tale in the first place, ya stupit Jambo moron."

"Christ, I'm sorry Jack, I'd no idea. I would never have done it if . . ."

"I should fuckin' well hope you would never have done it *if*. But you fuckin' well *did*."

"I'm so sorry, Jack, believe me. Really, really sorry. But you must understand I had to make the most of it. It was the scoop of the decade."

"No, Fraz. What I've got *now* is the scoop of the decade. Names and evidence of who killed Voss. Name and a motive for who needed him dead. And exclusive access to Tam McInnes, Paul McInnes and Cameron Scott."

Parlabane could hear Fraz swallow.

"I said sorry *before* you told me that, Jack, remember? I *was* sorry already. I'll give you whatever you want. You can name your price, within reason. In fact you can be reasonably unreasonable. Fuck it, you can have anything you ask for."

"I thought you'd say that. Well, you can get me a helicopter for a start."

"A helicopter?"

"That's what I said. Six-seater or bigger, ready to leave from Ingliston in one hour, or the story goes elsewhere."

"Two hours. I'll need at least two hours."

"Ninety minutes."

"It'll be there."

The helicopter swooped into the wide glen, banking around a truncated spur and down between the hills. Parlabane was leaning into the cockpit talking to the navigator, gesticulating at the map he had brought, and pointing out of the windows. They had received a stern police warning over the radio about twenty minutes earlier, telling them to change course and generally fuck off out of what was – temporarily – restricted airspace, i.e. the areas they were flying their own choppers around in search of the fugitives. Tam McInnes had told them the cops had hitherto agreed to look in the wrong places, but with the widespread realisation this morning that the game was a bogey, such cooperation had clearly been withdrawn as they endeavoured to bring the fugitives in and wash their hands of any complicity ASAP. It was like lunchtime in the Serengeti, there were so many birds hovering around, scanning the surface terrain for pickings. But happily, even with the security forces trying to look in the *right* places, they were still way off-target, and the restricted airspace did not include Parlabane's destination.

He glanced back, looking at Nicole as she stared through the glass at the landscape below. Her reddened eyes had the full Samsonite set under each, and her top lids had slid down a few times on the flight north, but she was wide awake now. Parlabane needed her to be there so that McInnes knew who they were and that it wasn't a trap, but even if this hadn't been the case, there'd still have been nothing could have stopped her getting on that helicopter.

The same went for Fraz. Parlabane had asked just how much of heaven and earth he had needed to move to get the 'copter at such short notice, to which he replied that he had merely phoned Angus Gilmore, who was very happy to assist. Gilmore had a lot of connections in the heaven- and earth-moving businesses. The bird was in the air shortly after dawn. Its proprietor would, Gilmore took open delight in saying, shit blood if he knew how many laws they would be using it to break, and its two crew were happy to hear no more than directions, allowing them to bail out on a "we didnae know" ticket if there were any future consequences, or even just future awkward questions.

Fraz sat at the back, next to the large ghetto-blaster he had insisted on bringing aboard, only to be told once airborne that he couldn't listen to it as it buggered up the flight instruments. Parlabane wormed it out of the navigator that this was actually a bit of a fib intended to protect him and the pilot from potentially dreadful music – "that beard, he looks a bit of a folkie; this is a strictly No-Runrig flight" – and got the go-ahead for Fraz to tune into Radio Four, which he jacked up loud to compensate for the noise of the engine and the blades.

"You know, you can actually *die* of smugness," Parlabane warned, watching Fraz lap up the broadcasts.

". . . stunned reactions to this morning's revelations in *The Saltire* which detail an attempt on the life of the lawyer representing the Voss Four, and draw a connection to the death of Finlay Campbell, also of Manson & Boyd – as well as claiming the four accused couldn't have carried out the murders of Roland Voss's two bodyguards . . ."

". . . has since emerged that three men are in custody following a further attempt on Nicole Carrow's life in the early hours of today, as well as attempts to murder John Lapsley, the journalist who wrote this morning's stories, and his fiancée, Dr Sarah Slaughter, at their Edinburgh home . . ."

". . . arrest of two men outside Strathgair late last night. Sergeant John Shearer has made a statement in the past hour that one of the men's fingerprints matches some of those found on the bus which crashed en route to Peterhead Prison on Tuesday night. However, police have no record of a fifth prisoner being on board . . ."

"Know what that sound is, Nicole?" Parlabane asked, with the most misanthropic smile she had seen this side of Jack Nicholson. She shook her head, not sure she even knew what sound he was talking about.

"It's the sound of the shit hitting the fan."

". . . who has been coordinating the search has said that these developments do not change his mission to apprehend the three remaining fugitives. 'Their guilt or innocence has to be decided in a court of law and it remains my job to make sure they appear in one' . . ."

". . . for Scotland, Alastair Dalgleish, told journalists that there was a real danger of media hysteria obstructing the investigation. 'We must wait for the full facts to emerge before jumping to conclusions.'"

"That would be a fucking first," Parlabane muttered.

"'The high profile of the late Mr Voss and the understandable level of public interest in these developments over the past few days has made everyone hungry for further sensation; and as the manhunt has not yet delivered a satisfactory conclusion, people are therefore likely to over-react to any fresh angle or apparently related event. The public – and the media – should remember that the only proven facts we have right now are that these men were apprehended at the scene of Roland Voss's murder, and that they subsequently absconded from a prison bus, leaving three more bodies at their backs.'"

"Prick," said Fraz.

"Well, we've made some impact on the pompous tit," said

Parlabane. "He's started referring to them as men rather than animals. Wonder if he'll call Michael Swan one when we prove he did it?"

". . . editor of *The Saltire* has said Miss Carrow is not under police protection because there is growing evidence that members of the police and/or security forces may have connections to the men involved. He has refused to reveal the whereabouts of the lawyer to the police and has defended harsh criticism of his newspaper's conduct from Charles Mo . . ."

The helicopter came in low over the small loch, the water's blue surface streaked with long orange lozenges, stray canoes, scattered and unmanned, bobbing on the waves. It dropped its speed and altitude further as it traced the south-running river, all eyes scanning the ground and the water below.

"There," said Parlabane with a laugh, pointing it out to the pilot. "It's you they're waiting for, Nicole."

She looked to where Parlabane had indicated. It was a small shore of grey pebbles, cut into the bank at a bend in the waterway, like a bite out of the land, not quite overhung with trees, a tousily unkempt field on the other side. A place the water would flood into and pound during the rains of winter, but for now a niche, where three orange canoes were arranged in an "N" shape.

The helicopter came down gently on the long grass, sheep scattering in reflexive panic. Nicole and Parlabane climbed out and ran across to the fence that warded the woollier residents away from the bank. Parlabane pulled a strand of wire up to allow Nicole to climb through, then ducked under it himself and jumped down the three-foot drop to the water's edge.

"Mr McInnes?" Nicole called, her voice almost lost in the noise of the rotor blades behind her.

Tam McInnes's head emerged slowly from inside one of the canoes, then with some effort he squeezed his body out of the hole and knocked on the other two vessels. He stood tall, defiant, redoubtable. Parlabane recognised Paul McInnes from photographs that had repeatedly popped up on news programmes, and recognised Cameron Scott from photographs that had repeatedly popped up on nature programmes. A cross between a sloth, Emo Philips and a broken umbrella.

The three of them waded quickly through the thigh-deep water to where Parlabane and Nicole helped them up on to the grass banking next to the fence. Tam McInnes clutched Nicole's wrists with both hands and smiled, saying nothing, just nodding his head. She laughed a little, sniffing as a few more tears found their way out of her overworked ducts' emergency reserves.

"This the double-glazing joker?" he said, indicating Parlabane.

"This is Jack Parlabane, yes," she answered. "He has his irritating moments, but he *has* saved my life twice in the past forty-eight hours."

Tam held out a hand.

"I'm sorry about your friend, Mr McInnes," Parlabane said solemnly, gripping it. "They killed a good pal of mine too."

Tam looked him in the eye and nodded again. "I'm very pleased to meet you, Mr Parlabane."

Parlabane pulled the door closed and gave a signal to the pilot, and the chopper lifted off again. There was a palpable release of tension around him as the runners left the grass. He sat down beside Tam, Nicole behind him in the seat next to Paul, Fraz at the back, his radio displaced by the invertebrate who insisted on answering only to "Spammy", which sounded about right to Parlabane.

Fraz began to pour cups of hot soup from a hideously cheerful tartan flask, passing them forward to each of the new passengers, who drank them down gratefully before moving on to some filled rolls he produced from a polythene bag.

As they ate, the three of them continued to scan the skyline restlessly, turning their heads back and forth to look out of the windows on both flanks. All eyes locked nervously on to the right-hand side as another helicopter came into view, before the fact sank into each of them that they were heading away – at speed and undetected – from where they were sought. In the distance they could see two more of the birds, intent and oblivious.

"What are they lookin' for?" Spammy asked.

"You three," said the incredulous Fraz, who really would have to learn.

"Why?"

Tam shook his head.

Fraz reached into his poly bag once more, this time lifting out some small disposable tumblers and a half-litre bottle of Glenfiddich, the squat green affair renowned of airport duty-free shops.

"It's a bit early in the morning, I know, but I'm sure you could do with something else to warm you up," he said. "It's the after-meal complimentary drink as part of the Air Saltire in-flight service."

Parlabane turned round to take hold of his and Tam's measures, catching a look at Nicole, who surprised him by knocking hers back in a gulp and gesturing for a refill. Fraz obliged. More relaxed, she began to sip the second glass. Paul beside her was smiling through tears as he cradled his drink, his mind and body being mercilessly racked by just about every emotion on the back-logged list, now that he felt safe enough once more to feel *anything*. Nicole's eyes filled up again too, then she laughed out loud at herself for doing it. Paul laughed also. Above the constant hum of the aircraft, Parlabane could hear them all start to chat to one another, as the fear and the danger dissipated in the helicopter's slipstream.

Tam had a slow, closed-eyed sip at the pale, golden liquid, then sighed and raised his glass to Parlabane, who lifted his own, mirroring Tam's unsmiling expression.

"This isnae over yet, you know that, don't you?" Parlabane said to him.

Tam nodded.

"Aye," he growled darkly. "You're fuckin' right it's no."

341

THIRTEEN

Knight got back into his car and pulled slowly away from the petrol pumps, then accelerated swiftly on to the slip-road, leaving the South Lakes service area behind and rejoining the motorway. Despite all the shit, he couldn't help but feel a thrill run through him as his mind and body reacquainted themselves with almost forgotten excitements. The buzz, the sense of challenge, the discipline, the exhilaration; damn it, *playing again*. He was the manager who had come off the bench and got stripped himself because the team were losing; all the old touch was coming flooding back, the rust and cobwebs shaken free.

It had gone wrong. It had gone very, very wrong, on a scale and at a rate that would have precipitated despair and inevitably panic in most others, but then he was a very long way different from most others. He had lost five men – his entire covert crew on this op – in the space of a few hours, and none of them had even managed to neutralise their targets in the process. They wouldn't talk – he could rely on that, at least – but it was nonetheless a disaster of such apparent totality that it had stretched even his nerve to remain calm and survey the situation dispassionately.

Discipline. This was about discipline. Remaining calm in the face of catastrophe was little more than a trained suppression of reflex, something even pampered politicos like Dalgleish had mastered. What took discipline was the ability to maintain your judgment, to be able still to move forward, even if that meant finding a path between the crashing pillars and burning bodies. And the first discipline was not to feel sorry for yourself, which was a bigger feat than it sounded. It was a dangerous weakness because it offered consolation, but consolation was for the defeated. The seductively comforting thought that you had done your best, done all you could, but had been the victim of astronomically improbable bad luck. We woz robbed, Brian. It was surrender with excuses; I lost but it wasn't my fault. Luck, fault, mitigation – none of it mattered, because your performance in this game was judged only by whether you got away with it.

He *had* been unlucky, devilishly so. But he wouldn't have been professional if he hadn't been ready for that. You didn't go ahead with an op like this if you weren't prepared for all the possibilities, and that included all-hands disaster.

That was what Dalgleish hadn't really grasped. You could plan something with micro-fine meticulousness, account for every contingency your experience and imagination can list, but it's never watertight. There's always the chance of a rogue, unforeseen factor, and there's always the possibility of simple, old-fashioned bad luck. And you've got to be ready to accept it and deal with it if it comes to that. Dalgleish had sat and listened to him say this, but he hadn't *heard*. That was the difference between them. Blokes like Dalgleish thought you *could* cover all the bases. Even if they knew they were playing the percentages, and that therefore there was still a minute chance of failure, they didn't really believe it would happen, and they never contemplated what they would do if it did. That was why his portable had been ringing non-stop since dawn, Dalgleish probably flapping around in his office, shitting himself since he heard, and trying to get through to him for reassurance that everything was going to be all right.

Well it was, kind of. But apart from the fact that he wasn't going to tell *anyone* what he was up to, Knight thought it would do Dalgleish good to sweat it out for a while. It would be a valuable exercise in panic-management, as well as reminding him starkly of where, who and what he was without Knight's assistance and patronage: respectively, lost, nobody and fucked.

Knight had been let down, badly, but the time for anger, self-pity and retribution was not now. Discipline. Professionalism. And downright maturity. You make a decision and you live with it, and you accept – from the word go – that you'll still live with it if it backfires.

The arseholes had contrived to miss the original barn door from ten paces. Unarmed, unsuspecting civilian targets. Fucking hell, talk about fish in a barrel. But he had harboured doubts for a while. He had already been thinking about a change of personnel, but then the Voss thing had come along. Very little notice; a matter of weeks. And stakes so high that he couldn't afford to pass on the job. Never mind the money; that was the slightest consideration. It was the threat to Dalgleish and the fortunes of his whole party posed by Voss's grip on their collective testicles. Whether they acceded or not, Dalgleish, Swan and the whole parade were going down. A corruption scandal that would sink their careers and scupper an already holed and sinking administration; or a political action – effectively legalising hard pornography – that would turn the stomachs of even their most traditionally loyal voters, for which the party chiefs would exact revenge . . . by which time they'd be in opposition. Which was the real threat. If the Tories went down, well, it wasn't exactly the end for Knight's ambitions, but it would certainly slow the pace for a while.

He knew they were past their best. Unfit, stale, and getting complacent through having things go their way too long and too easily. Thinking about their wallets and their stomachs, using their positions to line both, forgetting the real reasons they had got into their jobs in the first place. It was time for a clear-out, anyone could see. And if he had been given a couple of months' notice, he'd have done just that. Fired them all, got in a new crew. Guys who were young, hungry, sharp and out to impress. Guys who were in the job for the job's sake, not for the wages or because it made them feel important. Guys who just wanted the high, the excitement of carrying out an op, like those five stupid fuckers did once upon a time.

But nonetheless, it had still been his decision to proceed, to go with the current line-up one more time. His decision, pressured, high-stakes or not. He had known the risks, he had considered the implications, and he had gone ahead.

But not without devising a back-up.

He reached down to the passenger seat and took hold of the Mars bar he had bought at South Lakes, squeezing it up out of the wrapper with his left hand and biting off a ravenous mouthful. He hadn't eaten since that fish and chips yesterday evening, and he'd left half of it after seeing one of the local cops devour a deep-fried pizza. Bleeagh. Fucking pervert. He chewed noisily on the chocolate and tossed the wrapper to one side. It landed on top of the map, which itself sat above the unopened copy of *The Saltire* he had picked up at the service station. The story was all over the radio and the TV, but he had decided that a copy of the paper itself would come in useful.

He had actually phoned Swan *before* Morgan's unit got themselves arrested, and before he found out what *The Saltire* had blabbed. Bowman and Paterson's failure had caused too much damage on its own, and everything thereafter was to be geared towards limiting the consequences. Even if the lawyer and that hack had been plugged, even if Harcourt and Addison had made it to Strathgair and taken out the three runners, there were already too many question marks all over the place. Never mind whether the great unwashed were going to start questioning the Voss Four's previously indubitable guilt, he had to worry about what was happening on the inside. There were plenty of men who would do you favours and be happy (i.e. protected) not to know what was really going on or what it was really about, but if it went fugazzi, they didn't know you. That was no reflection on them, that was just the rules. While the op was under control, so was the information; everyone, from the top down, asked only the questions you let them ask. But now every last flatfoot in the highlands was a potential loose cannon; they would all be trying to work out why two covert agents had been found tied to a tree in front of a pile of guns, to guess why the prints of one of them were all over the prison bus, and generally wondering what the bloody hell was going on. And more importantly, so would their bosses.

He had phoned Swan at his Westminster flat, and the bastard woke up fast when he heard the situation. Knight let him babble a bit – lots of "Oh my God"s and "does Dalgleish know"s and "are you sure there's no chance"s – then told him to shut up and listen.

"I think I can still get you out of this," he said.

Swan shut up and listened.

"Dalgleish, I'm not so sure about. He might have to take his own chances, I don't know. It's nothing personal, just how the cards have fallen. Simple luck. There's a way to save you, and had it gone another way, I might have been having this conversation with him. But understand this: if I do this for you, you don't just owe me, I *own* you. Got that?"

Swan paused.

"All right, fuck you then . . ."

"NO! NO! Please, don't hang up," Swan blurted. "It's just . . . I don't know what you're trading here. I want . . ."

"You're not getting this, are you? I'm not asking for a trade, Michael. It's not a question of me getting you out of this and then you being bound to repay me as I see fit. Me owning you wouldn't be an agreement of this deal that you had to honour, or that you could try to wriggle out of. It would be a bare fact. That's what I'm telling you. I just want to hear you acknowledge and accept it before I do anything, because I'll need your full cooperation if this is going to work, and I don't want you wasting time looking for escape clauses." .

Swan sighed. He sounded resigned, broken. "Okay. I accept, I do. Whatever you want. You own me. Just tell me what I have to do."

"Not over the phone, you idiot."

"Where then? I thought you were in Scotland."

"I am. But we can meet halfway. Get in your car."

"But it's . . . I've got a meeting with Camelot in five hours in Westminster."

"Michael, get a grip. If you walk into the House today, there'll be a dozen coppers waiting outside for you by the time you leave. You have to act now. This is for keeps."

"All right. All right. Where?"

"Giggleswick. Your little cottage in the Yorkshire Dales you think no-one knows about, where you 'entertain' that Rugby League player from Leeds."

"Jesus."

"No, I don't believe that's his name. Get driving, Michael. Forthwith. I'll tell you how we're going to play it from there."

"All right. All right."

Knight could hear the trembling in Swan's voice. He sounded like he was about to cry.

"Now, we're not just going to have to work out our answers in advance, we're going to have to anticipate what the questions might be, and I'll need all the help you can give me on that. You'll have to bring whatever documentation is to hand about the FILM Accord, so that we can see where the danger is likely to lie."

"I've got . . . some stuff here, some papers. But most of it's at the Department. Should I . . .?"

"No. Just what's to hand. Time is going to be the most important factor here. Get driving. And talk to no-one. I mean it. I find out you've spoken to anybody – Dalgleish, anybody – and I walk."

"I won't, I won't."

"I know."

*

347

Knight turned up the car radio and allowed himself a smile of satisfaction as this morning's deft act of spin-doctoring took effect across the nation's airwaves and penetrated the nation's minds. It was so laughably simple. No-one believed it, no-one even listened to it if you sent some sod out to the front steps to make a statement. But if you called up the right person, told them it was utterly hush-hush and that they'd owe you heavily for giving them this, not only did they swallow it in one gulp, but they gave it top billing and practically the whole country bought it too. That was what this hack – this Lapsley or Parlabane or whatever he called himself – didn't understand. He had found out a few facts; so bloody what. But the fool thought the facts were the start and finish, like inert exhibits that everyone would look at and draw the same conclusions from. They weren't. They were materials. And the art of controlling information lay in *shaping* the materials.

". . . geant Shearer has come in for some heavy fire over his decision to go public with his information rather than take it directly to the detectives supervising the manhunt, but he has strongly rebutted this criticism, saying that as the finger of suspicion was pointing at unknown sources *within* the investigation, his actions were entirely in the public interest. This criticism comes in the wake of remarks by the Scottish Secretary, Alastair Dalgleish, warning against what he called 'media hysteria', but with police confirming that they are holding three men in relation to incidents last night at two Edinburgh addresses – one of which was the home of the journalist John Lapsley – and with accusations of conspiracy and cover-up more widespread by the minute, it seems Mr Dalgleish may have closed the door after the horse has bolted. Indeed, on the line now is our correspondent, John Crispen, who may be able to shed some new light on this morning's developments."

"Thank you, Sally. Yes, I spoke this morning with a very senior figure in the security services – someone who refused to be named, but someone who, I must stress, is involved in the Voss investigation at the highest level. And he admitted to me that suspicions had been growing among detectives that police and security-services personnel – possibly even figures *within* the investigation – were involved in the murder of Roland Voss and in the events that have followed. He pointed to the suicide of Craigurquhart security chief Donald Lafferty on Monday, and admitted also that detectives had already expressed fears that the prisoners' escape was not the opportunist outcome of a fortuitous accident, but the result of an orchestrated operation. He said he could not rule out the possibility that one or more of the men killed may have been party to the plan and subsequently betrayed.

"However, most dramatically, he told me that he still had no doubts over the guilt of the Voss Four, and believes that they have been continuously *assisted* – rather than somehow framed – by whoever these insiders may be. In response to some of the revelations and theories posited this morning, he asked what he considered the obvious question: why would a group of conspirators engineer the escape of the men they had framed for Voss's murder, when they were already set up to take the blame?

"I asked him, in that case, why the fugitives were not then evacuated from the area by car. He admitted he had no answer to that, saying he could only speculate that perhaps their plan had not gone off perfectly, and be grateful that this was the case."

"What of the two men arrested by Sergeant Shearer?" the newsreader asked.

"My source said detectives believe these men *were* involved in assisting the escape, but may have subsequently been double-crossed by the fugitives. However, he admitted he was not optimistic that the two men would avenge themselves by forwarding vital information, reminding me that Donald Lafferty had swallowed a cyanide pill rather than betray his superiors."

"And did your source have any response to the alleged attempts on the life of Thomas McInnes's lawyer, Nicole Carrow, and the suggestion that Finlay Campbell's death was also related to the conspiracy?"

"Yes he did, Sally. He refused to comment on Mr Campbell's

death until Strathclyde Police had concluded their own investigation, but he said he wholly understood Miss Carrow's reluctance to approach the police for protection. He admitted that in light of recent developments it was as well she hadn't, and said he believed she was among the innocent victims of this affair. He pointed out that Miss Carrow had only met McInnes once, having just joined the firm of Manson & Boyd a few weeks ago, and said he feared she had been unknowingly set up when she received the letter she presented to detectives on Monday. He said it would be entirely consistent with the ruthlessness the investigation had so far uncovered if the attempts on her life were a brutal and cynical ploy to cast doubt on the Voss Four's guilt by suggesting that they themselves were the victims of a cover-up.

"Finally, he warned that it would be suicidally negligent to be influenced by sensationalism and consider these three fugitives anything other than extremely dangerous."

Swan resembled something that had fallen out of a rolled-up mattress in a skip. He was wearing a blue Benetton sweatshirt which must have lain crushed in a drawer for the several years since it had been fashionable, and a pair of brown corduroys. For a man who usually looked like he had been born in a suit, it was a sartorial statement of distress and desperation. The normally immaculately coiffured mane of hair now looked like Heseltine in a wind tunnel, as if he had driven up from London with all the windows open, and his solarium-tanned cheeks had undergone a rapid bleaching process. He stood impatiently at the open front door like a kid bursting for the toilet, Knight having noticed him twitching at the curtains as he rolled the Scorpio up the driveway.

Knight was deliberately and demonstratively unhurried as he slowly climbed out of the car and locked it, even putting on the burglar alarm despite there being not a soul for bloody miles. He ambled up to the cottage's porch, patting Swan firmly on the shoulder and walking past him into the hall.

Swan patently didn't know what to say, not even how to greet him. Circumstances he wasn't programmed for. No protocol from the image-makers on this one.

"Christ almighty, man, fix yourself a drink and for God's sake relax," Knight told him. "You've got to play the unflappable statesman, not wobble around ashen-faced like you've just seen Banquo's ghost."

"Okay, okay, okay," Swan muttered, bending down and reaching into an antique lacquered cabinet as Knight sat back in an armchair. He poured himself a large brandy and gestured to Knight with a glass. Knight shook his head.

"Drink up," he instructed. "And then have another."

Swan sat down opposite with his second brandy, not relaxing but at least now attempting to give the impression that he was.

"So what are we going to do?" he asked, finally.

"The documents?"

"Oh yes, yes," he muttered, getting up and retrieving a folder from his briefcase, which sat at the foot of a hatstand just outside the living-room door. He handed it to Knight and then sat back down, picking up his drink from the carpet. Knight opened the folder and began to flip through the thick wad of papers.

"Hmm," he said. "I think we should be . . . look, do you have a desk or something?"

"Yes," Swan said, springing up, jumpy and over-eager. "I have a study, sort of."

He led Knight back into the hall and along past the kitchen to a cramped chamber opposite the bedroom. It contained an old desk and a chair, its back to the window. This last afforded a view of a stately oak in the garden outside, which blocked out a good deal of the light and contributed to the study's atmosphere of claustrophobic and depressing dinginess. A bookcase climbed to the ceiling on one wall, bearing several shelves of suspiciously neat and sequential legal volumes and encyclopaedia, which, along with the conspicuous lack of cup-rings and writing utensils on the desk, betrayed the room's phoniness. Swan never worked there;

probably seldom went in there. It didn't even have a phone. It was just a cover, an excuse for having the place if the wrong people found out about it. "Yes, I go there to read and work and be alone." Not to shag strapping young rugger stars.

"Have a seat," Knight commanded, placing the folder on the desk and standing over it as he began to sort the documents into piles. Swan finished his brandy and leaned back in the chair, tipping its spine against the wall.

"If you were listening to the radio you'll have heard the first part of my damage-limitation strategy," Knight said, looking up momentarily from the paperwork.

"Yes, I did," Swan confirmed enthusiastically.

"It'll dampen the hysteria down a little, but the questions are still going to pile up, even if we can neutralise the remaining three accused." Knight walked around to one side of the desk, staring through the window at the oak as he spoke. "The problem is that whatever conspiracy theories start flying around, about cops or MI5 or the bus crash, Voss, blah blah blah, the one thing they're missing is a motive. I mean, have you seen this, for instance?" Knight picked up his copy of *The Saltire* from underneath the now empty cardboard wallet and handed it to Swan, who unfolded it and placed it face-up on the desk in front of him.

"I've heard the radio references, of course," Swan said, looking down at the broadsheet, "but I hadn't seen the actual . . ."

Swan was unable to finish his sentence, due to his brain suddenly applying itself to the task of decorating the bookshelves in a glistening red and pink. Knight wiped his prints from the gun and placed it in Swan's right hand, which dangled at the end of his arm as it hung over the edge of the chair. He had a quick look at the corpse's right temple, satisfying himself that there was a powder-burn underneath the trickling blood. Knight removed a sheet of newsprint from inside his own jacket, and placed it among the piles of FILM Accord bumf, in front of *The Saltire*. It was a report from an American economics and business journal analysing figures sourced to a Dutch newspaper, detailing the

352

breakdown of Roland Voss's turnover for 1995, company by company. Messy slashes of luminous yellow highlighter pen picked out the pornography production, sales and distribution operations. The figures underneath each had a lot of zeros on the end.

"So, what we got?" asked Gilmore, standing up and walking towards them, Fraz moving quickly into the vacated seat on the settee.

Parlabane had returned to the office about an hour earlier. He had gone home with the purpose of joining Sarah in grabbing some kip, she having been persuaded that an attempt on her life and her part in a danger-fraught rescue mission was sufficient grounds for (for once) phoning in sick and taking the day off. She had been busy with the SOCOs while he had been flying the friendly skies. The cops found the missing section of their kitchen window on the roof, and took samples of the glass to match against fragments they might find on the suspects' clothes. They had also removed the duvet cover as it had Harcourt's bloodstains on it, and photographed some bootprints left on the stainless-steel draining board. When Parlabane showed up, she had gone directly to bed and left him to wait for the glazier, familiarly sacking out in about a second and a half despite the daylight pouring through the flimsy curtains like they were more a sieve than a basin. In fact, Sarah was so sound, she didn't even notice him climbing under the bed and re-attaching his gun and its clip to the boards below the mattress. After the new pane was in place, Parlabane tried to get his own head down for a while, but it was useless, with his brain still running like Kevin Harper on speed. He settled for a long bath, a change of clothes and a coffee, then walked back up the hill to *The Saltire*.

Gilmore's office was a picture. First, Parlabane had to wait for the security guard now posted outside to receive clearance to let him in. As far as he knew, there hadn't been a security guard outside the editor's office since 1990 when the then incumbent wrote an editorial backing Wallace Mercer's plan to buy Hibs and merge the club with Hearts. Parlabane almost tripped over the two camping mattresses and sleeping bags that lay on the floor of the ante-room where Gilmore's secretary, Catriona, normally worked, her desk now backed up tight against a wall and her chair perched on top of it out of the way. He later discovered a third such mattress just outside Gilmore's exec bog and shower-room, in the carpeted area where the coffee-percolator sat and gurgled.

In the spacious office itself, he had found Tam and Sadie McInnes sitting close together on one of two facing settees, clutching each other's hands tightly. Sadie was a neat wee woman, compact rather than small, damaged but not fragile. Her eyes were red and her face puffy with the passing of tears, but she was smiling as she spoke to Gilmore. Tam couldn't seem to take his eyes off her. Physically he dwarfed her, but he still seemed to be looking up to her somehow.

Fraz sat at the round conference table by one of the windows, where the failing glow of a strangely lilac sky could be seen reflected in the glass shop-fronts of Princes Street. At two more chairs sat Paul and Nicole, and on the table before them sat Fraz's tape recorder, amidst several piles of used dinner plates, coffee mugs and not a few beer bottles. Paul and Nicole were trying to make what they were describing sound real to themselves, its absurdity more striking now that the guns were gone and the blades were sheathed. Fraz was keeping them talking, just two of the five exclusive and sensational interviews that would have people fighting in newsagents tomorrow after the last copy was sold.

Spammy sprawled in a chair and leaned over Gilmore's ornate, antique desk, like an Illustrated Dictionary entry for "incongruity". He was pulling envelopes, papers and plastic boxes from a poly bag advertising a Paisley department store Parlabane knew for a fact had shut down in the early Eighties. The bag looked like it had been buried in a peat bog ever since.

The three erstwhile fugitives were clean-shaven, showered

and kitted in new clothes purchased by Catriona across the road – at M&S going by the ruff of empty green carrier bags sticking out of a bin near the door. Parlabane wasn't sure whether they had grabbed some shut-eye in the interim or whether the mattresses were for in case they had to lie low here overnight. Probably the latter. Gilmore had sent someone to pick up Sadie (and retrieve certain items from a Paisley address) as soon as the three of them were smuggled into the building, and he couldn't imagine Tam or Paul zedding out while they waited anxiously to see her.

They looked a bit like they'd not long come off a flight home from Australia – one that had taken the corporation bus route. Well dressed (almost leisurely attire), tearfully emotional to be with loved ones again, and looking like they'd sleep for three days if they shut their eyes for a second.

Parlabane had grabbed one of the beer bottles and stood by the desk with Spammy, poring over the haul of evidence. He was impressed with Gilmore, who was being generously solicitous towards Tam and Sadie, chatting away, reassuring them in any way he could, and insisting on getting things – food, drink, whatever – for them himself. He seemed humble before them, deferential as if they were so much greater than he for what they had come through. It made a change from guys in Gilmore's position who thought everyone they met should appreciate – (a) who, and (b) how important – they were. Fraz was right: the guy had the heart of a hack, enough to know that it's the tale that matters, not the teller.

Gilmore had stood up partly because Fraz was shooting him eager looks, keen to get more from Tam and some insight into what it must have been like for Sadie. If Parlabane knew Fraz, he'd put special emphasis on how she coped with the blood-thirsty baying of the other newspapers, as he always enjoyed a bit of quality self-righteousness when he could get it.

Gilmore pulled a chair over from the conference table and sat down at the edge of the desk, swigging at a beer bottle and rolling up his sleeves. Parlabane couldn't begrudge him his vicarious thrill; indeed he realised then, looking around the normally neat and sedate office, that in fact it wasn't so vicarious. Three men still wanted for six brutal murders, holed up right here. This whole thing went sour and everyone in this *room* could go to jail.

Parlabane stood back from the desk and leaned against the window, taking another mouthful from the bottle. He had warned Fraz and Gilmore that there was to be no arsing about with big-splash revelations, as Tam, Paul and Spammy couldn't wait for press deadlines; as soon as they had collated the evidence, it would go to Jenny, who would present it to the appropriate authorities. Parlabane hadn't told Jenny about the helicopter trip or what was going on at the office. He knew she'd have vivid enough suspicions, but as long as he said nothing, as a police officer she wasn't put in a compromising position. The issue of how Jenny would bypass Knight in presenting the new evidence looked like never being broached, as the last time Parlabane called her, she told him Knight hadn't shown up today, and *nobody* had any idea why not or where he was.

"I'd say we've got them up the arse with a blowtorch," Parlabane stated matter-of-factly. "Look. Maps, technical plans of Craigurquhart House, faked photos of Mr McInnes, dupes of the stuff stolen from Manson & Boyd . . . but that's just the veg. Here's the meat." He walked the five feet to where a compact midi-system sat on a low table, speakers either side, popped a cassette into the slot and pressed Play.

There was the recognisable bass hiss that identified a portable phone connection, but it seemed to dissipate each time someone spoke. The voices were a little distant, so Parlabane turned up the volume and adjusted the EQ until the words were clearer.

"Knight kill Voss . . . Knight takes Voss . . . Check . . . Knight and Harcourt . . . Harcourt . . . big hard-on . . . killing a billion . . . billionaire . . . doesn't make you any . . . any richer."

Parlabane cued forward on the tape and pressed play again.

". . . only reason yous cunts made it this far is because they

356

were followin' orders to look in the wrang places, an' because they knew *we* had yous in oor sights the whole fuckin' time."

"Good God," said Gilmore, eyes widening.

"That's Paterson and Bowman, the two men arrested in Strathgair last night," explained Parlabane. "Harcourt is the one who tried to kill Sarah and myself. He was planning to use a knife. I do believe that's his forte. The estimable Mr Scott here . . ."

"Spammy."

"Sorry, the estimable Mr Spammy here has also got tapes of the initial blackmail approaches and all subsequent instructions regarding the robbery of Craigurquhart, in which the caller is very specific about the date and time they had to be there, to the minute: 7:20 p.m., last Sunday. Voss was supposed to be heading out to that wankfest shindig in Perth right about then. Knight and Harcourt nip up the stairs while him and the missus are putting on their glad rags, kill everybody then saunter back down. A wee bit later someone goes to see why the VIPs haven't shown up at the waiting limo, and finds the bodies. The guy on the tapes uses a voice-disguiser, but it's what's being said that's important rather than who's saying it."

"It's absolutely incredible," Gilmore declared, shaking his head.

"Oh aye, there's this as well," said Spammy, reaching into a tattered brown envelope that Parlabane noticed was addressed to Sadie McInnes and pulling out a glinting, silver disc with no label on either side.

"What's that?" Parlabane asked.

"This is what was in the safe," Spammy said. "The only thing that was in the safe, in fact."

"You *got* into the safe?" gasped Gilmore.

"Of course. We're professionals," he grinned. "Check the postmark."

They did.

"Cute," said Parlabane. "So what's on it?"

"Fuck knows, man. This is the first I've seen it since Sunday night."

"It says 'McGoughan Technologies'," Gilmore pointed out. "Right there, very small letters. Is that one of Voss's companies?"

"Nah," said Parlabane, picking up the CD. "Disc manufacturer."

He placed it on the midi-system's awaiting tray and watched it slide smoothly inside, only to be greeted with an angry, sustained, strangulated electronic shrieking when he pressed Play.

"Wow!" Spammy laughed. "Voss was intae early Mary Chain. Mental."

"*What?*" asked Gilmore.

Parlabane shook his head, smiling at Spammy's joke and Gilmore's confusion. "Computer data," he explained. "It's a CD-ROM."

"I wonder what would happen if you did actually try to load some early Mary Chain intae a computer," Spammy was saying, unconcerned with whether anyone was paying attention. "Maybe subliminal messages would start appearin' on the screen, kinna the new-tech equivalent of playin' Sabbath albums backwards. 'Come and live in East Kilbride', it might say. Or 'Bobby Gillespie is Santa'."

If someone was listening to Spammy, it wasn't Parlabane. He had hooked up a CD-ROM drive to the PC on Gilmore's desk and was staring at the screen, right hand on mouse, left hand on keyboard, bottom jaw on floor.

". . ." he said.

"Any joy?" inquired Gilmore after a few more minutes, now sitting over at the conference table where Nicole was nibbling a chocolate bar, Paul having splayed himself across the settee opposite his parents.

Parlabane reckoned that if he concentrated really hard, he could maybe think of what to say *and* restore relations between his brain and his mouth long enough to say it.

". . ." he said again.

"Jesus, Jack, you look like you've seen a ghost."

He swallowed, gave it another shot.

"I have," he said, dazed. "But I'm not the one being haunted."

"What is it?" said Fraz, getting up.

"Proof."

"Of what?"

"Whodunnit."

"Swan?" Fraz offered.

"Swan, yes. Swan and another."

"Someone else? Who?"

"The Right Honourable Alastair Dalgleish MP, Secretary of State for Scotland."

Gilmore sprang to his feet, every eye in the room suddenly on Parlabane, whose own remained intent upon the monitor in front of him.

"Proof?" asked Fraz, walking towards the desk.

"Proof," confirmed Parlabane.

Proof – that landed gentry, Old Money, High Tory Alastair, free political thinker, "his own man" and self-styled independent spirit, would have been the Waldemere-Dalgleish who saw his forebears' legacies of land and business crumble if Voss hadn't been secretly propping them up since even before the '87 crash.

– that self-made Eighties-Thatcherite-Revolution success story Michael Swan had also been riding with stabilisers, so to speak, with a hidden benefactor assisting when his entrepreneurial genius inexplicably failed him or circumstances conspired against his otherwise inspired investment decisions.

But Roland Voss had never been in the business of altruistic philanthropy, and there was proof also

– that while a junior minister at the DTI in the late-Eighties, Dalgleish had massaged reports of Voss's liquidity while his bid to buy the Allied Newspapers group was under consideration. Irony number one was that Voss's empire was in ebulliently robust health at the time, but Dalgleish's report had nonetheless greatly exaggerated the extent of his arms revenues. This was to compensate for Voss's reciprocal concealment of the size of his European pornography interests. Irony number two, of course, was that the British establishment found dealing in weapons of torture, mutilation and death more acceptable in a potential proprietor of national newspapers than dealing in videos of a few consenting adults having a shag.

– that while both working at the Foreign Office in 1992, Michael Swan and Alastair Dalgleish had exerted diplomatic influence to stall and eventually scupper territorial peace talks between the military government and rebel guerrillas in the former British colony of Sonzola in western Africa, where Voss coincidentally happened to be on the verge of some massive weaponry transactions. (Voss was diplomatic himself, as well as exemplarily unpartisan – he was flogging hardware to both sides.)

– and that Swan and Dalgleish both owned undisclosed shares in the company which subsequently sealed those multi-million-dollar deals in Sonzola, where anti-personnel mines laid during the conflict, now ended for three years, were still killing and maiming civilians today.

And that was just the highlights. It was all there. Every last blind eye turned in government, every kickback, every hand-out, the works.

"Jesus, where does it tell you who killed Kennedy?" asked Gilmore, gazing transfixed at the monitor.

There were several folders on-screen, each with a general title, such as "Swan" or "DTI", and inside those were rows of icons with names and dates alongside. Every icon, when double-clicked, revealed a different secret. The document icons – depicting a sheet of paper with one corner folded over – when activated, filled the screen with copies of contracts, letters, agreements, certificates, memos; and these were photographs, not DTP files. Voss would doubtless have the originals deposited somewhere. Camera icons threw up photographs of Dalgleish, Swan and assorted others in meetings, with dates and locations printed in the top-left corners, the names and positions of all depicted personnel along the bottom.

Cassette icons played back secretly recorded conversations, a panel appearing centre-screen simultaneously providing a transcript plus (of course) namcs, dates, speakers, venues. And movie-projector icons activated Quick-Time video clips – again surreptitiously recorded – of segments of the meetings detailed in the tape play-backs, just to supply further evidence of who was present and what they were talking about.

"So what does it all mean?" asked Tam, leaning forward on the settee, Sadie and Paul either side of him. Fraz and Nicole sat opposite, Spammy and Gilmore at either end on chairs removed from the conference table. Parlabane stood at the far end of the room, by the window, taking a call on his portable phone.

"It means you'll all very shortly be free to go home," said Fraz. "And free to vote in the imminent General Election the Prime Minister doesn't yet know he's about to call."

"But what I don't get," interjected Nicole, "is why Voss black-mailed Dalgleish. I mean, this stuff proves Parlabane was right about Swan and the FILM Accord and pornography and all that stuff, but I don't see why the world's least-convincing Scotsman was brought into it."

"Leverage," said Fraz. "Voss might have reckoned Swan alone wasn't enough. Once the porn ramifications of the Accord were out of the bag, Swan couldn't have gone to the PM and said he was planning to ratify it because the PM would tell him no he bloody well wasn't. And if Swan insisted, the PM would either think he had gone mad, or worse, suspected he was being pressured from somewhere, and started asking questions. Either way, Swan drops it or he's fired, and Voss doesn't get what he wants. But the PM's long been wary of Swan and Dalgleish together, and he'd fancy a head-on with the pair of them almost as little as he'd fancy the opinion-poll consequences of having to fire two senior ministers."

"Maybe," said Gilmore, not sounding convinced. "But I'm not sure the Dutchman even believed the two of them could pull it off.

Knowing Voss, it probably just amused him to play God with their careers, watching them squirm as he squeezed them from both sides in the inescapable dilemma from hell. He made them, gaveth them political life in the first place, so maybe he decided it would be a giggle to taketh away. It's what his newspapers have always done: build 'em up then knock 'em down."

"Aye," contributed Paul, "maybe you should get somebody to root through reports of government scandals across Europe in recent years. Might find a few weird sackings and resignations wi' a hidden story behind them."

"Good idea," Gilmore said. "Bear that one in mind, Ken."

"Sure, sure. But for now I think we'll be pretty busy with events closer to home. Can't wait to see the court artists' impressions of *those* two bastards standing in the dock."

"That'll just be one bastard," corrected Parlabane, standing now behind Fraz and Nicole, holding the phone in his right hand. "That was Jenny Dalziel. Michael Swan's dead, in a cottage in Yorkshire. Acute allergic reaction to a bullet. She just heard down the jungle telegraph; it'll be all over the TV in about half an hour. Usual story, right now cops are only saying 'a forty-four-year-old man blah-blah-blah', but it's him. One to the head, gun in own hand, no apparent signs of a break-in or struggle."

"Jesus, he topped himself," said Fraz, gaping over the back of the settee.

"Like fuck he did," Parlabane sneered. "Even considering last night's shenanigans and today's media frenzy, Swan had absolutely no way of knowing anyone was actually on to *him*. Somebody took him out."

"Knight?" suggested Nicole.

"Well nobody's seen him today. Sounds good to me. Knight knows it's all going to buggery but he doesn't know he's been named. He gives the world Swan as a suicide then waits for people to make the connection – Christ, he could even be the one who 'discovers' the link from the Voss end – and he thinks he's in the clear. Then the only people who could incriminate him are his own men, who he's pretty confident will keep their mouths shut, Mr Knight not being familiar with certain properties of our native woodland fungi."

"What about Dalgleish?" asked Nicole.

Parlabane nodded, thinking, agreeing something with himself.

"He could incriminate Knight," she continued, "but only by incriminating himself. Of course if he was incriminated already . . ."

"Mr McInnes?" Parlabane said loudly, cutting off Nicole's musings.

"Aye?"

"Could I speak to you and your two erstwhile colleagues alone, please?"

Tam looked around at the gathering, finding confused but interested nods of assent from Paul and Spammy, while Fraz stood up and Gilmore offered to lead Sadie and Nicole out of the room.

Parlabane sat on the edge of Gilmore's desk, waiting for the others to leave. The door to the ante-room closed and he looked around at the three of them, Tam and Paul on a settee, Spammy defying a chair's attempts to support him.

"Gentlemen, I realise you've all had a rather stressful few days what with one thing and another," he began, a sparkle appearing in his otherwise tired eyes that would probably have scared the life out of Tam once; not now.

"But I was wondering if I could enlist your specialist services for one last job . . ."

He should have stayed at the Scottish Office.

He should never have left the building. Bloody hell. Jesus bloody Christ.

Dalgleish was crouched on the floor by the window in the semi-darkness, only the glow of the streetlights below picking out the outlines of objects in the room. He sat with his back to the casement, four feet from his desk, on the polished wide floorboards beyond the last tassels of the edge of the carpet, lifting the glass to

363

his mouth with two hands because either on its own trembled too much, and he had already spilled enough down his front to make his shirt cling to his chest. Or maybe that was just the sweat.

There had been no gin left in the house, and that parasitic Frog diplomat had finished the last of the brandy yesterday. His drinks cabinet back home would never have been allowed to run so dry, but as he considered the townhouse little more than a dormitory extension of his office up here, he had rather lacked enthusiasm for stocking up. There had been nothing else for it. The only spirits left were the bottles of single malt whisky people kept giving him as "wee gifties". Every time some bastard handed him one, he felt sure the sod somehow *knew* his publicised liking of it was a fraud. Christ. He had prised open the lid of the box, then mutilated himself trying to get the metal seal off the top of the bottle, a stiff sliver sliding neatly under his thumbnail and into the soft flesh below. Craigellachie, it said. Probably bloody Gaelic for agony. He had poured a large measure into a glass and then drowned it in Coke, which made it almost drinkable.

Enough to have two. And three.

But would St Andrew's House have been any safer? There were lots of people around, certainly, but they all went home sooner or later. Then it would have been just him and the security staff, and how could he be sure about them? Knight wouldn't necessarily come himself. He could send anyone. People with all kinds of passes, access, authority. He might not know his assassin until the moment of death. No-one could protect him. He couldn't phone the police because he wouldn't know which of them were in Knight's pay too, and besides, how could he enlist their protection without the risk of them finding out why he needed it?

He could trust no-one. Knight was like a Portuguese man-of-war, his lethal tentacles stretching out for miles, myriad and almost invisible. What had made him an invaluable ally now made him the deadliest enemy.

And he knew it was Knight. Swan had been told practically bugger-all about the mechanics of the Voss assassination. On the off-chance that there was any evidence leading the trail to him, the last person to have realised it would have been Michael, and he would be the last person on this *earth* to contemplate suicide. If it came to the crunch, Swan would have brazened it out with a display of bare-faced, squirming slipperiness that would put Aitken and Archer's side-windings in the shade. No. Knight's little thugs had blown it and now he was saving his own skin. Absolutely nobody knew where the bastard was and he simply would not answer his portable phone. Well, Dalgleish at least knew where he had been today. And where he must be headed.

Thank God he and Swan had a reputation for being close, otherwise his near-collapse on hearing the news might have seemed suspiciously dramatic. As it was, it probably scored some sympathy points with the voters for him to show such a human, emotional face when he spoke to the cameras later on, possibly the best on-screen blub by a senior politician since Thatcher's onion-in-the-hanky routine in the late Eighties. Except *he* hadn't been acting, though it wasn't Swan he was crying for. He had heard the report only ten minutes later, from a TV next door in the Press Officer's room.

"Mr Dalgleish, as you saw there, clearly *very* distraught by the news, having lost not only a colleague and a political ally, but a close friend too. The Scottish Secretary has asked that the media respect Mr Swan's family's need for privacy at this difficult time. [I.e. go and pester the fuck out of them in London and take a few eyes off the unravelling Voss disaster up here.] The Prime Minister has yet to make a statement on the matter, but he is likely to be deeply upset at the loss of a young and promising member of his cabinet."

Not to mention the loss of another MP and the government's Damoclean one-seat majority, Dalgleish thought. Swan's own majority had been 9,000, which made the constituency marginal by today's standards, so with the party's survival plan built around clinging on until June, the Ulster Unionists would be dusting down their wish list right now. Still, there would be consolation for the boss that it wasn't one of his more loyal ministers, and that Swan had been found with his brains blown out rather than with a bag over his head and half the Sainsbury's fruit counter up his arse.

But then Dalgleish realised the dreadful mistake he had made. He had played right into Knight's hands. He could hear the reporter already: "Mr Dalgleish appeared extremely upset late yesterday afternoon when talking about the death of his friend, Michael Swan, and Scottish Office staff said he looked close to collapse upon hearing the news. It has been confirmed that he left St Andrew's House soon after in a state of visible distress, and went home to his Edinburgh residence where . . ."

He had panicked. He had looked out of his office door and seen everyone in the building as a potential assassin, an anonymous hireling. He couldn't even trust his driver, so he had called a black cab and used all his restraint not to break into a run as he left the building. When he got to the townhouse, he sent the domestic staff home immediately, locked all the doors, turned off the lights and retreated to his study.

What else could he do? He couldn't tell anybody. Not only could he trust no-one but there was no-one who could help him anyway. Nobody could put shackles on Knight, not without everything becoming known. He couldn't flee the country either; he was a senior member of the cabinet, for God's sake, not Stephen Fry. Besides, any such dramatic act would only serve to more quickly precipitate discovery of what he had done.

But *what* had he done? Good God, what choice had he had? Voss had given him two options, but they were both routes to the same destination, and by Christ that was the terminus. What had been done was for the good of the party; for the good of the whole *country*. He had acted in good faith. They couldn't have Voss flooding England with filth, corrupting our children. And neither could they have one man exerting so much influence over government; it was unhealthy. Ending careers upon a whim, threatening to bring down the whole show and let bloody Labour

366

in. It was simply undemocratic. Voss *had* to be stopped, for the sake of Britain's future.

Oh God. Oh good God.

He heard a noise, a grinding, a thump. Footsteps. Oh God oh God oh God.

The glass fell from his shaking hands as he got up, spilling what was left of his drink all over his lap. He scrambled to the door, his steps unsteady with booze and fear, and locked it with a turn of the wrist. Then he backed away, still gripping the key as if it was electrocuting him, eyes fixed on the door as he heard more sounds from the staircase beyond.

So he had taken Voss's schilling, but who could judge him for that? How could he let what his ancestors had worked for and passed down through generations just disintegrate, or worse, be sold into other hands? – Just because Labour had run England into the ground in the Seventies, setting tax levels that forced many of his peers to leave for foreign shores while he stayed to tough it out because he *cared* for this country. Was he to be punished for that? Just because the Economic Miracle his party brought about – with not a little effort from himself – had come along too late to turn his own businesses around without a little help?

Oh God.

The door handle was turning, back and forth, someone trying to get in. Oh God.

A voice somewhere, inside his head. A voice he had ignored long ago, contemptuously shouted down like an opposition back-bencher. A voice of foreboding that never stood a chance of being heard in a time when no-one listened to such doom-sayers, like the luddites and cowards casting their weary words of pessimism over the new dawns of privatisation or health-service reform. A voice of reservation speaking as Voss offered his favour.

Get into bed with the devil, and sooner or later you're going to get fucked.

He heard strange, quiet clicking and scratching sounds at the door, and found himself frozen to the spot with fear, paralysed, helpless.

Sooner or later . . .

He'd thought he could escape by bringing Knight in to get Voss off his back forever, but nothing had changed. He'd only swapped one devil for another.

Sooner or later . . .

There was a dull thud of metal on wood, the bolt sliding back out of the frame. The handle turned. The door opened. And in he walked.

It was the devil, all right, but not quite the one he was expecting.

Much worse.

Parlabane had been surprised at Spammy's agility, the way those long limbs carried him steadily across the slates like a low, scuttling insect, and his reach and strength in pulling himself up where each adjoining building's roof was higher than the other. Paul had been the obvious choice to accompany Parlabane on this part of the job, but Tam insisted Spammy go instead. Parlabane guessed this was because Tam didn't fancy the role of sitting nervously in a car, worrying about what might be happening to his son, and reckoned that having to share that wait with someone like Spammy was probably a factor too.

Spammy had expressed confusion when Parlabane led him up to a close in Mansfield Place, when he knew Paul and Tam had been instructed to park in sight of an address in Drummond Place, a few streets away.

"It's my friend Jenny's flat," he explained, waiting for her to answer the doorbell. "And I'm afraid I don't have any pals who actually live right next door to Mr Dalgleish, so this'll have to do."

Parlabane knew the address from a story he had been sniffing around shortly after Dalgleish became Scottish Secretary. Some of the local papers made a big fuss over the fact that Dalgleish's wife and kids didn't move north with him, and that he hadn't bought a Scottish residence yet. Parlabane was less enthusiastic about the relevance of this because Dalgleish was reputed to see sufficiently little of his wife and kids for it to make bugger-all difference, the facade of a marriage only propped up for moral respectability in the party of dysfunctional family values. What Parlabane was interested in was the fact that the Scottish Office had bought the townhouse and furnished it for him to live in when in Edinburgh, and he had tried to wheedle it out of an increasingly nervous contact whether Dalgleish was paying any kind of rent.

"Well it is now a Scottish Office property, you know, as much as the more administrative buildings."

Parlabane had taken that as a no.

Jenny led them to the skylight, from where they climbed on to the roof, Parlabane explaining to Spammy the fringe benefits – for the burglar – of the architecture and distinctive geometric terraced layout of the New Town; benefits which were of course largely dependent upon having a top-floor address or being the friend of someone who met that criterion.

It took less than ten minutes to reach the roof of Dalgleish's equivalent of a council house. There was a museum-piece collapsible-circuit alarm trip where the small window slotted into the frame. Parlabane pulled his polo-neck out of his jeans, as if he was about to strip, which clearly startled Spammy until he noticed the canvas vest affair underneath, which harnessed a number of vital implements. He removed a compact blade and dexterously cut a hole in the glass, three perpendicular slashes making a rectangle against where the pane met the frame. He then levered the rectangle out, the rubbery, ancient paint and dried putty working like a hinge.

Parlabane pulled from around his chest a length of wire with a fine foil contact at each end, wiping some sweat from his forehead as he crouched over the window-frame. He placed the contacts flat together and slid them between the two white plastic cubes

369

that each housed half of the alarm trip, folding the foil back around them. Then he slowly pulled the skylight open and Spammy held it as he climbed in, Parlabane taking great care not to dislodge the wire.

Spammy clambered in after him, heedlessly dislodging the wire, indeed snagging it on his jumper and dragging it along behind him on the staircase. Parlabane unsnagged it from behind him and folded it up again, shaking his head.

"Guess the alarm's not switched on, huh, Spammy," he whispered, shooting him an attempt at a chastising glare. Pointless. Spammy just grinned.

He sent Spammy downstairs to open the front door for the others, and set about looking for Dalgleish. This didn't prove difficult, as he heard a glass crash to the floor in a room off the landing below when Spammy tiptoed loudly past it. Then he heard the bolt sliding home in the lock, which housed a keyhole from a Tom & Jerry cartoon and doubtless a mechanism installed in a gentler, less security-conscious age. He sighed at its innocent quaintness and pulled out his lock-picking wallet.

Dalgleish was standing in front of an antique bureau, holding the doorkey like it was a gun, quivering and apparently having pissed himself.

"Hi there," said Parlabane, turning on the light. "I'm selling *The Watchtower*. Does Jesus have a place in your life?"

"Wh-what? Who are you?"

"Joe Shmoe. Chuck Fuck. Who do you think?"

"I-I know why you're here, but listen to me, listen to me. I've got money. I can give you money. As much as you want. I'll double what Knight's paying you if you'll let me go. I'll treble it. Oh God, *please*."

Parlabane smiled. Dalgleish clearly didn't find it very comforting.

"I'm not from Knight, and I'm not here to kill you," he said. "I'm here in a kind of representative-stroke-advisory capacity. So take a seat."

Confused but tremulously wary, Dalgleish moved around behind the desk and sat in his chair.

"Good. Now there are some gentlemen here I think you should meet. Guys," he called, leaning back out of the doorway and making a beckoning gesture. Tam walked in first; followed by Paul, carrying a large black case, which he put down with an ominously heavy thump; and finally Spammy. They lined up behind Parlabane, Tam with his arms folded, Paul likewise, Spammy with his hands in his pockets. All of them were staring at Dalgleish. None of them quite looked delighted to see him.

"Just in case there's any confusion, Mr Dalgleish, this is Mr Thomas McInnes, this is Mr Paul McInnes, and this is Mr Cameron Scott. I take it that their names are familiar to you? Oh, tears, Mr Dalgleish? Perhaps you were moved by their dreadful ordeal?"

"Oh God, oh . . ." Dalgleish whimpered, gripping the desk as if it was the only thing preventing him being sucked backwards out of the window and into the Edinburgh night.

"These three men were framed for the murder of Roland Voss on Sunday night, along with a friend of theirs, Robert Hannah, who was murdered yesterday. They were supposed to be murdered too. So was I, in fact, along with my future missus and these men's lawyer, Nicole Carrow, whose boss, Finlay Campbell, was murdered on Tuesday. You know why. But more importantly, we know why too. And it would be safe to say we're not inclined to be very understanding about it."

"Look," Dalgleish said, sweating ruddily but mustering the last dregs of his professional composure. "I can pick up this phone and dial two numbers, an emergency code that will have the police here in moments."

"Aye, very good. Gaun yoursel'," Parlabane said, laughing coldly. "Mr Dalgleish, if you thought the police could protect you in your current plight, my guess is you wouldn't have been sitting in a locked room with the lights off, pissing your pants with fear. The police can't help you because it's Knight who's after you, and Mr Knight has, shall we say, certain influence in that profession."

371

Dalgleish seethed, allowing himself a moment of angry, out-raged hatred before the fear took over again. He tried to look at the four men in front of him, but recoiled every time he caught one of their stares.

"What do you want?" he asked, voice starting to break up.

Parlabane clapped his hands together, as if convening something.

"Well, here's the deal. Dinner is served."

"What?"

"I'm sorry, I was adapting the phrase for your unaccustomed ears, but it loses certain nuances in translation. In the native tongue it is – Mr McInnes, would you?"

"Your tea's oot," growled Tam.

Dalgleish perhaps didn't follow the phrase itself, but it was plain he understood the import.

"However, strangely enough," continued Parlabane, "much as they would dearly like to, and much as you eminently deserve it, my colleagues are not here to beat the shit out of you. In fact, ironically, we are all here to offer you some help. We are in a position to save what I was about to describe as your worthless neck, which would be inaccurate. Fortunately for you, the four of us tend to put a far higher value on human life than yourself or your associates. We also believe that, paradoxically, you consider your *own* life to be worth a great deal, so we are going to offer you the chance to purchase it. Obviously we'll take into consideration that your life's value has undergone a certain depreciation in light of the fact that you'll be spending the rest of it in prison, but we still figure even that's worth a few bob."

Parlabane's face became a cruel portrait of mock-sympathy as he noticed Dalgleish's confusion.

"Oh, I'm sorry, I don't think I made everything quite clear, and it would be unfair if I wasn't upfront about the whole deal. Paul?"

Paul opened the case at his feet and handed Parlabane a card-board folder from inside, which he placed on the desk in front of

Dalgleish, removing and spreading several sheets of paper across the wooden surface.

"You see, I'm afraid we're not offering you the chance to get out of this. I think you'll be able to grasp that from these documents and transcripts."

Dalgleish picked at the sheets, staring disbelievingly at them, mouth working wordlessly for a few seconds.

"But these . . . these prove nothing," he eventually stumbled. "Well, not nothing, but they don't prove I've anything to do with what you're accusing me of."

"Well, the picture changes when one takes into account where these documents came from, which was a CD-ROM locked in Voss's safe at Craigurquhart House and removed by the gentlemen before you. Add to that the fact that Voss stood to make billions if the FILM Accord was ratified by your chum Swan – who has subsequently rendered himself literally brainless rather than just metaphorically – and it starts to look pretty vivid, doesn't it? Except that we both know Swan didn't render *himself* brainless, don't we? Which leads us back to the current situation, viz, that you are well and truly humped. Knight doesn't know that, though. He still thinks he can walk away if he silences you. So as a future ex-Scottish Sec, your last major decision is a straight choice between violent death or a lengthy residence in one of those prisons you're always telling us are too cushy. Except that the latter option is going to cost you."

"You can save me from Knight? How?"

Parlabane shook his head.

"Afraid this is a seller's market, and you're going to have to cough up before I even tell you."

"What? You can't do that. It's absurd."

"Fair enough. We walk. After we've secured you in a very uncomfortable position and left the door on the latch for your big pal."

Dalgleish sighed furiously. "All right. Tell me what you want."

"Well, way I figure it, you couldn't write cheques out of your own account to Knight or any of his, er, subcontractors, and I

373

don't imagine they'd want the conspicuousness of depositing huge amounts in cash at their banks, any more than you would the conspicuousness of withdrawing it. So I figure you've got a well-hidden account somewhere – front company, difficult to trace back to your good self – from which you were going to pay them. An account which is, I would guess, still full, as one tends not to pay upfront for this kind of thing, and I don't imagine you'll be receiving a bill after the way it worked out. Now, an operation like this wasn't going to come cheap. Taking out one of the most rich and influential businessmen in the world, then organising a fake manhunt, plus unforeseen extras like murdering lawyers, journalists, yakka yakka yakka . . . *Lot* of bread. Make with the front company chequebook, Ally."

Dalgleish clenched his jaws together, bit his top lip and generally steamed.

"I'd make my mind up quickly, I was you. You're expecting a visitor, remember. And he could be here at any minute."

"Christ," Dalgleish cursed, and reached into his jacket pocket. He produced a set of keys and opened a drawer in the bureau, pulling out a chequebook. Parlabane took it from him and examined it.

"Very good," he said. "Now, we'll start with a cheque for one hundred thousand pounds made payable to Mr Thomas McInnes."

"A *hundre* . . ."

"Then a cheque for the same amount made out to Mr Paul McInnes, and a third hundred K to Mr Cameron Scott."

"And a fourth," said Tam flatly. "Payable to Mrs Veronica Graham, Bob Hannah's daughter."

Dalgleish looked up, face colourless, lost and hopeless.

"Oh look, just fuckin' get on with it," snapped Parlabane, sitting on the edge of the desk. "It's not as though you'll be needing it where you're going. Besides, according to what's in these documents, it's effectively Voss's money. Jesus, there's Tory gratitude for you. Somebody subs you and you use his cash to take out a contract on him."

374

Parlabane collected the cheques and handed them out.

"Right," croaked Dalgleish in a soul-broken whisper. "What are you going to do for me?"

Parlabane smiled. "We're going to help you," he said cheerily, "to help yourself. We can put you in the protective custody of some police officers we can guarantee are not under Knight's influence, and you can confess everything to them."

"*Confess?*"

"Yup. You see," Parlabane lied, "we don't have any evidence of Knight's misdeeds. We know *what* he did, sure, but we can't prove it. As I explained, we've got enough to nail you anyway, without a confession. However, if you do confess, and you name Knight, he'll be arrested as soon as he shows his face, and you'll be safe, but you can't name him and his crimes without confessing your own. And obviously your cooperation will be noted – judge might even knock your sentence down to a hundred years. Of course, if you don't name Knight now, well, he stays loose, and I can't see him gambling that you'll always stay silent. Can you?"

Dalgleish put his elbows on the desk and sank his head into his hands.

"All right," he moaned. "All right."

"Cool," said Parlabane. Tam tossed him his portable phone, which he used to call Jenny, who was waiting outside with Callaghan and Nicole. Paul opened the black case again and removed from it a cassette recorder, a video camera and some lengths of aluminium tubing. He placed the tape deck on the desk and plugged in a microphone as Spammy assembled the tubes into a tripod to support the camcorder. Spammy then took hold of the Anglepoise on the bureau and re-posed it to shine on Dalgleish, hopping back and forth from the camera to make further minor lighting adjustments.

Jenny, Nicole and Callaghan appeared in the doorway of the now very busy room, Tam and Paul moving into the hall to make space for them.

"These are officers Dalziel and Callaghan," Parlabane explained, "and this is Nicole Carrow, who is here so that there is a solicitor present. Storytime, Alastair. Secretary of State for Scotland's video diary, take one. Roll it, Spammy."

Dalgleish remained slumped over the desk, head resting on his forearms, as Callaghan completed his transcription of the statement and Spammy dismantled the video camera. Parlabane was replaying the tape, Nicole having retreated to the hall where she shared a can of Coke with Paul as Tam helped himself to large measures of the Secretary of State's Craigellachie.

The playback of Dalgleish's weary, shattered, monotonal voice provided a steady bass below the mutterings and conversations in and around the room, as Callaghan passed the papers across and Dalgleish signed them like a glazed-eyed automaton.

". . . to Craigurquhart House for a few days," burbled the tape. "That was to put him at ease, so that he'd think we were rolling out the red carpet because we were going to give him what he wanted with good grace. That's what he was used to. Conspicuous security, MI5, just to assure him we'd pulled out all the stops . . ."

". . . about Lafferty?" Parlabane's voice interjecting. "Did he say anything about his death?"

"Yes. He told me he killed him himself. He said it was 'a field decision', his words . . ."

Dalgleish got up from his chair compliantly as Jenny gestured to him with her handcuffs, which she proceeded to place on his wrists.

"So have you any idea where Knight might be?" he asked her anxiously. "I mean, where are you taking me? What if . . .?"

"He's in a cell over at HQ," she said. "He was arrested about two hours ago. We received a tape of one of his own men admitting Knight and – what was the name again? – Harcourt, I think, had killed Voss."

She smiled as Dalgleish's eyes filled with new fury and humiliation.

"What? Didn't Mr Parlabane inform you of this? Naughty boy. See, that's the problem, Mr Dalgleish. Bloody journalists. Like politicians. Can't believe a word they tell you."

Parlabane pulled the heavy grey steel panel aside on the cell door. Knight looked up, got to his feet as he saw the face peering in.

"Who the fuck are you, then?" he barked.

"Mr Knight? My name is Jack Parlabane. Donald Lafferty was a friend of mine, so I just wanted you to know that it was me who took you down. In fact I want you to remember both our names every day when you're slopping out."

"I'll remember your name all right, you little prick," he spat, walking up to the door and shoving his face in the slot. "I'll be coming for you, sonny. Mark my words."

Parlabane shook his head, as if pitying a fool.

"Mr Knight? Tell me, what gives you the idea that your parole officer's *father* has even been born yet?"

"Oh very smart. But you wait. I'll get you. I can have you killed with a phone call. You think I can't kill you just because I'm inside? Good luck sleeping, mate."

"Ehm, look, I don't think you've quite grasped the pattern here, Georgie. I know you're probably telling yourself that you're in here because you were unlucky, and that's fine, because we all need consolation in times of defeat. But that thought might turn into something more bitter when you've got years in prison to think about nothing else. So just to put your mind at rest and save you torturing yourself, you *weren't* unlucky. You were simply up against superior opposition."

"I'll look forward to hearing whether you say that while you're watching your girlfriend's throat being cut."

"You really don't get it at all, do you? Myself, Tam McInnes, Paul, Spammy Scott, Nicole Carrow – we *really* gubbed you. Stuck you inside, thwarted all the wee diddies you sent after us. What could possibly make you think it would be any different if we had a rematch? I mean, for instance . . ."

Parlabane raised his hand a few inches to let Knight see the dictaphone he had been holding just under the hole in the cell door. He pressed Rewind then Play.

"I can have you killed with a phone call. You think I can't kill you just because I'm inside?" it said.

"See? Another few years on to your sentence, just like that. Gubbed you again without even trying. And don't bother threatening me with your connections, arsehole, because I'm afraid you don't have them any more. All your one-time mates will already be off looking for the main chance elsewhere. You're finished. So, Georgie boy, understand this: if we were up against shite like you, again and again from now until the end of time, you'd still never even scrape a draw. Never mind the law of averages. Nicole, Tam, Paul, Spammy, Sarah, me? We're late Fifties Real Madrid. You? You're Cowdenbeath – any year you like."

. . . AND FINALLY

The judge cleared Thomas McInnes, Paul McInnes and Cameron Scott of all blame, even with regard to their conspiracy to and execution of a robbery at Craigurquhart House. He was remarkably understanding about why they took the law into their own hands by not going to the police when the blackmail began, appreciating himself how difficult it can be to act independently when a great threat is hanging over your head. The fact that Parlabane had recently sent him a package of photographs depicting the judge and an unnamed woman with an eye for discipline is probably only of tangential relevance.

The judge was less understanding of the dilemmas of Alastair Dalgleish. He sent him to prison for a sod of a long time, and unfortunately he'll have to serve pretty much all of it because certain of his cabinet colleagues had recently been making an awful lot of noise about "honest sentencing" and life meaning life. "If you can't do the time, don't do the crime" was the phrase, Michael Howard ingeniously utilising a soundbite that didn't contain the letter "L". Obviously the court case was not exactly a PR coup for the government, and their fortunes took a bit of a dip after that.

Parlabane and Sarah got married. Parlabane suggested Bogota for the honeymoon on the grounds that it would be comparatively quiet in terms of hired killers, but Sarah decided to put a slight dent in his generous remuneration for the story of the aeon with a deluxe tour of South-East Asia. She kept her own name.

Tam and Sadie bought a nice wee place in Strathpeffer, and moved up there after the court case. Given Dalgleish's reluctant contribution and the money The Saltire paid for their stories, they considered themselves retired, although Tam occasionally helps out at a garage in Beauly. Mostly they go for long walks, and Tam sometimes drives them over to Strathgair, where they follow parts of a familiar trail. It was painful the first few times, but he wouldn't allow himself to hate the place or spurn its beauty, and it helps him remember Bob.

Nicole got a bit more settled in her work, the job now apparently having struck a balance between excruciating tedium and life-threatening danger. She started seeing Paul, which was inevitable really, as they were about the only two people in the world who could understand each other. She had reservations about getting involved with a guy who was about to become a student, but it turns out he's a man of independent means.

Spammy arsed about the flat all day, smoked a lot of gear, did some acid, fixed a few tellies for folk, and occasionally helped out down the studio. Well, what the fuck did you think he was going to do?

All right, he was talking – talking – about setting up his own twenty-four track, but don't hold your breath.

The following is the Prologue and first chapter from

NOT THE END OF THE WORLD

Christopher Brookmyre's
latest novel

Available now as a Little, Brown hardback

PROLOGUE

Joey Murphy was a fisherman. He was the captain and proprietor of a small trawler that was the whole world to him, but which he knew to be merely a speck on the endlessness that was the Pacific Ocean.

He believed in God.

He believed in Jesus.

He believed in His death, resurrection and bodily ascension.

He also believed in ghosts, poltergeists, demonic possession, Satanic possession, flying saucers, alien abduction, Roswell, Bigfoot, the Loch Ness monster, the Bermuda Triangle, telepathy, telekinesis, pyrokinesis, spontaneous combustion, levitation, reincarnation, out-of-body consciousness and the rapture.

He believed Elvis was still alive. He believed the FBI killed Marilyn Monroe. He believed the CIA killed Jimi Hendrix. He believed the Apollo moon landings were faked. He believed Oswald acted alone, the Magic Bullet theory being far more divertingly outlandish than any of the conspiracy explanations. And he believed the world was going to end on 31 December 1999.

But, best of all, he knew it didn't actually matter a rat's ass what he believed, because he spent most of his time floating out on the waves, miles and miles from where all this shit was or wasn't going on. Truth was, if you were going to believe something, it was best to believe in stuff that made the world seem a more interesting place. That's what beliefs were for – reality you knew about.

Funny, though, the part of his brain that dealt with what he believed seemed able to keep all his beliefs separate from each other, allowing him to believe simultaneously things that were contradictory or even mutually exclusive. This meant that he could believe in Creationism, which he'd been taught in Bible class when he was a kid, while also believing that dinosaurs had once roamed the earth, which he'd been taught in science class three doors along.

Similarly, the part of his brain that dealt with beliefs seemed somehow separate from the part that generally got on with running the show. That was how it was possible for the former to believe the world had only about ten months left before God pulled the plug, while the latter forked out fourteen large for a refit that would keep the *Mermaid's Kiss* seaworthy for at least the next five years. He guessed it was also what stopped most everyone else who believed the same thing from abandoning their normal lives and setting off on oblivious sprees of spending, stealing, screwing, raping and killing.

But another vital factor that allowed him to believe this and all that other stuff was that he'd never once experienced or confronted anything that put any of it to the test. For all his fascination with the occult and the unexplained, Joey had never so much as heard something go bump in the night or seen a Flying Object that wasn't easily Identified as a civil or military aircraft. Long as that was the case, those two parts of his brain could just happily get along with minding their part of the store.

Problems only arose when something forced the two of them to show up in the same place at the same time, like running into your ex-wife at a mutual friend's funeral. During such uncomfortable and unavoidable face-offs, the casualties were invariably on the beliefs side: in his early years they had accounted for Santa Claus, the Tooth Fairy and the Easter Bunny; in his teens, for fears of self-inflicted myopia; and later in life for the notion that 'no new taxes' meant no new taxes.

The taking-care-of-business part of his brain had never been faced with anything that forced a comparable revision of its rule book and operating manual. That was really what made all that weird stuff so fascinating. With the exception of Reagan winning a second term, there had been a rational explanation for everything he had encountered on a personal basis.

Until today.

The ocean was dead, had been for two days now. That made it pretty to look at, but Joey didn't like it. You could forget where you were when the water was like that, especially with the sun shining. Start imagining you were on a lake or some other more forgiving body of water. You could forget how angry the Pacific got, start to lose your respect for it. And that was usually when the spiteful bastard decided to teach you a lesson.

There had been a request from the Coast Guard. A boat called the *Gazes Also* (dumb name), a science vessel or something, had failed to respond to its regular radio contact on the mainland, and they wanted someone who was in the area to go check it out. Just a transmitter malfunction, he figured, or a power failure – probably some floating laboratory with too many gadgets for the generator to deal with. The ocean had been so calm there was no chance of anything more dramatic having befallen the thing. Still, the *Mermaid's Kiss* wasn't so far from the vessel's last recorded position, and it was always healthy to be in credit with the CG. He gave Rico the co-ordinates and commanded him to change course.

They spotted it less than quarter of a mile from where it had been charted the night before, a solid, unmoving dark shape between the placid blues of the still sea and the cloudless sky.

As they approached Joey hailed the vessel over the radio, just in case they had sorted their radio glitch out and he was about to complete a wasted trip, but there was no response, and a quick scan through his binoculars showed no sign of crew above deck. As the *Mermaid* drew nearer, Joey switched to calling the motionless boat over his loud-hailer system, but this equally failed to provoke any human activity.

The *Mermaid's Kiss* pulled slowly and gently alongside the hull of the *Gazes Also*, close enough for Joey to notice that the oddly named vessel looked to have recently enjoyed a refurbishment way more impressive than the paint-job with fries he'd spent so much hard-earned on. Thing looked like it had just got back from a goddamn health farm. Everything about the boat looked neat, clean, fresh and in order.

Except the worrying absence of people.

Joey swallowed.

'I'm goin' aboard,' he told Rico. 'Hold her steady. Pedro, gimme a hand here tying up.'

'Sure thing, skip.'

Joey hopped carefully across the gap between the boats and tossed the *Gazes Also*'s mooring ropes back to Pedro.

'You want me to come with you?' Pedro asked.

Joey was about to decline the offer, but another look at the deserted decks changed his mind. He didn't know what he was expecting to find below but he was pretty sure he didn't want to find it on his own.

Pedro stepped across on to the *Gazes Also*, an iron hook in his right hand. Joey took a step forward, called 'Hello?' again, and began slowly descending the stairs to the galley.

He was bracing himself for every grisly discovery he could imagine, every last B-movie scenario and old salt's late-night tale, but what he found below decks was far more disturbing than any horror he could have anticipated.

He found nothing.

No-one. Dead or alive.

No-one.

They moved tentatively through the boat, fearfully pushing open every door. The cabins looked occupied. There were clothes in the foot-lockers, rumpled sheets on the bunks, Coke cans and candy wrappers in the trash-baskets.

Just no people.

Joey looked at Pedro, who was sighing slowly through pursed lips.

Neither of them said anything. Neither of them had to.

Joey turned back and began heading for the decks again. That was when he noticed. On the way in he had just been looking for people, not paying close attention to his surroundings.

'Jesus,' he said, and stopped dead in the galley.

On the table there were four mugs with cold coffee in them, an empty brandy bottle and some plastic tumblers containing the last shares of its contents. There were dinner plates in the sink, cutlery too, in water that was cloudy with detergent. There was a greasy frying pan and two empty pots on the hob. There was a CD/cassette player on the worktop, the power still on and the LCD readout indicating a disc in the tray. There were butts in the ashtrays, breadcrumbs on the chopping board.

'It's the goddamn *Mary Celeste*,' Pedro said.

Joey said nothing, just walked unsteadily back up the steps and on to the sun-soaked deck. He looked around himself. Apart from his own boat there was nothing but blue as far as the eye could see, and the *Mermaid's Kiss* itself hadn't encountered another ship in three days. There, was no suggestion of anything amiss on the boat, and there was absolutely nowhere anyone could have gone.

The crew of the *Gazes Also* had eaten Sunday dinner and then simply disappeared.

'You okay there, skip?' Pedro enquired.

Still he said nothing.

Then, for the first time in his life, Joey Murphy, whose stomach had survived twenty-eight years of the Pacific and twenty-five of his wife's chilli, leaned over the side of the boat and provided Davy Jones with a generous share of his lunch.

ONE

'Don't sweat it, Larry, it's a walk in the park.'

Oh, gee, thanks, Larry thought. He was sure it had the potential to be a walk in the park and a precedent for being a walk in the park, but now that Bannon had gone and *said* that, he figured he'd better be on the lookout for gang wars, serial killers, King Kong and Godzilla.

Not that Larry wasn't on the lookout for all of the above anyway, these days, although not for the same reasons as everybody else in this screwed-up town.

'Just as long as I ain't goin' down there to hear any Chamber of Commerce requests to lay off bustin' the delegates for coke on account of the valuable trade they're bringin' into Santa M.'

Bannon laughed, shaking his head. Larry figured if the captain had known him a bit longer he'd have placed a daddy-knows-best hand on his shoulder, too.

'Larry, for the most part, this is the shitcan end of the movie business. European art-faggots, Taiwanese kung-fu merchants and LA independents workin' out of fortieth-floor broom closets in mid-Wilshire. Unless they clean up at the Pacific Vista these two weeks, they can't *afford* any coke. Goin' by the budgets of their movies, you're more likely gonna be bustin' them for solvent abuse. There won't be any trouble, I guarantee it.'

Thanks again.

'The movie market moved down here to the coast from the Beverly Center about seven years back, and there's never been a hint of a problem in all that time.'

Yeah, keep it coming, Larry thought. You've just about got it thoroughly hexed for me now.

'These guys, they come here from all over the US and all around the world,' Bannon explained. 'They show each other their shitty movies, they press flesh, they schmooze and, if they're lucky, they do some deals. Close of business they hit the seafood restaurants, throw ass-kissing parties to impress each other, try and get laid, then it's back to their hotels and up at eight to start over. I did your job the first three years. No trick to it. It's a figurehead deal. In their minds you're kind of the LAPD's corporate representative, someone who'll show his face every so often, smile a lot, and tell them nothing of any substance if they ask questions.

'All the organisers need to hear is that we're maintaining a high profile, so the visitors ain't too scared of bein' mugged, shot, gang-raped or ritually cannibalised to walk around town. That means more uniformed beat officers in the pedestrian areas, plenty of patrol cars on Ocean Boulevard and along the beach, all that shit. Ironic, really. Our purpose is to reassure them that none of their movies will come true – well, not to them at least.'

Bannon sat back on the edge of his desk. 'Think you can handle that, big guy?' he asked.

'Guess so.'

'You don't look so sure. Would you rather be out with Zabriski today, maybe? Let's see . . .' He thumbed through some notes on his desk. 'Railway worker, laid off last Friday, walks into the AmTrak offices on Third at eight thirty this morning and deposits a black polythene sack in the lobby. It's one of these atrium deals, you know, with like three or four floors looking down on to the concourse. Telephones bomb warning eight thirty-five, detonates at eight forty-two. Sack contained a small but significant amount of explosive, probably basic demolition stuff. Not enough to cause any fatalities, but enough to distribute the contents of the sack approximately sixty feet in every direction, including up. Guy was, how'd they put it? a "sanitation engineer". Some of that stuff must have come all the way from Frisco before he syphoned it out the train. Four floors, Larry.'

'I'll just be getting down to the Pacific Vista, Captain. Got someone to talk to about this American Feature Film Market thing.'

'Attaboy.'

It wasn't paranoia, Larry knew. It was plain old insecurity. He'd have been suspicious of being given this AFFM 'liaison' gig anyway, simply because he was still very much the new guy, and it might well be the sort of shit detail everyone else knew to steer clear of. He knew the scene, could see the station house, smell the coffee:

'So who's gonna handle the annual fiasco at the Pacific Vista this year, then? Zabriski? Rankin? Torres? What's that? You already volunteered to escort a Klan rally through Watts? Shit. Oh, wait a minute. The new guy'll have started by then. Let's give it to him.'

Nah. Maybe not. He believed Bannon. It was just that everything new made him nervous these days, like he was a damn rookie again. Loss of confidence, loss of self-esteem. He could imagine the phrases on a report somewhere, sympathetic but scrutinising. 'Let's see if he can get it back together, but we better get a desk job lined up somewhere just in case. Poor bastard. Helluva cop once . . .'

He knew he'd be okay at the Pacific Vista. All Larry's shakes were on the inside. The AFFM guy would look him up and down and see a physically imposing and relaxedly confident police officer, rather than the learner driver Larry felt was behind the wheel. He'd handle everything calmly and professionally, and the market would go off without a hitch. Bannon would be correct. It would be a walk in the park.

He knew what was wrong. He'd lost the reassuring illusion of control. These days he was approaching everything with unaccustomed trepidation; not a fear that anyone was out to get him, but that he wouldn't see danger until it was already upon him. He kept experiencing *déjà vu*, recurring waves of it that would freeze him for a moment, deer in the headlamps. It was unsettling, but at least he could recognise it as a symptom, and from there make the diagnosis:

Fear of the future.

Larry knew *déjà vu* wasn't any mystic or psychic phenomenon, just crossed wires in his head. Signals went from the senses to their regular destination in the brain, except that they took an accidental detour via the memory synapses. What you got through your eyes and ears you thought you were getting from deep inside your mind. It happened to everyone now and again, but to Larry it happened a *lot* when he was under a certain, specific kind of stress: the stress of not knowing what happens next. Not ordinary worries about dreaded or hoped-for possibilities, like before starting a new job or moving to a different city, but the vertiginous, isolated blankness of facing a future you couldn't even speculate upon. A confused helplessness of not even knowing *what* to dread or to hope for, because you just can't envisage what's ahead in any way, good, bad or indifferent.

The part of his mind that normally occupied itself with constructing models of possible futures – next year or even just next week –was left grinding gears, and the *déjà vu* was probably a resultant malfunction.

Sophie had gone for more tests last Thursday. She was the pregnant one, but it was Larry who felt he was going to be sick all the way to the clinic.

Why did he have to feel surprised that everything was fine? Or feel that the doctors were lying to them, maybe until they felt they were strong enough to hear the tragic truth? Why, when he looked at the ultrasound scan, could he not believe he would ever see the child depicted in its hazy image?

Maybe the future was blank because he was scared to let himself hope. He already knew how scared he was to let himself dread.

Larry had worked hard at resisting the 'impending fatherhood' variant of cop psychosis. He had seen it around him on the job and its self-corrosive ugliness provided a vividly appalling warning. Decent cops, guys you thought you knew, underwent a shocking transformation, as the man you used to work with barricaded himself in behind barbed wire, broken glass and howling dogs. It was as if they suddenly saw every crime, every murder or rape or mutilation, as a personal affront, fucking up the perfect world they had planned to bring their new child into. Every lowlife they dealt with on the street was no longer just some scumbag, but a direct potential threat to their delicate offspring. They couldn't see a victim any more without seeing their kid. They got hardened. And then they got brutal.

He had worried he might succumb this time, let the poisonous fears and insecurities transmute within him and secrete themselves as armour and weaponry on the outside. Instead he just felt kind of helpless. As if the future was rushing towards him faster than he had anticipated, and all he could do was watch; watch events develop, even watch himself take a role and play his part. It felt like the old-time raceway down at Disneyland. It might look like you were steering the car, and you could even pretend to yourself that you were, but if you let go of the wheel it would follow the track around anyway.

He and Sophie hadn't been trying for a baby. He didn't think they were even at the stage yet where they could *have* that conversation. Guess it just happened. One or other of those tearful clinches where they just held on to each other in the darkness, pressing their bodies always tighter, where neither of them noticed

393

the moment when holding became caressing, pressing became grinding, and the emotional need for closeness became an animal need for penetration.

So maybe it was partly that he didn't feel ready, but Jesus, when were either of them ever going to be ready? What was ready anyway? Was it when you stopped crying yourself to sleep sitting on the floor in David's room? When you stopped waking up in the night because you saw him dying once more in your dream? When you stopped hearing his voice among the laughter every time you passed a schoolyard?

When you stopped feeling?

Larry had to jump on the brakes as he turned his car into the horseshoe driveway in front of the Pacific Vista. The hotel was split into two seven-storey wings either side of an elongated hexagonal lobby. The first floors of the wings extended inwards to create a wide gallery overlooking the central concourse, but the remaining storeys were glass-walled about ten yards back on either side. This was to accommodate the towering centrepiece, a steeply sloping canopy of glass, rising high above the lobby on four sides to a flattened summit, into which, in an unsurpassed feat of architectural piss-taking, there was sunk a rooftop swimming-pool. The bottom of this was, of course, also glass, allowing the sunlight to continue down through the chlorinated water and dance shimmeringly around the lobby. Up top, the effect was supposed to be of the pool having vast and glistening depth, which was probably true. However, the anticipated further spectacle of bethonged babes floating above the desks, shops, cafés and restaurants had legendarily failed to materialise, as visions of plunging through water, glass and then a hundred feet of nothing at all proved sufficiently discouraging to most guests, however many safety assurances were advertised.

The other architectural oversight was that at certain (i.e. most) times of day, due to the angle of the sun, the whole thing turned into some kind of giant refractor lens, blazing white light out at the front or back like a laser blast. This made the horseshoe avenue a popular hang-out for personal-injury lawyers, as suddenly blinded drivers rear-ended each other, shunted bell-hop carts (and bell-hops) and occasionally ran over guests handing their car-keys to the blue-uniformed valets. If you came in on foot, you felt like a bug under a cruel kid's magnifying glass.

Larry had been there once before, investigating a bombscare. He'd turned on to Pacific Drive from Santa Monica Boulevard and thought the thing must have gone off, because the bomb-squad truck and two black-and-whites were zigzagged wildly across the blacktop, which was littered with debris from smashed headlamps and tail-lights. Turned out they had all rushed to the scene in the usual blue-light scramble, then concertinae'd each other when the big beam hit. Damascus Drive, folks called it now.

Larry remembered just in time. He brought the car to an abrupt stop, pulled down the shade-panels and slipped on his sunglasses. Now, through the windshield, he could make out a host of silhouettes against the fierce glow, like the last scene in *Close Encounters*. He edged forward slowly, glancing nervously into the rear-view mirror for advance notice of the architect's next unsuspecting victim. A blue courier truck came rapidly into view, but a paint-scored dent in its fender assured Larry it wasn't the driver's first visit. The truck slowed to a crawl and limped tentatively towards the main entrance behind Larry's four-door.

Larry climbed out and slung his jacket over his shoulder, the concentrated blast of sunlight having briefly turned the inside of his car into a microwave. The hotel had a 'greeter' on duty, standing on the blue carpet in front of the sliding doors, a white-bread blonde in a short skirt and a jacket, her smile almost as fake as her surgically sculpted nose. She was the covert first line of defence, ostensibly welcoming visitors to the premises but actually delaying them a moment while the security desk checked them out via the camera eight feet behind her head. She had an earpiece and a wire-thin mike following the line of her jaw. The say-cheese face and the confidence wavered momentarily as Larry climbed the few steps towards her. The reaction was almost tediously familiar, but some days he still enjoyed the look of helpless discomfiture. This was one of them, and he'd even switched the jacket to his right shoulder so that his holster was visible.

'Giant bald black guy carrying a gun at twelve o'clock. Mayday. Mayday. No information on this. Repeat, no information on this.'

The greeter had clocked the valet accepting Larry's keys, which somehow validated him for Official Greetee status. She took a quick breath and went into action. 'Good afternoon, sir, and welcome to the Pacific Vista hotel. How are you today?'

Larry smiled. Angst-ridden, bereaved, paranoid, nervous, strung-out and suffering mild symptoms of *fin-de-siècle* cataclysmic psychosis. Also known as . . .

'Fine.'

'And what is your business at the Pacific Vista today, sir?'

He pulled his badge out of his shirt pocket and pointed it beyond the greeter to the video camera. 'I'm Sergeant Larry Freeman of the LAPD, Santa Monica first precinct. I'm here to see Paul Silver of the American Feature Film Marketing Board.'

Larry watched her eyes stray from him for a second as she listened to a message through her earpiece.

'He'll be right down, Sergeant Freeman.' She smiled, suddenly back on-line. 'Would you like to come inside and take a cold drink while you wait?'

'No, thank you,' he said, turning back to face the horseshoe. 'I'd prefer to stay here just for the moment, if that's okay with you guys.'

'Of course, sir. Would you like a cold drink brought out to you here?'

'Why, that would be most civilised.'

A waiter appeared, in an unfeasibly short few moments, carrying a tray bearing a pitcher of fruit punch and a tall glass with ice in it. He poured the drink and handed it to Larry.

'Thank you,' Larry told him, then held up the glass to the security camera. 'Cheers,' he mouthed.

The fruit punch was pink in a way that no fruit had ever been (not *that* kind of fruit, anyway), and Larry noticed with a grin that it perfectly matched the pink beams that highlighted the hotel's exterior decor. Glass, glass and more glass, with all opaque materials either a soft aqua or this peachy-pink. He figured there must have been a serious paint production surplus in these colours back in about '92, because every new building in the city had sported them since. Sophie's alternative theory was that some real camp guy got elected the city's construction-materials regulator, and you just couldn't get anything else past his Garish-Guard chromatoscope. 'Green? *Green?* By the *ocean*? Are you kidding me? Pleeeease!'

Larry sipped the punch and looked back down the drive, where trucks were being unloaded of chipboard partitions, cable drums and aluminium stanchions by squinting young men in white T-shirts, all bearing the AFFM's logo. Tempers were beginning to get frayed by the frequent incidence of light-dazzled collision. After a while they sussed a system of using the boards as sun-shields, with the guys carrying the other equipment falling in behind.

More vans were pulling up all the time and stopping suddenly, either in quick reaction to the glare or because they had encountered a stationary object up-front. Their drivers handed boxes, packages and cardboard tubes to T-shirted workers or occasionally to stiffly coiffured women in sharp suits. Clipboards were signed. Receipts were dispatched. Everybody had a laminate. Everybody had a mobile.

Across Pacific Drive there was more scurrying busyness going on, with temporary construction under way on the expansive concrete of the parking lot that used to be the Ocean Breeze Retirement Home, before it became the Ocean Breeze Hotel, before it became the Ocean Breeze whorehouse, before it became the Ocean Breeze insurance fire. Zabriski had worked the case, saying it set a new textbook exemplar in obvious torchjobs. There was a light scaffold being erected, creating what looked like a platform, even a stage, plus more chipboards, perhaps for concession-stands. White sheets were being draped around the wire fence that separated the place from the messy back lots of First Avenue, and horizontal banners were being laid out on the ground in preparation for being hung up someplace. He couldn't make out what they said.

More legibly, vertical banners bearing the AFFM legend and this year's dates flapped gently from flagpoles along the horseshoe driveway, as they did from streetlights all around Santa M. This event was a big deal. Larry thought again about Bannon's assurances, weighing them up in the context of the growing ferment around him. He estimated that the trouble factor was indeed low, but the embarrassment and repercussion factors were in the ionosphere, given the high profile any fuck-ups would certainly receive. He figured that if shit met fan – or demolition charge – he should remember to be a politician before he was a cop.

'Sergeant Freeman?'

He turned around to find a short white guy with a real bad perm, big and shaggy yet somehow rigidly neat, like he couldn't decide whether he wanted to be in Motley Crue or The Osmonds. When he smiled, he definitely had Osmonds teeth.

'I'm Paul Silver,' he said, extending a demonstratively confident hand. He was faking it. The little guy was shitting himself, and unusually it was nothing to do with Larry's presence, size or colour.

'Larry Freeman. You the man in charge of this show?'

'Yes, sir, that I am. I'm Chief Co-ordinator of Logistical Onsite Market Activities for the American Feature Film Market nineteen ninety-nine.' Larry could *hear* the capital letters.

'First time in charge?'

'That, too. How did you know?'

'Because you're shitting in your shorts.'

The smile switched off. Pauly clearly feared We were about to have a Problem.

Larry grinned to defuse the situation. 'Don't worry, me too,' he said, gripping the now less certainly offered hand.

'First time, or, er . . .?'

'Shitting in my shorts, yeah. But hey, everybody assures me there's never been a problem before.'

The little guy rolled his eyes. 'They keep telling me that, too.'

Silver led Larry inside, through the vast lobby with its diamondoid canopy. The orchestral music being pumped through the place was fighting to be heard amid the clamour of hammers, power-screwdrivers, staple guns, raised voices and the chiming of mobile phones. Stalls and stands were being erected, or finished off with promotional material, posters and cardboard cut-outs advertising company names and movies. Many of the flicks looked like the kind of stuff that always filled the lower shelves at the video store, past the New Releases and All-time Classics: Titles for the Undiscerning Viewer. *Musclebound White Guy with a Big Gun II: Hank Steroid's Revenge. Kickboxing Vigilante with Serious Unresolved Personal Conflicts IV: Showdown in a Burbank Parking Lot.*

The shimmering light of the sun through the rooftop pool painted its own changing shades on every surface. Even the wide-spread tackiness of the market's paraphernalia couldn't detract from the elegance of the effect. Larry had to hand the architect that one. Still nobody swimming in the damn thing, though.

Larry followed Silver through the doors at the far end, out on to a wide terrace that overlooked the beach and the ocean at the rear (or did that make it the front?) of the hotel. Silver pulled up a chair for him and sat down opposite. A waitress arrived with a pitcher and two glasses. This time the fruit punch was aqua bluc. Larry laughed, declining his drink, but took up the little guy's offer of a club sandwich and a Seven-Up.

Silver listened to Larry's assurances about police visibility, more officers on the beat and other half-inspired bullshit with sage nodding. He clearly didn't care. He was too wired about the market itself being a success to have any head-time left for worrying about what was happening to the delegates when they weren't engaged in On-Site Market Participatory Activities.

'Well, I guess it ain't me who should be doing the worrying,' Larry said, popping a stray piece of cooked chicken back between two levels of his impressively towering sandwich. 'Looks like you got a bigger operation running across Santa M than *we* do.'

Silver smiled, but there was an Oh-Christ-don't-remind-me wince in the middle of it. 'Biggest one for years,' he said. 'These events kind of shrank after the video boom of the eighties died off, but with new end-users taking up the slack – satellites, digital delivery, fibre-optics – the worldwide appetite for product is growing year-on-year. AFFM 'ninety-nine will have more accredited participants than any of its predecessors since the event moved to Santa Monica.'

Larry tucked heartily into his sandwich. He'd correctly anticipated that the right stimulus remark would precipitate little Pauly's prepared PR response, thus buying him time to eat.

'Almost every room in the Pacific Vista will function as an office for one of our participant companies, while all of the cinemas in downtown Santa Monica are screening scheduled programmes of market product, from eight in the morning through to six at night. That's a total of almost fifty screens, showing an average of five feature titles per day. Plus, as a new development this year, two of the hotel's function suites have been designated Video Galleries, with a total of thirty-eight booths where delegates can view tapes of non-premiering product – that's titles already screened at previous markets but with certain rights still available – on widescreen format monitors with digital-quality sound channelled through headphones. We've also installed a product-and-rights database with access terminals on every corridor so that delegates can find out what territories and formats are still available on a particular . . .'

It was a mighty sandwich, but Larry still managed to finish before Silver did. He took a big gulp of Seven-Up and wiped his mouth with a napkin. 'Plus you got all that stuff across the street in the parking lot, too,' he said. 'What's that about? Promotional events? Stunts? Star appearances?'

Silver's brow furrowed and his head shook. It was weird watching all that hair move as one. This guy didn't have a stylist, he had a topiarist.

'Oh, that's nothing to do with us, Sergeant Freeman,' he said. 'It's a real headache, actually. We normally annexe that lot exclusively for participants' parking, and this year we've had to rent a place half a mile down the beach and organise a free-and-frequent shuttle-bus service. The lot changed hands recently and the new proprietor said he already had the whole place rented out for the market's dates.'

'So what have they got planned there?'

'We didn't ask. But unless it's the world's first outdoor film market it's unlikely to give us much concern.'

'Guess not,' Larry said, thinking he'd better check it out when he was through here.

It was much the same deal as across at the Pacific Vista. Guys in matching T-shirts, chipboard screens, electrical cables, laminates, mobiles. Except these T-shirts said, 'Festival of Light – Santa Monica 1999', and it wasn't just the material that was uniformly white. The focus of the lot's layout was a stage at one end, facing north. Workers were assembling an elevated aluminium structure around it, a construction Larry wasn't too old to recognise as a frame for a lighting rig. There was a big truck backed up to one side of the stage, and through its open rear doors he could make out some black boxes that he figured for a PA system.

Larry walked through the gap in the low fence where cars usually went in and out, ducking under the ticket-activated barrier. He made it half a dozen yards into the lot before two T-shirts made their hasty way from the stage to challenge him.

'Excuse me, sir, but I don't believe you have a personnel pass.'

Neither of them looked more than twenty. It was the smaller one who spoke, shiny straight white teeth probably enjoying their freedom after years behind bars. He didn't look like he'd be getting his hands dirty on any of the heavy lifting work. That – and

401

associated tasks – seemed the remit of his high-school linebacker buddy.

Odd thing to say, even as polite intimidation. Not 'Can I see your personnel pass?' or 'Do you have a personnel pass?', but '*I don't believe you have* a personnel pass'. Pretty confident about who does, then. Either there weren't too many of them or there was something about Larry's appearance that made it unlikely he'd be carrying one. What could that be, now?

'It's okay, kids, I got access all areas,' he said, producing his badge.

'I don't understand, has there been some kind of complaint?'

'No, I'm just takin' a look around. Wonderin' what you've got in mind with all this stuff.'

'What do you mean? We've already cleared everything with the police *and* the mayor's office,' the kid said, folding his arms. 'We've got the fire department coming down tomorrow for safety checks, and we've got an official police liaison officer dropping by to—'

The kid was cut off by a hand on his arm. An older man, maybe mid-thirties, had appeared behind them from a partially constructed stall nearby. He was dressed identically to his junior companions – sneakers, jeans, T-shirt, teeth - but his laminate was a loudly important red.

'Who's our guest, Bradley?' he asked, smiling widely at Larry in practised PR mode as he spoke.

'Sergeant Larry Freeman,' Larry said, showing him his ID. 'I'd just like a quick look around.'

'Well, we weren't expecting the police department until tomorrow afternoon, Sergeant, and yours wasn't the name we were given, but long as you're here, why don't I give you the tour? I'm Gary Crane. Festival construction supervisor.'

He put a hand on Larry's back and began walking him away towards the stage. The welcoming committee retreated, shrugging.

'What's the party for?'

402

'Party? Oh I see. Well, I guess you could call it that. I'm right in assuming you're not involved with the Festival liaison?'

'I'm involved with a different liaison, 'cross the street. Just want to see what the other star attractions are in the neighbourhood this week.'

'Certainly nothing as big and impressive as the AFFM, Sergeant.'

'So what is this . . .' Larry indicated the man's T-shirt, '. . . Festival of Light, Mr Crane?'

'It's a celebration. A youth and family event. We're having music, singing, speakers – hence the stage. There's going to be bleachers that end. We're putting them in that big space behind the sound desk, which will be in that booth there. There'll be cooking, concession-stands, face-painting,' he continued, indicating the stalls taking shape around the lot.

Smily Gary was being persistently vague around the point of interest. Larry listened to him describe a few more things his eyes had done a pretty good job of noticing for themselves, then interrupted. 'Yeah, but what are we celebrating?'

Crane stopped, looking Larry pityingly in the eye, as if he couldn't believe he didn't understand, then smiled again. 'The light of Christ. What other light is there?'

He felt relief flow through him like a flushed cistern. Terrifying visions of biker conventions and Klan rallies dispersed from his thoughts, washed away in that glib piety emanating from Crane.

Larry looked back at the lot from the sidewalk on Pacific Drive as he waited for the WALK sign on his way to retrieving his car. One of the horizontal banners that had been laid out face down in the lot was being raised towards supports above the stage; there were similar brackets all around the concourse. The banner, folded lengthways, was being hauled up by some of the T-shirts and secured in place at either end. Then it dropped open to reveal its slogan.

'Festival of Light –Santa Monica '99.'

Larry had a little smile to himself. In an ideal world this would

403

still be the AFFM's parking lot, but Happy Clappies he could live with.

He was about to look away again when he noticed another fold of the banner doubled up behind what already faced out, with T-shirts untying the strings that would let the last section drop down. It unfurled with a slap against the frame.

'American Legion of Decency'.

Uh-oh.

This wasn't a movement or an organisation Larry had specifically heard of, but he suddenly didn't feel quite so comfortable any more.

Something about that last word had always scared the shit out of him.

QUITE UGLY ONE MORNING

Christopher Brookmyre

Winner of the 1996 Critics' First Blood Award

Yeah, yeah, the usual. A crime. A corpse. A killer. Heard it.
Except this stiff happens to be a Ponsonby, scion of a venerable
Edinburgh medical clan, and the manner of his death speaks of
unspeakable things. Why is the body displayed like a slice of
beef? How come his hands are digitally challenged? And if it's
not the corpse, what is that awful smell?

A post-Thatcherite nightmare of frightening plausibility, *Quite
Ugly One Morning* is a wickedly entertaining and vivacious
thriller, full of acerbic wit, cracking dialogue and villains both
reputed and shell-suited.

'The dialogue is a joy throughout and the plot crackles along
with confident gusto and intelligence . . . an assured debut
by a talented writer'
The Times

'Very violent, very funny. A comedy with political edge,
which you take gleefully in one gulp'
Literary Review

'A wicked satire . . . excellent plotting and a
goodly amount of acidic one-liners'
The Scotsman

'A sharp, funny novel, with strong characters and
some smart dialogue'
TLS

Abacus Fiction
ISBN 0 349 10885 4

THE CROW ROAD

Iain Banks

'It was the day my grandmother exploded. I sat in the crematorium, listened to my uncle Hamish quietly snoring in harmony to Bach's Mass in B Minor, and I reflected that it always seemed to be death that drew me back to Gallanach.'

Prentice McHoan has returned to the bosom of his complex but enduring Scottish family. Full of questions about the McHoan past, present and future, he is also deeply preoccupied; mainly with death, sex, drink, God and illegal substances . . .

'Riveting . . . exhilarating . . . its pace, development, intensity and, above all, its hip and sexy humour never allow it to flag. With *The Crow Road*, Banks reinforces his credentials as one of the most able, energetic and stimulating writers we have in the UK'
Time Out

'Done with considerable imaginative subtlety and a fine touch . . . As fine and ambitious a novel as any from a Scottish writer since the 1960s'
New Statesman and Society

'Beginning with a bang and ending with an exclamation mark, Iain Banks's tenth book in eight years would seem to confirm his position as the enfant explosif of the Brit pack'
Scotland on Sunday

'He continuously proves himself master of two tricks: he marries pacy plot-lines with languorous literary diction, and he mixes a wealth of straight social realism with flights of gothic fantasy'
TLS

Now you can order superb titles directly from Abacus

☐ One Fine Day in the Middle of the Night	Christopher Brookmyre	£6.99
☐ Not the End of the World	Christopher Brookmyre	£6.99
☐ Quite Ugly One Morning	Christopher Brookmyre	£6.99
☐ Full Whack	Charles Higson	£6.99
☐ Getting Rid of Mr Kitchen	Charles Higson	£6.99
☐ The Crow Road	Iain Banks	£7.99
☐ Complicity	Iain Banks	£7.99
☐ Whit	Iain Banks	£6.99

Please allow for postage and packing: **Free UK delivery.**
Europe; add 25% of retail price; Rest of World; 45% of retail price.

To order any of the above or any other Abacus titles, please call our credit card orderline or fill in this coupon and send/fax it to:

Abacus, 250 Western Avenue, London, W3 6XZ, UK.
Fax 020 8324 5678 · Telephone 020 8324 5517

☐ I enclose a UK bank cheque made payable to Abacus for £ ....
☐ Please charge £............... to my Access, Visa, Delta, Switch Card No.

☐☐☐☐☐☐☐☐☐☐☐☐☐☐☐☐☐☐☐

Expiry Date ☐☐☐☐   Switch Issue No. ☐☐

NAME (Block letters please) ....

ADDRESS ....

....

....

Postcode ....Telephone ....

Signature ....

Please allow 28 days for delivery within the UK. Offer subject to price and availability.

Please do not send any further mailings from companies carefully selected by Abacus ☐